The Golden Anaconda

AND OTHER STRANGE TALES OF ADVENTURE

By Elmer Brown Mason

Off-Trail Publications

Elkhorn, California

Dedicated to those Kings of the Lettered Road, Wanderin' Walker and Amblin' Ed.

With thanks to Norm Davis, John Gunnison, and Rob Preston.

Front cover art by Elliott Dold from
The Danger Trail, April 1927

Back cover illustration from
Elmer Brown Mason's "Twisting Roots,"
The Frontier, March 1925

OFF-TRAIL PUBLICATIONS
Elkhorn, California
offtrail@redshift.com

Printed in the United States of America
First printing: September 2009

CONTENTS

Wandering Smith

Remote Corners

Elmer Brown Mason and the "Biological Romance"
By John Locke

ELMER BROWN MASON WAS AN ENTOMOLOGIST who had a side-career writing fiction for magazines. His stories appear from 1911-26—at least as far as current records show. He hit several of the "better" magazines, *Harper's Weekly*, *McClure's*, *Munsey's*, *The Saturday Evening Post*, but the bulk of his modest output was to be found in the pulps. What claim he has on our memory and interest mostly comes from a series of short "scientific romances" published in *All-Story Weekly* and *The Popular Magazine* over a year spanning 1915-16—the subject of this anthology.

The scientific romance, spurred by the success of the Edgar Rice Burroughs novels, became a specialty of the Munsey pulps in the period from the publication of Burroughs' *Tarzan of the Apes* in *All-Story* (October 1912), to the end of the decade. In his book *Under the Moons of Mars: A History and Anthology of "The Scientific Romance" in the Munsey Magazines, 1912-1920*, Sam Moskowitz explored the term "scientific romance," which actually predates the Munsey years. He provided this concise definition:

> The term "scientific romance" . . . meant science-fiction love stories. The love or romantic element is an integral part of the story, but the boy-meets-girl, boy-loses-girl, boy-gets-girl formula is forwarded on a jet stream of adventure and action, against immensely colorful backgrounds like the dry ocean beds of Mars or the unknown world of the future.

Science fiction had been well-established by 1912 in the works of Verne, Wells, and others, but appealed to a predominately male audience. The scientific romance opened up the genre to female readers.

The "science" in the scientific romances usually involved the mechanisms of travel to exotic destinations like other planets, the inner earth, other dimensions; and the exotic technology encountered in these places. Exotic life-forms were found in these places, too; however we don't usually think of biology as the central science at issue. This may be the main reason why Elmer Brown Mason, whose stories push Earth biology past its known limits, has been overlooked as part of the school of scientific romance. His small output, and shorter story length, doesn't attract much attention either. Most of the scientific romances were novels.

Curiously, Mason received no mention in Moskowitz's book, despite a generally thorough treatment of the subject. But a reading of Mason's two-part Borneo saga in *All-Story*, "Black Butterflies" and "Red Tree-Frogs," should leave little doubt that Mason was following the formula, in combining exotic locations, fantastic elements, and romance between scantily-clad individuals. Mason's five Wandering Smith stories for Street & Smith's *The Popular Magazine* follow the same general formula but, again, the output is small, and, additionally, Street & Smith was not known for scientific romance.

The details of Elmer Brown Mason's life form a sparse, sometimes contradictory patchwork. He was born in Deer Lodge, Montana on September 30, 1877, or September 30, 1880, depending on which account you believe. Most of the information comes from Yale publications that listed brief biographies of their students. His father was Captain Roswell Henry Mason, a Civil War veteran and one time surveyor-general of Montana. His mother Mary's maiden name was Brown. His grandfather, Roswell B. Mason, was a railroad builder and Mayor of Chicago at the time of the great fire (1871). By 1895 at the latest, the family appears to have relocated to the Chicago area.

As a prep, Elmer studied at the University School in Chicago, and also studied abroad, which implies family affluence. One account lists his service in the Spanish-American War (1898), "as second lieutenant of Company B of Colonel Koch's regiment of United States Provisional Volunteers." The timing of his college years is a bit murky. He did his freshman year at Yale with his brother, Roy M. Mason, both in the Class of '02. Then Elmer did his second year with the Class of '03. He was published in *The Yale Literary Magazine*. In 1900, Elmer transferred to Princeton, where he worked on the *Princeton Tiger*. He graduated with a B.A. in 1903. (One account has him transferring to Princeton after his freshman year at Yale.)

(Brother Roy appears to have published some commercial fiction while still at Yale, and afterwards for *The Yale Monthly Magazine*. However, he could not be connected to the artist and writer, Roy Martell Mason, who was of a similar age.)

After graduation, Elmer was employed by the publisher, Dodd, Mead & Company, and then with Harper & Brothers. Eventually, he became a real estate broker in New York City. He also worked in lumbering. Our best account of his life, in his own words, comes from *Adventure's* Camp-Fire column, on the occasion of his one and only appearance in the magazine (November 30, 1925). (His letter is published in full following this section.) He describes how he used his jobs, and later his fiction-writing income, to finance extensive world travel, including to places like Borneo which would reappear as settings in his stories.

From 1909-10, Elmer undertook graduate studies in Botany at the Yale Forest School. After finishing, he became a Forest Entomological Assistant for the Bureau of Entomology, specializing in forest insects. (The Bureau was a division of the U.S. Department of Agriculture from 1894 to 1934.) In

1912, he wrote of his life-to-date:

> Have been in literary work, newspaper work, real estate, lumbering, forestry, and am now permanently in forest entomology. Made a success of lumbering and forestry and am quite happy with bugs. My one and only real achievement was a campaign against the Southern pine beetle, which threatened to kill all the pine in the South last year. From July 1 to December 15, had a station at Spartanburg, S.C., where a campaign was carried on against said beetle. It appears to be under control this year. Emerge from the woods now and then to make an address on forest insects, but spend most of my time in the timber.

In 1911, he made 49 speeches on the Southern pine beetle problem, all over the South. In a separate account, he wrote:

> Was in charge of forest insect field station at Spartanburg, S.C., from August 20, 1911, until the closing of the station, December 15, 1911. Went there as last man and came away in charge. Since then have been engaged in editorial and investigating work in Washington.

The responsibility he came away with put him in charge of the South Atlantic and Gulf states. He also wrote articles for lumber journals and newspapers. His conclusion:

> It's a fine life, extremely healthy, interesting and unremunerative. As one cannot spend any money in the woods, however, the college man's burden (i.e., debts) is gradually decreasing.

That last reference gives us a final clue as to why he began writing fiction on the side. His literary inclinations, professional writing responsibilities, privacy, unmarried status, spare time, and debt, may all have combined to ignite his initiative. Our first record of a commercial fiction sale is the short story, "Flaherty—Road Monkey," in the April 1911 *Hampton's Magazine*, a dialect-heavy tale of lumbermen, who he also calls "pulp men" since their lumber is going to the paper mills. He has two known shorts in *Harper's Weekly* in 1913; and another in *Lippincott's*, 1915. At some point, as his Camp-Fire letter implies, the writing income financed his travels.

That brief record of sales gives no precedent to the fantastic stories that appeared in the pulps over the course of a year. Starting with "The White Gorilla" (*All-Story*, June 5, 1915) and ending with "Red Tree-Frogs" (*All-Story*, August 12, 1916), he made ten sales to either *All-Story* or *The Popular*, in generally increasing length. The shorter pieces run from 6-9,000 words;

the novelettes climb to 12-13,000 words; and the longest story, "Black Butterflies," runs almost 20,000 words. Although we have not examined all of his published stories, these ten appear to constitute an explosion of creativity that is distinct from the majority of his output.

In the introduction to "Black Butterflies," *All-Story's* editor, presumably Bob Davis, described Mason's stories as: "weird adventures in weird places with weird animals and men." That's a pretty good description; it zeroes in on the novelty that makes Mason's stories so entertaining. In the Camp-Fire letter, Mason wrote of the places he had visited:

> In the past I have covered the world fairly well: Borneo, the *Sunderbund* in India, South America, Europe thoroughly, my own country in various capacities. . . .

The ten stories collected here have the following settings:

The Fighting Man	*Bayous*
The Dancing Mulatto	*Florida*
The Golden Anaconda	*Columbia*
The Black Flamingo	*Everglades*
Saint and Señorita	*Amazon*
The White Gorilla	*French Congo*
The Albino Otter	*Everglades*
Lost—One Mylodon	*Patagonia*
Black Butterflies	*Borneo*
Red Tree-Frogs	*Borneo*

The four stories set in the Florida or the Bayou country fall within his Bureau of Entomology jurisdiction. Three are set in South America, two in Borneo, leaving only "The White Gorilla" with an unvisited setting, unless—and this is hard to believe—he forgot to list Africa on his travels-list.

The heroes of the stories are usually naturalists, fascinated with the scientific implications of their exotic surroundings. We can presume that these men represent Mason himself, or Mason as he idealized himself for the purposes of thrilling fiction. In many cases, these naturalists are searching for specimens, often to be obtained for museums, e.g.:

> I envy people in New York having such a place to go [the Museum of Natural History]. There is everything there, and then some more. Days wouldn't have been enough for me to thoroughly examine its treasures. And then I had an especial interest because bird, beast,

insect, and reptile I had had a share in taking were on exhibition. ["The Black Flamingo"]

He doesn't say so in The Camp-Fire, but perhaps specimen-gathering was a prime motivation in his overseas travels. Given his outdoor skills, and, after 1910, his academic grounding, he certainly would have been qualified for the job.

We might also presume that many of the odd characters in his stories were based on people he met in his travels.

In Mason's era, the attitudes of white westerners toward members of other racial or ethnic groups often ranged from the impolite and condescending, to the harsh and even cruel. That's not news. And the presence of racial awareness in Mason's stories should come as no surprise since it was a common element in the pulp fiction of the time. However, Mason's sensitivity to racial differences is so omnipresent, and takes so many forms, that it rises to the level of a preoccupation.

The most obvious evidence is Mason's use of the slang "nigger," e.g. "At the first words of the song, Mose turned whiter than I ever saw a nigger do before" ("The Fighting Man"). The word appears in the first four Wandering Smith stories from *The Popular*, particularly the first two. We should note that in those days, "nigger" had a broader definition, meaning not only African but any dark-skinned people, so that it's use in, for example, "The Golden Anaconda," could simply have been a substitute for "Indian." Curiously, "nigger" *never* appears in his *All-Story* pieces. Given the African setting of "The White Gorilla," in particular, this seems odd. "The White Gorilla" uses terms like "natives" and "savages." This suggests that *All-Story's* publisher, Munsey, had an editorial policy that barred the use of "nigger," a policy not shared by *The Popular*'s publisher, Street & Smith.

Dark-skinned people aren't the only ones to receive second-class characterization. Van Dam's servant is described as "his Jap" ("The Albino Otter"). Asians, commonly, are distinguished by their color: "In a yellow avalanche the coolies piled over our frail barricade" ("Black Butterflies"). Mason lays his views on the line in this passage while also conceding the finer points of primitivism:

> I'll not deny that the Anglo-Saxon is the greatest of all races, but being one has its disadvantages at times—we talk when we should act. To save a cartridge Gomez should have had a knife stuck into him, and a savage would have applied that practical solution to his problem. White men are civilized beyond logic, however. ["Black Butterflies"]

If dark skins are second-class, white skins must be first-class:

> The girl wore a long, pink, silky dress that accentuated her slimness and made her skin whiter, her hair and eyes blacker by contrast. Gosh, but she was beautiful! ["The Black Flamingo"]

The deification of whiteness reaches a symbolic pinnacle in the treasuring, by naturalists, of albinoism, a rare form of literal whiteness, in people and animals, that derives from a lack of pigment. The glory of albinoism is a central theme in "The White Gorilla" and "The Albino Otter." Given Mason's preoccupation with race, it becomes more than a scientific curiosity:

> Van and I dined luxuriously on what I took to be very young lamb and afterward adjourned to the den, on the walls of which are ranged the cases containing his albino collection—the traditional white blackbird, the enormous, glittering, white toucan, the snowy raccoon, the white panther, and that last acquisition in a huge case by itself. There was a roaring wood fire, and before it, partially covered by a snow-leopard's skin, twitched, while he slept, the coffee-colored slim cannibal boy. Once he reached up a long, bare foot and scratched his ear exactly as a dog attends to a flea. ["White Gorilla"]

The majesty of the white animals is put into stark relief against the crudity of the "coffee-colored cannibal boy."

Still, one can have too much of a good thing:

> Once the jungle has cast its spell over you, once you have sweated to torture in the wet, enervating gloom of its tropic growth, you are lost forever to the world of cities with their dull skies and flat pavements over which stream unceasingly the endless, white-faced throngs. ["Red Tree-Frogs"]

But . . . on the other hand:

> White men are not only polite to one another in the jungle through motives of policy, but also because they are generally really glad to see a face of their own color. ["The Golden Anaconda"]

Mason's racial references really mount up through the course of the ten stories. He doesn't seem to express any race-based hostility to people, i.e. a desire to commit violence for purely racial motives; he simply engages in endless classification, putting people in their proper place. We could disparage him as a writer for resorting to the shorthand of stereotypes, while failing to employ more descriptive language. But it's noteworthy that he writes as an educated man and a naturalist. One of the foundations of his scientific knowledge is taxonomy, the ordering, ranking, classification of living organisms by their degree of relatedness, the fitting of all types into the great tree of life. Mason seems to be engaging in this exercise with racial identities, a dubious scientific exercise since, as a minimum, it indiscriminately mingles genetic characteristics with social and environmental factors. But was Mason much different than contemporaries who shared similar backgrounds and experiences? It's a hard question to answer from the distance of so many years.

Between "Red Tree-Frogs" and the start of the American involvement in World War I, we know of only two Mason stories that found print, both in the middle of 1917. Then, at the age of 40 (or 37), Mason went off to war. He served seventeen months in France, as a Lieutenant in the 30th Division, winning the Croix de Guerre. He refers to his war experience twice in the Camp-Fire letter. The war robbed what was left of his youth, but the first mention gets at that rather obliquely:

> I used to be an active member of your fraternity but the war rather put me out of the game for these last years—not to mention the years themselves. The only roaming I have done since 1918 consists of a swordfishing trip on a schooner to the banks, not a startling adventure but an extremely interesting experience.

The second instance admits the physical damage:

> I used to be a fair field shot with rifle and shotgun but German gas made that a "used to be."

"I have given a hostage to fortune," he concludes, with characteristic understatement. We can only imagine what health problems might have ensued from his gassing. If he couldn't use a rifle, was it because nervous problems prevented him from holding it steady, or that his eyesight wouldn't let him aim? In any event, it's clear his life was severely impacted.

His publication record picks up again in 1919, but his stories are of a much tamer variety. Gone with the adventuring were the stories inspired by the adventuring. He had a number of shorts in *Telling Tales*. He hit *The Popular Magazine* several more times. He appeared with shorts in *Munsey's* through 1925. Of note, *Munsey's* was the only magazine of the Munsey chain that celebrated editor Bob Davis still remained involved with after the rearrangement of his duties in 1920, which suggests that Mason and Davis retained good relations. Mason's stories for *Munsey's* could be characterized as light social dramas. Examples: "A to Z" (August 1921), examined the question of whether women were interested in business; "Lucky Numbers" (January 1923) centered around two families in Palm Beach; "Atmosphere" (March 1923) contrasted country joys and city comforts.

Several of his postwar stories were based on ocean fishing, which he alluded to in The Camp-Fire. These include: "Fisherman's Luck," *Munsey's*, July 1922; "Cullin's," *Argosy All-Story Weekly*, January 17, 1925; "On Gorges Banks," *Argosy All-Story Weekly*, March 14, 1925. He published an article on swordfishing in *The Saturday Evening Post*, November 17, 1923.

He hit *Short Stories* a couple of times in this later period, and appeared once in the unsuccessful Macfadden magazine *Fighting Romances from the West and East*. His only book, *The Night Rider*, was published by Doubleday in 1924; it reprinted his story from the October 25, 1921 *Short Stories*.

He had a new tale of Borneo, "Twisting Roots," in the sixth issue of *The Frontier* (March 1925). In "Black Butterflies," he had described a favorite hangout in Brunei, the British Protectorate:

> The entertainment furnished at the Devil's Club is rather unique. Everything starts with a good dinner, of course, and plenty of drinks. Then comes gambling on a rickety roulette wheel, fan tan, or just drinking. If none of these amusements appeal to you, you watch the show.
>
> Dyak girls, teeth blackened and ornamented with tiny gold stars let into the enamel, ears bored around the edges with holes from which dangle rings and pendants, wave their long hands, the nails dyed to a crimson, and dance to the slow beat of the native instruments. Chinese girls, always smiling out of their slanting eyes, play toy-like banjos and never cease to wonder at European kisses. Perhaps there are wrestlers, or two sailors from rival ships put on the gloves and fight to a knockout while men from every corner of the earth stand around the ring.

It's made clear from his letter to *The Frontier's* monthly column, *The Trading Post*, that this new story was selling old memories:

> To those of us who have roved, and most of your contributors seem to belong to this brotherhood, it is manna to read of far places described exactly as our eyes have seen them. And THE FRONTIER is a vivid example of "the nearer the truth, the better the tale." I should be willing to wager a large percentage of the check that came to me for "Twisting Roots" that several of your readers who have been in Borneo

will recognize Li Fo—still more the Devil's Club. Li Fo—which isn't his real name, of course—long ago set out for his Buddhistic heaven with the knife of a river pirate between his ribs. I'm sure the Devil's Club still exists, however. As a matter of fact I last heard of it in the front line trenches before Ypres from an English subaltern.

Mason's only appearance in *Adventure* (November 30, 1925) came late in his fiction career. His novelette, "Jerias," was not so exotic, though. It was an animal story set on a small island off the coast of Maine. His last known new fiction was a short story, "Smoke of Dreams," in the January 25, 1926 *Short Stories*. There his writing career ended, as far as we can tell. A near quarter-century later, though, he had a mini-revival in *Famous Fantastic Mysteries* and *Fantastic Novels*, which reprinted a lot of Munsey scientific romance. In 1949 and '50, they reprinted the first four *All-Story* tales in this collection, "Red Tree-Frogs" being the omission. The stories were beautifully illustrated by Virgil Finlay. We have no date of death for Mason, so whether he was around to enjoy his rediscovery is an open question.

We do have scattered details of his post-writing life, however. By 1926,

On Gorges Banks

By ELMER BROWN MASON
Argosy All-Story Weekly, March 14, 1925

he was married to May Stanley, a poet and fiction writer. Our earliest record of her is a verse collection, *A Minnesota Christmas*, in 1914. She published fiction in women's magazines like *Pictorial Review* and *Good Housekeeping*. Like Mason, she published shorts in *Munsey's*. Her last known publication, *Blue Meadows*, was a 1932-33 serial in *The Delineator*, and was reprinted as a book.

Curiously, the narrators in two of Mason's stories refer to their past loves: "I have had two romances in my own life, both ending happily" ("Lost— One Mylodon"); "The one real love comes to all of us sooner or later. It had come twice to me in my life" ("Saint and Señorita"). These comments seem a bit too similar to be coincidental; perhaps Mason was talking about his own experiences as of 1916, when the stories were published.

The remaining details about Mason's life are more problematic. There were more Elmer B. Masons in the country; and even Elmer Brown Masons. So one is loathe to combine bios without cause.

Here is one tantalizing set of possibilities. On October 31, 1929, Marie Curie spoke to the New York City committee of the American Society for the Control of Cancer. The mayor and other dignitaries attended. Another speaker at the dinner was an Elmer Brown Mason. A year later, this Mason spoke again at the committee's dinner. Our Mason was an experienced public speaker, so he can't be ruled out. Perhaps he was speaking as a victim of cancer. In 1930 and '32, in New York, an Elmer Brown Mason worked for an advertising agency, managing the account of the Committee on the Cost of Medical Care. . . . The dots are out there, floating around; we simply can't connect them reliably.

Adventure, November 30, 1925

Excerpt from The Camp-Fire

FOLLOWING CAMP-FIRE CUSTOM, ELMER BROWN MASON rises to introduce himself on the occasion of his first story in our magazine ["Jerias"]. Like many others he has sat with us before joining our writers' brigade.

Mineola, New York.

It is an honor to stand up in such company on this, the occasion of the first story I have sold to ADVENTURE. Some of you I know; one of you I met in Borneo many years ago; one, whose name is on the tablet (in ADVENTURE's anteroom) of those who have hit the last trail, once did me more than a favor.

I used to be an active member of your fraternity but the war rather put me out of the game for these last years—not to mention the years themselves. The only roaming I have done since 1918 consists of a swordfishing trip on a schooner to the banks, not a startling adventure but an extremely interesting experience.

In the past I have covered the world fairly well: Borneo, the *Sunderbund* in India, South America, Europe thoroughly, my own country in various capacities from timber cruiser to lecturer for the Bureau of Entomology on beetle damage in the South Atlantic and Gulf States. In those salad days I used to accumulate a stake, first from jobs, later from the writing of fiction, pick out the two places I wanted to go worst, and toss a coin between them. I remember one trip to Brazil where there was no limit to the poker game going down—table stakes. I came back on the same steamer several months later as assistant to the assistant's assistant deck steward. For a brief and inglorious period I was a general during an earnest but misplaced attempt to furnish a South American Republic with a better government. I do not cling to the title, however.

As to personal tastes, I like the woods, any woods in any country. I like all animals, wild or tame, with the exception of pug dogs and goldfish. I know a little about butterflies and beetles. I used to be a fair field shot with rifle and shotgun but German gas made that a "used to be." As to sports, all outdoor ones.

Perhaps the best thing in this best of all lives, now that I have given a hostage to fortune, is to read about what other younger men are doing and seeing in the places I have been. And these young men speak most vividly through the pages of ADVENTURE.

—ELMER BROWN MASON

Wandering Smith

The Fighting Man

A tale of moths and the Luna Girl. A colorful picture of life among the bayous of Louisiana. An unusual bit of fiction.

I AM A PERFECTLY PLAIN MAN WITHOUT ANY EDUCATION, but I have wandered more than a little, from the tip of South America through Lower California and into most of the corners of the southern coast of the U.S.A. That coast is all corners, so I have covered a lot of ground. In spite of my lack of education, I know a great deal, have picked it up from real authorities. You see, my lot has mostly been cast with scientists, men who are looking for something in out-of-the-way places and have a definite idea what that something looks like. Chapman has taught me about birds. I have hunted snakes with Ditmars, a man who is by way of being the prince of a little European country, where they run the biggest gambling hell on earth. He spent nearly a year with me collecting fishes and the tiniest of sea things.

They all come to me. Any one who wants to go after something unusual in a strange place telegraphs me at Père Guerrin's restaurant, in New Orleans. If I happen to be there, and feel like going, I wire back:

> Come a-hooting.
> (Signed.) WANDERING SMITH.

My real name is Isaiah Ezekiel, but somehow I have lost it in the shuffle and only my banks know it. Every one else calls me Wandering, and I don't care, because I call men by the name that best suits them. Most people have fool names, anyway. Imagine naming anything but a Persian tomcat Montmorency, or calling anything but an oyster De Haven!

I had been in New Orleans about two months, taking in all the fights, cocking mains, and horse races, but eating—and drinking—too much, when Old Bug's letter came. Old Bug isn't his real name, of course, but it's what I call him, so will have to do.

The letter read that he would like to send me a young man who hadn't had much experience in the wild—his word; he meant in the sticks, along the bayous, outdoors, in short—and if I felt like it, would I take him out of the cities to collect moths and butterflies?

I had about made up my mind to go alligator hunting, anyway, and, though I don't hold much on risking trips with tenderfeet, I like Old Bug, so I wired: "Come a-hooting!"

It was two nights afterward I was sitting downstairs in Père Guerrin's, at two in the morning, wishing I hadn't drunk the last four high balls, and watching a party of sailors getting ugly by drink degrees. Père Guerrin's place is no palace, either, in regard to the restaurant or the hotel above, and its patrons are not among our best people. I'm kind of used to it, though, and never go anywhere else. The front door was shut, of course, at that time in the morning; and when some one began to pound on it from the outside I didn't pay any attention but put it down to some souse after just one more. The pounding stopped, and, after an interval, the side door opened and there entered six feet and a half of pink kid crowned with a black and white plaid cap above a round, baby face, black and white plaid—very plaid—suit, gray gloves—it was hot summer—white shoes and socks. Père Guerrin looked him over and walked forward on his toes, the way he does when he is getting ready to throw some one out.

"I'm looking for Mr. W. Smith," the checkerboard volunteered.

"No such gent here, monsieur," answered the père, sidling nearer.

"But, my good man, I'm just off my train, had an appointment with him at this address, can't wait to see him."

"No such gent here, monsieur." The père balanced forward.

"Mr. Wandering Smith?"

"That's different," the père grumbled, obviously disappointed that there was no excuse for exercising his bouncing talents.

"Wandering!" he yelled, and I haughtily beckoned over to my table and indicated a chair.

"Mr. Wandering Smith?"

I nodded while sizing him up more carefully, and one of the gray-gloved hands promptly tendered a card on which was scribbled Old Bug's signature and embossed in Dutch letters:

MONTMORENCY DE HAVEN ETHERIDGE.

I motioned the card away and signaled Père Guerrin.

"My name's Wandering," I said to the boy; and to the père: "Take my friend Shorty's order."

Montmorency De and the rest of it looked kind of thunderstruck at first; then he grinned, and with that I couldn't help liking him. It was the kind of grin a kid wears when he tears his pants on a picket fence. He knows it isn't right, but he can't help it.

Père Guerrin brought the bottle of Scotch, and for my guest beer, which he drank promptly, as though to get it out of the way. Then he asked me when we could start and how soon we would get there; if I had a motor boat ready, or a sailing craft, and was it sloop or knockabout rigged; didn't I think it a good idea to take along two canoes in case one was busted; had I ever noticed there, by chance, a moth, fore wings maculated with white on black,

black hind wings, tuft of red hairs on end of the abdomen; was the rice in blossom, or didn't it ever blossom—

I managed to cut him short with the information that it was fourteen million miles to the moon, and the *Great Eastern* had seventeen masts. Then, before he could break in again, explained I hadn't the slightest idea where we were going, and no one but a natural-born idiot would think of using a canoe among cypress knees when he could get a light, strong skiff.

Then we settled down to business. The kid wanted to cruise in and out along the coast of lower Louisiana, sugaring for moths—I was to find out what that meant later—and he had no more idea of what it was like or how to get there than a red-headed Irishman has of crocheting. I explained ways and means to him at great length while he listened as though I were reading his mother-in-law's will, and then there occurred what Père Guerrin calls a *divertissement*. Three of the sailors were dead to the world, and the four remaining had finished the bottle left them, when the old Frenchman had gone upstairs at three o'clock. Now these four souses came over to our table and offered to buy from me or fight me for the quart of Scotch from which I had mixed my last high ball. I don't like being interrupted when I am talking, and I won't fight drunks—they are liable to stick a knife into you—so I simply tipped the bottle onto the floor with my elbow, where it smashed to pieces.

The sailors swore a good deal, and were pretty ugly, but there wasn't really anything doing since I spoke to them politely. I glanced at the kid while they were making up their minds, and got one of the most disagreeable shocks of my life. His face was dead white, covered with perspiration, and his gloved hands were clenched on the edge of the table. I had begun to like him, too, but not as much as I hate a coward, and I guess I sneered when I spoke:

"Want these gentlemen removed from your august presence?"

"Yes, they—they are noisy and probably dangerous."

To say I was disgusted was to put it mildly. I left my chair and went upstairs. The sailors would leave for Père Guerrin, and I don't like fighting drunks.

The père cussed me proper for disturbing his sleep, especially as everything was quiet below, but he came just the same. We went downstairs into the restaurant and stopped suddenly.

There wasn't a sound in the room save the snoring of the three men who had passed away. The other four lay heaped in a corner beneath the fragments of a table, and my fearful friend was ruefully contemplating a pair of gray gloves burst into shreds over the knuckles.

"Were your dangerous friends struck by lightning, Shorty?" I queried.

"They got abusive," he acknowledged, and, in plaintive tones: "I've split a brand-new pair of gloves all to pieces."

In the morning I left Shorty snoring in pink pajamas and slipped over to the water front to see what I could find. Luck was with me, and I chartered a nifty forty-foot knockabout with large cabin and cockpit, and a sweet little kicker behind, ordered some stores, and then went after Mose, my cook.

When I had corralled him—no slight task, since he always marries anew after every trip and lives with his wife's relatives—the expedition was ready to start.

Shorty had a raft of dunnage—luggage he called it—a great part of which consisted of cork-lined boxes for insects, cyanide killing bottles, and a whole library of scientific books. It didn't make much difference, however, since there was plenty of room in the boat. On general principles I should have liked to kick, but when I got back he tickled me to death by standing the père on his head—something I never could have done, old man though the Frenchman was. Just a jujutsu trick, the boy explained—depended entirely on one's adroitness! So does lifting a safe—that and brute strength!

Our supplies and dunnage were stowed away by one o'clock, and we dropped down the Mississippi. Then, throwing Mose's last bottle of gin overboard and putting him at the helm, I cornered Shorty, extracted by the roots all his ravings about the sea, the sky, the what nots, and pinned him down to what he wanted to do. Briefly his program was as follows: We were to anchor near the shore each night, and, taking the skiff, sugar trees through the swamps, rowing from one to another until it was light, catching the moths that came to the bait. During the morning, we were to mount our catch on spreading boards—Shorty was sure I could help him a lot with this—and the afternoons we would hunt butterflies on the higher ground. Great program, wasn't it? The idea was evidently to save up all our sleep until we got back!

By night we anchored close in near the mouth of Bayou Lafourche, with a wet tangle of swamp in front of us. Shorty nearly went crazy at the sight of it, and made sounds indicative of joy that he called yodeling—something like a bull alligator shot through the lungs. He could hardly wait for supper, and, before it was dark, we were in the skiff among the cypress knees.

I've carried strange freight in my life, but nothing odder than that boatload. The big, pink kid was in the bow, two butterfly nets by his side, and between his knees a pail of hell brew consisting of four pounds of brown sugar, a stale bottle of beer, and half a pint of rum. He had about a hundred two-foot-square white napkins that he soaked in this mixture and tacked to the trunks of trees. The rest of the boat was full of large pickle bottles with tight glass stoppers, their bottoms holding cyanide of potassium beneath a layer of paper. There was also a large, flat box with a cork bottom, on which to pin the moths after they were dead.

It was a crazy performance; but I'll try anything once, and Shorty was so excited and happy tacking up his beer-soaked doilies that I hadn't the heart to tell him how many kinds of a fool he was. We covered over two miles close to where the water brush was thickest before all our cloths were up, and then it was dark. Shorty switched on an electric searchlight like a small automobile lamp, and we rowed out of the swamp into open water and back to where we had commenced. Then the fun began. The first bait was literally covered, and the air full of pale-green moths with two long, flowing tails to their wings like old-fashioned coats. In the glare of the electric light, they looked unearthly beautiful, seemed dreams from the depths of greenish-amber absinth.

"Why don't you grab your net?" I whispered excitedly.

"Luna moths; very common," he answered calmly. "Hope they don't crowd out everything else. They breed in the sweetgums, persimmons, and hickories along the shore."

The next tree and the next were covered with lunas. Then came quite a stretch of open water, in which we surprised an otter hunting, before the square of white cloth tacked to a giant cypress. As the powerful light fell on it, there appeared to be only a moderately sized brown moth hanging to the edge.

"The Cypress Sphinx," breathed Shorty in tones of positive awe, rose to his feet, slammed the net over it, and fell into the water. Everything was soaked, including me, and the boat half swamped, but he didn't seem to mind a particle. Holding the net well up, the bag turned over so his prisoner could not escape, he clambered onto a cypress knee and raved. Only three or four specimens yet known in collections! Reported from Georgia and Florida alone, his was the honor of adding another state to its range. Rare, rare, ultra rare! Did I appreciate how lucky we were? How fortunate a day it was when we met!

Farther along we captured a Giant Sphinx—all of two inches long! Big-game hunting, this!—a brownish-yellow, pretty thing that looked kind of like a gold nugget. The next outburst was over a Galbina Silk Moth, brown marked with white, and he had another fit over a pink, brown, and yellow Zephir, its fat body barred with crimson. After that, I lost count while he had an elegant time and only fell out of the boat once in the next three hours.

When we came to the end of the doily-marked line, he suggested that, while he stuck some of the deadest moths on pins in his cork-lined box, I row to the other end, instead of going back immediately over the same ground. I swung the skiff out into the open water while he impaled the pretty night butterflies, his tongue wagging like a tickled dog's tail, and just as he pinned the last one, something went wrong with the electric lantern. It was black dark for a moment, and then our eyes got accustomed to the opaqueness of the night, and I rowed through a sea of silver moonlight while he tinkered with the battery. Rounding the point where our trail began, I saw a glow on the water and heard voices. Cautioning Shorty not to switch on his light, I silently dipped my oars and slid toward the sound. Closer the radiance lay behind us, and there were still voices. I pushed the skiff through the swamp growth and came unexpectedly to the abrupt rise of a hill straight from the water, and the murmur was replaced by a quavering old voice raised in a kind of chant:

> *"Butt'fly, butt'fly, floatin' goe,*
> *Reckon thar ahn't no blood in yo'!*
> *No blood, no bones, nothin' 'tall,*
> *'Cause yo' is so lightsome an' small.*
> *Nigger touch yo' full ob de moon,*
> *Him boun' up an' die right soon.*
> *Nigger dahr in de dahk eat yo',*
> *Him can doe what de white folks doe."*

Other voices joined in a shrieking chorus:

> *"When de moon am pale, white folks' blood am red;*
> *All de niggers be happy when de white folks dead!*
> *Dah's butt'flies cahved on de voodoo stick,*
> *Kill all de white folks, kill 'em quick!*
> *Dah's butt'flies cahved on de voodoo stick,*
> *Kill all de white folks, kill 'em quick!"*

The voices rose in higher and higher shrieks:

> *"Kill 'em, kill 'em, kill 'em quick!*
> *Dah's butt'flies cahved on de voodoo stick."*

And that fool kid burst into a roar of laughter!

There was instant silence, followed by the hiss of water upon fire, and then a scurrying through the underbrush.

"What a comical song!" he exclaimed. "Rather odd, too. An uproarious but innocent amusement."

"Uproarious but innocent rattlesnake!" I answered indignantly. "That's the voodoo butterfly song; and the rice planters would shoot a nigger on sight that they heard singing it—it means murder or even worse!"

Shorty dropped the subject out of politeness, and I immediately shut up. It was more than evident that he did not believe me, and we rowed back to the first of the doily moth traps in silence!

There were even more of the valueless lunas about than formerly, but every little while a prize would be captured and I would be called upon to help rejoice. Once I nearly went to sleep, but a four-foot moccasin dropped into the boat, and after that I kept my eyes wide open. The morning mist was rising from the water before Shorty regretfully suggested our return to the knockabout, and then only because the game had ceased to fly.

The entire morning passed extending the gauzy wings of the moths—there were more than a hundred of them—and I watched his deft fingers manipulate the infinitely delicate things without tearing, drawing them out with fine needles placed behind the stoutest veins and pinning them in place beneath bits of thin pasteboard.

By noon, however, all were mounted and identified, and we hoisted sail and turned on the kicker.

A mile around the point where we had begun our night's hunting, a dock ran out into the water, and off it we anchored. Provided with two butterfly nets and leather-cased cyanide bottles, we had Mose row us toward the shore. Shorty was just as excited and yodeley as he had been during the night, and, as we landed, began to hum:

> "Kill 'em, kill 'em, kill 'em quick!
> Dah's butt'flies cahved on de voodoo stick."

At the first words of the song, Mose turned whiter than I ever saw a nigger do before. He gave a gasp and a gulp, and his voice sounded scared to death:

"Fo' de Lohd's sake, Mistah Shorty, don't sing dat! More niggers done gone crazy over dat song than am libbin'. It done been wicked vodo!"

Shorty stopped instantly, and I saw he was going to ask some questions, so I tried to stick a butterfly net kind of carelesslike in his eye, thus distracting his attention. It's rotten bad luck to even mention vodo to niggers.

Butterfly hunting wasn't as good as the sugaring game, though Shorty was mighty pleased with what he did catch, especially a crimson, black-speckled thing he called the Mexican Silver Spot. You see, our territory was very limited because we couldn't penetrate the swamp land along the shore, and all the rest of the landscape was rice with one solitary, sticky road running through it off into the distance. Mighty desolate outlook, I thought, and it was breathlessly hot. Besides, I was tired, having contracted the habit, in early youth, of sleeping some small part of every twenty-four hours.

The paddy fields were full of niggers working to drain the soil so it would be dry enough for a reaping machine to cut the ripe crop, and I couldn't help wondering how many of them had been on the swamp hill at midnight singing the vodo song.

We went on and on up that rotten road, catching a butterfly now and then, but not often enough to keep my head from nodding, until at last we left the sickly green fields behind and came to higher country. There were butterflies to burn, and Shorty yodeled his head off, till, tired as I was, I caught some of his enthusiasm. We flew through the brush like two maniacs, losing all count of time; and then suddenly it began to rain!

It was no ordinary rain. The sky changed from sunshine to jet black, the drops fell faster and bigger, while the thunder roared overhead, and the lightning played around like the darting of a snake's tongue. I caught Shorty's hand—we could hardly see, so thick was the downpour—and led him to the road up which we staggered toward a large house in the distance. We stumbled through a heavy iron gate, fortunately open, and up onto a broad porch, unable to hear ourselves speak above the hiss and drum of the falling water.

Shorty grinned at me like a naughty small boy who has gotten wet on purpose, and then his face changed at something he saw over his shoulder. Sweeping me aside with his left arm, his right fist shot out to meet the impact of an immense mastiff, silent and grim as death, springing at his throat. The dog went over backward, the door opened behind us and then slammed shut, revealing a glimpse of a white-wooled nigger with square spectacles, yellow vest, and a tailed coat. The animal, recovering itself, crouched, sprang again, and Shorty's big hands caught its throat, swinging it at arms' length, while the forepaws ripped the shirt from his chest. Released again, it flew up the steps, and I yanked my automatic from under my arm only to have Shorty slap it out of my hand. He caught the brute back of the neck, swung it up into the air, and I saw his fingers turn white as they tensed into the flesh. For a full minute he stood poised, the beast above his head, and then slung it sideways the length of the porch. In a flash it was on its feet, but Shorty took two steps forward. The dog drew back, hesitated, then, turning, jumped out into the rain.

During the whole performance, I was conscious of two sharp eyes peering out from a little window in the door. Now the eyes disappeared, and, in a moment the door itself opened to the white-wooled, spectacled old darky who, bowing grandly, announced:

"Cunnel Fairfield begs yo' will honah him by bein' his guests. He has instructed me to lead yo' to youh apahtment, where yo' will find dry habiliments."

We followed up a broad staircase and into a big hall with doors on each side, one of which, open a crack, closed noiselessly as we passed. Both of us were dripping mud and water at every step, and Shorty was nearly naked to the waist, his chest all scratched and bleeding.

Ushering us into a big room with a nice tiled bathroom off it, the darky opened a cupboard and put a bottle of whisky, some glasses, and a siphon on the table, which already held a bowl of cracked ice, and excused himself to get "dry habiliments."

Two little nips kind of restored us, and we got into the dry things as fast as we could. After we were dressed, Shorty told the negro to present Mr. Wandering Smith's and Mr. Montmorency de Haven Etheridge's compliments to Colonel Fairfield, and we would like an opportunity to express our appreciation of his hospitality.

We were met at the foot of the stairs by a little, dried-up man, whom I recognized at once. Those eyes were the same ratty ones that had watched the fight with the dog through the trap in the door—and not interfered! I fitted a name to him, of course, as I always do to people, but I didn't call him by it. He was Sir Rat without question. "Sir" because of his fine manners, "Rat" because he was one.

Shorty said something about lost wayfarers at the mercy of the elements, Southern hospitality, and suchlike dime-novel stuff; and Sir Rat, talking along the same lines, told us to forget it; he was glad to see us. He added that we must not think of leaving that night, and we would dine at once as soon as his daughter came down.

There was a rustle at the head of the stairs, and she came. Yes, she came. I never held much for blondes, but she was the exception. Her hair was straw color, looked awfully soft, and glinted as though it had caught raindrops. Her eyes were blue-black, and her skin was even pinker and whiter than Shorty's. She was very tall, and wore a light green dress with a tail to it—reminded me of something I couldn't put my tongue to just then.

Sir Rat introduced us:

"Daughter, Mr. Montmorency de Haven Etheridge, Mr. Wandering Smith. Gentlemen, my daughter, Marcella Carter Fairfield." And Shorty gave her his arm, while her dad and I followed into the candle-lit dining room.

The conversation was beyond me, but I was so sleepy I didn't care. It was all I could do to keep awake. The food was served by the white-wooled nigger with his yellow vest and long-tailed coat. He looked like a big moth moving outside the radiance of the candles. Finally the talk switched around to something I could follow. Sir Rat began to tell of the labor troubles of the rice planters, his sharp little eyes like hot pin points, while Shorty listened politely, though I could see he would much rather have heard the girl's voice.

Niggers were growing worse and worse each year. It was actually necessary to send to New Orleans to get enough to plant and gather the crop. The colonel found it impossible to use the same laborers more than one season. They seemed to get mysteriously corrupted; some even went mad, and he had had two foremen murdered. There was voodoo about the plantation, some malign influence, he'd give ten thousand dollars willingly to put his finger on the exact trouble. This year it was worse than ever—there had even been threats—

Miss Fairfield butted in here and turned the conversation to moths and butterflies. She was perfectly lovely; there is no other word, and neither of us could keep our eyes from her. Then Shorty told of our adventure during the afternoon, not mentioning the mastiff, and worked back to the previous night, while it grew harder and harder for me to keep awake and I tried to think what she reminded me of. With the beginning of the description of the sugaring I knew. Pale-green wings with long, graceful, feathery tails, pure white body—the Luna moth, of course. It came to me in a flash as I raised my eyes to look at her. But what was that shadowy fluttering above the candles? The conversation had stopped abruptly, and all eyes were upon it. For a moment it was lost in the darkness, swept back, and a great Luna moth circled twice swiftly around the lights, and, hovering above Sir Rat's plate, settled nearly against his hand.

I heard the girl give a gasp, saw the colonel turn pale, and behind him the old darky, peering down on his master over his spectacles, triumph, hate, and fear in his eyes.

There was a long silence, broken by Sir Rat in a voice scarce above a whisper:

"Absalom, where did—that come from?"

" 'Clare to goodness I don't know, Massa Frank!"

"Take it up!"

The old darky, advancing a shaking hand, withdrew it, and then let one beautiful moth cling to his black finger, murmuring beneath his breath something about "de full ob de moon."

"Marcella, gentlemen, you will excuse me for a few minutes," said Sir Rat, and motioned the trembling nigger to follow him.

"Perhaps I owe you an explanation," said the Luna—I mean the girl. "That moth is the sign of the voodoo, and we have been threatened it would be sent us three times—and then death! Father received one in a letter; this is the second. Of course it sounds extraordin—"

The last word was cut short by a scream from the next room, followed by a swishing sound I had heard before, the unmistakable hiss of a black-snake whip, that cruel instrument of punishment of the old slave days. There was another scream, and Shorty sprang to his feet.

"Please, *please* sit down!" the girl breathed, her imploring eyes full upon him.

The kid's face was white and covered with beads of sweat, exactly as it had been in Père Guerrin's café—and I knew now what that meant—but he sank back into his chair. Then, while scream after scream echoed through the house, those two young things sat tense and motionless, gazing into each other's eyes.

The shrieks ceased, and the girl relaxed with a whispered "Thank you, oh, thank you!" The door opened, and Sir Rat entered and took his seat as though nothing had happened, but his eyes had the bloodthirsty look of a hunting ferret.

A younger nigger appeared, and the dinner went on as before, interminably, while my eyes that would close seemed to see the girl float from her seat and fly away like a great Luna moth. Then I would come back with a jerk and eat something else I didn't want. At last the meal came to an end, and, waiving the smokes, we all went into the parlor. I found a seat in a dark corner, and the Luna Girl went to the piano and began to sing:

> "By de ole bayou a yaller maid
> Am waitin' in de mag'olia shade.
> Night owl hoot in de cypress tree.
> Oh, but dat girl's sweet toe me!
>
> "Louisiana, whar de dahk waters flow!
> Louisiana, whar de wil' rice grow!
> Dah's whar am waitin', mah yaller deah,
> Sweeter fahr dan cohn in de yeah.
>
> "Père Guerrin bring another drink.
> Underwing moths as black as ink.
> Moses, luna, vodo, snake,
> Darn you, Shorty—"

These last four lines may sound rather queer, but they didn't to me because I heard them in my sleep.

When I awoke, the room was empty, and I stumbled drowsily up the stairs. Shorty was undressed and in bed, snoring mightily. I slipped off my clothes, crawled onto a cot, and was asleep before I could throw the extra pillow on the floor.

No full night's rest was coming to me, though. I suppose I had been out of the world for a couple of hours, just taken the edge off slumber, when something woke me. I lay still, trying to think what it was, when through Shorty's snores came a sound as though two bricks were being rubbed together, followed by a deep groan. I was out of bed in a second, and felt all around the room to try and locate the disturbance. It seemed to come from beyond the bathroom, and I stole out into the hall and down where a tiny shaft of light shone from a keyhole. From behind this door came more grating and another groan. I bent down and applied my eye to the aperture, and this is what I saw:

The room was lit by a single candle, and beside it sat the old, white-wooled butler, his bare back toward me, and that back was covered with long, raw welts! With a file he was grating a piece of red wood, and as soon as he had accumulated a little dust he sprinkled it over his shoulder onto the wounds and groaned. I watched this performance for a few minutes and then silently opened the door.

"Look here, you fool nigger," I whispered, "you quit this business and go to bed, or I'll tell Sir Rat—I mean the colonel—about it in the morning. It looks like voodoo to me."

At my first word he was on his feet and snatched up a heavy, carved, black stick, which he hid behind him when he recognized me. Then, down on his knees, he simply prayed to me to say nothing, that he was only applying some "right powerful soothin' "—sounded "soothin' " from his groans—to where he had been beaten. I finally promised not to peach on him. Honest, I was sorry for the old black; those raw wounds were pretty bad.

Back in bed, this time I slept through till morning.

At breakfast, where our host looked more like a rat than ever, the Luna Girl did not appear. Her dad informed us, however, she was to drive us back later, and also expressed the hope that this would not be our last visit to the plantation. Shorty said we should certainly pay our respects often, since we expected to be in the neighborhood for some time—which was news to me.

Afterward we were led out to look over the grounds and buildings, and there were sure enough of them. The nigger quarters consisted of a lot of miserable pine shacks about half a mile away; but the house, outbuildings, and barn were all that any one could ask for. There were a pack of seven bloodhounds kept there, and the big mastiff was chained to a kennel.

When we got back to the house, there was the Luna Girl in a trap waiting for us; and at sight of her, Shorty's face lit up like a bright tin dipper in the sun. That fool kid could no more conceal what he felt than he could realize that ordinary men needed to sleep once in a while.

It was a mighty rough road, but the girl drove well, so all I had to do was to wedge myself sideways in the rear seat to keep from falling out. As for those two in front, it might have been the smoothest asphalt for all they noticed it. Tall as she was, Shorty overtopped her; and I am here to maintain with rifles, shotguns, automatics, axes, knuckle dusters, or bare fists that a handsomer couple never rode over rice clay.

They talked every minute, without saying a thing, just as birds make noises together, and it was only as we reached the dock that anything really pertinent was said.

"May I come back very soon?" Shorty asked.

"If you care to, after—after last night," she answered.

"I do," he said, "and would after a thousand such nights!"

She gave him a queer little look, the kind a woman sometimes gives a baby, and, nodding her head, quickly drove back over that desolate road.

Mose was in a blue funk when he rowed us to the knockabout, bursting with something he had to tell, and simply tickled to death to see us. When Shorty had spread out his butterflies of the day before, and was mounting them, I took Mose out in the skiff to pick up the sugaring doilies. There he unfolded his tale.

It seems that two niggers had paddled out to him as soon as we were gone and told him all about the Fairfield plantation. It was known as Niggers' Hell, so he said, all along the coast, because once a hand was lured there he never got away until the rice crop was in, and, in addition, was treated like a dog, whipped on the slightest excuse, tracked down with bloodhounds if he tried to escape. It was regular slavery, of course, but the law permitted it since labor was contracted for at New Orleans covering the entire season. Worst of all, voodoo was prevalent throughout the plantation, and a nigger who did not profess that mysterious and loosely defined cult was persecuted not only by the whites but by those of his own color, while Colonel Fairfield paid no attention to actual killing among the blacks so long as the field work went on. There were rumors that murder was to be done, and the two niggers begged Mose to let them hide on the knockabout and escape farther down the coast. He threatened them with a shotgun until they went away, and that night a butterfly-carved voodoo stick was thrown on board, though the moon was full and there was no craft or swimmer in sight.

Of course, I called Mose a fool and would hear no more of it, after I heard it all, but I did some thinking nevertheless. No wonder Sir Rat could not use the same niggers two seasons running! The wonder was how he got any at all!

We set sail at noon for farther down the coast, where there were no rice fields, but highlands back of a broad belt of swamp, and anchored just before dark near the shore. The doilies soaked in sugar, beer, and rum were tacked up, and the night's work began. It differed little from our first collecting. Shorty fell overboard twice; he wasn't really awkward, but several sizes too large for the skiff; we didn't see a single luna, but we did see and capture a Juno Moth, fore wings maculate with white on black, hind wings black, a tuft of red hairs on the end of the abdomen, exactly as it had been described to me at Père Guerrin's, and our rejoicings must have disturbed the alligators for miles. We took nearly two hundred specimens, and you can bet I was weary when the light came.

Sleep was impossible during the morning, Shorty yodeled and sang so uproariously while mounting moths; and in the afternoon we hunted butterflies till nearly dark. Back on board the knockabout, the kid promptly began to prepare for another night's sugaring, and then I kicked.

I explained to him carefully, in simple words mostly of one syllable, that I was not interested in perpetual motion, that I had reached an age when I felt I was entitled to an occasional luxury—sleep, for instance!

He seemed very much surprised, but was extremely nice about it, and I forgave him—darn the fool kid, anyway! Evidently he wasn't able to keep still, however, because he suggested that Mose sail us back to the Fairfield plantation during the night, the kicker not working so I could sleep. Back we went, and I actually had twelve hours of unbroken rest for the first time since we started.

We hunted butterflies till four o'clock next day, and then returned to the boat, where Shorty said we had better doll up and pay a duty call at the Fairfield mansion. Duty call nothing! He wanted to go. I took that opportunity to tell him what I knew of Sir Rat, and he didn't seem a bit surprised. "Of course the Luna Girl is quite a different kind of a horse," I concluded.

"Luna Girl! You noticed it, too?" he answered quickly. "I'll give you credit, Wandering, for acute perception."

There were a lot of people at Sir Rat's, and—very bad sign—they were none of them neighboring planters. In fact there was hardly a Southerner there. It was a distinctly sporty crowd, the women playing bridge and a nice little poker game going on among the men.

Here I am going to skip a lot. We stayed in that neighborhood for three weeks, and about every other night the Luna Girl had one perfectly good, six and a half feet of pink kid courting her. For a time I kept away, until Shorty happened to mention that he had dropped a thousand dollars in the card game. Then I made it my duty to hold up the poker-playing end of the combination—scientifically.

Of course it was a red-hot love affair on both sides, and the prettiest one I have ever seen. I liked the kid; he adored the Luna Girl, and they were as suited to one another as possum and 'simmons to a nigger.

We hunted butterflies and moths persistently during the intervals; but there was more love than entomology in the air, and there could be but one ending to it all. It came quicker than I expected. One night the kid and I hiked for the boat, with him yodeling his head off, and I knew what had happened before he told me. He was to tackle Sir Rat the next night, and we were both too excited to sleep, so we tacked up a dozen sugared doilies in the best places and collected till morning. The moon was on the turn; it was very dark, and, strangely enough, not one luna moth came to the baits where there had been thousands before. Also we heard, from the hill in the swamp, the voodoo song come floating out over the water:

"When de moon am pale, white folks' blood am red;
All de niggers be happy when de white folks dead!
Dah's butt 'flies cahved on de voodoo stick.
Kill all de white folks, kill 'em quick!"

and then the frenzied

"Kill 'em, kill 'em, kill 'em quick!
Dah's butt 'flies cahved on de voodoo stick."

faster and faster rising to demoniacal shrieks.

I was all for breaking up this party, but Shorty said to let 'em enjoy themselves. I suppose he had a fellow feeling for them through his yodeling.

Then a wonderful thing happened. Shorty's net brought in another Juno Moth. But it wasn't a Juno; the tuft of hairs on the abdomen was not red, but white!

"A new species!" he breathed. "Wandering, a new species! I'll call it Hemileuca Etheridgæ. What a beautiful, be-autiful world it is!"

Don't remember how we got through the next day—we were both as nervous as selling platers—but, toward evening, we reached the Fairfield mansion. There were no other visitors this time, and we dined *en famille*—which means only four of us.

When Absalom had brought on the coffee and cigars and gone, Shorty detained the colonel, "something of importance" to say to him. The Luna Girl and I started to leave when the old butler shot past us back into the dining room like a scared cottontail.

"The sup'ntendent like to see yo' at de do', Massa Frank," I heard him say, and Sir Rat followed him out into the hall.

The white-wooled darky threw the door open and dived into the darkness. At the same moment a perfect flock of Luna moths came fluttering in. Sir Rat dashed to the porch, there was the sound of scuffling feet, the beat of a horse's hoofs, then silence. The girl, Shorty, and I rushed outdoors to find it light as day, the negro quarters and barn burning, the flames mounting higher and higher. One of the two superintendents stumbled out of the smoke toward us.

"Bill has been murdered," he gasped, "the bloodhounds and mastiff poisoned, and there isn't a nigger left on the place!"

Sir Rat was clean gone; there was no use trying to fight the fire, and we were all alone save for the countless luna moths that were wildly circling about our heads. There was only one thing to do. Arming ourselves from the weapons in the house, we hastened down the long road toward the landing.

Twice we heard scurrying in the rice, and I emptied my automatic at the sound, and, as we approached the water, the chorus:

> *"Kill 'em, kill 'em, kill 'em quick!"*

followed by the roar of both barrels of Mose's shotgun from the boat.

On board we drew breath and tried to think what to do. There was not another plantation within ten miles, and the nearest town was twice that distance away. Every building on the Fairfield estate was unquestionably doomed. Sir Rat was irretrievably lost. No, there was one faint hope of saving him! We sailed the knockabout well clear of the shore, and leaving the Luna Girl under Mose's protection, Shorty, the superintendent, and I got into the skiff. Muffling the oars, I pulled toward where we had sugared in the very beginning, pushed through the swamp growth, and came to the foot of the hill. Sure enough, there was a great fire burning among the trees as we stole up through the underbrush, and, just as we reached the edge of the circle of light, the voodoo song burst forth:

> *"Butt'fly, butt'fly, floatin' goe,*
> *Reckon thar ahn't no blood in yo'!*
> *No blood, no bones, nothin' 'tall,*
> *'Cause yo' is so lightsome an' small.*
> *Nigger touch yo' full ob de moon,*
> *Him boun' up an' die right soon.*
> *Nigger dahr in de dahk eat yo',*
> *Him can doe what de white folks doe."*

In a great circle about the fire were crouched some thirty niggers, a pannikin of rum before each of them. Sir Rat, naked to the waist, was tied, his face against a tree, and a black-snake whip at his feet. Old Absalom, his yellow vest gleaming in the firelight, and his white-wooled head bare, was going from pannikin to pannikin dropping a luna moth in each, but a luna moth that was blood red.

> *"When de moon am pale, white folks' blood am red,*
> *All de niggers be happy when de white folks dead!*
> *Dah's butt'flies cahved on de voodoo stick.*
> *Kill all de white folks, kill 'em quick!*
> *Dah's butt'flies cahved on de voodoo stick,*
> *Kill 'em, kill 'em, kill 'em quick!"*

With the last words of the song the niggers drank down the rum, holding the fluttering moths between their thick lips.

"No use to tackle that bunch," whispered the trembling superintendent. "We'd better beat it."

"My God, Wandering," fairly shouted Shorty, starting forward, "do you see those lunas are *crimson*, a new species?"

"Come back, you fool!" I yelled. "They are only powdered with red dust." But he was among them, and I settled down to shoot.

A big buck nigger met his first rush, and went down in the fire. Another and another fell before him. They clawed toward him, all that I could not wing, in a swaying, maddened throng. Some he whirled over his head, some fell before his fists, others he crushed or laid out with his knees in a way never learned in any gymnasium. The crowd broke, giving me more open shooting, hesitated, and the woods were full of fleeing niggers. A cask of rum burst into roaring flame, upsetting a large, covered basket, from which rose a cloud of luna moths, dashing into the flames, filling the night with the soft whir of their wings.

Sir Rat was quite dead, without a mark on him. We took his body to the boat and set sail for New Orleans.

That is really the end of the story. The rest is a kind of an introduction that you find at the end of a book to say they lived together ever afterward without throwing dishes.

The Luna Girl hadn't another relative on earth but her father—and he was dead—so she and Shorty were married in New Orleans as soon as we got there. I was witness, best man, gave away the bride, and ordered the wedding supper—cocktails, oysters, rare steak, French fried potatoes, lettuce salad, champagne, and cigars.

One thing I forgot. It happened as we were kicking up the Mississippi and just goes to prove what a king Shorty is.

"Wandering," he said, "you remember that new species, a variation of Juno, that I was going to call Hemileuca Etheridgæ? Well, it is going to be known to science as Hemileuca Wanderingi, the Wandering Moth."

The Dancing Mulatto

*Another story of "Wandering" Smith, whose adventures
with moths and the Luna Girl were related in the December
7th POPULAR. Here "Wandering" makes the acquaintance of
a stage beauty and a mad negro in the shark-infested waters
of the Southern Coast.*

I'M ALWAYS CRAZY TO GET BACK TO NEW ORLEANS from the water or the sticks
and grab onto the bunch of mail waiting at Père Guerrin's restaurant. There
is something mysterious and exciting about letters to me. Even the circulars
from promoters of fake mining stocks are full of romance—I'm strong
for romance—and there never fails to be at least one letter from "Shorty,"
otherwise Montmorency de Haven Etheridge, and the Luna Girl, who is now
Mrs. Shorty. Then I like to read what the people who want to go exploring
or collecting have to say, and sometimes one of them hits me just right, and
I wire:

> Come a hooting.
> (Signed)   WANDERING SMITH.

Mostly, however, I stay in the city a while, taking my fill of metropolitan
delights: prize fights, cocking mains, horse races, moving pictures, and have
the père's tough waiters bring me drinks I don't want, and more food than I
can possibly eat. It soon begins to pall, though, and I get indigestion. Then
I'm off again to South America or poking around in the unfrequented corners
of the southern coast, generally with some scientist or other.

I went through the usual program when I got back from the trip that filled
in the six months after Shorty married the Luna Girl. There was nothing
really interesting in the mail waiting me, but I had only been in New Orleans
two days when a letter came from Old Bug:

> MY DEAR WANDERING: I am tempted, on the grounds of our very
> real friendship, to ask a great favor of you.
>
> One of our most esteemed patrons, the Honorable Charles Kurtz,
> of the Kurtz Packing Company, has asked my advice in regard to an
> unfortunate attachment formed by his only son, Philip. He seems to
> feel that the lady in question, an ornament of the vaudeville stage,
> is not actuated entirely by motives of disinterested affection in this
> matter, but is unduly influenced by the glamour of the large fortune
> which will ultimately come to the young man.
>
> Philip Kurtz, though possessing an unenviable reputation for

wildness, has one redeeming virtue. He is a great fisherman, and from the point of view of a naturalist, I am sending you under separate cover his monograph, "The Breeding Habits of the Tuna."

The Honorable Charles Kurtz has pleaded with his son not to rush into a hasty marriage which he might regret, and obtained his consent not, for six months, of his own volition, to try and see the lady in question or correspond with her.

Here is the rub, however: Philip is filling this interval, expressed in his own words as reported to me, "by keeping a lot of silly asses from drinking too much by drinking as much as I can myself with the laudable purpose of materially reducing the available supply."

It has occurred to me, and I really think the idea a bright one, that if you should take him for a five months' collecting and fishing trip where he could catch quantities of fish, his mind might be taken off his trouble. I should feel he was perfectly safe, in every respect, with you, and it would place me in the enviable position of actually doing our illustrious patron a distinct favor.

Yours sincerely,

A. DELMAR JUMPKINS,
Curator of Entomology,
Museum of Natural History.

P.S.—I trust I am not asking too much of you!
P.S. No. 2.—The museum is *very* short of funds.

A.D.J.

Can you beat it? He trusted he wasn't asking too much! Very darned trustful, I took it! Me steer a lily-handed young souse, who wanted to marry a chorus girl, over the face of the waters that he might forget his troubles while catching little fishes! Still, Old Bug *was* a friend of mine, Pa Kurtz swollen with wealth, the museum "*very* short of funds—"

I cussed myself for a double-dashed fool; but, nevertheless, wired "Come a hooting," then drank three high balls, one after the other, and went to a nigger prize fight.

Philip Kurtz appeared at the père's on the third day. It only took a glance to identify him. He was medium size, with broad shoulders, very black eyes, and dressed in one of those perfectly fitting suits that you know cost at least a hundred dollars just because of its plainness. He saw me watching him, and came straight for my table with outstretched hand.

"I'm Philip Kurtz," he announced simply, "and I know you are Wandering Smith. Let's have a drink!"

Of course it wasn't etiquette for him to order the first one, but he showed his breeding and that he recognized his mistake by letting me pay for it unquestioned—and ordered another. We hardly said a word, just sized each other up, as two strange men will. A single swift glance seemed to satisfy him; then he leaned back and submitted to my scrutiny as though he were used to being on exhibition.

He wasn't really a man, after all, I decided; just a fool boy with little more on his mind than he could conveniently carry. There were great circles around his eyes, and the eyes themselves looked tired. His hands twitched slightly, and I noticed a big bunch of muscle stood out between his thumb and forefinger. As we sat there, wordless, somehow I got to feeling so sorry for him that I began to like him, and, since I could think of nothing to say, just to break the silence, ordered another drink. That's the way the afternoon went. Every twenty minutes or so one of us would say something, then we'd have more booze. We dined at the père's, and afterward, simply in self-protection to get away from the liquor, I suggested that we charter a hack and look around a bit. I defeated my own object. Can't remember all the places we went, but I'm sure of two shows, a cock fight, four gambling houses, aside from innumerable cafés, with drinks, drinks, drinks, till I could hardly see.

We ended up at Gray Jake's dive about midnight, and I'll agree with any man, woman, or child who will even hint I was all in. There was a great hulking nigger in the ring, who offered to forfeit twenty dollars to any one who would stay with him for three rounds. Positively I was so lit that it looked like easy money to me, but Tank—yes, I was calling him Tank by that time—beat me to it. And it was some fight! The boy was at least twenty pounds lighter than the black man, but he could hit like a streak of lightning. Everything was crooked as a ram's horn, of course. It went two rounds; then Kurtz slipped and fell, and the referee counted him out, though he was up at six.

Finally we went home. I remember wanting to ride the horse and being restrained. The next I knew it was morning, and the père was beside my bed with a nice, long, cool mint julep as an eye opener.

I found Philip downstairs in the cafe, sipping his third—he had omitted breakfast—and he greeted me as though he hadn't got the hardest-headed man in Louisiana soused to the eyeballs the night before. Not so yours truly! I spoke hard and fast, and the burden of my remarks was that if he wanted to see any more of me we were going to start for the fishing grounds that very day; that if he ever asked me to have another drink I'd kill him; that I was old enough to be his father, but thanked God I wasn't, and that he ought to be ashamed of me!

I must say he took it like a little man, and it wasn't an hour before we were on the train for St. Augustine.

Of course I got over the night before after an extra sleep, but the boy didn't; he had evidently been at it for some time—and there wasn't a drop of drink to be had on the cars. He tried to sleep, but couldn't; just sat there looking at nothing and making a noble effort to control his nerves.

I've seen the black dog get his fangs into several men in my time, and it isn't a pleasant sight. Some see things, some do things, others go plumb crazy. The boy was different, however, from any I had known, and I wondered how he was going to get relief. It came in a new way—he just talked.

At first it was to me, and then he kind of forgot that I was in the stateroom, and babbled to himself. I learned all about the girl—from what he said I judged she must be right sweet—and I also learned something that his pa, the Honorable K., would have been glad to know, namely that the boy had a very good reason for agreeing not to see or write his sweetheart for six months— she wouldn't let him! There was a mixed-up lot of conversation between them, all about how they loved one another, but she had a fortune within her grasp and wanted to bring something to him, how dangerous it was to dive into a shallow tank, her brother was a fool, and all Spanish documents were liars. He talked himself out finally, and just sat and twitched, and you can bet he was suffering!

At last we reached St. Augustine, and it was a very shaky, white-faced lad I had in tow. We went straight to the Ponce de Leon, where we chartered a private dining room, and it was there ended the chapter on drinks.

"Wandering," said the boy, "I am now going to have my last one for an indefinite, longly indefinite, period, and it is going to be the rajahs' peg."

"Fly to it!" I agreed. "Were it any one else I'd hit him over the head with one of these carved and gilded chairs, but I know you will keep your word. I'll have a bottle of beer myself."

I had my bottle of beer, and he had his fancy drink. It consisted of a pint of champagne mixed with two ponies of brandy all in one big glass. Rajahs must be a short-lived race if they hit that combination with any regularity.

Next morning I had quite a different man with me, and one who apparently had nothing on his mind but getting out onto the water after fish. I always make a point of selecting my own craft, but this time I gave in. Really, he knew more about what he wanted than I did. The boat I chose was condemned as too small, and he chartered a sloop with three-foot draft, steel center board, and a crew of four niggers. What he didn't put on board in the way of tackle, nets, harpoons, and even dynamite, I have yet to see.

Of course we didn't get started that day or the next, but the third night we finally set sail.

I say night advisedly. It was I who selected that time, and the reason was that I didn't want the niggers to get too clear an idea of where we were going. My fishing grounds were less than fifty miles from Miami, but I preferred to sail from St. Augustine in the interests of secrecy.

You see, these fishing grounds are unique. The limestone formation that underlies the Everglades crops up there, a mile or two out at sea, where it is overbuilt with coral. Within this protected water, which you enter by a broad and very deep channel that goes to the very edge of the mangrove-bordered shore, the fish fairly swarm. There are three small islands, strung out like the three stars in the handle of the Dipper, within this reef, and it was on the farthest out of these that I intended to establish our headquarters.

The wind held steadily, and I timed myself well, so it was night again when I swung the sloop through the reef and anchored.

To say Philip was delighted with the place was to put it mildly. The surface of the water was all phosphorescent in the night with the breaking of fish, and the fins of sharks—more sharks than I had ever seen there before—left long trails of light as they cut through the calm sea. From the distance came the crashing slap of an enormous Florida devilfish as it slid out of the water and then came flapping back to its native element, and we filled the air full of shrieking birds with the splash of our anchor.

The boy could not wait till morning to get closer to the water, and nothing would do but that we go out on it. We rowed slowly down the channel in the darkness, though really it was perfectly light from the phosphorescent fishes, a bodyguard of sharks' fins all about us. As we neared the black line of the shore mangroves, just behind the last island, our escort turned swiftly back and I looked around somewhat puzzled for the reason. The answer flashed quickly before me, the broad back fin, like a small canoe sail, of a spotted tiger shark, the king of them all. I slapped the water with an oar, the fin sank, and at that very moment, from the shore tangle of undergrowth, came the weirdest sound that I have ever heard.

It was gibberish, yet wasn't gibberish. Had a certain regularity about it, a suggestion of the rush and slap of waves far out at sea, ending with the shriek of the storm wind:

> "Swish ole, swish ole, ayaha, whe-e,
> Swish ole, swish ole, ayaha, whe-e,
> Ayaha, whe-e, swish ole, swish ole,
> Auguhahah, eh-e-e!"

The dark-green foliage parted, and onto a yard-wide, sandy beach glided a dim human figure. First it ran swiftly from one end to the other of the white sand, returned in a looping series of figure eights, then standing, its face from the water, began to hop about in the mad dance the Seminole Indians have borrowed from the flamingos. For fully five minutes it gyrated silently, while I held the skiff motionless, the oars barely dipped against the tide, and then it began to sing:

"Mah babe she hungry fo' hah mahn,
She watch him 'cause she lub him so.
He brung hah all de bes' he cahn,
He feed hah high 'cause he hah mahn,
Hah mahn who will not let hah goe!"

There was an interlude of swaying dance, and then another verse:

"Mah babe lub fisch, mah babe lub meat,
Mah babe lub mos' de blood all hot.
Red blood is hah especiales' treat,
Hot blood she reckon mighty sweet,
De bestes' food she got."

The song broke off short as his mad whirl brought the singer facing us, and he spied the boat lying silently on the water. With a final maniacal "Eh-e-e," he jumped straight backward into the underbrush and disappeared. At that very moment the water boiled beside us, up came the canoe-sail-shaped fin, and the small, emotionless gray eye of the great fish glared into mine as it turned sideways in the water, its seriate rows of teeth cutting clean through the oar just above the blade.

"Out of here for mine!" I exclaimed emphatically.

"Me, too," said Philip. "And I only hope you aren't even half as scared as I am."

I stuck the remaining oar from side to side of the boat like a paddle—any kind of a shark will snap at a sculling oar, and I wasn't talking any chances—and we progressed slowly against the tide. The fin of the tiger shark did not reappear, but our former bodyguard of ordinary sharks soon picked us up, and we reached the sloop and hoisted the skiff without a word spoken between us.

On deck, the boy turned to me and held out his hand.

"Thank you for a whale of a time, Wandering," he said.

The whole performance bothered me. To begin with, a lot of sharks, though it surely meant the fish were there, promised unpleasant fishing. Then that dancing maniac was something new to me; there had not been, to my knowledge at least, a human being within miles of the place on my last trip. One man would attract others, and I visualized a canning factory taking toll with nets and dynamite from my pet fishing grounds. The tiger shark was worst of all. A fish of that species has an unbelievable appetite and will soon drive every finny thing out to sea if it lingers long in one place.

Philip had turned in, and there was nothing for me but to do likewise. My mind full of gloomy forebodings, I climbed into the bunk, and, all night was pursued through my dreams by the hideous, cold, dispassionate eyes of legions of tiger sharks.

Dawn broke the way it does on the east coast, in such a blaze of glory that heaven no longer seems a myth. It is utterly impossible to sleep after the first light comes, there is so much to be seen and even more to be heard. The sea is full of breaking fish, the air of screaming birds, while the wonderful Florida sunshine plays so brilliantly over all that you can nearly hear its chiming in the voices of a thousand tiny silver bells.

Nevertheless, it was with rueful countenance that Philip and I gazed over the side of the sloop. The water, all within the reef, was literally sown with the fins of sharks, and we well knew what that meant for the fishing.

"Do you suppose it's a convention or just a rally of the Smith shark family?" the boy asked.

I had no answer ready, but went below and brought up a high-power rifle. For half an hour we enjoyed—no, I can't say enjoyed; it was too gruesome— a new species of sport. The water would have flattened and turned lead bullets, but I had some steel-tipped shells, and no sooner did one of the great fish turn, exposing the white of its belly, than I fired. There was little chance of killing outright; the shot must be placed in a vital spot for that, but the slightest wound accomplished the same result. In a flash the one hit was surrounded by scores of its brethren, and, while the water seethed and tossed, literally torn to fragments.

We soon tired of this gruesome amusement, however, and, since there was no use in attempting to fish inside and the tide was on the flood, hoisted sail and put out through the channel to sea. I left Mose, my cook—whom I had torn from his last matrimonial adventure, probably his twentieth, to go with me—and two of the other niggers to prepare quarters for us on the island.

Within the reef it must have been a shark convention, after all, since there was not a single fin outside; but, on the other hand, all the fish in the world seemed to have emigrated there. The Gulf Stream swept in close to the shore at that point, bringing with it dolphins, iridescent and brilliantly marked, agile bonito—these last two the most graceful of all fish—blowing and wheezing schools of porpoises, and we even spied a great swordfish ranging to and fro. Of the lesser dwellers of the deep there was legion.

The skiff was quickly over the side, with a powerful negro to row it, and we made our casts. Instantly both baits were taken, and when the fish were landed they proved to be amberjack. Then I lost my bait, and the boy hooked onto a barracuda. No use going into details. Never have I seen such sport. There were tuna, mutton fish, groupers, drum, everything you can possibly imagine, though it was only later in the afternoon that we saw tarpon. Then came a gleaming school of them surging out to sea, and Philip cast into their midst. His pole bent, and a seven-foot silvery fish sprang, at the sting of the hook, clear of the water. Then there *was* a fight! Foot by foot the line would come in, only to go out twenty times that length. The run carried us a full mile, until we worked in shore off the mouth of the channel, and gradually the fish tired. Foot by foot again, even inch by inch, the line came in, and the rushes were becoming shorter and shorter, when I happened to look toward the channel opening in the reef. It was alive with speeding fins, the sharks even piling out of the water in their haste to escape to sea.

"Here comes your shark Smith family reunion," I sang out; "better get your fish in quickly!"

I spoke too late. A twenty-foot monster rose from the depths and snapped the seven-foot tarpon clean in two. From a live pull the strain on the line changed to a dead weight, and Philip brought the half-portion fish to the side of the boat, not, however, before another shark had clipped off an additional section.

The fishing was over, of course, and surrounded by shark fins we rowed back to the sloop, and, beating in through the reef, and anchoring close to the island, went ashore.

I thought it strange that no fins showed inside until I spied the unmistakable dorsal of the tiger shark in pursuit of a school of mullet.

Mose, not a talkative nigger from having been married so much, had quite a story to tell. It seems that as soon as we had put out to sea a dugout appeared, paddled by a mulatto, and escorted by the fin of a tiger shark. The nigger landed on our island, turning to curse the monster that wove back and forth in circles near the shore, and came up to where my men were pitching camp. There he had begged food, in payment for which he had sung and danced. He told them that fish had been plentiful inside until the tiger shark, with a million other species, had come in with the last storm, but since that time it had been nearly impossible to catch anything, the sea scavengers snatching the fish from his lines or tearing his nets to pieces. Mose gathered that he had a mate on the mainland back, some place among the mangroves, but aside from the fact that he was a "rhymin' niggah"—that is, he made up the words to his songs as he went along—and seemed nearly crazy with fury against the tiger shark, there had not, up to that point, been anything wildly unusual about him.

The extraordinary part came late in the afternoon, and certainly was rather ghastly. Mose chopped off the head of a fowl in preparation for our dinner, and, at the sight of the blood, the mulatto turned into a maniac. Every drop of it he caught in a jar brought from the dugout, and then followed Mose around, begging him to cut off the head of one of the other niggers, who was somewhat portly, and let him have the blood. The fat coon was first indignant, then scared to death—my cook probably entered into the spirit of the thing, though he took care not to tell me so—and finally grabbed up a gun and tried to shoot our queer guest. The mulatto ran for his rude craft, the jar of blood under his arm, and, snatching up on the way a large carving knife that he had much admired, pushed off into the lagoon. The tiger shark was still waiting, and twice, before the dugout had reached the shore mangroves, made a rush, nearly upsetting it, while the paddler beat it off with a broken oar and a stream of imprecations, to finally land and drag his craft out of sight in the underbrush. Then, half an hour before the sloop returned, the tiger shark had chased all the other sharks out through the channel.

"We must get that fish somehow, and to-night," I remarked to Philip; "there will be no peace or comfort while it is around."

"Better fill the mulatto full of arsenic and feed him to it," the boy suggested, "and we'll be rid of two nuisances at the same time."

With that he went off to measure and dissect the day's catch, having the scientist bug as bad as any of 'em, and being much more interested in a tiny fish with a misplaced scale than the largest, healthiest thing that ever swam.

After dinner, when it was too dark for young Kurtz to smear himself with fish scales any longer, we held a consultation anent the tiger shark. He was all for going out that night and harpooning it. I put the kibosh on that at once. A friend of mine had ironed one the year before, and it had chewed the end off his boat. It seemed wiser to me to take our rifles and try to kill it, or at least maim it sufficiently so that it would flee out to sea, if not torn to pieces by the others.

As we pushed off the skiff, from the distance came the sound of the mulatto's singing, and, approaching the shore, we saw him prancing up and down the strip of white sand, waving the purloined carving knife. I held the boat by the oar tips, and pointed. As the man moved from one end of the beach to the other a fin paralleled his course in the water. Floating a little nearer, we could distinguish the words of the song:

"Debil, debil, don'feah yo'!
Mah babe's fed bu'yo'mus'goe.
Mah babe's fed with blood all red.
Debil, debil soon be deahd!
Don'feah yo', don'feah yo'!
Eat de fisch so yo'mus'goe.
Wan'mah babe fo'mah set free.
Debil, yo'goin'heah from me!"

Out of breath, he paused for a moment; then, the knife in his teeth, dove straight off into the water, while the tiger shark's fin slithered sideways toward the splash.

I grabbed my rifle and fired, but the bullet went high, drilling through the fin, and the mulatto, rising by the shark's side, poised and drove his knife downward. A phosphorescent streak of light enveloped the monster as it went under our boat, and we could plainly see the negro clinging to the haft of the deeply buried knife. Up they came, not five yards away; the man-eater rolled over, and I emptied my magazine into its ugly head, while Philip darted a harpoon into the white of the throat.

All this happened in less time than it takes to tell, and we dragged the dead beast up on the beach, the negro still clinging to the knife in its side. In spite of sinister appearance and the evident fear it had inspired in all the others, its length was only about nine feet, a pigmy by the side of the shark that had chopped in two the big tarpon.

"Dante's Inferno was *some* place from the description," Philip said, "but it can't touch yours. We'll christen this charming spot Wandering's Hell."

"Dis Blood Inlet," came the mulatto's voice as he rose unsteadily to his feet, "an' dat done been mah fisch."

"You're welcome to it," Philip answered, "but I want to look it over in the morning, so don't cut it up."

"Mos' cehtain, sah; mos' cehtain! Now yo'-all he'p mah drag him whar de ole buzzahds won' get him."

"Come on, Wandering!" commanded the boy, grabbing hold of the harpoon. "It's nothing but a nightmare, anyway, and it will be all right in a minute. Nurse will wake us, and we will find we are safe in our little beds."

We pulled the carcass along the beach and into a path that opened through the mangroves. A couple of heaves and we were beside a fifteen-foot broad lane of water, into which we pushed our burden and where it promptly sank. The color of the water showed it very deep, but I knew gases would accumulate within the dead thing and bring it to the surface in the morning.

We picked our way back to the beach, the negro preceding us, and, as his feet touched the sand, he whirled away in the flamingo dance, singing:

> *"Blood an' meat, blood an' meat,*
> *Mah babe she eat, an' eat, an' eat!*
> *Auguhahah, eh-e-e,*
> *She eat, an' eat jus' 'cause ob me.*
> *Eh-e-e, eh-e-e!"*

Philip and I tumbled into the skiff, leaving him howling and whirling on the sand.

For a month we settled down to steady fishing and collecting, the mulatto always hanging about until we really became quite used to him. Of course he was mad as a hatter, but apparently harmless after he had been deprived of his only weapon. This happened in rather an odd way.

The morning after the death of the tiger shark, Philip rowed over by himself to examine it, his skiff loaded with collecting jars and smelling horribly of formaldehyde. He was gone three hours, and came back radiant. It seems that the great fish itself had not proved especially interesting, but on its belly were stuck three remoras—flatish, parasitic fish that fasten themselves by a sucking disk to the bodies of sharks—that told an interesting story. They were of different species, one found hitherto only off the coast of India, one that had never been taken north of Brazil, and the third—oh, delight and ambition of every naturalist!—undescribed in the annals of science.

While he was holding forth on this extraordinary piece of luck the stolen carving knife slipped from his pocket and tinkled on the deck.

"Did our friend have an excess of conscience and return this?" I asked, picking it up.

"Well, not exactly," he answered judicially. "It was rather strange, that part, and, for a moment, somewhat exciting. The mulatto, when he wasn't carried away by an attack of his dancing mania, simply hung over me. He was more than afraid that I was going to slice off at least half his 'fisch,' I daresay. I happened to cut my finger in removing the last of the remoras. Naturally I stuck it in my mouth, but not before that human whirligig had seen the blood.

" 'Don't waste hit! Don't waste hit!' he yelled. 'Ah wan' hit fo' mah babe.'

"And then he pulled out the knife and flew at me. He was about four times as strong as I am, a regular gorilla, but I happened to catch his left hand in mine, and pulled it back of him, so he had to face from me. One thing I have and that is a grip"—I remembered the bunch of muscle between thumb and first finger I had noticed in Père Guerrin's—"and I simply squeezed till he dropped the knife. At once he calmed down, and I watched him tow the shark out of sight up that odd lane of water. By the way, I found a minimum of thirty feet in that channel over a half mile of water, sounding it with a harpoon line, and it seems to go on indefinitely as straight as a die."

Then Kurtz began to talk of his remoras again. All scientists are more or less, generally more, cracked, but I like 'em.

After that we kind of got used to the maniac, as I said before, and he was always around. Of course we watched him, were careful not to leave edged tools within his reach, and chased him away when there was any blood spilled, even that of fish. One person alone remained absolutely unreconciled to him, namely the fat coon whose blood he had demanded, and the mulatto kept his distance, though he watched him furtively, evidently gloating over his size.

We used the nets a great deal, letting most of the catch go, and keeping only what we needed for scientific purposes. The "rhymin' niggah" furiously resented the escape of the smallest fish, and would gather up every scrap, and even steal from the net if we did not watch him. Once, at nightfall, we took a whole school of tarpon in the big steel net, and staked it out for examination in the morning, with the fish crowded close together. During the darkness the mulatto helped himself to our largest skiff, and must have filled and emptied it a dozen times during the night.

We had some trouble with sharks, of course, though they never reappeared in their former numbers. Also, Philip hit on a way of handling them that he wondered he had not thought of before. A quarter of a stick of dynamite attached to copper wire was concealed in a dead fish. Mister Shark swallowed the bait, Philip switched on the current from an electric battery, exploding the bomb, and that was the end of another sea scavenger. It was funny to watch the little pilot fish that always accompany sharks as their guardian angels go back and forth between their charge and the bait, plainly, through some wonderful instinct, feeling that all was not well. Appetite generally overruled caution, however, and there was one shark less in the sea.

The mulatto was awfully interested in this sport, the remains being his perquisite, and we even caught him sending out pieces of bloody fish with the tide to lure sharks within the reef, a trait of cunning for which we had not given him credit.

It was a splendidly healthy life, the weather held beautifully, and we worked very hard.

I don't think that Philip forgot his girl for a moment, though, and I know he grieved deeply at times. The fit would come on hardest in the evenings, when there was no more work to do, and it was then that the dancing mulatto proved a real blessing. He was always ready to sing his strange improvisations, and it would have been impossible to keep him from dancing.

Where he came from I never definitely found out—he told a different tale each time he was asked—but I strongly suspect he had escaped from some negro asylum—there is one, I believe, near Miami. I speculated a good deal also on what the black woman was like that he kept so carefully hidden in the mangrove swamp, and wondered if she really had the enormous and perverted appetite for the strange food he brought her. The idea was somehow monstrous, but then she might be only one of his hallucinations. Any reference to his babe drove him into a wriggling agony of embarrassment. He acted in exactly the same way a dog does when it greets its master after a long absence, ending up always with the flamingo dance.

We had a full month of wonderful sunshine, and then the weather changed. The fish gave the first intimation; the tarpon, and then all the other species, running out to sea. I knew what was coming, and prepared for it as best I could. The sloop was moved into the deeper water of the channel and double anchored fore and aft, with plenty of chain. On the island we made all snug, driving additional tent pegs.

The norther broke with all the fury of the tropics, and it was bitterly cold. For three days we saw no more of our maniac; he disappeared on the mainland with a dynamited shark in tow. And what a three days! Our tents went flat, fire was literally blown from the island, and finally we were forced to take refuge on board the wildly tossing sloop.

It was during the third night that the storm blew away, and we awoke to sunshine. Philip and I hurried up on deck to take our morning plunge— providing there were no sharks about—and stopped, and stared. Piled up on the edge of the shoal water of the island was a little white knockabout, her mast gone. It was not the wreck, however, or the man in golden yellow tights and swimming shirt letting himself down into the water that held our eyes, but a girl! Clad in a brilliant crimson one-piece swimming suit, she was poised for a dive on the stern of the boat. I doubt if I have ever seen anything lovelier or more graceful. She was a sunbeam incarnate, if you can imagine a blood-red sunbeam!

The man soused himself gingerly into the little waves, the girl cut the water in a beautiful, lithe curve, and Philip, with a yell like a Comanche, went over the side of the sloop. Up he came, shouting: "Marion, Marion!" and a red-turbaned head rising above the water turned toward him. A dozen strokes put them in each other's arms, and they sank lip to lip.

Here was romance! Romance with a vengeance! And I'm strong for romance. I tumbled into the skiff and rowed to where they were now treading water, hands clasped and talking seventeen to the dozen.

"Marion," said Philip, "this is Mr. Wandering Smith, my very good friend and present chaperon. Wandering, this is Miss Dupuis, the unconscious cause of my wanderings."

Rowing a boat, I could not "rise and bow," as the etiquette books have it, so I just said I was glad to meet her, and grinned. She tore her eyes from her lover long enough to smile at me, but that smile did the business. Young love, young love! I've been through it myself, and married twice, besides.

Ultimately we reached shore and sanity, and sat down on the sand.

Miss Dupuis, or, rather, Marion—I was calling her Marion before I knew it, and neither she nor Philip seemed to mind—had been blown into the inlet, with her brother, on the tail end of the storm. Their trip was after treasure; they had come alone, and were quite confident of recovering the gold, even were it deep under water, since Marion was a professional swimmer and gained her livelihood by diving from the top of theaters into a tank. I remembered, then, Philip's unconscious conversation when he was on the verge of D.T.'s.

At this point the man in yellow waded in to us from the knockabout and greeted Philip.

"You seem to have turned up again, Tank. How is your good father?"

"He is very well, thank you, Carlos, and would undoubtedly be touched by your interest. How is rhyming?"

Then they just glared at one another, and it was evident no love was lost there.

At last Philip remembered his manners.

"Mr. Wandering Smith, Mr. Carlos Livingston Dupuis!"

I nodded curtly—my friends' enemies are my enemies—while he examined me coolly.

"Wandering! Ah, yes, a kind of modern Smith-Æneas, I take it. By the way, I, too, have a title. Leaving off all the other names, I am generally known as Tough Dupuis."

I refrained, with difficulty, from telling him he looked it, which would have been a lie. As a matter of fact, he was as handsome as a patent-medicine chromo—the after-taking picture—and looked exactly as one would imagine the virile Whitman type of poet should.

An embarrassed silence fell upon us, the exquisite girl in her close-fitting crimson suit, the handsome, bearded poet dressed in yellow, and us two ordinary fellows in faded trunks and jerseys. It was broken by the grating of a keel on the sand, and the mulatto stepped from his dugout. For a moment he stared at Marion, a vivid blotch of red against the glaring white sand, and then sprang toward her with a frantic yell.

"Eh-e-e, gib knife, gib harpoon! Ah kill hah, Ah kill hah! She blood, blood, blood, red blood! Mah babe lub hah, mah babe lub hah!"

I jumped forward, but the poet was in front of me, and, with the most perfect grace and ease, knocked the nigger sprawling. Marion flew into Philip's arms. The black man rose in a flash and gyrated over the beach as he sang, varying his dance by flinging himself imploringly at our feet:

> *"Mah babe lub blood, she lub hit so!*
> *Mah babe lub blood all boilin' sweet.*
> *Don' let de red blood thing toe goe,*
> *Tha' red blood thing, tha' red blood meat!*
> *Mah babe don stahve until she seek.*
> *Ah get hah food as bes' ah cahn.*
> *Ah cotch de turtle in de creek,*
> *Ah feed hah buzzahds, ah, hah mahn."*

He stopped, and seemed to come back to some semblance of sanity.

"Cotch po' niggah some fisch in de net," he pleaded, "mah babe done been stahvin'. Nothin' bu' ole buzzahds to feed hah for fo' dahys!"

"Kill that fool thing, Wandering!" said Philip over his shoulder as he waded with the girl into the water.

I took the mulatto to the camp, and, when next I saw Marion, she had slipped a white skirt and middy waist over her crimson sea costume, and was sitting on the deck of the sloop, obviously quarreling with Philip.

I put an end to that with the call for breakfast, and, rowing out, brought them ashore.

The meal was distinctly an unpleasant one. Philip was sulky, the girl pouting, and the mulatto kept interrupting us to go fishing until I had to set the fat coon on him. The poet was the only one that talked, and I can't say much for his conversation. He professed a great admiration for the dancing mulatto, called him a bard of the wilderness, hazarded that the babe of whom he raved was probably beautiful beyond words, a bronze Venus! Mad, yes, but were not all geniuses mad! He was a genius and mad himself. Perchance soul would speak to soul! He would read him some of his own verse—

After breakfast, Tough, the poet, went off to his wreck and began to put it to rights. I'll give him credit for evidently knowing something about boats, and he was the strongest man I have ever seen. By sheer bull strength he hauled the busted mast out of the water, and, when I left, already had a jury rig under way.

The mulatto tagged after me as I walked up the beach looking for the lovers, again imploring "fisch."

I found them at it again, quarreling like two children, tears in the girl's eyes, Philip's face red as a tomato, and I didn't see where I was called upon to stand for such doings.

"Look here!" I said. "I'm perfectly willing to act as chaperon to you two to the north pole or beyond, but I am not going to referee a continuous prize fight. If you have troubles tell them to Uncle Wandering and he will make it all right."

Really they were glad to be interrupted, and both began to talk to me at once. It took some brain work to figure out what it was all about and to separate what each one was driving at.

Philip wanted to sail right back to Miami and get married. She acknowledged that she wanted to all right, all right, but if they did Father Kurtz would disinherit him—not that she cared for the money, but "dear" was so extravagant.

The boy maintained that ten thousand dollars a year, which he had in his own right, was quite enough for them to live on with economy, and it would be fun to be poor. He also hotly denied the charge of extravagance.

Perhaps he wasn't. Everything is relative in this world, and the cigars we had taken with us only cost thirty dollars a box.

The girl appealed to me: Was it not the sensible thing for her, with her brother, to sail farther down the coast and pick up the half million in gold—half million in gold! Just like that!—that was waiting for them. She had a map that showed the exact spot, in addition to translations of Spanish documents giving all details. It had come into her possession—

Here the mulatto appeared and implored us to go fishing. He wept, threatened, and finally became so abusive that I chased him to the dugout and heaved a piece of driftwood after him.

This broke off the conference, and we adjourned till the afternoon, when the brother was to be present. Meanwhile, the two kids started courting, as was right and proper, and when they began to hold hands and forgot me I went away, satisfied.

It was too rough for fishing, though growing rapidly calmer, so I rowed out to the wreck and helped the poet. He certainly made me work. Also, his line of talk gave me more than a pain. I asked him what he thought of the treasure hunt, and he reproved me as an iconoclast and barbarian for mentioning material things on such a beautiful day. Then he recited about a yard of his poems, word colors, he called them, that sounded something like this:

> *"Golden, cream, pink, rose,*
> *Her hair, brow, cheek, lips.*
> *Oh, to be the wind that blows. . . .*
> *Golden, cream, pink, rose,*
> *Ah, to be the wind that blows,*
> *And this rainbow sips!"*

He pronounced wind like you wind an alarm clock. I preferred the crazy nigger's verse.

In the afternoon, we all met under the dining-room tent, and the girl produced a formidable sheath of documents.

"First, I must tell you about it," she said eagerly. "During the last century a ship sailed from Spain with half a million in gold for the purchase of lands in Louisiana. It was wrecked, and the sole survivor—"

"Skip that part," I suggested.

"All right. The map and documents came into my possession in a remarkable way. While a young girl of the Spanish nobility was in New York her father fell dreadfully ill. Their remittances did not arrive—"

"Skip," I suggested again.

"Of course it was pure gratitude on his part, for I only gave him two hundred dollars, and—"

"Skip," I repeated wearily.

"Well, look at the map, anyway," she snapped. "Don't skip that!"

It was a perfectly good map, well drawn, and covered with little pictures, as such maps always are—dolphins, trees, and the treasure ship itself, with an arrow pointing to it. I have seen hundreds like it. They make 'em in New Orleans to sell to the tourists. In one respect it differed from the usual run, however; the latitude and longitude were given. And when I read the figures I groaned. They exactly indicated the location of a fresh-water lake, a little farther down the coast, and two miles inland. Fighting for time, I asked the poet's opinion.

"What care I for gold when there is sunshine all about?" he answered.

"But what do *you* think of it?" demanded the girl. "Wouldn't it be a sin not to go and get it?"

"I—well, I—" But the sentence was never finished. There was a shout from the beach, and the mulatto staggered toward us.

"Yo'-all won' gib po' niggah fisch. Then Ah buy fisch fo' mah babe. Get de net, get de net, get de net!"

From his closed right hand he flung several tarnished gold pieces on the table and whirled away, dancing.

"Ariel showering gold," said the poet.

"Great goodness!" exclaimed the girl.

Philip said nothing, but picked up one of the coins, while I looked over his shoulder. It was larger than a double eagle, stamped with the head of rex something, and a lot of Spanish words; the date was worn away.

"Get the large mesh steel net," I yelled to our niggers—I knew the mulatto preferred quantity to quality—"and catch this nut a lot of fish."

"Where did you get this money?" I shouted to the dancing man.

"Is yo'-all goin' toe gib mah fisch?" he asked doubtfully.

"Yes; where did you get this money?"

For answer he began to sing:

"Eh-e-e, mah babe shall eat
Ob fisches. Eh-e dis niggah glahd!
Above de gold she always sleep,
Don't touch or yo' be deahd!"

I caught him by the shoulder, and made him stand still.

"Who is this babe of yours, and where did she get this money?" I demanded sternly.

Instantly he began to cringe and wriggle in horrible embarrassment, exactly like a dog, and no more words came from him. Disgusted, I turned back to my friends.

"We'll pick up this treasure first," I stated positively.

"We haven't got it yet," warned Philip; "haven't an idea where it is."

"Let finding out be my part," volunteered the poet. "I'll take my brother bard fishing out beyond the reef, while your men are drawing the nets. He'll yield up his secret to me, and then I'll rob him ruthlessly. My name is Tough Dupuis!"

"Go to it!" I agreed heartily. "There will be two of you. Meanwhile, I'll take advantage of his absence to explore that lane of water up which Philip saw him tow the dead shark."

We followed out this program exactly. The poet took the mulatto, somewhat dazed by the honor, off with him in a boat, and, as soon as they disappeared outside the reef, I rowed for the strip of white sand on the mainland.

It proved an easy task to drag the light skiff through the path in the mangroves, and I was soon rowing up the deep, straight channel. The water was running out furiously with the tide, so that I made but slow headway. Nor were my surroundings cheerful. Not a fish rippled the surface—the water just flowed smoothly and swiftly on between banks where the luxuriant, tropical vegetation met overhead—and there was no sound of bird or beast.

A mile and a half of hard rowing, and the current slackened. Then came a sharp turn, where I spied, on the bank, a wretched hut, door open, and quite empty—the dancing mulatto's babe was evidently nothing more than a figment of his diseased brain—and I looked ahead to find the channel blocked. Square across it lay an old, old, queer ship. Rowing nearer to the water-flush bulwarks, I looked beyond. Spread before me was a great pool a hundred yards broad by two hundred long, surrounded by ghostly white, dead cypress trees festooned with countless, motionless buzzards, and the wind brought me an indescribable stench of carrion.

It was a ghastly place, the most ghastly part of it the awful silence. My heart began to pound, and I looked fearfully over my shoulder. There was a splash that sounded to my overstrained nerves like a crash of thunder, and, turning the skiff with one oar sweep, I never stopped rowing until the mangroves hove in sight.

Out on the inlet the mulatto passed me, his dugout loaded to the gunwales with fish, and towing something behind. The moment he saw me he began a song of exultation:

> "Ah feed mah babe on bestes' bes',
> On blood an' meat, on blood an' meat.
> Ah feed mah babe on bestes' bes',
> On everything tha's feet.
> Ah got hah all de bestes' food,
> 'Cause ah got gold—"

Heaving an extra rowlock at him, I caught him on the side of the head, and he shut up.

The news of the old ship stranded far up the lane of water nearly sent the girl into hysterics of joy. She was all for going there at once, but I thought it wiser to wait till morning and get the mulatto out of the way.

The poet alone showed no excitement. He was plainly peeved that he had not made the discovery himself, and, besides, the fishing trip had proved neither profitable nor enjoyable.

"I recited the greatest poem that has ever been written—one of my own," he explained, "and it left him utterly unmoved. All he cared for was 'fisch, fisch, fisch.' Then we came on the floating carcass of a dead steer, thrown from some cattle boat, and he insisted on taking it in tow after beating off the sharks. He is just an ordinary, uninteresting maniac."

You may well believe Philip and I were up before dawn. We had decided not to let the negroes into the secret of the treasure and ourselves row the skiff to the old ship. It was barely light when we loaded the boat, putting in, as well as lunch for four, canvas bags for the gold, several sticks of dynamite with caps, some copper wire, and the electric battery. The purpose of this last combination was to blow up any obstruction that might be in our path to the treasure.

The sun was just above the horizon, the mulatto's dugout silhouetted against it as though framed in a disk of gold, when the girl, in her one-piece crimson swimming suit, dove gracefully into the silver water, and Philip was over the side of the sloop with a loud splash. Next appeared the poet and let himself lazily down from the bowsprit, his great muscles standing out like rounded lumps of marble. The words of the dancing nigger's song came to us clearly over the water:

> "Mah babe she lub hah mahn,
> She lub, she lub hah mahn.
> He treat hah powerful lubingly,
> He brang hah fisch from out de sea.
> Mah babe she lub hah mahn."

"Race you to him, dear," cried Marion to her lover, and clove through the water with beautiful long strokes. The boy was after her, falling farther and farther behind, and, as she approached the dugout, the mulatto rose to his feet. A sudden premonition of evil flashed over me.

"Keep away from him!" I shouted. "Keep away from him!" But I spoke too late.

"De live blood thing, de live blood thing!" the maniac shrieked. "Oh, how mah babe lub hah!" And he brought his paddle down on the red-turbaned head.

I saw her go limp, start to sink, his arm shoot out, clutch and drag her into the dugout. Saw him tie her hands and feet with two twists of a cord, and paddle madly for the mainland.

It was like a nightmare, all happening in a flash, and I found myself in the

skiff, rowing as I had never rowed before. The poet climbed over the stern
and caught up a pair of sculls, dropping them for a moment to pull Philip into
the boat as we surged past. There was no sound save the laboring of our breath
as we bent to the oars; not a word was spoken. The bow grated on sand, and
we rushed the boat through the mangroves to the lane of water. The dugout
was a dim shadow far ahead, driven on by the maniac's powerful strokes. Up
that silent mile and a half we sped, had gained when we reached the turn, and
whirled around by the wretched hut—then we stopped rowing.

The black madman stood on the old, old ship, the crimson-clad girl limp
across his shoulder.

"Eh-e-e, mah babe, mah babe!" he called, and from the pool beyond
slowly rose, inches at a time, a great six-foot fin, the fin of a tiger shark
enormous beyond belief.

"Mah babe, mah lubly babe!" he shrieked, as the awful monster turned
on its side in the water nearly beneath his feet. "Ah brang yo' blood—red,
live blood!"

The poet slipped quietly into the channel, and disappeared on the shore.
Philip threw himself face downward in the boat. I jerked my automatic from
under my arm, yet dared not shoot lest the senseless girl go, with the fall of
her captor, into the waiting jaws of the shark, now lying its forty-foot length
flush with the surface.

The mulatto shifted his burden, and I thought the end had come, but it
was only to his other shoulder.

> "Look, mah babe, look, look at de meat,
> Young thing, blood red, won' she be sweet!
> Look, babe, wha' yo' mahn brang toe yo',
> Yo' mahn who lub, jus' lub yo' so!"

I was conscious, out of the tail of my eye, as I waited for a chance to
shoot, of the poet creeping along the outer bulwarks.

The mulatto broke into his mad dance, balancing, with his crimson
burden, along the edge of the wreck, the greedy monster below following
his every movement. For just one second he pirouetted, his back to the shark,
and, in that second, the poet was upon him. One hand caught and flung the
girl into the water by my side, the other flew to the dancer's throat. There
was a wild medley of legs and arms, from which the nigger shot over his
opponent's head into the pool.

They say that sharks must turn on their sides before they can injure a
man, but this one cut the mulatto clean in two with a straight lunge, then rose
again to finish his work.

The girl was not dead, only stunned, and came back to consciousness in her lover's arms. We rowed them to the sloop, and then Dupuis and I went back—we had a task to perform.

From the deck of the old wreck we called out, and the giant fin rose from beneath the water. Slowly the forty-foot leviathan swam toward us, half turning, showing row after row of teeth in its sinister, oblique mouth, and lay, expectant, gazing up at us from a small, hideous gray eye.

I took the fish we had prepared with two sticks of dynamite inside attached to a long copper wire, and hurled it far out into the pool. The giant fin jiggered to the bait, the wire tightened. I switched on the current, and that, in a lather of foam, was the end of the dancing mulatto's babe.

We found that the treasure lay nearly beneath our feet. From the rotted hull of the ancient ship gold fairly seeped out into the pool. Evidently the cargo had all shifted to that side in the mighty tornado that must have driven the ship inland, and, at the same time, imprisoned the tiger shark within the pool, all more years ago than a man can realize.

We could never persuade Philip and Marion to return there, and, for ten days, the poet and I dredged out the gold alone, ten days in which the buzzards feasted on the tiger shark, blown in two by the charge of dynamite, and grounded in shoal water at the upper end of the pool.

Of course there was no half million of gold; but, when it was finally turned into modern money, the rarity of most of the coins commanded prices that brought the total not far from that sum.

Philip and Marion went back to New York and were married somehow, also with Pa K.'s consent.

Tough Dupuis lingered on with me all summer, fishing and reciting poetry. I took turns admiring his magnificent physique and hating him for the things he said. Twice I attempted to lick him, totally without success, and he threatened that if I tried it again he would spank me until I howled. I, therefore, abandoned the idea, and, by making allowances for what he said, we became very good friends.

My share of the treasure gave me more money than I knew what to do with.

The poet refused to take a cent. Said he wasn't going to crush the flower of his genius beneath a weight of bloodstained gold. So we sent his part to Old Bug for the museum.

It's funny, but Philip is never associated in my mind with the girl, the mulatto, the shark, or anything that happened to us together, but only with that last drink of his, the rajahs' peg.

When I got back to New Orleans, and Père Guerrin inquired about the boy and asked me to have a drink, I told about Philip's last one, the champagne with two ponies of brandy in it. The père listened politely until I was through; then, calling one of his tough waiters, ordered two beers.

The Golden Anaconda

Wandering Smith comes in touch with the relics of a mighty race—a race dwindled to a few poor survivors, but a race that left its imprint on the world thousands of years ago. Wasn't it Ferguson who told us about the Golden Man in one of his novels? Here you will meet the Golden Woman, a beautiful voiceless thing who seems like some goddess of the olden days to Wandering Smith and his fellow adventurers whose throats are full of the dead dust of long-forgotten peoples. There is a suggestion of Rider Haggard in this striking novelette.

THE PROFESSOR CAUTIOUSLY RAISED HIS FLAMING RED HEAD above the side of the boat, reached back, picked up a felt-wrapped wire loop attached to a thick cord, and lunged over the bow.

"Got him!" he yelled, and I threw my weight on the cord. Instantly there was a terrific splashing. The jungle awoke to the chatter of monkeys, shrieks of gorgeously colored macaws, and the clear-toned clang of a bell bird's voice. From a lather of foam emerged the head of an anaconda, the great water boa of South America, lashing the river with its sides as it swam from us. The professor calmly began to row against the great snake, while I dragged at the rope, using one of the seats as a lever. The boat slid over the captive, and the prof, dropping his oars, imprisoned its tail in another felt-protected loop. Then we caught the wicked head in a steel mesh net, hauled it on board, and tied it up—it was a little one, only about ten feet long.

Easy, wasn't it? But it didn't always work out that way. Nothing on earth has a worse disposition than an anaconda, save, perhaps, an angry bee. The day before, we had hooked onto an eighteen-foot monster and not been able to gain an inch on it. Reddy finally gave me a little slack by rowing with its pull. The anaconda decided to come into the boat of its own accord, mouth wide open, looking as though it didn't need a dentist. I shot its head to pieces and a leg of the prof's pants, with a load of No. 6, and we spent some time plugging up the bullet holes in the forward part of the skiff.

Nevertheless I liked the excitement, and the whole proposition was certainly a sporting one. Professor Ritchie McKee had blown into Père Guerrin's café in New Orleans, red head and all, with three hundred dollars, orders from every zoological garden in America covering several tons of snakes, and the proposition that I help finance an expedition up the Magdalena River into Colombia. He was a little middle-aged Scotchman, with china-blue eyes, the flaming red hair I have already mentioned, and an argument that he needed the money.

Somehow he hit me just right, and we were calling one another Reddy and Wandering within the hour while quarreling over the respective merits of different brands of canned goods in a tropical climate. The upshot of the matter was that I now found myself in the upper reaches of the Magdalena River, navigating, with the assistance of three mestizos and Mose, my cook, a flat-bottomed, broad-beamed, wood-burning thing built like a house boat and loaded with snake cages.

Don't think for a moment that we got where we were without the slightest difficulty, just paddled along, fanned by tropic breezes. We didn't. And the worst of our troubles began and never ended when we picked up the orchid hunter.

There was nothing much doing until we were well up the Magdalena, past where you take the overland route for Bogotá. The river, before that point, had been alive with alligators, which made it unhealthy for anacondas, and, as anacondas were our main objective, we did not waste time on shore looking for other kinds of snakes. Once beyond the Bogotá connection, however, we anchored and put off in a skiff to explore a small tributary. There we took our first big water snake, right at the mouth, and a pretty struggle we had, too. After carrying it aboard our flatboat, we went up farther, and, a mile from the main river, came upon the most incongruous craft, deserted and tied to the bank, that you can possibly imagine in the middle of South America. It was a thirty-foot launch, decked over, brave with white paint and brass fittings, the simple engine built to burn wood, and the most perfectly appointed thing I have ever seen.

Hardly had we finished examining it and got back into our own boat when there was a wild chorus of yells from the jungle, the spat-spat-spat! of an automatic, and a lanky white man jumped on deck, cast off the line, and, dodging into the cabin, let the launch go down with the current. The air was instantly full of that sharp whistling sound that I had learned, on a previous trip, to associate with the tiny poisoned arrows the natives shoot from their bamboo blowguns, and I promptly yanked our boat around under the protection of the bulwarks of the larger craft. For five minutes, as we were carried swiftly down the stream, we all lay low, and then the white man put his head over the side of the launch.

He had about as disagreeable a face as I have ever looked upon: very high forehead, long pointed nose, thin lips, and the longest curved white teeth I have ever seen in a human being's mouth—they were more like an animal's than a man's—and his first remark was quite in keeping with his appearance:

"Who in the devil are you, pray?"

It made me mad, of course. White men are not only polite to one another in the jungle through motives of policy, but also because they are generally really glad to see a face of their own color.

"This is King Robert Bruce, late of Scotland," I answered, "and if you include me in your polite inquiry, allow me to present myself as the Archbishop of Canterbury."

"None of your nonsense!" he snarled. "I want to know who you are," and he actually threw an automatic on us.

There was not one thing to do. I just ached to get my hands on him, but you can't rush a twelve-shoot gun from a skiff onto a launch. I swallowed my mad as best I could, and was just beginning to tell him our entire family history when there was a whistling whir in the air, the automatic clattered to the deck, and a pretty little poisoned arrow was sticking in his wrist. He grabbed up the gun with his left hand, turning it loose into the jungle, and by that time we were both on board.

In a few moments the wounded man turned a sickly green, and we certainly had one time over him! Reddy was always loaded up with snake-bite dope, and we treated him with the dissolved purple crystals of permanganate of potash and injections of strychnine, praying, at the same time, that the arrow was tipped only with snake poison, and not the deadly *wourali* for which there is really no antidote. We pulled him through finally, but only after five hours' work; and meanwhile we put several long miles between ourselves and that unhealthy locality, the launch towing behind our flat-bottomed side-wheeler.

When our involuntary guest came to, he was frankly distrustful, but somewhat more polite. He volunteered the information that his name was Hiram Jones—Hiram Jones nothing! I know a John Doe when I see one, and he certainly belonged to that indefinite family—that he was collecting orchids, had discovered what he recognized as a new species—all collectors are nuts over new species—on a tree of a native graveyard, and that the natives had jumped him when he tried to get it. Also that he was rather obliged to us, hoped to make it all right, would do as much for us under the same circumstances. We were collecting reptiles, were we not? Reptiles *exclusively*, hey, what!

I disliked the man exceedingly, felt that he was lying in other ways than about his name, and piously looked forward to getting rid of him as soon as possible. At that time he was too weak to turn off, however, and during the night his launch blew up and burned to the water's edge.

The man positively had a fit! He raved of *Cattleya Mendelli, Dowiana aurea, Odoratum coronarium*—I know something of orchids, and these certainly were valuable ones if he had 'em—and beat at the fire with his one good hand. We finally had to drag him away, and all that we saved was a little ammunition, some clothes, and a bunch of English bank notes. The orchids were between decks forward, where the fire was hottest.

At first he suggested that we take him back to the Bogotá connection, which, of course, was out of the question; and then, much to my disgust, made a deal with McKee to go with us and have the privilege of the extra skiff to carry on his work.

The neighborhood where we took the ten-footer I began this yarn with was a fine place for the big snakes. There were many little tributaries running into the river, and each one seemed to have its pair of anacondas. Sometimes we missed them when they were stretched out along a branch over the water, their rich olive-green bodies with the two alternate rows of large oval spots along the back and small white-eyed spots on the sides blending perfectly with the lichen-decked limb of some giant tree. Mostly, however, they lay with just a fraction of their heads above water; and the prof was a wonder at picking out, from yards away, just the ripple that showed where a great snake was patiently waiting for what the current might bring. Then, with a few cautious oar strokes, we'd drift down on it, and the rest was purely mechanical.

Reddy, who was a cheerful, even-tempered little cuss, grew happier with each successive captive, and the one of which I have just spoken making our sixth sizable snake, we rowed back contentedly toward the main river. At the mouth of the tributary, a chorus of wild yells broke on our ears, and, quickening our stroke, we shot out into the river to see Hiram Jones climbing onto the steamer, the opposite shore lined with furiously gesticulating savages.

"We'll have to go from here!" I exclaimed angrily. "That imitation English boob has been monkeying around the graveyards of the simple peasantry again."

"He shouldn't have done it," complained Reddy. "Now we have lost a good hunting ground. You had better speak to him, Wandering, while I am stowing away the snake. I'm not big enough to quarrel with him, and two men shouldn't jump on one."

Very tactfully put, I call it. The hint wasn't lost on me. I rolled my sleeves up as I got on board, and the prof dove down the companionway, dragging his net full of snakes.

"Look here, alias 'Iram Jones," I said, taking care to get close enough to him so he couldn't use his gun, "we've had enough of this graveyard work, and of stirring up the natives."

What I was aiming to do was obvious, and I'll give him credit for being no coward. The fight lasted several minutes. He was a better boxer than I, but hadn't been through the school of lick-'em-or-get-half-killed I had been brought up in. When he yelled, " 'Nough!" I got off him rather pleased with myself and willing to listen to what he had to say. It proved to be the same story. Native cemetery—you tell 'em by rags tied to sticks—rare orchid on tree, niggers popping out from every direction when he went for it. The only difference was that this time he had brought away what he was after, and it certainly was a marvelous thing! The flower, already fading, was about a foot across, olive-green, regularly blotched with black, while the stamens were pure gold color and gave off a musky odor.

"It looks for all the world like an anaconda," said the prof, who had come on deck as soon as the noise was over.

"Just the ticket! I'll call it *Oncidium anacondæ*, Barlow"—Barlow, mind you!—said the so-called Hiram Jones, and, unconscious of the name he had let slip, picked up the tangle of aerial root-lets among which the strange flower bloomed. Something round, about the size of a tennis ball, fell thumping from the mass to the deck, and, making sure it was not a reptile, I picked it up while the other two men crowded nearer. Pulling away a few dead leaves, I held in my hand an infinitesimal mummy head, too small to be even that of a baby, looking as though it must have belonged to the tiniest of pygmies or else a gnome. The features, absolutely perfect in every detail, though shrunken beyond belief, were those of an old, old man, and in place of eyes were two crimson crystals sunk deep beneath the parchment-covered forehead. The whole thing was hard, like a lump of rubber, without a sign of a bone in it.

For several moments we gazed, astounded, at this gruesome object; and then Barlow, alias Hiram Jones, spoke:

"Look here, you blokes, do you know what this means—a fortune for every one of us! I saw hundreds of heads hanging to this one tree—thought they were weaver birds' nests. My word! *Look* at those bloody stones! They are rubies!"

The nearest I have ever come to engaging in the ghoul business was when I helped an old scientist to dig up the bones—and part of the skin and fur—of gigantic antediluvian lizards and mammoths in a salt marsh of the Brazilian coast. They say that rubies affect people's brains, however, and I'll admit for a moment I was tempted. Not so the little Scotchman.

"You dirty Sassenach!" he roared. "Do you think I'm going to turn corpse robber for all the red crystals in the world? I—I have a good mind to feed you to my anacondas. Don't you dare open your mouth to make such a suggestion again!"

"No, don't you dare!" I echoed shamefacedly, and there the matter rested.

Of course I had heard of the little mummy heads. Everybody who has been south of Panama hears the tale. But I had never seen one before, hardly believed in them. The tribes along the Magdalena are reputed to remove the skull from the heads of their own dead as well as their enemies, and shrink them to the size of small oranges by some mysterious process that keeps the features in proportion and as clear cut as in life, preserving them indefinitely. Why they were hung in trees, and how they were protected from bird and beast, was still an unwritten chapter.

II

While all this was going on, there was an awful hullabaloo from the shore, yells, beating of native drums, and the ear-splitting bray from a bamboo horn. The river was at least a mile broad there, however, and we were anchored in the middle of it; so I did not fear an attack in the daytime—savages don't come out after steamers when it is light; they have learned better. We had loaded up with wood for fuel the day before, and I didn't propose to stop again until we reached the Rio de Sucuriu—native for River of the Anaconda—a fork of the Magdalena about which I had some rather vague information, and which was really our ultimate destination.

After the crew had piled enough wood under the boilers to get up steam, I left Mose to tend them, and went forward to see what I could pick up from the mestizos in regard to local burial customs. It was little enough. They knew of the mummy heads, of course, and of the substitution of bright crystals for eyes, the standing in the community of the preserved deceased being indicated by the kind of stone, but they could tell me nothing of where these same stones came from—they were sacred things in possession of the priests alone.

I had only been forward about ten minutes when a yell from Reddy told me something was wrong below.

At the door of one of the cabins I found the little Scotchman hauling the unconscious Englishman out by the legs. The olive-green orchid lay on the floor, and from it emanated an odor of musk, only muskier, that caught you by the throat and simply choked you. We soused the senseless man over the side, and by the time he took in coming to he certainly must have been pretty near to cashing in. Then we fished out the deadly orchid on the end of a long pole, and should have thrown it overboard had the sick man not begged with actual tears that we save it. Later he tied it to the end of a stick and fixed it firmly over the bow. Outdoors, the odor was not so oppressive, but we came stern, nevertheless, where we could not smell it.

Steam was up by that time, but another factor upset our calculations. The wind and river began to rise, both coming straight down on us, and finally I had to steer our unwieldy craft into the backwater near the shore to avoid being rammed by the trees that came booming down the current; and just as we anchored, the black tropic night shut down like a curtain.

You can't fool with a storm in that latitude. The river lashed into foam, great sheets of water were bodily torn from the surface and whipped to shreds in the air, whole trees came whirling down, rearing and plunging as though alive, while the heavens were rent with lightning and shaken by thunder. The worst of it was over in thirty minutes, but the river rose and rose till our anchor began to drag. With full steam I could just keep head to it, but no more, and I had to feel around for hours before I could find bottom where the anchor would hold. Thankfully my crew then turned in, and I went forward to take one last look to see we were not drifting, when through the blackness I saw what appeared to be a large log coming swiftly down on us. It struck the anchor chain, split, and I had only time to recognize it as a native dugout before a naked savage described a parabola over the bow into my arms.

After a brief struggle—he was slippery as an eel—I caught his wrists and escorted him down to the light of the main cabin, calling to McKee and the Englishman.

Of course the naked wild man must have been scared to death, but he gave no sign of it, just stood up swaying with the pitch of the boat, and waited, apparently unperturbed, for what was to come, his eyes fixed on Reddy's flaming topknot. He was only about four and a half feet tall, gracefully formed, with features so far from being negroid that they appeared as clear cut as a young girl's, and he was not black, but a clear light chocolate. Through his elaborately arranged hair were stuck several of the tiny poisoned arrows, though he seemed to have lost his bamboo blowgun.

We all stared at him with nothing to say. As a matter of fact, he was much more at ease than were we, and then I bethought myself of asking some questions about the Rio de Sucuriu.

There are about twelve different and distinct languages spoken along the Magdalena, but there also exists a kind of *lingua franca* common to all the tribes of the river banks. I called in one of my mestizos and through him began to interrogate my captive.

The Rio de Sucuriu was only three canoe days farther up—he had come from there himself, caught by and driven before the storm. Yes, there were many serpents there, but they harmed not man since man was their brother and the son of "she who was married to the golden one, queen of all serpents."

I gave him food, which he wolfed down ravenously; and then, just as the mestizo turned to leave, a strange thing happened. From a shelf where the Englishman had placed it, the tiny mummy head fell to the floor and bounced to the savage's feet. He made a quick grab for it, but Barlow was before him, snatching it to himself with a fierce: "It's mine!" The speech was unintelligible to the naked man, but the gesture was unmistakable. He flew to his feet and pointed with two quick words.

"He says 'dead stealer,' " translated my interpreter at my look of interrogation; and then, listening to a stream of passionate sibilants, continued: "He has heard of the white man, and death is waiting for him as a slave who murders his master. At once he must give him the head that it may hang again on the sacred tree, lest another head he dreads come to him. He wants it now."

"Give him the thing!" I ordered. "We can't afford to quarrel with the natives, especially with one who comes from where we are going. He'd put us in wrong at once."

"I won't!" snarled the Englishman. "Kill him and throw him overboard. Dead men tell no tales."

And he actually meant it. Just as cold-blooded as that. I made a snatch for the mummy head, missed it, then struck it out of his hand, and the prof picked it up and gave it to the savage.

He took it into his cupped hands and made a kind of a salaam, turning it face upward, and we saw that the rubies were gone from the eye sockets, gouged out.

I believe I should have killed Barlow, alias Hiram Jones, then and there had we been alone. As it was, I turned and struck him across the mouth.

"Get out of my sight, you unclean ghoul!" I shouted, and he slunk quietly away.

I presented the little naked savage with a square of red cloth—it pleased him immensely—to wrap the head in, which he did with the greatest reverence; and, while he squatted on the floor, one hand on the bundle to keep it from rolling with the pitch of the boat, I made him a regular oration.

I told him we were capturing snakes, which, strangely enough, did not seem to astonish him, and that we hoped to find many big ones in the Rio de Sucuriu. I also tried to convey to him that the Englishman was quite mad, and that in no way had we been parties to the taking of the head. He made no comment, except to ask why we didn't burn the madman to drive the wickedness out of him; and then, after a parting look of admiration at the professor's red head, tactfully terminated the interview by curling around his precious bundle and going to sleep.

Reddy and I talked till daylight, and the upshot of our conversation may be epitomized into two paragraphs.

Though we had no intention of gouging rubies out of the mummy heads of the native dead, we hadn't the slightest objection to negotiating with the priests for them.

He wished to Heaven there was some way of getting rid of our English incubus without handing him over to the vengeance of the savages.

III

The river sank as quickly as it had risen, and we skirted the current for two whole days before we came to the fork that had been dubbed the Rio de Sucuriu. Our savage pointed out the channel all the way, and we thus avoided the usual hang-ups on sand bars.

Rather strange and most self-contained person, that naked wild man! He was outwardly quite unimpressed by the boat and its contents, all of which must have been new and very wonderful to him, but he seldom took his eyes from the prof's red head. Me, he evidently considered Reddy's subordinate, despised the Englishman, and classed the mestizos as slaves. Mose, my cook, who was a very black, black man, plainly puzzled him. The orchid stuck up in the bow was familiar to him, and he looked on it with mingled feelings of fear and disgust.

At the mouth of the Rio de Sucuriu, our guest left us, taking along the mummy head in its red wrapping, and promising to return after two darknesses to show us where we might capture more snakes. I for one was glad to see him go. He would put us in right with his tribe, and it would not be necessary to keep constantly on the alert for the vicious little poisoned arrows. Neither did the Englishman grieve over this departure. We hadn't treated that gentleman with undue consideration these last days, had hardly spoken to him at all in spite of his attempt at an apology. He had tried to explain his eccentric behavior in regard to the mummy head on the grounds that he did not know what he was doing from the time the deadly orchid overcame him—even claimed that he did not know what had become of the rubies. All this was mixed in with whining over the loss of his launch and orchids—at least a thousand pounds' worth—and, after talking interminably, he ended up by borrowing some clothes from me with the excuse that his own we had saved were so shrunk by the water he could not get into them. I let him have some, of course, but I'll be dog-goned if I wanted to.

Opposite where we anchored, a spit of rock, some twenty feet broad, ran out into the water, so perfectly reproducing in shape the head of an anaconda that had the idea not been ridiculous I should have called it the work of man. Also the Rio de Sucuriu was well named. We took three anacondas the first day, one sixteen feet long, and located a pair of monsters that we simply did not dare to tackle alone. Reddy was crazy to get them, and suggested wild scheme after wild scheme for their capture. Having no desire to trouble the digestion of a thirty-foot snake, I turned all his plans down, urging that we wait until the natives appeared and then enlist their assistance. In the meantime, Barlow hunted orchids by himself, and he certainly brought in a heap of them.

At sunrise of the third day, we were awakened by a most infernal din, the throbbing beat of native drums, the savage braying of bamboo horns, accompanied by the splashing of paddles. Before the mist had gone, we found ourselves surrounded by dugouts, and, as the sun rose, a state craft paddled underneath the stern of our side-wheeler. Hewn out of a single log, it was fifty feet long, with thirty paddlers, and in the bow stood the savage whom we had picked up farther down the river.

"Grab your guns!" gasped Barlow.

"Guns nothing!" I answered, and I was scared. "There are hundreds of them. We'd be torn to pieces in ten minutes. Wits alone will get us out of this."

I summoned my mestizo interpreter, and the savage in the bow of the state canoe began to speak.

I can't give his exact words, but the substance was as follows: The Red God with his friend and slaves was welcome in the territory of the Sucuriu people, though not the one with him who slew from behind and respected not the dead. There would be feasting, and many serpents would be bestowed upon us that we might be honored.

Plainly the prof was the Red God, and our best card, so I shoved him up on the bulwarks, meanwhile orating all I knew through the mestizo. I said we much appreciated the honor done us and should be tickled to death to have the snake donation—we'd make some donation on our own side—that we had only six days to linger, then the Red God and us, his servants, must return whence we had come; that the wicked one among us had been driven temporarily mad by the flower of death and was not responsible for his actions, but would be punished when we returned to our own land.

Then we permitted—indeed, I don't see how we could have hindered—the naked savages to swarm all over the boat. Not one thing on board was taken or even touched, however, and we all rowed to shore feeling as though we were part of some fantastic dream.

The feast was no worse or better than others of its kind, and liberally watered with palm wine. The entertainment following consisted of the customary savage dances. Our party and our former guest, now host, sat, or rather squatted, a little apart from the rest of the Sucuriu people, and were served by young slaves of whom there seemed to be a large number. The entire performance was something new to the prof, and he enjoyed it all hugely, also the palm wine—until I had to warn him. You see, I had been up against it before, and knew it was not to be trusted. Like all Scotchmen, he knew best, however, and when I discovered, in the gloom, that he had his arm around an attractive but more than lightly clad brown girl, the party broke up. Savages believe in love at first sight, rapid wooings, and absolute sincerity. Besides, I'm darned if the girl wasn't extremely good looking.

The prof was cross as a bear the next morning, and took occasion to insult me seventeen separate and distinct times. I took it all gracefully, though; I've had palm-wine heads myself and know what they mean. Finally, however, he accused me of being jealous of his "way with the weemen," and myself having an eye on "yon mud-colored lassie" of the night before. This was too much. I'm a respectable widower—twice—and couldn't afford to have my name scandalously coupled with a brown girl—Père Guerrin might hear of it—so I soused him over the side until he told me he felt good-humored again. Reddy had come on the trip with a single crash suit, so we routed out some of Barlow's shrunken clothes. They surely had shrunk, fitted the little Scotchman exactly, and he was just half the size of the orchid hunter.

By this time several dugouts were alongside, and we prepared a dozen or so of the felt-wrapped wire loops and explained their use to the natives. They caught on at once, and we started toward where Reddy and I had seen the snakes that were too large for us to tackle alone. Anacondas, in addition to their devilish bad temper, are about as shy as you make 'em; but the savages paddled along, singing and whooping as though the game was a deaf stone idol instead of the alertest reptile that swims. The mestizo interpreter could not check them, and they did not seem to understand my signs for silence— on the contrary, whooped the louder. As we pushed into the backwater, where we had seen the monsters, the reason for this lack of caution was apparent. Far from being alarmed, a thirty-foot anaconda undulated swiftly toward us. A native rose in the bow of the leading canoe, and, holding a dead capybara above his head, began a kind of a chant. I got the translation later. Here it is:

> "Brother, thy brothers come,
>   An offering bear to thee.
> With fear the jungle is dumb,
>   Sucuriu people are we.
> Brother, the golden one
>   Watches, where crowned with gold,
> She sits and basks in the sun,
>   Wrapped in HIS golden fold.
> Brother, we bind you free,
>   Bitter though be your strife,
> Though you our brother be,
>   We pay the debt for a life."

The anaconda raised five feet of its body out of the water, and the singer cast the capybara into the waiting jaws. Before the snake could dive, a felt-wrapped wire loop circled it, then another. The dugouts swarmed about it, the lashing tail was imprisoned, and, in less time than I can tell, Reddy slipped the steel-mesh net over the wicked head. The female was not so easily captured, one savage losing a large chunk of his shoulder; but, within two hours, both reptiles were safely ensconced within our damp hold—and they measured respectively thirty-one and a half and twenty-eight feet.

In three days we had as many big snakes as we could cram into the large cages, while the savages were eager to catch more, and delighted with our gifts. It had been necessary to establish a tariff, so rapidly were serpents brought us; not only anacondas, but the gentler, beautifully marked boas that reach a length of ten feet and take the place of our own domestic cat as rat catchers in the native huts. We paid so many yards of cloth, according to length, and added an alarm clock when an especially fine specimen was taken. Reddy became jubilant and more jubilant with every addition to our collection, forgot all about the "mud-colored lassie," and I was pretty well pleased myself. Barlow alone of our party was not happy, and with cause. No sooner was he out of sight of our side-wheeler than ping! a little arrow would stand up, quivering, on the side of his skiff. These missiles were not poisoned, but this did not prove that the next one might be harmless. The Englishman took the hint and spent his time morosely moping on board, and begging us to go farther down the river. Selfish ugly brute he was—though, I grant him, brave enough; he had fought me—and I heartily wished us well rid of him.

The professor now began to think of smaller reptiles, and was specially desirous of grabbing onto a few fer-de-lances. These are pleasant snakes, known by the Spaniards as *rabo de huesos*—bone tails—from the curiously colored and spike-like tip at the end of the body, about the deadliest things in the reptile line, and so temperamental that only one ever survived to reach the New York zoo, where it died of excitement.

We tried a hunt on dry land, equipped with wire loops and very close mesh metal nets. Only three specimens resulted from the entire day's tramp, and these did not amount to anything, were as common as savages, Reddy said. An attempt to enlist the natives in this new sport, something we had shied away from at first for fear of being deluged with the commoner reptiles, was entirely unsuccessful. Our former guest, who seemed to be the chief of the Sucuriu people in spite of his youth, lucidly explained that all the lesser snakes had been captured long ago and taken to the place of the dead. Requests for information as to the location of said place of the dead met with the same chilling silence that I well remember having had from a fat lady at the only ball I ever went to in my life, when I apologized for tearing a yard off the rear end of her dress.

Not only did we fail to make a single capture the next day, but, in addition, the prof got badly stung by a large blue wasp, and the savages plainly looked with disfavor on our land expeditions. Furthermore, on the boat, the Englishman exhibited three tiny arrows, distinctly tipped with poison this time, that had been shot on board during our absence. He asserted, with unnecessary profanity, that he was going wherever we did from that time on.

Oddly enough, not one of us suggested moving on, and, when you come to think of it, it wasn't so odd, after all. You see, we were all fundamentally fighting men, and the fact that the savages obviously wanted us to pull out just got our dander up. Besides, I was mighty curious to see that place of the dead to which all the land reptiles had been transported, and unquestionably the prof felt the same way. That little red-headed devil had something else on his mind, however, as I was to find out later.

Before I forget it, since you always hear Scotchmen spoken of as hard-headed, I should like to state right here that the man who says Scotchmen aren't at the same time sentimental is a liar—they invented sentiment.

Barlow, of course, really wanted to stay, because he was crazy for another shy at the orchids, with which the woods in that neighborhood seemed to be crammed.

Each of us kept strictly to himself that night. The Englishman took the poisonous orchid from the bow of the boat—it smelled worse during the darkness, too—and boxed it up carefully. The professor got into a skiff and went ashore. I turned in and dreamed of thirty-foot anacondas, their heads covered with flaming red hair and their mouths full of long curved teeth.

IV

Before sunrise, the mestizo interpreter woke me with the news that there was a canoe alongside with some savages in it who wanted to talk to me. I stacked up the pillows under McKee's head; he was breathing heavily and had a way of sleeping flat that invited heat apoplexy—and went on deck. It was just getting light as I looked down into the native boat, and what I saw there came near to doubling me up with mirth at the same time that I recognized its seriousness. In the bow sat the young chief, simply trembling with rage; the paddler was an old white-wooled brown man, evidently the father of the pretty chocolate-colored girl in the stern. For her part, she had been weeping, held her head very high, and wore, by a string around her neck—and indeed she wore little else—an unmistakable red object, an ample lock of the professor's auburn—by courtesy—hair.

The young savage shot out a stream of *sssss's* that sounded like an angry anaconda, and the interpreter elucidated. Briefly the substance was that Reddy was trying to steal his girl, that she was ready and anxious to be stolen, and that we were therewith ordered to beat it at once, if not sooner. Through the mestizo I promptly told his nibs to forget it; we'd stay as long as we pleased.

The answering flow of sibilants was less virulent and shorter, and translated into a query as to what we would take to go away.

Then I had an inspiration. Slowly, word by word, I had my man impart to this autocratic savage a promise that we would leave the moment the Red God had secured all the land reptiles he wanted, and there must be many;

that he wished to visit the place of the dead and see what crawling things he could find there, and that if both these requirements were met he would shake the girl.

For a long time the savage hesitated, and when he finally spoke I could only gather from the rendering of his words that we were to go with him that morning, prepared to stay several days, and with everything we owned that would hold reptiles. The rest of his speech was a jumble to me: The Golden One might blast us—breath of death—sacred road—

The dugout sheered off, and, going below, I beat a brisk tattoo with a pair of military brushes on the side of the cabin.

"Awake, my red-haired Lothario!" I yelled. "Awake! I have good news. Jump into your clothes, and don't wait to brush your hair; you've ruined your beauty, anyhow, by that gob you cut out of your bang. Come and catch little snakelets; we're going where there are oodles of them."

Reddy sat up, somewhat blear-eyed; then, scrambling out, looked at himself in the four-inch mirror on the wall.

"I dinna see it has changed my appearance," he remarked. "I mind some palm wine— What were you saying about wee snakes?"

I told him. The serpent made Eve forget her Adam. The mere promise of venomous reptiles made Reddy forget his Eve. The little Scotchman turned into a whirlwind, and, when the dugouts arrived, had enough collecting paraphernalia piled up to load three of them to the guards. Every one of us, except Mose, whom I left behind in charge of the boat, mestizos as well as the Englishman, went ashore at the anaconda-head-shaped outcrop, where we found the young chief awaiting us with a dozen slaves for porters.

For an hour we followed a jungle trail, single file, the chief evidently steering by a lofty peak in the distance. Then the trail broadened out, and we found ourselves walking upon rock the like of which I have never before seen. It was a road, or, rather causeway, thirty feet broad, built of ten-foot square blocks of stone, and winding back and forth up to the highlands. No twenty men could have lifted one of those square blocks; no, not fifty men; and there were millions of 'em. Furthermore, the middle of the stoneway was worn smooth by the footsteps of thousands exactly like the flagstone in front of the swinging doors of Père Guerrin's café.

Not one of us said a word until we had passed along the two half-mile undulations, and then the Scotchman spoke the conclusion of his thoughts:

"We-el, 'tis Aztec. I'll say no more."

"It's a bloomin' snake miles long," said Barlow; "miles, miles long, with its head in the river."

I had nothing to say. To tell the truth, it kind of made me feel religious, awed me, especially the wearing away of the solid rock by those countless feet. They must have been bare feet, too, and their owners dead for the Lord knows how many tens, hundreds, even thousands of years!

We followed the great sweeping curves of this mighty road till noon, now to the right, now to the left, always rising, until finally the mountain loomed above us, and just then the causeway broke off short in a chaos of tumbled blocks of stone. On either side were acre-large enclosures that looked as though they might once have been water tanks, terraced one above the other to the base of the mountain, two miles away. Above the ruins of this ancient road a way of more recent origin had been fashioned. Zigzagging from tall forest tree to tall forest tree were a pair of thick long bamboos, one above the other, the lower a path to which bare feet might cling, the upper a handrail.

Where the road broke off, the chief halted, pointing to the splintered and shattered blocks of stone below. My eyes followed his gesture, and, ten feet beneath me, a yellow serpent was stretched out in the sun; another crawling lazily from a fissure in the rocks; a third lay coiled. There were snakes large, snakes small, snakes of every hue of the rainbow. The place was alive with reptiles.

"This is heaven," stated the professor positively, picking out a wire loop and collecting box and preparing to climb down to the jumbled bowlders.

"This is the nearest to hell I have ever seen," I remarked, getting ready to follow him.

We could not stay among the ruins; the reptiles were too thick about us. And, after Reddy had come within a hair's breadth of being struck by a fer-de-lance whose head I shot off, we climbed back again. The broad walls of the tank furnished us with a four-foot path, however, and from it we angled, trapping snakes in a loop on the end of a bamboo pole exactly as you snare suckers with a copper wire. It was unpleasant, but exciting, sport. I, for one, was perfectly willing to land my snake on the wall, perfectly unwilling from that time on to have anything to do with it. Barlow limited his activities to toting the collecting boxes and swearing. He cursed the savages, the snakes, the sky, the earth, Reddy, and me, until the Scotchman, after a few moments' deep thought, told him such language was "fair weeked" and it would be no sin to tip him over into the reptile den.

We took fifty snakes, ten of which were the dreaded fer-de-lances, a German flag—immortalized in Kipling's tale—three species of coral snakes, a green racer, two bush masters, and others whose names I simply can't remember. Then night came.

As the light went, a strong breeze blew down from the mountain onto our camp; but, far from being laden with the scent of flowers, it brought an aroma that to me suggested ten thousand alligators. The Englishman recognized it, however, from the first whiff.

"Death orchids!" he exclaimed. "There must be a hundred burial trees near here, and perhaps rubies—"

"Which you will leave alone," I interrupted, "or I'll give you a licking that will make the last one seem like love taps, and hand you over to the savages afterward."

Of course Reddy was primarily a snake collector, and that was his dominant interest, but he was all of a man besides, and, as such, crazy to see what was at the end of the long bamboo road. It was obvious the chief did not intend that we should go farther, and so we made our plans without consulting him. The wall of the next tank was five feet higher than the one in which we had done our strange fishing, and on it grew a tree to which ran the bamboo bridge. We decided that the next morning we three—the Englishman being unwilling to leave us for a moment—would climb this tree and follow the swaying airway to the mountain. With this purpose in view, we turned in early, after sending back the mestizos and some porters with our boxes of snakes.

V

In the morning, our project was simplified by the withdrawal of the savages farther down the stone causeway. Very evidently they did not at all care for that neighborhood. Immediately after breakfast, we set out, taking a few snakes first in case any one might be spying; and then, scrambling up the five-foot wall, looked down into the next tank—and stood transfixed.

For a moment—as had the Englishman—I thought the dead trees of which the enclosure was full held an enormous colony of weaver birds' nests. On every branch and twig hung a tiny mummy head, the sunlight glinting here and there on jeweled eyes, and an odor of musk floating up to us—though more faintly than during the night—from the foot-wide, olive-green flowers of the death orchids, the only living thing, save reptiles, that flourished in that gruesome place.

"Let's go back," Barlow begged, in a whisper; "not even rubies are worth it!"

"I'm afeered," simply stated the Scotchman.

"We're in for it now; let's go on," I urged; and then I added, since I saw both of my companions were scared to death, and so, indeed, was I: "*I'm* not afraid!"

"You're a le-er!" promptly responded McKee, and began to climb the tree we had selected the night before.

From the fragile bamboo bridge we looked down for a full two miles on enclosure after enclosure full of dead trees hung with the shrunken heads. There were thousands; and, as we progressed, they became unquestionably more ancient, had fallen to the ground—even the trees themselves had sometimes fallen—and lay heaped like the debris of blackened combs and litter beneath a century-old wild bees' hive. On one tree I counted two hundred heads; there were fifty trees in that section, thirty separate sections in all, making, at a low, *low* estimate, three hundred thousand of these tiny relics of what had once been human beings. It was the vast graveyard of a mighty race, a race dwindled to the few poor survivors of the present day—the Sucuriu people.

From the swaying bamboos we stepped at last onto solid rock, a continuation of the great causeway, but narrowing like the tail of an anaconda. At its very tip lay a fifty-yard, sand-bordered pool from which it seemed the twelve-mile-long stone serpent might have emerged.

Tired and breathless, we sat gazing into the clear water that backed up against a sheer cliff, and then from a small cave across from us, its top just above water level, came a ripple. Something split the surface of the water, and there emerged a head as red as Reddy's own, followed by a woman's face and arm, her hand resting lightly on the neck of a nine-foot anaconda, and her body swaying from side to side through the water with the undulations of the swimming serpent.

"I'm going crazy!" gasped Barlow. "Do *you* see it, you blokes?"

" 'Tis extraordeenary," vouchsafed the prof.

The swimmers struck shallow water, the girl stood up, and the anaconda curled about her till its head rested on her shoulder. Snake and woman, save for her flaming hair, were both a golden yellow, and it would have been hard to say which was the more beautiful.

Quite unafraid, she approached us, her eyes on the prof's glowing head, and then stopped. I rose and bowed, which was ridiculous; couldn't think of anything else to do; but she never even looked at me.

One arm she raised and pointed at McKee, and in some mysterious way the gesture asked a question as plainly as though she had traced an interrogation point on the smooth white sand. For a moment she stood pointing, and then, raising both her hands, pressed two fingers across her lips. Again the gesture needed no interpretation, was as clear as though she had put it into words—the woman was dumb.

"Puir, puir lassie!" said the prof, with infinite pity. "Puir bonnie lassie!"

And I felt my own heart go out to the beautiful voiceless thing standing like some goddess of the olden days, the golden snake coiled about her golden form.

"Let me talk to her," said the little Scotchman, and, beckoning her nearer, began to trace pictures on the sand.

The Englishman may have thought he was crazy, but I *knew* I was as I watched Reddy drawing the story of our voyage. According to his pictures, we came from the rising sun—"rising" indicated by a series of dashing rays—she glanced at his hair—then came up a broad river in a great canoe—

It was a fine series of drawings, and covered ten yards of sand. When it was finished, the woman put her hand up to her hair and drew from among the thick tresses a small skin bag. This she opened, and took out a pear-shaped stone, with which she began to mark on the sand, and that stone was an inch-long ruby!

Barlow made the sign of the cross and rose to his feet.

"Let's look around a bit, Wandering," he begged, "while the children draw pictures. Perhaps we'll find a ten-headed lion with a basket of diamonds in each mouth. I'm in for what there is to see before I'm locked up in the dippy house."

I needed a chance to collect my thoughts myself, so followed him, leaving Reddy and the girl bent absorbingly over their tracings.

To the left of the stone snake's tail, rude steps were cut in the living rock, and up these we scrambled. They led to a small platform, and again in the rock was hollowed out a little house, with windows and doors, stuck there on the cliff like a swallow's nest. Inside were jars of pottery, hammers and knives fashioned from flint, and wood evidently stacked for burning that went into dust at our touch. No human could have dwelt there for years and years; everything was too quiet, too motionless, too covered with the dust of ages. We stole silently out into the sunlight again, and, by the doorstep, the Englishman picked up a ruby carved in the likeness of a coiled snake.

More steps led to another rock-hollowed house, differing in no respect from the first, and we climbed up from terrace to terrace, exploring the countless long-abandoned dwellings of a dead race. The sun was well to the west when we reached a shelf broader and longer than the others with no doors or windows cut in the rock, only a long line of bathtub-shaped depressions. Each depression held the crumbling bones of a skeleton, and every skeleton was headless! Our faces turned from this row of open graves, we walked to the far end of the shelf and came to a great hole on the brink of which, scattered among flint knives, hatchets, and little round balls of clay, were small rubies, red snakes' eyes they looked like, which Barlow eagerly gathered up. Together we peered into this pit, and mixed with the clay balls were thousands upon thousands of skulls each split neatly in half, while here and there, adhering to the clay balls, was a piece of parchment-like skin.

"I'm sick!" I whispered. "Let's get out of here."

"I'm dead with thirst," Barlow answered through parched lips, his face pasty white in spite of the heat.

No nightmare could be more awful than our descent from those endless silent terraces. We slipped and clung to the edge of thousand-foot precipices, slid down the rude steps, skinning hands and knees, and our throats were full of the dead dust of long-forgotten peoples, our lips swollen, our tongues thick. Twice the Englishman abandoned his bag of rubies; twice, sobbing, he went back for it. The sweetest music I have ever heard was Reddy's voice from near below, calling and cursing by turns. And then the sun sank, leaving the world bitter cold.

It was darker than pitch down by the pool, the only sign of light a sheen from the still water that made our faces look like white blurs in a big splash of ink. By groping around rather at haphazard, we collected a few pieces of wood for a fire, and, shivering, huddled over it. As the flames rose, picking our faces out of the gloom, it became more than apparent that the prof had somehow acquired a black eye. It was a beaut, covered all one side of his face, and very naturally I asked how he got it.

" 'Tis nothing," Reddy answered; "a wee bump against yon stone."

"It's a right-handed swat," I insisted. "You got fresh and the lady biffed you."

"You're a le-er," he flared; "the lassie no laid hands on me; 'twas the snake."

It isn't the easiest thing in the world to get a Scotchman to tell what he doesn't want to; but I finally gathered in his story, what there was of it.

The girl had understood his drawings, but hers were quite unintelligible to him, a series of snakes, fishes, triangles, and complicated geometrical figures. More by gesture than anything else, he gathered that food was brought her over the bamboo bridge by the savages; that she dwelt in a cave rising from the other side of the pool, and that she had been there for fifteen complete sun revolutions. " 'Tis then an unfortunate thing happened," he continued. "To encourage the lassie, I put me hand on her shoulder. 'Twas by no means a caress, ye'll understand; more like a pat. And then the snake struck me with his head on the side of me face. The lassie was fair angry and drove it into the water. I dinna blame her; it spoiled the pleasure of the whole day for both of us. At sundown she became greatly agitated, pushing me toward yon bamboo bridge, and then, when I would not go, swimming back and forth from me to the cave across the pool, making signs for me to follow her. I would have humored the puir lassie had ye two not been away pleasuring all the day."

"Pleasuring?" repeated Barlow. "A peach of a lot of pleasure we had while you were philandering, and we've brought back a fortune."

Come to think of it, so we had. The rubies simply slipped my mind. Things get kind of out of proportion in the wilderness. We had out the bag and felt and hefted it—it was too dark to look at the stones—and it weighed all of ten or twelve pounds. Quite a hunk of jewels, and yet somehow it failed to impress me. I couldn't think of the little red things in terms of money; only as eyes of the horrible shrunken mummy heads. Reddy didn't show any undignified amount of joy over them, either; refused to commit himself to any undue enthusiasm until he knew exactly what the stones would bring "within a thousand dollars, say," a question on which we naturally could not enlighten him. With the Englishman it was quite different. He fair lusted over the bag in the darkness. They would buy him a boat of his own, brass fittings and all, air-tight compartments that would preserve orchids forever. He'd travel in Borneo, Brazil, India; there should be money enough to go everywhere. His thoughts took a sudden twist—

"Look here, you blokes," he whined, "at least half of what they bring belongs to me. I was the one that found them. Any court of law would uphold me."

"We-el, let's submit it to a court of law," suggested McKee.

"We'll divide these rubies into three parts when we get back to the boat," I stated positively. "Meanwhile, since you found 'em, you can carry 'em."

The moon rose, and at the same moment we saw the golden maiden swimming toward us, the anaconda in her wake. She came straight to Reddy and tried to lead him into the water, carrying her hands to her nostrils, pointing out into the darkness, and beckoning imploringly. Never have I seen anything more tragic than the look of agony on her face, of striving to make the Scotchman understand.

"Puir lassie!" he said pityingly. "I'll be back. She canna bear to have me leave her."

"And you're going now," I insisted; "it won't be the easiest thing in the world to travel that thread of bamboo by moonlight, and the sooner we reach our flat scow the better."

The woman followed us, the great snake coiled about her body—she must have been as strong as an ox as well as impervious to cold—and importuned Reddy with imploring gestures to return. He shook his head, however, and, slipping off our shoes and tying them around our necks, we fitted our stockinged feet to the slippery bridge.

Hardly had we gone a hundred yards, with me leading, when I stopped and held up my hand.

"Nothing doing!" I shouted. "Beat it back as quick as you can, praying that the wind doesn't change!"

And I had reason! From beneath me came the indescribable odor of the death orchids, only a hundred times stronger than I had ever smelled it before, forming a deadly barrier that no breathing thing could hope to penetrate. Already I felt my head reeling as I climbed back toward the mountain, and that with the breeze blowing from us. We reached firm ground none too soon, the girl clinging to the prof's hand and striving to drag him into the pool, for at that very moment the wind changed.

"To the pool for your lives!" I yelled, plunging in and wading out until only my face was above the surface. The poisonous miasma from the death orchids was blowing down on us like mist above a marsh, and lay suspended not six inches above the water, sinking lower and lower every second.

"We're all done for," sang the Englishman, "just as I was rich, too. I'm no coward, but I refuse to die with my sins unconfessed. Listen to me, Wandering! I intended to murder you and that fool of a snake-collecting Scotchman so I could keep all the rubies. I shot the top of the man's head off who hired me for this trip. He knew nothing about orchids; intended to claim all the credit for what we found; and, besides, I wanted that launch. Two years ago—"

"Can your childish babble!" I screamed. "Who cares a hoot for what you were going to do or have done? Where's Reddy? Hey, Reddy! Reddy! Reddy!" I yelled.

The water swirled; I felt a hand clutch my arm, and the golden woman rose beside me.

"Where's Reddy?" I screamed in her face, and the poor dumb thing actually smiled at me, pulling my hand.

"They say drowning's easy," droned the Englishman. "I'll just take a whiff of that corpse flower and flop over into deep water."

He stuck his head out into the grayness, and I saw it drop forward just as I caught him beneath the arm. Following the pull of the girl's hand, I swam with her, towing the senseless man after me. Once the lash of the anaconda's body touched my leg, and then there was darkness. I felt, rather than saw, rock above me; next was conscious of space, inky blackness, but room all about me. My feet touched bottom. Hauling Barlow with me, I staggered forward and fell face downward on smooth dry sand.

It was Reddy's voice that brought me back.

"Are ye there, Wandering?" he whispered.

"Yes. Are you all right, Reddy?"

"Yes, the lassie saved me. Feel around till ye find me; I'd like to touch something human."

Barlow's body across my knees quivered, and I raised him to an upright position. He groaned and slid down against me. My groping hand found the little Scotchman, pulled him to me, and I threw an arm over his shoulder. Once my other hand touched the smooth wet body of the anaconda, and I snatched it quickly away. And then—wonder of wonders!—I slept dreamlessly, beautifully, blissfully!

VI

The moment of waking brought with it a full consciousness of all that had taken place. The morning came filtering in through the water that blocked the entrance to the cave, lighting it with the dim gray quietness of an empty church. Pressed against my right side lay Barlow, breathing naturally.

McKee's red head was pillowed on my left shoulder, and crouching near by, her fiery hair spread on the sand, slept the girl. There was some one else, or, rather, something else, awake beside me. The golden anaconda lay curled about the golden woman, its diamond eyes fixed unflinchingly on mine.

I shook Barlow, and he sat up while slowly the meaning of his surroundings came over him.

"I say, this isn't hell, after all!" he ejaculated, getting to his feet. "Now ain't this a rum go! I say, Wandering, I was out of my head last night. You mustn't pay any attention to what I said. I'm really very fond of you and Reddy." And he smiled at me, showing all his long curved teeth.

My hand on McKee's forehead made him open his eyes, and at the same time his teeth began to chatter.

"The lassie saved us," was the first thing he said. "Wake up, bonnie one!" But she was already awake, looking up at him with adoring eyes.

"The sunlight for mine!" I chortled. "Never expected to see it again. You first, prof!"

Teeth chattering, the little Scotchman waded into the water and dove under the arch of rock, the girl and snake following him.

"Now you!" I directed Barlow.

"We'd better look around and see if she hasn't some rubies hidden here," he answered, and then splashed into the water just in time to avoid a vigorous kick.

Never did sunshine seem so blessed as that shining upon us outside; never did the whole world seem more joyous or beautiful! I just gave myself up to breathing and soaking in the warmth, gazing up at the sun till my eyes blurred.

When I finally turned to my companions, Barlow was coming out of the pool with the bag of rubies that he had dropped there the night before, and the look on his face as he gloated over the open sack was that of a demon.

Then Reddy claimed my attention. He was leaning against the golden woman, her arm about him, and, though his face was red as fire, he was shivering like a leaf. It didn't take a second glance for me to realize what was the matter. The *calentura* fever had him, and it behooved us to get back to the boat and quinine, lots of quinine, as swiftly as possible. The knowledge of his condition was in the girl's eyes as she looked anxiously at me. Indeed she raised her hand, palm down, moving it, shaking, in front of her face; and if that is not a good symbol for fever I have never seen one.

Had Reddy been less far gone, that two miles of climbing would have been agony for him. As it was, he moved along the slippery bamboo as only a drunkard of a man spurred on by fever could have done. At times he was delirious, shouted and sang, apologized to several imaginary "weemen" for making them love him. The girl kept her hand beneath his elbow, indeed carried him the last quarter of a mile, looping the anaconda around him to ease her burden. Barlow and I kept one bamboo length to the rear. The weight of snake and woman plus Reddy must have been considerable, and we did not dare put too severe a strain on any one section of the seemingly slender bridge. Down our tree we climbed at last, first the girl with her now raving burden, which she laid tenderly on the wall to draw breath, then yours truly, and last Barlow.

From behind me came his voice:

"Great heavens, Wandering, look below you to the right!"

I glanced over the edge of the wall, and immediately beneath me lay coiled a fer-de-lance that must have been all of twelve feet long—the most absolutely venomous object I have ever seen.

"Glad Reddy doesn't want—"

My words were drowned by the bang of an automatic, and I felt a sear of fire along my side. Spinning on my heel, and at the same time ducking low, I dodged the second bullet and caught Barlow's gun arm at the wrist in both of my hands. He snapped his left hand to my throat while I strove to twist away his weapon. Deeper sank his fingers in my flesh, deeper and deeper. I felt my eyes popping from my head, my tongue protruding, and swung him in front of me in a last furious effort to break free. From the girl's lips that I had never before heard utter a sound came three distinct hisses. Dimly I saw the anaconda uncoil from her body, writhe forward, and, quicker than light, cast a coil around Barlow's neck, while I wrenched from him, falling face over the edge of the wall. There was a mighty crunch of breaking bones, and man and snake went over me inextricably mixed, straight down upon the fer-de-lance below. The poison reptile struck three times, sinking its fangs once in the body of the anaconda and twice in the Englishman's thigh.

We did not even attempt to retrieve the dead man; left him where he lay. Reddy was our first care. Turn by turn that wonderful golden woman and I half carried, half led him the mile-long undulations of that mighty causeway, until we finally reached the stone snake's head jutting out into the river. There the golden anaconda joined us, apparently none the worse for the venom from its poison cousin, and wrapped itself around its mistress. Not a savage had shown the tip of his nose all the way, and at my hail Mose came ashore in the skiff unmolested.

For ten days the girl and I fought off death from the little Scotchman, and at dawn of the eleventh day the fever broke.

Reddy was a good little man, but "weemen" were his weakness. I had pieced together disconnected fragments of his ravings with rather astonishing results. Not only did he have a wife in Scotland, but also one on the Continent. The upshot of my cogitations was, again, that Reddy was a good little man, but that was no reason why he should take all the goddess of a golden woman had to give. At present his plan was to settle down in the wilderness with her and forget the world—I was to deliver his snakes. I knew, however, that sooner or later he would return to civilization—they all do—and then what would she have left?

My mind was slowly made up, and, though I hated the plan worse than death, I began to put it into execution at once. Under my direction, the mestizos got up steam, and then I went to the woman and told her by signs to go ashore and get Reddy wild grapes, a thing she had often done before. Like a child she obeyed me.

No sooner was she out of sight than up came the anchor and we steamed away. Just in time, too, for as we rounded from the Rio de Sucuriu into the main river, the girl's crimson head showed above the water, coming swiftly after us. It was impossible for any swimmer to catch our side-wheeler, however, when it was going with the current, and the last I saw of her was her beautiful nude golden body, with its crown of flaming hair raised half out of the water, her arms held out imploringly while her dumb lips worked, the head of the great snake making an arrow-shaped ripple by her side.

Reptiles and all, we reached New Orleans without adventure. It was not a pleasant trip for either of us, though. Reddy refused to speak to me when he learned what I had done while he was sick and helpless. He expressed himself as absolutely certain that the "puir dumb lassie" would pine away and die for love of him. God help me, but I can never be sure that he was not right!

Back in civilization, I took the bag of rubies—Barlow had dropped it on the wall during his last fight—to a jeweler to get them valued. However well the Englishman may have known orchids, he was distinctly not up on precious stones. His fortune in rubies proved to consist of garnets—very fine ones, it is true, but nevertheless nothing more than garnets.

One last word in connection with Barlow. The day after Reddy's fever broke, the chief of the Sucuriu people paddled out to us and threw something on board. It proved to be a package done up in the identical red cloth which I had given him to wrap the mummy head. Inside were two objects. First Barlow's head, shrunken the size of a small orange, all the teeth gone save two that overlapped the wrinkled mouth like the curved tusks of a peccary, while from each socket protruded the fang of a fer-de-lance; second, also a tiny mummy head, its top blown away, leaving it roughly flat, the features unmistakably those of a high-bred Englishman, rubies—garnets I now know them—for eyes, and attached to it by a slender gold chain was a monocle.

We had given back the savage his dead; he returned ours to us.

I heard indirectly, one month after our return, of Reddy's marriage, in New York, to a widow with four children. Wonder if he sent cards to his other wives? I know none came for me. Could I have foreseen this, I never should have taken him from the golden woman, but left him in the wilderness with the pious hope that the golden anaconda might make a meal of him some dark night, mistaking him for a hog.

The Black Flamingo

*In which Wandering Smith takes a bird man into the heart
of the Everglades in search of a black flamingo and comes
upon a mystery that smacks of ante-bellum days.*

THERE WAS A HEAP OF MAIL WAITING FOR ME at Père Guerrin's café when I got
back from the snake-collecting trip I had taken into Colombia with McKee,
the Scotchman. Letters are much more exciting to me than poker. You see,
you *may* draw anything in them, and from anywhere, while even in the
greatest American game you have only fifty-two cards—if you are honest—
from which to fill your hand. The second one I opened gave me a bat right
between the eyes. Inside was an engraved card:

MRS. ALFRIEDA DE MILLE
and
DOCTOR A. DELMAR JUMPKINS
announce their marriage on Friday, May the twenty-first, at high noon.
Church of the Resurrection, New York City.

Doctor A. Delmar Jumpkins was no other than Old Bug, a special friend
of mine, and he was sixty if a day! All the old fools weren't dead yet, I
decided. And who in the dickens was Alfrieda?

The next letter in the pile was from Old Bug himself, and it kind of
warmed my heart to think he had remembered me even in the midst of his
passion.

> MY DEAR WANDERING: Among the first of my friends I desire
> to advise you of my approaching matrimonial alliance with a most
> estimable and attractive woman. The cards will doubtless reach you
> before, at the same time, or shortly after the receipt of this letter. It
> would give me the greatest pleasure if you could come to New York
> on the twenty-first of May, and be present at the ceremony.
>
> I am in a state of extreme felicity, and could, were there time
> and space, expatiate at great length on the charm and many estimable
> qualities of the future Mrs. Jumpkins. I have, however, a matter of
> real importance to communicate to you.
>
> I am sure you will share my delight when you read that, in looking
> over some of the material we collected together, under the bark of a
> piece of cypress I came upon a new species of *Ips*; indeed, I am not
> sure that I shall not claim for it a new genus! It approaches, in some
> respects, the large *Ips calligraphus*, but differs in being golden yellow

instead of light chestnut, and in that its wing covers have twelve regular indentations on the margins instead of the five or six coarse teeth of the later species.

Herewith the technical description: . . .

(There was a whole page of it.)

I am gratified beyond words at the find, and know you will share my pleasure. It does, indeed, mark an epoch in my life, since it has been taken for granted that the genus *Ips* had been thoroughly covered.

I look forward with the greatest pleasure to showing you this new and rare beetle, and hope this letter will catch you *ad interim* your frequent trips. Yours sincerely,

A. DELMAR JUMPKINS.
Curator of Entomology,
Museum of Natural History.

Of course there was only one thing to do. I never desert a pal in trouble, and, besides, I was curious to see the beetle and Alfrieda. The date of the wedding was such that I had to catch next morning's train, so I packed a suit case, got the père to fill my flask, and went out to buy myself suitable clothes and Old Bug a wedding present.

The trip to New York was uneventful, and a taxi landed me at the Museum of Natural History, where Old Bug seemed a heap tickled to see me. We looked at the new *Ips*, which I admired as was expected of me, and then went over the museum together. Honest, I envy people in New York having such a place to go. There is everything there, and then some more. Days wouldn't have been enough for me to thoroughly examine its treasures. And then I had an especial interest because bird, beast, insect, and reptile I had had a share in taking were on exhibition—it was just like meeting a boyhood chum in some bar.

Old Bug turned me over, when we reached the bird-habitat groups, to a young, good-looking cuss with gray hair and the most enormous voice I have ever listened to—sounded like the boom of a great bittern. He was introduced as "Professor de Mille, my best man," and I figured him out as Alfrieda's brother. Together we wandered from bird group to bird group until the beautiful flamingo nesting collection was reached, and there we stuck while he told me how he had been with Chapman and helped to secure these specimens, the whole museum echoing to his voice.

"They breed only in the Bahamas now," he continued.

"They breed in the Everglades today; I have seen them," I interrupted, "and a jet-black one among them."

"What!" he roared.

I repeated my statement.

"Couldn't be a black flamingo," he flatly contradicted me; "it's unheard of!"

One thing led to another, and, before I realized it, we were quarreling like two entomologists. Honest, I thought of the wedding just in time, or I'd have biffed him and then the best man would have had to officiate from a litter.

There is only one way, short of a fight, to stop an argument when neither side will give in. I owe this valuable piece of knowledge to Père Guerrin, and I put it to use.

"Let's have a drink," I broke in on his seventeenth reason why I hadn't seen the black flamingo, which I *had* seen.

For a moment, he looked puzzled, and then grinned.

"I'd forgotten you were Wandering Smith, for the time being," he boomed. "I seldom indulge, but this—er—the wedding—"

"We'll drown our grief," I suggested, and we did, under several layers of wetness. Also I wondered, not without a certain amount of respect, how any human being could drink five cups of black coffee one-quarter laced with brandy at that time in the morning.

The wedding went off fine, and Alfrieda was a darling, fat as you make 'em, but a very great lady just the same. Not the kind that's great just because she has clothes and money, but that's born so. You'd take off your hat to her instinctively even were she serving drinks behind a bar. She was plainly very much stuck on Old Bug, and I was content to leave him in her hands. Perhaps she might even cure him of his pet vice of swilling down boiling water with every meal.

I'm so sentimental that it's all I can do to keep from crying at weddings, and I was glad when this one was over. Afterward, we had a breakfast at the bride's home, and, believe me, it was some feed! Every kind of a scientist you ever heard of was present, herded together by groups, the entomologists fighting one another like wild cats in one corner, the piscatorialists swapping fish stories in another, and the bird, beast, archæology, and all the other ologies segregated each according to his kind.

I found myself with the ornithologists, De Mille, the best man, booming away on my right, and an authority on humming birds smoking countless cigarettes on my left. It was a wet feast, and, the occasion being an unusual one, I lapped up everything that was put before me.

De Mille roared out my story of the black flamingo, and it sure caught every one's attention. They made me tell how I had managed to lose myself in the Everglades, how I had found the birds nesting, and how, while I was being guided out by a Seminole Indian, I had seen the black flamingo.

During all this talking, either seventeen or forty-six more drinks came my way. I remember a heated argument with the mammoth-voiced man, a taxi, and then I woke up, the next morning, in my hotel, with my new silk hat under my head by way of pillow.

Hardly had I put down the second pitcher of ice water when the telephone bell rang, and De Mille shattered my eardrums with a request to be allowed to come up.

Dog-goned if I remember it, but it seems I had agreed to take him into the Everglades to study birds, and especially to try and get hold of that black flamingo.

Of course there was no backing out then—and I had intended to do the social act at two prize fights in New Orleans, just had to forget 'em—so we took the train that same night for Fort Lauderdale, on the edge of the Everglades.

I was mighty doubtful about that trip. You see, the mere fact you have once been a certain place in the Everglades doesn't mean by a whole lot that you can go there again. The whole country is nothing more than an eight-thousand-square-mile shallow lake of fresh water that seeps up through limestone, and is overgrown with the most vicious five to ten-foot saw grass that you can possibly imagine. There are islands of marvelous fertility lost in this grassy wilderness, but only to be reached by nearly blind channels that the Seminole Indians alone know. And you can't get a Seminole for love or money to guide you into the Everglades, though they'll lead you out quick enough when you get lost there.

Nevertheless, I had a general idea of the direction in which I wanted to go. A flat-bottomed, twenty-foot scow, provisioned for two months, was hired, and we set out up New River.

For a day, we followed a more or less straight channel in a generally western direction, and then turned off boldly into a slight opening between the grass stems that seemed to lead southeast with the surface flow. At first it went in the right direction, then turned, stopped, and we struck a cross current and thick barrier of ten-foot grass. Pushing into this, we found another open channel; and by night, as completely lost as two people ever were, we tied to a small, very wet island where grew a single tall, wild rubber tree.

To tell the truth, I was completely discouraged and ready to look for a way out as quickly as possible. Not so Noisy de Mille! He had gone quite mad over the teeming bird life all around him; olive-brown and white limpkins, Louisiana herons, little blue herons, white ibises, snake-necked water turkeys, peach-blossom-shaded spoonbills, and a hundred others. Also it seemed to be the mating season for the majority of these birds, floating grass and mangrove bush holding many a nest with its treasure of quaintly marked, delicately beautiful eggs. The crown to the ornithologist's happiness came, however, when, with a metallic honking that sounded like a dozen brazen horns, seven flamingos drew a scarlet streak across the sky, flying toward the setting sun.

"We'll follow them if we have to grow wings to do it," De Mille roared. "They are in their mating plumage, Wandering, in their mating plumage! Do you realize that they may be nesting here in Florida?"

What could you do with a nut like that? All scientists are crazy, anyway. I contented myself with killing seven moccasins that showed a tendency to roost in the boat, and went to sleep, lulled by the crying of the limpkins and the hen-like notes of the Florida gallinule.

Don't know whether it was the rain or the roaring of the bull alligators that woke me, but I opened my eyes to look straight up into a dead-white human face not a foot from mine. For a moment, I thought I was still dreaming, and then the face popped out of sight like a diving loon. On my feet, I jerked my automatic from under my arm and snapped on the electric torch. It was darker than pitch in the drizzle, but I saw, and it was no fancy, the tall grass in the water waving as though something had just pushed through, and there was a peculiar smell in the air. A smell—well, a perfume—darn me if it wasn't cologne!

Mystified and rather frightened, I sat down in the stern of the boat; and then, from not a hundred yards away, came a shrill "Co-he-e-e!" to be answered by another "Co-he-e-e, co-he-e-e!" from behind the island.

Noisy woke and sat up.

"Don't speak!" I whispered. "There is something going on I don't understand. Just get out your gun."

For a moment nothing happened; and then, from every side, came a perfect chorus of "Co-he-e-es!" Something whistled through the air and fell into the boat, and—silence, save for the pattering of the rain.

An hour we waited, neither of us saying a word, till finally—and I nearly jumped out of the boat at what he meant for a whisper—De Mille spoke:

"Your friends seem to have gone."

"They knew you were going to coo at them and went away not to be deafened," I answered crossly. "I don't like this at all. Were they Seminoles, I wouldn't mind, because Seminoles never hurt a white man; but those 'Co-he-e-es' never came from an Indian's throat; sounded more like niggers. The Everglades are a hiding place for every escaped convict and bad black man in Florida. I'm not even sure they were niggers, because I saw—" But there I stopped. I was ashamed to mention the white face that had peered at me over the gunwale; felt I must have been dreaming.

"Let's see what came on board," I suggested, to change the subject. "Be careful, though. Perhaps moccasins fly in this mad place."

I snapped on the electric torch and swept its radiance over the boat. On the middle seat quivered an arrow feathered with the brilliant plumage of a flamingo, its point sunk deep in the wood.

We stared at this strange object for a moment, and then De Mille plucked it out.

It was about a yard long, feather and oyster-shell point bound on with deer sinew; and halfway up the shaft was rolled a slip of paper on which was written, in a small, beautiful script:

> We mean you no harm, but you had better follow the Indian who will come to you in the morning. Though we mean you no harm, I cannot answer for my slaves.

"Co-he-e-e!" came from the distance, and I promptly pressed the button, shutting off the light.

We spoke no more that night, neither did we sleep.

The rain ceased. Morning came at last, and glad indeed were we to see it. The dry, yellow grass changed to a sea of molten gold, the clear brown water to liquid amber. Bird after bird awoke, first to sleepy twitterings, then to full-throated song. Just as the sun rose, the seven clanging flamingos trailed scarlet across the sky, flying out of the west.

Incredulous of the night's happenings in the brilliant morning light, De Mille and I turned with the same movement toward the middle seat of the boat. The flamingo-feathered arrow was still there, a large moccasin comfortably coiled beside it.

We killed the snake and settled down to talk over the situation while the teakettle came to a boil over its spirit lamp. I was all for devoting our energies exclusively to finding a way out. My companion argued, on the other hand, that being lost didn't matter in the slightest. Hadn't we plenty of provisions and the best of drinking water all around us? Why not seize this opportunity of a lifetime to study the birds, and, above all, to run down the seven flamingos? He left the final decision to me, however, and was far too much of a gentleman to mention that no black flamingo had been flying with its pink kinsfolk. I simply don't know how I should have decided were it not for what followed.

So silently that I could hardly believe my eyes, the grass stems parted and a yellow canoe slid over the amber water toward us, guided by a Seminole Indian.

"Come show you way out. Long, long way," the paddler remarked laconically.

"Thanking you very much for your kindly interest in our welfare," I said sarcastically, "but we are not going out."

"You die," came the indifferent answer, and the yellow canoe whirled about to disappear in the saw grass.

We spent the day collecting nests and eggs and taking photographs. The birds were so tame that we could snap a brooding mother, and then afterward the very eggs or young which she had covered. And many of the eggs were certainly very lovely. There were full nests of white ones, spotted and speckled with rufous brown that the hen gallinule left with an explosive *chuck*, pale limpkin eggs blotched and stained with light cinnamon brown, eggs green, eggs mottled with pink; and we even found, on a mangrove branch above the water, the tiny, lichen-decked nest of a ruby-throated humming bird with its two infinitesimal white eggs, iridescent twin pearls.

De Mille simply wallowed in happiness, and I must say I was little less interested than he. During our collecting, we tried to keep a general westerly direction, but tempting vistas through the high grass continually lured us from our course, until, at nightfall, we found ourselves in a ten-yard-wide pond among broad water-lily bonnets. The pond was not over a foot or two in depth, and, making the best of the situation, we anchored in the middle.

The great marsh went to bed with cluckings, twitterings, and sleepy ends of song; flamingos sounded their horns for a brief moment above our heads, and the darkness came.

There were no mosquitoes—indeed, mosquitoes are rare within the Everglades—it was warm, and the little circle of light from our lantern really made a very cozy kind of shut-off place from the rest of the world. Supper eaten, and pipes drawing, we stretched comfortably in the bottom of the scow.

"Don't blame Ponce de Leon for expecting a fountain of youth in this climate," lazily remarked De Mille; "it breeds dreams. Before last night's concert began, I had a vision of an exquisite child face floating above me, and actually seemed to feel a kiss, soft as mist, upon my lips."

"Barring the kiss"—my face ducked—"I had the same pipe dream," I answered, sitting up. "But I went you one better. My girl used cologne."

Noisy sat up, too.

"That's a little more than odd. Now I think of it, my dream lady seemed addicted to perfume. I put it down to the magnolia blossoms this morning. Do you suppose a mermaid has been fascinated by our unquestionable charms, Wandering, and is following us around?"

"Showering the boat with cologne and flamingo-feathered arrows, while her pet alligators shouted 'Co-he-e-e!' in the distance," I added to his sentence. "I tell you, Noisy, there is something happening that I don't understand, and I do *not* like it. If we have the same kind of a concert to-night, I'm going to sprinkle the Everglades with a few steel-capped bullets."

It didn't rain that evening. The stars came out; the moon rose, flooding the golden marsh with silver, and it was very light. Even the birds seemed half awake, twittering softly now and then, as though turning over in their sleep. Stretched at full length, looking up at the stars, for a long time we listened to these gentle noises; then we, too, slept.

I seemed to be in a storm. The ocean splashed all around me, and then a wet mass of water came down on my face. My eyes open, I realized that the boat had drifted against the tall grass, and heard De Mille sputter: "I'm half drowned!"

"An alligator slapped the water with its tail when it saw—" The words froze on my lips. Above the reed tops rose a fearsome thing, a white, shivering shape with large, fiery eyes glowering down on us.

"Bang-spat-spat-spat!" went my automatic. "Co-he-e-e, co-he-e-e, co-he-e-e!" echoed from every side.

"Gimme that pump shotgun," I yelled to Noisy, swung it around by the barrel he tendered me, and turned it loose toward the flapping apparition before the stock was well against my shoulder.

There was a scream, unmistakably feminine, the white horror disappeared, and our boat rocked gently from the recoil of the gun.

"By the great horn spoon, the place is bewitched!" cried De Mille, and his voice was several octaves above its normal pitch.

"Bewitched or we have both got 'em," I ejaculated furiously. "What does it all mean?"

The anchor rope had been cut clean in two, I found, when I went up to the bow, and I navigated our boat back into the middle of the lily bonnets, and tied it to push poles sunk deep in the mud. The circle of high grass was unbroken as I swept the electric torch around it; even the broad lily pads seemed to have been undisturbed.

"Load every gun on board, Noisy!" I ordered. "We'll give your mermaid and her friends a warm reception if they come back. You might tell her so in that gentle voice of yours."

"Come and get shot!" De Mille promptly roared. "We're going to fire at anything we hear or see."

"Co-he-e-e," floated mockingly back to us over the reeds.

In the morning, we hadn't much to say to one another. What was there to say, anyway? There was nothing to tie to, just mystery. People don't go into the Everglades to play practical jokes. Besides, there aren't any white people in the Everglades, and no one could possibly conceive of an Indian cutting up such foolish didos. And yet, just beyond the pond, we found something that rightly belonged in a boys' boarding school. It was a sheet on a long pole, two big holes cut in it for eyes, and simply peppered with my shot!

That day was much like the previous one, save that we were both distinctly nervous, prone at times to keep silent, just listening. About noon, as we were skirting an unusually high and thick wall of grass, along which ran a narrow lane of shallow water, a consciousness that had been growing on me crystallized into a certainty. Some one, or something, was following us. Twice I had seen the grass tops on our back trail move, barely, but yet move.

"You go on and then come back fast as the devil when I holler," I whispered to De Mille, and, behind an elbow in the wall of vegetation, slipped out of the scow into two feet of water.

I hadn't long to wait. With a nearly imperceptible rippling, the bow of a yellow canoe pushed by me, then came the arm, the body of our Seminole visitor, and I had him down under the water before he could utter more than a surprised "Gugh!" The noble red man was no weakling, but I am not a subject for a sanitarium myself, and he was half between being choked and drowned when I set him on his pins and yelled for the scow. We hauled him on board and sat him down none too gently on a seat, and then I orated.

There were many words to what I said, but the sense amounted to what he meant by following us, who was he, why had he made all those crazy noises and rung a spook in on us? I paused for breath.

"Show you way out," he grunted stolidly. "Long, *long* way now. Long, long, *long* way to-morrow. Long, long, long—"

"And it will be a 'long, long' time before you get back to your wigwam, if ever," I announced angrily. "You take that pole and push along this floating egg crate, and, remember, if you try to run—swim away—I'll shoot you as full of holes as a Swiss cheese."

The entire afternoon, his canoe towing behind, that impassive buck poled us along the high, impenetrable wall of grass, while we poked into the domestic affairs of coot, duck, rail, and warbler. When night came, our involuntary gondolier was sent up into the bow with some food, and we settled ourselves in the stern, talking in whispers.

It was plain that the Seminole could not have been responsible for one-tenth of the night's racket, and we easily deduced that he must have other companions, probably white men. How to find out who and where they were was the problem. Short of boiling the savage alive, I, for one, could think of no way of drawing this information from him, and Noisy was equally at a loss.

It began to rain at sunset, and we huddled under a tarpaulin. I picked up a rope and rubber blanket, starting forward to tie up our prisoner and protect him from the wet. At that very moment an inspiration came to me, and, flinging the covering into the bow, I went back to De Mille. A few whispered words and he understood. Gently we drew the Indian's craft to the stem of the scow—once it scraped on the bottom, the water was so shallow—and, after listening breathlessly in the darkness, I slipped into the canoe and lay flat.

It was a crazy scheme, but it worked. About midnight—and, Lord, how hard it had been to keep awake—a shadow loomed beside me in the blackness and the canoe began to move noiselessly forward through the rain. The Indian was towing it, the painter over his shoulder, and I sat up, training my gun on the dim outline of his back. Not two hundred yards from where we started, he began to grope in the water, grunted with satisfaction, pulled up something from the bottom, and turned to find my automatic against his stomach.

I took what he had picked up out of his hand. It was a chunk of iron, and to it was attached a wire that led straight into the thick of the high, reed wall.

It was too dark, and besides I was too sleepy to follow the wire that night, so, tying the painter of the canoe firmly to it, I marched Mr. Indian back to the scow, bound him hand and foot, and was asleep in two minutes.

Binding the Indian, and leaving him that way all night, was not a sporting proposition. The reason we could do it was that we were scared. Not of anything we could see or might be brought bang up against, but of what we couldn't put our hands on, or understand the why and wherefore of.

I was ashamed of myself when I unbound the Seminole in the morning, and I hated my companion because he had let me tie the Indian up. It's true I should probably have biffed Noisy the night before if he had objected to what I was doing, but I hated him for not having objected just the same.

In silence, we ate our breakfast, and, still in silence, each of us, the red man without orders, picked up a pole and pushed the scow down to where the canoe was moored.

As might have been expected, the wire served the same purpose in the water that blazed trees do on dry land. It marked a trail, one that a canoe could easily follow but that was really too narrow for our bateau. Breaking through the first barrier of reeds was the hardest part, but the rest was no motor-boat ride. We sank to our thighs in the mud while hauling the scow over the shallow places, cut hands and faces on the cruel saw grass, and it was breathlessly, burning hot. The vegetation swept and raked the boat, finally pulling the trigger of a gun which came within an ace of blowing my head off. Warned by this, while the Indian and De Mille were in the bow, I slipped all the shells out of the shotguns, and even unloaded my automatic, which I wore under my left armpit. Till early afternoon, we pushed and shoved forward, and came at last to another barrier of reeds higher even than the previous one that had blocked our progress. Both of us flopped down exhausted, Noisy leaning over the side to dash water in his face, and the Indian passed behind my back down to the stern. I turned just in time to see him make a grab for one of the guns.

They say that no Seminole will injure a white man, but I'll never put that "they say" past one of them again. This one did not wait to threaten, just brought the gun to his shoulder and snapped both empty barrels at me. I yanked out my automatic—it was empty, too, but he didn't know it—and covered him.

"Drop that gun," I said disgustedly—somehow I couldn't get mad—"and go up into the bow and pole."

Pushing the blunt nose of the scow against the twelve-foot grass, we gained inch by inch, till suddenly light showed through, the boat shot forward, upsetting me on top of Noisy, and the Indian dove over the bow into open water.

We were floating in a small lagoon a hundred yards from a large island. The shore was well above water level, and on its gray sand stood an evenly spaced orange grove of the largest trees I have ever seen. A dock, near which were several canoes, bottom up, ran out into the water, and from it a broad avenue stretched up to an ample, colonial house, its roof and pillars, instead of the conventional white, painted the exact shade of the yellow reeds. Over the door hung an old, old flag, solid blue, with one white star, the first battle flag of the Confederate States of America.

"Come on!" I said to Noisy, loading both shotguns and handing him one. "We've just busted back sixty years into the past and are going to pay our respects to Jeff Davis."

The avenue between the orange trees was swimming in the heat as we walked up it, and, in the house, a fresh young voice began to sing:

> "We are a band of brothers,
> And native to the soil,
> Fighting for the property
> We gained by honest toil;
> And when our rights were threatened,
> The cry rose near and far—
> Hurrah for the Bonnie Blue Flag
> That bears the single star.

> "Hurrah! Hurrah!
> For Southern rights hurrah!
> Hurrah for the Bonnie Blue Flag
> That bears the single star.

> "As long as the Union
> Was faithful to her trust,
> Like friends and like brothers
> Both kind were we and just;
> But now, when Northern treachery
> Attempts—"

There was a furious shout of rage, followed by a shot, then a long "Co-he-e-e!" A dozen blue and white-clad figures appeared and disappeared among the orange trees.

"Forward into the asylum!" I commanded. "Hurrah for the Bonnie Blue Flag and all the little flaglets!"

Up the steps we marched, laid our guns on the porch, and Noisy raised a brass knocker and let it fall. The door opened, and a Chinaman—yes, that's what I said—a Chinaman bowed before us.

"Will you please tell your master that two men who have lost their way would be glad to speak to him?" said De Mille.

"I ketchum master," the Oriental answered, and slammed the door in our faces.

"Let's sit down," I suggested, beyond surprise at anything, and turned back to where we had left our guns—they were gone.

Noisy was abnormally calm. He made three remarks one after the other:

"What a beautiful old house!"

"The oranges look as though they might be ripe for picking."

"Do you think it will rain to-night, Wandering?"

"Have you read *Dare-Devil Dick, the Boy Scout*, and do you know how to do the crawl stroke?" I asked in my best society tones. He shut up.

After ten minutes, the door opened violently, and an old, white-haired gentleman came swiftly out onto the porch.

"A thousand pardons, my dear sirs," he whispered, "a thousand, thousand pardons! We receive so few visitors that my servants simply lose their heads when we are fortunate enough to have guests. You must come inside at once and I will see you are provided with fresh garments; yours seem to have suffered. Afterward, and not before, we may talk."

While he was speaking, I had an opportunity to examine him, and he sure was a curious specimen. Aside from his voice, which was remarkable enough in itself, being a mere whisper, he was very, very old and more wrinkled than I have ever seen a human being. His goatee and mustache were dead white, his eyes the exact color of a lemon, and his skin saffron yellow.

"We are imposing on you," answered De Mille, "appearing quite unannounced, but I fear we have no alternative," and we followed within.

I have been in most of the famous bars and gambling houses—places on which the owners don't care how much money they spend—in the United States, but their gorgeousness in comparison to that house was as the little deuce of spades in a ten-cent pack of cards to the king of hearts in a faro deck. The walls were hung with shining swords and shields, with red, yellow, and green silks embroidered with flowers, the floor was covered with the richest carpets, and, at the end of the hall, was enthroned a double-bellied idol sitting cross-legged on a gilded altar. The chairs were bamboo, their backs fretted with gold, silver, and scarlet, and there was a pleasant smell of sandalwood in the air.

We were ushered into a room with two low beds, and, with a whispered intimation that a servant would bring us fresh garments, the little, old, wrinkled man bowed himself out.

An impassive Chinaman brought us some white clothes, and we fixed ourselves up as best we could. Noisy's face was covered with cuts from the cruel saw grass that made it look as though he had tried to shave with a dull razor in the dark. My principal injury was to my nose, and it had begun to swell horribly.

Again the Chinese butler appeared, this time with the information:

"Master send when ketchum tiffin."

We sat down to wait. It was one o'clock. An hour passed, then another. De Mille stretched himself on a bed and went to sleep. For the hundredth time I catalogued the room in my mind, walls hung with dull brown silk, two beds, two washstands, a clothes press, several chairs, and that was all. Hardly enough to hold an active man's attention for half a day. French windows opened onto a vine-shrouded porch—we were on the second story—and finally, careless of politeness, I stepped outside and looked around. The porch was at the back of the house, and I could see half the island. It was one great orange grove set in a narrow frame of sunlit water beyond which stretched the unbroken yellow of the saw grass. The gray-white sand was hidden, for the most part, beneath the polished green of the leaves, but around the house it was bare. A small shed stood about fifty yards away, throwing a long shadow to the west, and, just beyond the shadow lay a man, face downward, our Seminole guide. There was no mistaking the meaning of that huddled sprawl, I've seen it too many times. The Indian was dead, shot through the head.

I moved to the other end of the porch. From a window just beyond the railing came a soft hiss:

"I'm sorry I scared you—had the men scare you—but you nearly shot me. Don't tell father or I shall be kept in my room and—and I want to see the gray-haired young man again."

"I won't tell," I whispered, trying to lean far enough over the rail to catch a glimpse of my interlocutor's face, but a Chinaman in a blue blouse emerged from beneath the trees, and I dodged back through the French window. Before I could more than wake Noisy, the door opened—none of the Chinamen seemed to have been taught to knock—and a Celestial beckoned to us. We followed him downstairs and into a yellow silk-hung dining room.

The little old man rose from the head of the table.

"I regret that my wife and daughter will not share our meal; they have already lunched. You will meet them this evening at dinner."

De Mille bowed. I imitated him, and we sat down.

Of course, the first thing to do was to tell our host our names and business, and Noisy did it perfectly. He explained that we were after birds, especially flamingos, for scientific study, had lost our way—he did not mention our night terrors—and a Seminole Indian had guided us, under compulsion, to the island.

Our host listened carefully, but made no comment, save to ask in a whisper if we were connected in any capacity with the Federal government, and seemed pleased at our negative.

The food was delicious and watered with the hottest and strongest Tokay I have ever tasted. General Carter—it transpired that this was his title and name—talked every second in his tiny, whispering voice, talked as though this was his first opportunity for speech for years.

We learned that he had gone to China after the Civil War, prospered and married there, and returned to America to spend his remaining days. The reconstructed South did not please him, so he had moved into the Everglades to this hidden island, bringing with him Chinese coolies and house servants to use instead of niggers. "They are practically slaves, you know, which makes it seem so homelike, quite the old days over again."

Noisy managed to hint at our departure. The old Confederate would not hear of it. As a matter of fact, he explained, one of his retainers, a Seminole Indian, who alone could guide us out, had met with an accident. We should have to wait until another Indian, who was delivering a few boxes of oranges at Miami for shipment, returned, but he hoped to have us as his guests much longer. Come to think of it, several flamingos had nested on a small islet near by for years. That might interest us.

It certainly did interest De Mille. He ate no more lunch, was mad to get started, to the old fellow's rather ill-concealed annoyance, it seemed to me.

Anyway, I hadn't been happy during the luncheon's whispered monologue. Our host may not have been lying in what he said, but he certainly was in what he did not say, and in the impression he aimed to leave on our minds. Men who like to talk as much as he did don't hide away from their fellows without some good reason. All this jabber about Chinese coolies sounded fishy to me; it was simply too crazy, and then there was that dead Seminole lying out in the sun. I couldn't make head or tail of it, and I did not like it at all, not one little bit.

Luncheon over, De Mille assumed that we were going straight to the flamingos. The saffron-faced old man had an ugly glint in his eye, but he did not attempt to gainsay him. We all walked to the eastern end of the island, and there, a few rods away, on a mud flat, were the birds—eight of them. There were hundreds of the old, stool-like mud nests going into ruins—the rookery must once have been an enormous one—and four flamingos sat on new nests, their feet tucked under them, not hanging down outside as you sometimes see them in pictures. Seven of the birds were a beautiful, rosy pink, and the eighth was jet black.

The ornithologist just looked and looked, and then he breathed a sigh of utter bliss.

"I'm going for the cameras," he said, and left us without another word.

The general insisted on showing me all over his domain. He was wonderfully spry if he were the age he appeared, and his little, whispering voice never ceased for a moment.

The island was about a mile long, and half of that broad. It was planted with every kind of citrus tree I have ever heard of, and manicured to a frazzle by the Chinese laborers, seventeen of whom I counted. In addition to the large colonial mansion, the small shed behind it and a miniature fruit-boxing plant, there was a group of servants' quarters at the western end.

The conversation was utterly one-sided until we got back to the house, and then I managed to slip in a question as to how he shipped his oranges. There was a clear channel two miles away, I was informed, that ran to the Miami River. The boxes were transported there by canoe, and placed on a barge that landed them at Miami.

Inside the house, General Carter regretfully left me at my door. Within, I put a chair beneath the knob and hurried out onto the porch. The body of the Seminole was gone from the shadow of the shed, but I thought I could still make out a dark stain on the sand. Busy with most unpleasant thoughts, I turned to leave the porch, and came face to face with a young girl, her fingers against her lips cautioning silence.

Have you ever seen a play called *Madame Butterfly*? If so, you may have some idea how that girl—child—looked. She was dressed in a white kimono sprinkled with pink flowers, and there were seed pearls on the sleeves, from which her slender, bare arms protruded like the white stamens of some wonderful orchid. Her mouth was a tiny, crimson thing, her hair and eyes jet black, and her eyes, placed slightly slantwise like a Chinaman's, were full of tears.

"You won't anger father, will you?" she pleaded in a whisper. "You will do everything he even hints. Such a little thing sometimes maddens him. Osceola is dead," she choked on a sob, "and he couldn't help your getting here. And, oh, don't, don't let the gray-haired young man cross him! Please, *please* don't! I—I kissed him in his sleep when I went out with the men to scare you away, he looked so clean and young," she broke down, sobbing uncontrollably beneath her breath.

"That's all right, my dear; that's all right," I tried to comfort her. "No one will make your father mad—" But she didn't wait to hear the rest of my sentence, ran into our room, pulled aside the silk hangings, and disappeared through a door that closed noiselessly behind her.

De Mille came in shortly afterward, his handsome, young face, with its incongruous crown of gray hair, radiant with happiness and his arms full of cameras.

"Shake, Wandering!" he chortled. "Shake twice! I've got the finest lot of photographs you have ever seen. And think of finding an example of Mendelism among flamingos! No one will believe in that black bird. I'll simply have to shoot it, which I hate to do, and take it back with us."

"If you ever get back," I interrupted, and then I told him all that had happened, except, of course, about the girl kissing him. She hadn't really meant to tell me that; it had just slipped out. "So, you see, it behooves us to mind our p's and q's and all the rest of the alphabet," I concluded, "or we'll find ourselves out on the sand with a bullet through our heads."

Noisy gave a low whistle, and then sat silent, digesting my information.

"We'll just have to do the best we can," he mused aloud. "Never heard anything so crazy in all my life. The wicked old rabbit! Suppose the Chinamen *are* practically slaves, as he said, and would cheerfully commit murder for him."

The door opened abruptly, and a Chinaman stuck his head in.

"Ketchum dinner," he announced, and popped out again.

General Carter was waiting for us in the hall, and guided us into a drawing-room. There sat an enormously fat Chinese woman, and, behind her, stood the girl.

"My dear Esther, Mr. Philip de Mille, Mr. Wandering Smith! Gentlemen, my wife, Mrs. Carter; my daughter, Miss Carter!"

We bowed, and I said it was pleasant weather. Noisy, as usual, said nothing, but his eyes were very busy. The girl wore a long, pink, silky dress that accentuated her slimness and made her skin whiter, her hair and eyes blacker by contrast. Gosh, but she was beautiful! Delicately, like a flower!

We got seated in the dining room somehow, and then the old man began to talk. There was no one else in it. That whisper went steadily, evenly, monotonously on till I began to think of it as an endless slender wire and wonder if it couldn't be snapped by a quick blow, or would have to be cut with pliers. Once De Mille said something aside to the girl in that booming voice of his, but she raised eyes so full of fear to him that he did not attempt to address her again.

That was a great feast all right, all right. We sat like dummies, not saying a word while the old, yellow-faced gentleman whispered steadily at us.

After dinner, we adjourned to a room with a piano in it, and the general asked his daughter for a song. De Mille followed her and turned over the music, and, for the two verses, we had a respite from that whispering voice.

"The years creep slowly by, Lorena;
    The snow is on the grass again;
The sun's low down the sky, Lorena;
    The frost gleams where the flowers have been.
But the heart throbs on as warmly now
    As when the summer days were nigh;
Oh, the sun can never dip so low
    Adown affection's cloudless sky.

"A hundred months have passed, Lorena,
    Since last I held that hand in mine,
And felt the pulse beat fast, Lorena,
    But mine beat faster far than thine;
A hundred months—'twas flowery May,
    When up the hilly slopes we climbed,
To watch the dying of the day,
    To hear the distant church bells chime."

"Quite enough, my dear, and thank you," the old man broke in. "That song always reminds me of the night before the First Battle of Bull Run—" He was off again.

Coffee and cognac were brought to us, and Noisy gulped down more than one of his favorite coffee-laced-with-brandy drinks. I could plainly see his nerves were getting frayed to the raw by everlastingly acting the part of audience, and I waited for something to happen. It did.

"May we not hear Miss Carter sing again?" he broke in on the continuous flow.

The general turned his pale, lemon-colored eyes on him, and they became suffused with blood.

"I am talking, sir," he whispered, and the whisper made it sound worse than if he had shouted: "Be so good as not to interrupt me again."

De Mille turned a deep scarlet; the girl gasped; the old man went calmly on and on and on with his reminiscences.

Suddenly he came to a full stop, looking interrogatively at me.

"Most interesting," I said, without the slightest idea of what he had been talking about.

"You agree with me, then?"

"Bet your—I mean, entirely."

He rose from his chair.

"We keep early hours here. It is our only house rule. To bed by ten and lights out by half past."

He clapped his hands, and two Chinamen appeared with lighted candles.

"Good night and sleep well," our host whispered as we went up the stairs.

Once inside our room and the door shut, Noisy began to roar.

"Go to it, old top!" I encouraged him heartily. "You can't call that human phonograph anything that will hurt my feelings."

The man was fair eloquent, as my Scotch friend, McKee, would have put it, but right in the middle I had to clap my hand over his mouth. The door opened, and the butler appeared with two glasses on a tray.

"You ketchum nightcap and put out lightee," he droned, and was gone.

My, but I slept hard! I tried to wake and couldn't, though some one seemed to be calling me. Finally, through a kind of stupor, it penetrated to my consciousness that something was thrashing around the room like an angry boa constrictor. Instinctively, my hand sought for the gun which I had put under my pillow. It was not there. Broad awake now, I struck a match and lit the candle. De Mille and a Chinaman were wrestling all over the room, the latter trying to escape, the former hanging to him like a bulldog. A well-directed kick in the stomach quieted the intruder, and I retrieved my automatic from inside his blouse. Opening the door, I applied my foot where it would help him along the fastest, and he scuttled out of sight in the dark.

"What in thunder does this mean?" gasped Noisy, nursing a bruised shin.

"They wanted my gun for a souvenir, that's all," I answered. "Go to bed. To-morrow we'll plan to get away from here, even if we have to ride your pet flamingos."

The general did not appear at breakfast, but his daughter did. She presided over the coffee cups as though she had been used to receiving strange, battered guys that blew in from nowhere all her life, and she chattered like a flock of sparrows.

Ten years had she lived on the island and was only eight when her father left China. She didn't remember her mother—father had married a second time—but she had a miniature of her, and she was very beautiful.

Noisy said he could well believe it, and got the snub he deserved in her prompt reply that she took after the male side of the house.

Of course, it was a strange life, living away from the world and seeing no men—people, but she had never known any other. And father had promised her that next year she should go to Paris. Books kept her happy. Father gave her lots of them. Had we read *Ivanhoe* and *Lorna Doone* and *Henry Esmond*? She thought they were just splendid! Then there were her pets. We *must* come and see Richard Cœur de Lion immediately after breakfast. Father never appeared till noon—he had been sick a good deal lately—and she could have us all to herself.

Quite a bunch of conversation! I made a mental note that she really did take after her dad in at least one respect, though Noisy didn't appear to mind her chatter; in fact, seemed to like it.

I'll give it to you! I am romantic, and the way that he looked at that slanty-eyed, vibrant, fresh young girl tickled me nearly to death. It was love at first sight, if I have ever seen it, and most kinds of real love start exactly that way—right on the jump. My courtships did—both of them—and I had so cared for each of my wives in turn that I never married again.

Out in the sunlight, the girl put up a parasol, walking by De Mille's side, while I trailed along; behind. She laughed and talked every minute, and, as now and then I heard his voice in about the ratio of sixteen to one, I decided they were getting along famously.

Meanwhile, my eyes were busy, and I noted two very pertinent things: first, that four of the Chinese coolies were following us at a respectable distance, but none the less following us; second, that not only had all the canoes disappeared from the neighborhood of the landing, but also our boat was gone, its contents piled orderly on the dock.

By this time, we had reached the eastern end of the island, where the flamingo rookery was located, and Miss Carter asked us to stand back among the orange trees. She walked to the edge of the water, and, raising her hands trumpetwise to her lips, sent a long "Co-he-e-e" over to where the birds were nesting.

You may believe me or not, as you please, but this is what actually happened: Seven of the flamingos rose in the air with a metallic clanging, trailing off across the sky, the eighth, and it was the black one, waded, with slow dignity, across to the girl, and there she fed it something she took from her pocket, its queer, hooked beak between her cupped hands.

"He's Richard Cœur de Lion," she explained, coming back to us, while the great bird moved majestically off through the water, "and he's a dear, just as tame, as tame! You see, the others fly away each day to where they can get the little shells they feed on, but we keep Richard's wings tied down, and I feed him with the tiny clam things the Indians get for me." She held out some miniature spiral shells to Noisy. "It's so ingenious the reason we keep his wings bound," she continued, "I just must tell you. When the Indians get in from Miami with supplies, we turn him loose, and he flies with the other flamingos. The Seminoles see him and come from all over the Everglades in their canoes to take away the orange boxes. You see, father is afraid of flooding the market, so he sends out his oranges one box by each Indian. Then they are shipped from different places and don't get to New York or San Francisco all at the same time. Isn't that clever? And he gets enormous prices—five hundred dollars for a single box—"

"Your mother wants you at the house, Esther," came a whisper from behind us, and we turned to find the general standing not a yard away. And the sight of him nearly made me take to my heels. The man was loathsome, positively loathsome! Shaking and trembling, he stood before us wrapped in an old gray dressing gown. The pupils of his eyes seemed to have entirely disappeared, leaving them a liquid mass of light yellow pigment, quite expressionless, horribly nonhuman; his lips were drawn back, revealing in his upper jaw a palpably false set of teeth, while a few stumps stood out from his lower gums; his saffron skin was mottled, damp, and dry in alternate patches, and from him emanated a sickly sweetish odor that caught you by the throat and gagged you.

"I'm sorry this thing happened, gentlemen," he hissed in his painful whisper—the girl had fled—"but it leaves me no alternative. I must tell you the reason I isolate myself and my family here. I am bearing a heavy burden of sorrow. My daughter is quite wanting, quite insane. She suffers from the hallucination that we live entirely from the sale of the oranges for which she believes I get extraordinary prices. Really I sell none, just ship a few boxes to my friends, my Chinese friends." He paused a moment as though to let this sink in. "I suppose it is just as well for you to know, however, as it may not be practicable to send you away from here for some time. You will excuse me now. I am not a well man and seldom leave my room before noon."

We spent the rest of the morning examining the nests and watching that great black bird. It was true enough about its wings being bound. They were loosely confined by a light leather strap about the body, not so as to deprive it entirely of their use, but tight enough to prevent flight.

How much more of what the poor girl had told us was fact, and what did it all mean?

Luncheon was much the same as the day before, the only difference being the presence of the ladies. They might just as well not have been there, however, as far as adding to the verbal gayety went. The general did all the talking, or rather whispering, and that whisper never ceased. Afterward he marched us out to inspect the packing plant, and, while I was being lulled into a state of pure imbecility by a description of the Battle of Manassas, the cowardly ornithologist sneaked away and left me alone with this human whispering machine.

Later in the afternoon, when my brain was reeling, the general suggested that we go out on the water, summoning two Chinamen by clapping his hands. They produced a skiff from somewhere, and we rowed around the island. Then it was that that old scalawag put one over on me, Wandering Smith, who should have known better. The manner of it was as follows: An alligator was sunning itself in the reeds; in the most natural way in the world, my host asked me for my gun to take a shot at it. I handed it to him, all unsuspecting. His back to me, he pulled the trigger and there was a splash.

"So sorry," he whispered remorsefully; "it jerked out of my hand and went overboard. There are twenty feet of water here. I'll send some men out later to dive for it. Now, at Bull Run, when the Yankees broke, I—" Can you beat it? And when he left me at the door of my room I plainly saw in the breast pocket of his coat the outline of a gun—my gun!

It was too late for more than a hurried word with Noisy before dinner, and he was simply bursting with something he had to tell me.

Merciful heavens! What an evening! I listened to the history of the Civil War, detailed with a minuteness even beyond Old Bug's scientific description of a beetle. We had no music—the general's head ached—just whisper, whisper, whisper till my brain reeled, and, when ten o'clock came, I was so tired I saw black.

Up in our room, Noisy could hardly wait for the door to shut.

"That exquisite thing is no more mad than you or I," he burst out. "She simply has never been away from this cursed, mysterious island, and takes for gospel truth everything that old devil tells her. She is as innocent and far sweeter than a child, and, you must acknowledge, talks extremely well."

And a lot I should have liked to add, but didn't. I've heard them talk that way before, and I knew what it meant. Noisy was a goner all right. When a man compares a woman to a child, you can take it from me that it's all over but the wedding tears. It certainly was a pretty romance, but it didn't help clear up matters for us.

"Did she say anything about her father?" I asked.

"Only that he was very good and kind, except sometimes in the mornings. The blessed child says she loves him—without knowledge of what love means," he sighed.

"When you meet her to-morrow, try to get her to talk about him."

"How did you know I was going to meet her?" he asked in amazement.

"Go sleep or I'll tell you 'bout Battle Bull Run," I answered, and immediately closed my eyes.

Perhaps I had been out of the world for two hours when I woke to a house echoing with yell after yell of agony. Out of bed and into my shoes and pants with one jump, I felt around for some weapon. The candlestick, a heavy, silver one, came under my hand, and, cautioning Noisy to stay where he was, I slipped out the door. The yells ceased, to be replaced by a succession of thin, chuckling laughs, and I followed the sound downstairs, beyond the dining room, back of the altar that held the ugly, double-bellied god. Creeping on all fours, I parted a heavy curtain and peeped through.

The fat Chinese woman was bending over a tiny lamp, holding something in the flame that gave off a thick, greasy smoke. The general lay on a couch in his dressing gown, propped up with pillows, and it was from him that the low-toned, senile mirth came. Against the wall, his hands tied to iron rings above his head, half hung, half stood a Chinaman, his bare back toward me, and that back was covered with long welts. Beside him was the shaking butler, a wire-lashed whip in his hand.

"Three more!" commanded the yellow-faced old gentleman.

The whip rose and fell three times.

"That's all," whispered the old man. "Sent you for the Yankee's gun last night. You failed to get it; had to get it myself. Let this be a lesson to you to obey me in future. Unloose him!"

The butler reached up and cut the thongs from the iron rings. His face was toward me, and I saw he was licking his lips with fear. The bruised man salaamed three times to the floor and backed out past me.

The Chinese woman finished what she was doing over the flame of the lamp, and, holding a ball of sticky, smoking stuff on a long knitting needle, took from a little table a foot-long bamboo fitted with a tiny metal bowl—an opium pipe. Plunging the reeking mass into the bowl, she handed it to the saffron-faced old man, who greedily carried it to his lips.

Most opium smokers, I believe, reach the poppy coma after three or four pipes. The whispering man smoked ten, the butler cooking the pills, the woman crouching by the couch and handing him the pipes, the last three of which she had to hold to his lips. Then the smoker's eyes closed and he sank back among the cushions. For several moments, the woman watched him, lifted his eyelid with her finger tip, and then dismissed the butler with a low-spoken word. He passed so close to me between the curtains that I could have touched him.

Cooking another opium pill, the fat woman stretched herself on a lounge near the small table. Thrice she replenished the tiny bowl, and, the last time, I saw my automatic lying on the table beneath her hand. Four pipes, the bamboo receptacle slipped to the floor, and she, too, slept.

The candles were gutting low. Through my peephole floated the nauseating sweet fumes of the opium. The house was very still. Inch by inch I rose to my feet and reached my hand to the edge of the curtain, then withdrew it quickly. There were cautious footsteps stealing up the hall. Holding my breath, I waited. A shadow crossed the slit of light from between the curtains. The curtains themselves were slowly drawn back, and a Chinaman, a long knife in his hand, tiptoed past me. Shifting my candlestick, I brought it down with all my strength on his skull, jumped over his falling body, snatched my gun from the table, and swiftly, silently, sped upstairs.

The first light of morning was just beginning to filter in through the long French windows. From outside came the soft twitter of early-rising birds. Within, the house was silent as the grave.

We breakfasted late and alone the next morning, and, out under the orange trees, laid our plans for the day. I was to try and locate the boat or any other available craft, and, if possible, pump some of the Chinamen. Noisy, who had a date with Miss Carter at ten to feed Richard Cœur de Lion, was to encourage her to talk as much as possible—a rather easy job, I thought, though I kept that opinion to myself.

There were no boats or canoes of any description on the island, and I finally decided they must be hidden in the saw grass, to be produced only when needed. All the Chinamen, under the direction of the butler, who also seemed to be a kind of a foreman, were busy packing oranges. The orange boxes were ranged in a long row, the covers leaning against them, and on each cover was stenciled the name of the consignee, always a Chinaman. No two boxes went to the same address, and their destinations ranged from Houston, Texas, to Chicago, Illinois, even including San Francisco. The manner of the packing was rather odd. One of the two compartments of each box was filled full, the other received only a layer of oranges in the bottom, and then, with its cover, was carried inside a room with a lock on the door, and placed on a long table.

I watched the work going on for some time, and then the butler passed behind me.

"You ketchum spring. I come," he said in a low voice, and mingled with the workmen.

As nonchalantly as I could, I sauntered off among the orange trees until I could no longer see the packing plant through the shiny green leaves, then hurried straight to where I had been directed. The Chinese butler was waiting for me, and, with a "You come," led the way to the western end of the island behind the servants' quarters. There he paused and pointed to seven little round mounds, two very recently made, decorated with pieces of shell, gay scraps of paper, and bundles of faded flowers.

"All dead," he indicated, with a sweep of his arm. "T'ee, fo', fiv' China boy, Indian, 'nother China boy this morning. Gen' Carter kill. You lookee!"

He raised his blouse, and turned his bare back to me. It was covered with half-healed welts, exactly such wounds as I had seen inflicted the night before by the steel-lashed whip in his own hands.

"You ketchum way from here?" he asked.

I shook my head, thinking rapidly. Evidently the old, saffron-faced opium fiend not only beat his men, but even killed them at his pleasure. Also, they did not know how to get away. The saw grass formed an impenetrable maze that only the Seminoles could thread, and they, in some mysterious fashion, were evidently bound to the old Confederate. It was too much for me.

"You no ketchum way out," begged the butler again. Again I shook my head sadly. For a moment, he stood thinking, and then, once more, spoke:

"China boy ketchum Indian. Burn him fleet and hlands till he show way out. You kill Gen' Carter. We alle glow way."

I was willing to listen to a poor brute who wanted to escape from being flayed with a wire whip or, perhaps, even killed, but when this same brute suggested that I murder my host and connive at the torture of an Indian, it was quite a different matter. I told him there was nothing doing, and turned and went back to the house.

Noisy was waiting in our room and had a lot to report from Miss Carter. A Chinaman, whom her father had punished, had tried to murder him the night before and had been knocked senseless by the faithful butler. Faithful butler! I remembered his expression after he showed me the welts on his bare back. Later, the Chinaman had died. She was all broken up over it. How could any one want to hurt her good, kind father? "Then a wonderful thing happened, Wandering," De Mille continued. "I tried to comfort her, patted her shoulder, and, before I knew it, I had her in my arms. I am the only man she has ever kissed—how many girls can truly say that of their lovers?—and we are going to tell her father this evening."

"You are going to tell her father no such thing, young man," I announced firmly. "First, we are going to find a way out of here back to civilization. You can take the girl with you if you wish. It won't be the first time, or, I hope, the last that I act as chaperon for two young fools. We are going to find a way to get out of here, first of all, though, you understand! I haven't the slightest desire to be buried with six Chinamen and an Indian in the middle of the Everglades."

The general did not come to lunch. Miss Carter did. Whenever the butler was out of the room—I was uncomfortable every time he passed behind my back—the lovers held hands, and I know I beamed on them. Give me a good, old-fashioned love affair every time for real enjoyment; it beats horse-racing, cocking mains, and even prize fights.

Just as the dessert was being served, there was a chorus of "Co-he-e-es" from the water. The girl sprang to her feet with a cry of pleasure.

"It's the Indians bringing things from Miami. There will be books and new dresses for me. I must run and untie Richard's wings."

We followed her out of doors, then walked down to the dock, where were four dugouts, and watched the coolies unload four large boxes which they carried into the packing house. The girl returned quickly, and, as we went back to the house, followed by the butler carrying her bundles, a great black flamingo flew eastward across the grassy waste of the Everglades.

The general met us at the door, wearing all his teeth, but looking frightfully sinister and rather ill. He apologized in his usual whisper for neglecting us, and regretted that he would not be able to spend the afternoon with me—he had forgotten to give me the aftermath of the Battle of Chickamauga—but the packing house would claim him till the evening.

Noisy and the girl wandered off. I established myself on the front porch with a copy of *The Life of "Stonewall" Jackson*—local color—that I had no intention of reading.

Almost immediately, Seminoles began to arrive at the dock, pushing out of the saw grass from every direction. I had hoped to locate the opening of a channel, but either the canoes could slip between the reeds like snakes, or there were countless water trails abutting on the island. Chinamen came from the packing house, each with a box of oranges on his shoulder, which, unloaded in a canoe, was whisked out of sight into the saw grass. I watched thirty-eight thus disappear, and sauntered down to get a nearer view of the operations. Ten more boxes went away, not one word exchanged between Seminole and Chinaman, and then there was an accident. One of the coolies stumbled, down came his box on the heavy planking of the dock, split, from one side rolled out the yellow fruit, and from the other, breaking through a casing of oranges, cascaded a dozen two-inch square tins.

I walked quickly back to the house, not wishing the general to know what had been revealed to me. A glance was enough. Once before, seized on a ship from India, I had seen those little square cans, and I knew they contained opium.

No wonder the orange boxes were addressed only to Chinamen! No wonder the general kept the secret of the way to and from his island inviolate!

The Indians continued to arrive and take away the oranges in a steady stream, until Noisy returned, and we went upstairs.

"Sorry, Wandering," were his first words, "but Esther is going to tell her father of our engagement. Couldn't persuade her not to, couldn't persuade her, then, to let me do it. She says if he gets angry, he won't hurt her, while he might kill me."

I whistled. What was there to do about it, though?

"I'll lend you my gun," I offered.

"Never saw the time I needed a gun yet," he answered haughtily, "especially against an old man."

"That listens noble," I remarked. He made me kind of sore. "But allow me to suggest, just as a precautionary measure, and in no way as a reflection on your courage, that you wear a geography in the seat of your pants—I mean trousers."

He was about to answer me unkindly when the butler stuck his head in the door, intimating briefly that it was time to catch dinner.

That was one nervous meal! No one said a word. The fat Chinese woman never took her eyes from the general; the general glowered at Noisy, his daughter, and me, turn by turn. I watched him out of the corner of my eye, my automatic stuck in the waistband of my trousers. The lovers just mooned at one another.

We all rose at the end of the meal, and the old gentleman detained us, while the ladies went into the drawing-room.

"I understand you want to marry my daughter," he whispered at De Mille.

The boy bowed, flushing pink.

"You have known her three days, you have abused my hospitality, and you are a d——d Yankee cur. Go to your room! I'll deal with you tomorrow, as I deal with my servants."

Gosh! I got to my feet, and Noisy stood up, just trembling with rage. His mouth opened and shut without a sound coming out, and then he suddenly bolted. I started to follow him.

"Just a moment," came the whisper. "You remember I was going to tell you about the end of the Battle of Chickamauga."

"You ain't," I shouted, and, jumping out the door, ran upstairs.

In the drawing-room, Miss Carter was singing:

> *"Wake! dearest, wake! 'Tis thy lover who calls.*
> *List! dearest, list! The dew gently falls,*
> *Arise to thy lattice, the moon is asleep,*
> *The bright stars above us their bright vigil keep."*

"We're in for it now," I said to Noisy, who was striding up and down the floor, his voice rumbling like an earthquake, "and as soon as it's light, we are going to beat it. That opium fiend isn't much good in the morning."

"We're not going to beat it without Esther," firmly spoke De Mille.

"Oh, bring her along, the black flamingo, and the family cat, too, if you wish," I answered crossly. "The more the merrier!"

Before we turned in, I jammed a chair back under the doorknob and arranged an artistic fortification of wash-stands, chairs, and bric-a-brac that would go down with a crash at the slightest touch in front of the French windows. Then I turned in and slept till nearly daybreak.

Just before dawn, when it is darkest, I woke with a feeling of insufferable heat. There was a roaring noise outside like the wind through a tree-top, and suddenly it was light—red light.

"Philip! Philip!" cried a voice. "The house is burning! Come quick!"

Out of bed, I touched the girl's soft shoulder, caught her hand, and, dragging Noisy to his feet, we slipped through the door I had forgotten, behind the silk hangings. Quickly we were in the hall and down the stairs. A sheet of flame burst from behind the curtains above the hideous god on the altar, and a fierce chorus of "Co-he-e-es" came from outside. The Chinamen were massed before the front door as I flung it open, and greeted us with a yell.

"Pick up your girl and make for the landing!" I commanded, and fired two shots into the thick of the crowd. It broke, scattered, and we found ourselves running down the long avenue. There were plenty of canoes near the dock. Launching the largest one, we prepared to push off.

"Father! Get father!" begged the girl from her lover's arms. "They'll kill him!"

"Good riddance!" I said beneath my breath; but, nevertheless, jumped to the dock, shoving off the canoe and shouting, "Wait at the flamingo island," sped back toward the house, now a roaring volcano of flame. As I reached the edge of the shadow, the butler appeared on the porch, holding something in his hand. He raised it that all might see—a saffron-faced head, the eyes closed, the skin mottled. Turning, I ran eastward through the orange trees, and, splashing through the water, crossed to the mud flat, beyond which showed the dim outline of the canoe. Something rose before me, and I caught it in my arms. There was a protesting squawk, and I tumbled into the boat, the black flamingo clasped to my bosom.

How we got there through the maze of tiny waterways I don't know, but in less than two hours a little lane opened out into a broad, strongly flowing channel, down which we paddled. By noon, we were on a river I recognized—the Miami—and the rest of our journey lay clear before us.

Noisy married the girl, of course. I should have shot him if he hadn't. You can't arrive at a thriving Southern resort in your night clothes, accompanied by a lady, also in her night clothes, and a black flamingo, without compromising said lady, even when chaperoned by such a respectable old party as yours truly.

It was several weeks before it occurred to us to report the shipments of opium to the Federal authorities, and, since I couldn't remember any of the Chinese consignees' names, the investigation did not come to much. They easily evolved the theory that the stuff was floated ashore just beyond Miami, on the edge of the Everglades, and taken in by the Indians—a very clever scheme for distributing it in America, since Florida was the last place from which you would expect opium to be shipped. A year later, the island was even located, but found to be deserted. Whether the Chinamen got away, perished in the sea of saw grass, or were slain by the Seminoles, I don't know.

The black flamingo was on exhibition in the Museum of Natural History, and for some time attracted considerable attention. Then a meddling old fool of a scientist found that it was only dyed, not really black at all.

This nearly broke Noisy's heart, but about that date the first baby came to distract his attention. Esther insisted on naming it Richard.

Saint and Señorita

*The meeting of the Saint and the Señorita was as nothing to
the meeting of the Saint and the Black Iguana. A story of the
South American jungle, told by Wandering Smith.*

I LIKE ANIMALS IN THEIR PROPER PLACES, i.e. cooked, in cages, or wild in the jungle. I do not like to find an armadillo under my bed and a pea-green monkey scrubbing the ceiling with my only toothbrush.

The boat was a Noah's Ark within a week from the time we started. Doctor Myron T. Jessup collected everything—birds, beasts, reptiles, insects, fishes—and I'm sure he would have put a different brand of Indian in each of the big cages, if he had dared. There were three professional collectors working for him, not to mention my humble services, and you know what the banks of the Amazon River are—just crawling with life.

I shouldn't have minded the variety—rather enjoyed having so many different kinds of beasts around—if they had been kept in cages; but they weren't. The naturalist tried to tame everything, from the tiny wistiti monkeys to a tapir that looked like a cross between a hog and a baby elephant, and didn't have enough brains, to begin with, to be really wild.

I must say he generally got away with it, though. Animals seemed to recognize him as a kindred soul, and used his body as a kind of neutral territory. I have seen a parrot sitting on one shoulder, a monkey on the other, while an iguana crawled across his lap and squirrels were asleep in both his side pockets. He never handled the iguanas when there was sunlight, though. Sunlight seemed to affect those ugly lizards like whisky does most people. After they had soaked in it a little while they'd bite anything.

Darned if he wasn't the gentlest little fellow I have ever known, and just as simple and modest as though he wasn't the greatest living naturalist, to whom even T.R. tipped his sombrero. I named him "the Saint" before I had known him a day, and he certainly looked and acted the part.

As a matter of fact, it was sure ungrateful in me to complain of a few harmless animals lying around promiscuous. I'd never been more comfortable or happier in my life. The sixty-foot, broad-beamed, flat-bottomed boat was built solely for collecting purposes, with a big kicker behind and an entirely adequate crew. Everything in the world that spelled comfort had been provided. I even had Mose, my own cook, on board, and, take it from me, the combination he puts together would make the Czar of Russia jam his napkin under his collar and forget all else. There was hardly a thing for me to do: just keep a roving eye over the boat and crew, shoot game for the captive animals, pick out our route, watch the natives didn't get ugly, navigate the boat, check up the commissary, and help catch wild animals.

In the evenings, after dinner, the Saint and I would loaf and smoke, telling one another of the things we had seen outside of cities, or, maybe, play a game of chess. Mostly we just sat silent, though, comfortable in having each other around, and watched the brown river flow steadily by while the shore rustled with night noises. Then, 'bout ten o'clock, the Saint would turn his young-looking, smooth face, with its great brown eyes, toward me and say:

"Another beautiful day ended, Wandering, and still another coming in the morning. Let's sleep, so as to get to it quicker."

Of course, no large animals were to be expected until we were well up the Amazon, and it was only after the tenth day we anchored near the bank and prepared for a real hunt. Though the Saint collected everything, he was especially anxious to secure a series of iguanas, largest and ugliest of the lizards, and half a dozen jaguars to distribute among the various American zoological gardens. The place where we stopped was ideal for our purpose—jungle to the water's edge, and several hundred acres of brush-overgrown clearing reported in the middle of it. Six of us—the Saint, the three professional collectors, an Indian guide, and I—made up the party, and almost immediately we found traces of an entire jaguar family, for which we set traps.

The unbelievably luxuriant tropical jungle was only penetrable through the narrow animal trails, and it was with the greatest difficulty we finally forced our way to the comparatively open, brush-overgrown clearing; and here we found lizards beyond counting, numerous as insects. There were thickset, broad-headed geckos, with glistening, catlike eyes, fleeing in every direction, their throats pulsating as they filled the air with sharp, clicking sounds; alligator lizards, brown, yellow, vividly shaded with green; yard-long basilisks, upright, comb-like protuberances extending from head to tail; swifts, skinks; tejus banded with yellow and white; and then the iguanas, thousands of them, brilliantly colored, twelve inches to five feet long, with strange crests the length of their bodies, and still stranger swelling throat pouches.

Had there been a single specimen, we never should have secured it, but the lizards were so numerous that as soon as we lost one, another was beneath our hands. Some we simply grabbed, others we netted; the big fellows were nosed, and a pretty struggle they gave us, even after we had caught them. My hands were bleeding from a dozen bites before all the collecting sacks were full, and the assistants, together with the Indian, had been sent back, heavily laden, to the boat.

The Saint and I lingered on, pushing forward as cautiously and noiselessly as possible. The naturalist wanted a specimen of the black iguana, one of which we had surprised basking on a rock, whence it had crashed into the brush, and, running nearly upright, disappeared with more noise than a frightened cow. The walking was very bad, and we were forced to be continually on our guard against snakes. Nearly across the clearing, another black iguana went through the bushes like a railroad train, leaving behind it a chorus of indignant squeals. I had heard those same squeals before, and knew what they meant. With a yell of warning, I took to my heels for the nearest tree. A drove of peccaries, the little, wild hog of South America, before which even the jaguar turns aside, swept toward us, and I hauled my companion up into the branches barely in time.

There must have been fully two hundred of the fierce little animals glaring up at us when we were finally perched on adjacent limbs. Of course, we could have shot a good many of them. My automatic held eight shells, and we had, between us, a score of cartridges for our guns; but what was the use? The more we killed, the closer the remainder would stick, as I knew from experience. It simply resolved itself into a waiting game, and the Lord only knew how long those obstinate hogs would keep us in a state of siege.

Of course, I grumbled and cussed, but the Saint took the situation more calmly. Within ten minutes he had collected half a dozen tree toads and some insects, and was so deeply absorbed that I doubt if he even realized we might have to spend the night like a couple of roosting hens.

The morning wore slowly on, then the afternoon, while the peccaries still hung together beneath us. The sows dug dry wallows and suckled their young; the boars rooted, sniffed up at us, or fought fiercely among themselves. Not one animal showed the slightest indication of leaving.

The jungle was very still. Even the wild hogs had relapsed into peaceful, barnyard-like gruntings. From afar came the faint, insistent clang of a bell-bird. The Saint selected one of the tree toads, packed it in a neat tin box, and let the others go.

"Time we were getting back to the boat, Wandering," he suggested.

"Very true," I agreed, "but I've left my folding, pocket aeroplane at home. How are we going to manage it?"

"Let's try a big noise."

We did. Firing off our guns brought the peccaries in close ranks about the foot of the tree. Yelling seemed to amuse them. I worked the bullet out of a shell, chewed a piece of linen from my shirt, sprinkled it with powder for a fuse, and, attaching it to the cartridge, chucked the whole makeshift bomb down among our besiegers. It was gobbled up before it got a chance to go off. Another explosive suffered the same fate. Then one did burst, and the peccaries tried to climb up to us.

"The only thing to do is for you to try and tame them," I told the Saint, giving up my efforts in disgust.

Far off in the jungle a jaguar screamed. Night was approaching; in two hours it would be pitch dark. Again the jaguar lifted up its voice, and the sound was followed by a faint "ow-ou-owh, ou-owh!"

"Dogs, by all that's holy!" exclaimed my companion.

The baying grew nearer, increasing in volume. The little hogs faced about and listened uneasily, some even trotting off into the underbrush.

"Ow-ou-owh, ou-owh, ou-owh!" and a gigantic black jaguar burst across the clearing, scattered the peccaries, and spun up to the top of our tree. On its heels came a dozen dogs, but dogs the like of which I had never dreamed. They stood, on an average, four feet at the shoulder. The yellow hair had been shaved from their bodies so the pink skin showed through, and their heads, with enormous, slavering jaws, were as big as buckets. Around the tree they raged, in such a fury of sound that we could scarce think, while from the highest limb the jaguar glowered down on them.

A score of horsemen appeared, circled around the dogs, and a rifle spoke. The jaguar came tumbling through the foliage, caught in a crotch at my very elbow, and hung there, dead.

The dogs were caught, one by one, and led away, long ropes around their necks, and the Saint and I slipped from the tree.

Those cavaliers couldn't have been more surprised if two camels had descended in their midst. They just stared. Then the Saint, who had the manners of a prince, addressed a handsome young chap who appeared to be the leader, and explained our predicament. At once two of the servants were dismounted, and we were offered their horses, with an invitation to ride to the hacienda. It was getting much too dark to think of returning through the jungle to the boat, so we found ourselves threading the brush until a good road was reached, down which we galloped. After an hour's ride, we swept into a clearing, and drew rein before a large, rambling house. The servants, with the dogs and the body of the dead jaguar, went around to the back, and, dismounting, we entered the broad veranda.

It was instantly apparent to me that we were on one of those fabulously rich Brazilian estates that cover thousands of acres, and are ruled after the fashion of small kingdoms by their all-powerful owners. The house was enormous, modern in every respect, and crammed with native servants. There were actually electric lights, and manufactured ice tinkled in the drinks that came to our rooms. The Saint and I changed quickly into the white garments provided for us, and then dinner was announced.

You can't beat a well-born South American for manners. I was seated on the right of the young man, Don Roderigo Cervantes; at the other end of the table, the Saint was placed next to his sister, the Señorita Anita. Opposite him, and on the lady's left, glowered a middle-aged, mustached cuss in the gorgeous uniform of a captain of Brazilian cavalry, and there were seven other people at the table, including the señorita's duenna, who had a very downy upper lip, and an old padre.

It was terribly formal, at first. Our host proposed the health of the President of the United States, the Saint that of the President of Brazil. Then we drank to our hostess, the army, the church, and to each other in turn. Nevertheless, it bogged down into a pleasant dinner toward the end. The girl at the head of the table was one merry peach. Once the ice was broken, she simply flashed like a sunbeam. It was very evident that the soldier was completely infatuated with her, and she took the greatest delight in maddening him by flirting most outrageously with the Saint, who played up beautifully. There was lots of good food, quantities of good drinks, and everything was very jolly.

After the coffee and liqueurs came on and the ladies had gone, we men all drew closer together and got better acquainted. It transpired that young Don Roderigo Cervantes and Señorita Anita were the sole heirs of countless acres of forest, plain, and swamp, the owners of rubber, cacao, cattle, and a lot of other things. They were, of course, awfully rich—simply did not know their wealth. Also the hacienda and estate were unusually fortunate in having an old Englishman for superintendent, thus cutting out the usual South American graft. Over this domain the boy and girl, neither of them much over twenty, ruled with rights of high, low, and middle justice, hunted, raced thoroughbreds, gave great entertainments to which guests came from hundreds of miles around, and, when all this palled, took trips to Rio de Janeiro, New York, even Paris and London. Contrary to the storybooks, that always picture riches burdened down with discontent, they seemed the happiest people I have ever known.

Of course, the Saint told them all about our boat and the purpose of the expedition, and they were awfully interested. As a matter of fact, every one is interested in anything concerning wild animals. It must be an inheritance from our ancestors of the Stone Age, when beasts undoubtedly furnished all subjects of conversation. They laughed over our scrape with the peccaries, but when the naturalist began to expatiate on the subject of iguanas, a queer silence fell over the group. Don Roderigo broke it with rather a nervous laugh.

"You have come to the right place, señores," he said. "Our ancestral home is known as the Hacienda of the Iguanas, and it certainly deserves its name from the numbers of those lizards around here. Furthermore, we keep one as a kind of fetish. My father left its care to me, the same as his grandfather did to *his* father. The padre, here, calls it a species of idolatry, and hopes the beast will die. I think it is the devil, myself, though, and will live forever. There is a queer old legend about it, too. Would you like to look at the animal?"

The Saint said he certainly would, and we followed through several rooms out into a large patio around which the house was built. The entire court was a tropical garden, beautiful under the moonlight, and it didn't seem to me to fit in with the character of the place to have Don Roderigo switch on a multitude of electric globes hidden in the foliage, that made it light as day. In the center of the enclosure we paused before a kind of masonry cellar sunk in the ground, with a fence of pointed iron pickets curving over the edge like the bear pit in a zoo. Shrubbery grew at the bottom, with quite a large tree in the middle, its top on a level with our heads. At first, our eyes saw nothing, and then became riveted across the pit on something whence came a hissing like a thousand snakes.

Great Cæsar's ghost, but the fetish of the Cervantes was an awesome thing! Fully seven feet long, a crest of large, lanceolate spines tipped with pink, reaching from the neck to the base of the tail, compressed so that it looked like a mighty sword, the iguana raised a wicked head toward us, beneath which its enormous, comb-like pouch fluttered with rage.

Save for the pinkish tips to the crest, it was black, jet black, black as the core of night. Hissing furiously, the reptile rose on its hind legs, and, half upright, dashed against the side of the pit, the two-foot-long nails of its middle fore-claws scratching white lines in the stone walls.

"Pretty, isn't it?" our host exclaimed, but there was an uneasy look in his eyes that belied the lightness of the words. "If you really want to see it angry, though, just hum any little tune. It's a deadly foe to harmony." And he puckered up his lips to whistle.

"No, my son," reproved the padre, "remember your promise to the señorita!"

The boy shrugged his shoulders; but, nevertheless, turned to the house.

Back in the cheerful dining room, the Saint simply babbled over with questions.

Did he ever remember it as smaller?

No. It had always seemed the same size to him.

What was it fed?

Fruit, and sometimes fowls, which it tore to pieces.

Had it ever attempted to escape?

No. Why should it?

Had it attacked any one—hurt any one?

It never had the chance.

"One of the dogs, and you know our breed is rather formidable," Don Roderigo continued, "once jumped into the pit. It was dead within a minute."

That ended the interrogation, and I must say I, for one, was glad to stop thinking of the reptile. Then we joined the ladies in the next room.

Gosh, but that was a pleasant evening, and certainly a queer one for the middle of a South American jungle. One of the women sang, and she did it very nicely, in that high voice that kind of splashes like a waterfall. The officer played the piano till the house shook, and then a big Victrola was turned on, and every one—save yours truly—danced. And that's where the Saint won out with heaps to spare. He was the lightest man on his toes I have ever seen. It simply did my heart good to watch him whirl that pretty Spanish girl across the floor, her black eyes sparkling up to his big brown ones, her little, red mouth curving in a smile while he talked down to her. I certainly enjoyed the sight, but there was some one else who certainly did not. The gentleman in uniform looked as though he might burst any minute.

Up in our room, the Saint conversed at great length about the black iguana. It was the queerest legacy a family ever passed down from father to son. How old was the great lizard, anyway? And there were no records of one anywhere near that size. Simplest thing in the world, if it wanted to get out of its prison. Just had to climb the tree that grew in the middle of the pit, and jump. Black iguanas were normally arboreal, too.

I stood this monologue as long as I could, and then exploded:

"Don't you ever think of anything but animals, Saint? Can't you find something better to talk about than a dirty black reptile, after dancing the entire evening with one of the prettiest girls you have ever seen?"

"Why, I had no idea you were romantic, Wandering!"

"I am, and proud of it," I announced sulkily, and snapped off the electric lights.

"She really dances very well," came apologetically out of the darkness.

I let such insipid praise pass without comment, as it deserved, and turned over. Something like a suppressed chuckle came from the other bed.

Our room opened into the patio. I was just dropping off when the tinkle of a guitar came from outside, accompanied by the half-muted tones of a man's voice.

> *"The red rose is wondrous fair,*
>> *The lily white as heavenly grace.*
> *But the rose cannot with thy lips compare,*
>> *Nor the lily with thy face.*

> *"The trill of a bird in the dark,*
>> *The night breathing perfume.*
> *But the very stars to thy voice hark,*
>> *And the—"*

"*Sis-s-s, sis-s-s, sssss,*" came from the middle of the court, and the captive iguana began to rage around its prison. There was a muttered malediction, and the serenade ended abruptly. From somewhere in the hacienda came a soft laugh. Then I really went to sleep.

In the morning, nothing would do but that we send word to the boat, and spend the day at the Hacienda of the Iguanas. The boy had taken a violent fancy to the Saint, and demanded to be taught "everything" in regard to lizards at once. The girl, though not so effusive, volunteered the information that there would be dancing again in the evening.

Word dispatched to the boat, we spent the day in the woods collecting, but more often simply observing. The neighborhood fairly swarmed with lizards, not surprising considering that the natives looked on them much as their master regarded the black iguana.

Back at the house, the evening passed like the previous one, save that the Saint danced practically every dance with Señorita Anita, even swiping one that plainly belonged to her soldier admirer. That gentleman looked daggers, but apparently couldn't think of anything to do about it.

The next day found us on the boat, but under a promise to return for a great masked ball that was to be given the end of the week.

Our jaguar traps brought us three captives, a female with two kittens. They were healthy beasts, and the delighted naturalist began to try and tame them at once. It was certainly wonderful the power he had over wild animals. The mother was taking food from his hands within twenty-four hours, and didn't seem to mind at all his handling of her offspring.

For the next few days, lizards proved our main prey, and we finally succeeded in capturing two mature black iguanas, as vicious brutes as I have ever seen. We also paid a formal dinner call at the hacienda, during which the Saint got lost with his hostess for two hours, much to the horror of the duenna.

The fifth day, the one preceding the ball, we were hailed from the shore by Don Roderigo, and he came on board too excited for even the usual polite amenities.

"The black iguana has escaped from the patio," he burst out, "a thing that never happened before within the history of our race! It *must* be recaptured, or some great misfortune will befall us! You may laugh at my superstitions, but it *must* be found."

Of course, we were too polite to laugh, and asked for further details. There weren't any.

Horses were waiting, and we rode back with the boy. The señorita, very pale, but glad to see us—or rather the Saint—led the way out into the court. The cement pit was empty, a great hole in the bottom coming out beneath the shrubbery near the house. The patio had been carefully searched, the house ransacked, but there was no trace of the black iguana.

"We'll try the dogs," announced the naturalist.

"They won't track it; they have been trained to leave lizards alone," answered Don Roderigo.

"It attacked one once, and might do so again," explained the Saint. "That is the only way I can think of to locate it."

All that afternoon we scoured the surrounding country, the dogs ranging ahead, and, though we put up quantities of other game, not an iguana was seen. As evening approached, we rode back slowly toward the house, and, just as we turned at dusk into the avenue, there was a howl of agony from one of the great dogs. Spurring toward the sound, we burst through the underbrush. An upright, black horror tore past us, and we drew rein by a dead hound, ripped open from jaws to tail. In vain we hunted the neighborhood of the hacienda in the twilight. The black iguana had disappeared as completely as though the earth had swallowed it up.

Dinner, that evening, was very quiet. No one there, save the Cervantes, the señorita's duenna, the padre, and ourselves. The boy was especially silent and preoccupied, and the burden of the conversation fell on the Saint.

By this time I was beginning to get fed up with that mad hunt after a lizard. A fer-de-lance had all but struck me during the afternoon, and I was dog-goned tired. It seemed to me there was more fuss, being made than was necessary. What if the ugly reptile *had* been a family fetish for several generations? It was bound to die some time, even were it recaptured. Lots of worse things might happen. I caught myself just in time to stifle a prodigious yawn.

After dinner, coffee was served out in the patio. Don Roderigo excused himself on the plea of looking over some accounts with the superintendent, and took the padre with him. The duenna, as all good duennas should, promptly went to sleep. I stepped inside the house and stretched myself out on a couch, leaving the señorita and the Saint alone in the moonlight. At once I found I could distinguish their words from where I lay, and started to move, when something the girl said stopped me.

"Perhaps you think it silly, señor," she began, "that my brother should be so distressed, but we really have been brought up with the feeling that the iguana would always be with us."

"I, too, should hate to lose such an extraordinary animal, if I owned it," came the Saint's voice.

"It's not that; it's the legend! I believe I shall tell it to you, and perhaps you will understand."

It was at this point that I settled myself unblushingly down to listen. The girl went on:

"The first Don Roderigo Cervantes came over with Cortez to Mexico, but, disgusted with the conquistador's cruelty and insatiable lust for gold, left him, taking along his own followers, and coasted down South America, then up the Amazon River. The natives were very gentle and friendly, and brought him gifts of gold, pelts, and strange animals. The king, who was at the same time the chief priest, was especially attached to my ancestor, and they even hunted together in the jungle. It seems there then existed reptiles that are not known to-day, among which was a gigantic lizard, much like the one we have lost, but thrice as big, and very fierce. On a hunting expedition, the native king was seized by one of these reptiles, and would have been torn to pieces had Don Roderigo not succeeded in hewing its head from its body, receiving an awful wound during the struggle. When he had been drawn back from the very gates of death, the priest king gave him a tiny green iguana—which has since grown into the enormous black one you have seen—with the prophecy that as long as it was in our family we should keep our estates on the Amazon, prosper, and mate only with the bluest blood of Spain; and so it has always proved. The prophecy has grown into a kind of a folk song."

Glancing cautiously at the sleeping duenna, the girl began to half sing, half chant, beneath her breath:

> *"Green shall turn to black as night,*
> *(Guard your trust full well!)*
> *Broad lands spread to left and right.*
> *(Guard you your trust well!)*
> *Riches, honor, health, and fame,*
> *Shall make glorious your name,*
> *Naught shall cause Cervantes shame.*
> *(Hold you your trust tight.)*
>
> *"Should the jungle claim its due,*
> *(Should your trust break free.)*
> *All your world begins anew.*
> *(When your trust lost be.)*
> *Spain shall know you never more,*
> *Comes one from an alien shore—*
> *Heed the mystic, ancient lore.*
> *(To your trust be true.)"*

A tree creaked, the foliage rustled. "*Sis-s-s, sis-s-s, ssss!*" came from the center of the patio. Don Roderigo sprang past me and switched on the lights in the court. We rushed to the concrete pit and peered through the iron pickets that curved over the edge. The black iguana, mold on its shoulders, a broken vine tangled in its crest, glared up at us and then dashed furiously against the stone walls, scarring them with its two-foot-long claws.

The hole through which the gigantic lizard had emerged into the patio was filled with great rocks, and an all-night guard stationed by the side of the pit.

Don Roderigo and his sister were too pleased for words. We stood in a chattering group, all talking at once, trying to evolve some reason for the return of the reptile. In the excitement, the señorita's right hand was clasped tight in the Saint's left. She drew it away finally—suddenly seemed to notice it—but she drew it away very gently.

The Saint had nothing to say while we were preparing for bed; just kind of mooned. Out of the corner of my eye, I watched him surreptitiously slip a tiny handkerchief under his pillow.

Oh, well! The one real love comes to all of us sooner or later. It had come twice to me in my life, and I knew how he felt.

In the morning, people began to arrive simply in hordes, and we went back to the boat. On the way, the much-uniformed officer passed us, accompanied by a guard of ten little brown soldiers beautifully mounted. Their leader bowed most formally, hesitated as though he would speak, and then, evidently thinking better of it, rode on. I didn't care a whole lot for that fellow, and his looks were a little more than murderous. South Americans are rather impulsive, too.

On the boat, the Saint, after petting the jaguars and playing around generally with all the other animals, concentrated on the black iguanas while I sat around and watched. The two vicious lizards had been confined in a large cage, well shaded from the sun, and the naturalist began proceedings by simply stepping inside and then standing perfectly still. They made a furious rush at him; but, since he didn't move a muscle, stopped short of sinking their claws in his flesh. It was a curious spectacle—the man perfectly motionless, the reptiles quivering with energy, but clearly at a loss to understand his pose. I rather think they had the same feelings that come over a man when some one he has just insulted won't fight, and, while he longs to, he can't quite bring himself to pound an unguarded face.

Then the naturalist began to whisper, his lips not moving at all, an even, low sound, infinitely soothing, like a flow of water just heard from very far away. The tense animals started, hesitated, then gradually relaxed. The whisper changed to a low, plaintive whistle, hands weaving slowly from left to right. Gradually the lizards' heads began to follow the moving hands, while the sibilation grew slightly louder, monotonously lingering over a single note, and the Saint bent down and passed his finger tips over the ugly heads.

"Bring me a few bits of meat," he demanded, in a quick aside, keeping his palms moving down the crests, that sank beneath their touch.

When I brought the meat, both reptiles were half on his knees, and they fed from his fingers.

It sounds kind of mad, doesn't it? But that was always the way he handled wild things. Just kept still, and then got them interested in some little, soft sound, or even monotonous movement. Perhaps he mesmerized them. I don't know. Anyway, I have never seen another man who could do it, and I certainly can't myself. Finally I was forced to decide it was something in the nature of the Saint, a kind of a blessed gift, like being able to sing wonderfully or stack cards.

"Now bring on your family fetish, Wandering!" he exclaimed triumphantly, stepping from the cage. "The Cervantes' pet is certainly a wonderful animal, may really be a link between the extinct *iguanadon* and the present-day iguanas. I shan't be happy till I get my hands on it."

"Enjoy yourself," I encouraged him heartily. "If you don't mind, though, I'll sit on the side lines while you give your taming exhibition."

Then it was time to think of dressing for the ball, and we set our minds to improvising costumes, and nearly laughed our heads off.

Finally, however, I hit upon the clever expedient of going as an organ grinder, and having the naturalist dress up in skins as the monkey, but he objected.

"What show would I have with the señorita, or even of getting a dance with her?" he demanded.

"She'd think you were right cute, and might pet you."

"I'd rather go as something more heroic, Wandering, if it won't disappoint you too much," he answered diffidently.

"Go as Goliath in the lions' den, if you want to," I snapped. I *was* rather disappointed, my idea had struck me as so original.

The Saint fixed himself up as a native warrior—Inca chief, he called it—with skins, feathers, and his arms bare. They were darned husky arms, and looked capable of shoving the fish spear he carried clean through a whole cow. It was surprising how like a savage he managed to look, in spite of his great, calm brown eyes, and how the air of gentleness that was his in civilized clothes completely disappeared under the jaguar pelts.

I wound myself in yards of Turkey red, to represent a flamingo. The color was horribly off, though, and made me look exactly like the devil; so I hung a sign over my shoulders:

FLAMINGO
EATS ANYTHING

and let it go at that; and we slipped on our masks and made our way to the Hacienda of the Iguanas.

It was sure a brilliant scene, and a whooping good time was being had by all, as the U.S. society papers would put it. There were any number of devils who tried to chum with me, until I haughtily turned my back on them so they could see by my sign I really was a bird.

Monks were dancing with chorus girls; the Queen of Sheba was quarreling with a gent made up to represent Bryan, a green-and-red parrot, labeled "dove of peace," shouting "never bite a lion, never bite a lion," from his shoulder. Bull fighters, kings, Arabs, and aviators were making love to bo-peeps, gypsies, vivandières, fairies, and birds of paradise, while the whole crowd fizzed with joy, like the champagne every one was drinking.

The Saint made his way straight as an arrow to a Carmen, unmistakably the Señorita Anita, because she was the prettiest and most graceful girl in the room.

I watched the dancing for a while, and then stepped out into the patio. There were couples on every bench, none of whom showed the slightest indication of asking me to come and sit down beside them.

The only place that wasn't crowded with people was the railing around the pit in the center. There I strayed, rather forlorn in the happiness, youth, and love that seemed everywhere, and gazed down into the enclosure. The black iguana, crest erect, throat pouch purple and pulsating, was moving from side to side, jumping to the tree in the center and running halfway up the trunk, an ugly, fearsome thing, in striking contrast to all the laughter and joy around it. For a while I watched the seemingly tireless beast, and then strayed back through the rooms and out onto the front veranda. Standing in the shadow, words came to me from a dark corner.

"But, chief of the Incas, are you not overbold in wooing a daughter of Spain—your worst enemy?"

"Why should not two brave races be united by the ties of love?"

"You *are* bold, indeed! And since when have the Incas proved themselves as brave as the cavaliers of Spain?"

"Are there no dragons here to tame, that I may prove my worth?"

"None save the iguana of the Cervantes'. And I do not think your daring would go that far."

"Come, and you shall see."

Some fox, the Saint! He had simply shaped this highfaluting masked-ball language to his own ends. I knew perfectly well that he intended to try his power on that enormous black lizard, but it had never occurred to me that he planned to further his wooing by the same means. I stalked through the crowded rooms after the Carmen and the Inca chief, and out into the patio, now deserted at the beginning of a dance. A gorgeous toreador joined us, and we moved to the edge of the picket-protected pit.

Honest, I had my doubts if the Saint could get away with any soothing stunts on the Cervantes' fetish, and the most I expected was an attempt to calm it down from outside its prison. Nothing so undramatic for him, though. Without a moment's hesitation, he vaulted into the pit and stood upright among the shrubbery, the blunt end of his spear held from him. I yanked my automatic from under my left armpit, quite prepared to use it, if necessary. The señorita tore off her mask, the better to see, and bent eagerly forward, lips half open, eyes sparkling.

The black iguana, hissing furiously, rose on its hind legs and hurled itself toward him. The spear distracted its attention for a moment as it bit and tore the haft to slivers. It whirled like lightning toward the absolutely motionless man, paused—and that was all there was to it. Beginning with the thread of whisper, and ending with the monotonous whistling, the Saint had the black monster climbing lethargically over his knees within five minutes.

"Santa Maria!" exclaimed the señorita, and I noticed she had tight hold of the toreador's hand—must have been a habit with her—"is this a man or a devil! I'm afraid!" And darned if she didn't run back into the house still hanging onto the toreador.

I spoke to the Saint severely when he climbed out of the pit. Not that I wasn't proud of him, all right, but he had nearly scared me to death. My words I shan't repeat, because they were right bitter, and I was awfully ashamed of them a moment afterward.

"It may have been an—ahem—reckless thing to do, Wandering," he agreed, in that gentle voice of his, "but love makes even the most cowardly man daring—and I have some power over animals."

I wanted to tell him that love would never have made me that daring, even doubted if drink would; but what was the use? As a matter of fact, we just plunged back among the maskers—where I could see he was crazy to go—and I promptly lost him.

Yum! But there was some action by that time! Every one was having twice as much fun, and whenever you turned round, a little brown servant handed you a glass of champagne. A large lady, disguised as what I thought was a cauliflower, until she told me she was a very sweet cream puff, singled yours truly out for attention, and we got on famously—she seemed to have lots of brains. Somehow, we became separated from the rest of the crowd, since I didn't dance, and wandered off to a kind of conservatory full of flowers, palms, and parrots in cages. Just as we reached the door, the toreador and the Carmen slipped out by us. My companion gave a start, and drew back into the shadow until they had passed, then we entered. I don't suppose it was the gallant or proper thing for me to do to switch on the lights, but I'm a widower—twice—with my heart in two graves. Anyway, I wish I hadn't. Every parrot in the place woke at once, and began to make a noise half between a hiss and a man eating very hot soup.

"What the dickens are those fool parrots doing that for?" I demanded.

"Does not the señor know?" asked the cream-puff lady, looking soulfully up at me.

"Can't say I do."

"The señor makes me blush for his innocence! Are not those birds of God trying to imitate the sound of many ——" But what the "many" was I never heard, because there came a perfect roar of merriment, mingled with the peal of bells and the sound of firearms, from the house. It was midnight, and the time to unmask. My companion let hers fall, revealing the downy upper lip of the señorita's duenna, and, snatching away the piece of black velvet from my face, with an ejaculation that sounded like "*caramba!*" except that Spanish ladies don't use the word, simply ran from me, throwing back over her shoulder:

"I thought you were the English superintendent!"

In the hacienda, the fun became more fast and furious without the masks than before. The señorita danced, turn and turn about, with the Saint and the toreador, who proved to be the Brazilian cavalry officer.

I drank so much champagne that it made me thirsty, and I couldn't dig up a real, hard drink anywhere. Dawn began to whiten the sky, and the dancers thinned out. Suddenly I missed the Saint. He wasn't on the floor or the front veranda. I wandered out into the patio. Dimly, in a spot of shadow by the iguana pit, I caught sight of him, a girl's arms around his neck. After all, the funniest thing about a kiss is the sound.

We woke late, next morning, on the boat, and, for some reason I can't understand, I felt morose and had a headache. Not so the Saint. He simply effervesced, tried his hardest for an opening to tell me what he had on his mind. I fenced him off for a while, out of pure ill humor, but finally relented.

"Don't tell me you are the only man she has ever kissed!" I commanded. "And how about the iguana prophecy—the best blood of Spain, and all that?"

"I am, but how did you know it?" he burbled. "Since I have conquered the fetish of the Cervantes', she says the legend does not count. Oh, Wandering, how wonderful it is—" For an hour this went on.

The collectors came on board with the early-morning crop—two young peccaries, a few snakes, and a capybara, this last a queer kind of a beast, much resembling a rabbit, slightly smaller than a hog, and with short ears. The Saint began his taming stunts with this last. Somehow, they didn't seem to work. That usually timid creature simply went for him, finally biting a nice chunk out of his wrist. I could see the naturalist felt awfully humiliated, after taming jaguars and seven-foot iguanas, at being bitten by something little more formidable than a rabbit, but I couldn't think of anything comforting to say. Then the two young peccaries simply chased him out of their cage. Evidently something was wrong.

"Look here, Saint," I asked anxiously, "what the dickens is the matter with you? Do you suppose it is because you are thinking of that girl all the time—can't concentrate?"

"Nothing at all to do with it!" he snapped. "Never thought of her at all—at least very little. Those animals just happen to be plain idiots."

He opened the door of the jaguar cage and picked up one of the kittens, dropping it with a howl. It had raked all five claws across his cheek. Then, I regret to say, he swore—swore in a manner no saint could ever dream of, and few sailors equal.

I kept away from him till afternoon, after managing to elicit the information that we were to pay a call at the hacienda later, and that he had secured Don Roderigo's approval of his suit the night before, as well as the senorita's consent. Pretty fast traveling, it seemed to me.

Somehow, this love affair didn't hit me quite right, though. I am as romantic as a middle-aged chorus girl. I realized what word would have followed the duenna's "many" of the night before, and that word was "kisses." Also the one I had seen, or rather heard, the señorita give the Saint had a kind of a practiced, finished sound. You can always tell, especially if you are twice a widower. Now, I don't mind a girl being kissed once in a while, but when the very parrots start to imitate her— And what if she really had affected the Saint's wonderful power over wild animals? Of course, I only thought all this, did not say it aloud. It doesn't pay to interfere in love affairs. But I wasn't happy.

The Saint certainly did not look the gay and joyous, accepted lover as he walked to the hacienda, one wrist done up in a white bandage, and five long pieces of court-plaster on his cheek. I lured him a bit off our usual line of approach, so as to pass the conservatory where were the parrots, and then tried to hurry him on when I got there. Those brainless birds were making the same sounds as they had the night before, and with reason. Some one was being kissed under the shadow of a banana tree within the glass enclosure, and we both plainly saw who it was. Without a word, the Saint passed on.

No servants admitted us to the hacienda. The door stood open. We passed from empty room to empty room and out into the patio. There was a strange silence over the place. Little brown servants stood everywhere, tense, motionless, not daring to breathe. On the ground, bleeding from a slight wound in his shoulder, lay Don Roderigo, and above him towered the black iguana, seven feet of upright, hissing fury, yet hesitating in what direction to vent its rage.

"Every one keep perfectly still," quietly ordered the Saint, and then he whistled shrilly. The black horror came down on all fours and spun around, facing him. Slowly waving his arms from left to right, the naturalist approached, and the reptile's head began to follow the weaving of his hands. Deliberately he unwound the bandage from his wrist, stooped down, tied it around the lizard's neck, and led it through the hacienda out into the broad avenue.

Don Roderigo had followed us to the front veranda, and, wordless, watched us go. The señorita and the Brazilian officer stood at the door of the conservatory. While we were passing, both made the sign of the cross.

As our boat swung out into midstream, the Saint stepped into the jaguar cage and deliberately cuffed the largest one. Nothing happened. Then he hauled the fetish of the Cervantes' out into the broad sunlight and sat down on it.

"Would you like a little dynamite to smoke in your pipe?" I asked, from a safe distance.

"No, Wandering," the Saint answered gently and sadly, rising, and pushing with his foot the seven-foot lizard toward its cage. "I'm through playing with dynamite. I *would* like a drink, though—that is, if it isn't champagne."

Remote Corners

The White Gorilla

FOR EIGHT MONTHS NO WORD CAME FROM MY FRIEND VAN DAM.

Those of us in his debt virtuously assured ourselves that we had intended to pay him back at once, and tried to bear up; others who wished to borrow were naturally somewhat resentful at his absence. As usual, he had given no intimation of his flitting, and all who called at his diggings—so he designated the enormous top-story apartment where he dwelt among his countless trophies and collections—were met by the always smiling Jap with the information: "Mr. Van Dam, he will be back—oh, quite soon some day."

This same phrase had excused a two years' disappearance of his master in the interior of Borneo. Gradually we ceased to think of him, and each little life traveled around its own restricted orbit as though the absentee had ceased to exit.

My own affairs were going rather well and orders simply poured in. This halcyon state was due to a Hercules, for which Van had provided me with an extraordinary model, and a Pittsburgh millionaire bought because it was the image of a fellow steel worker he had known in his undollared youth.

These orders, however, were entirety for portraits, which I do not like doing—my forte is large allegorical canvases, though Van thinks differently—but never having had any money, I developed a lust for it and painted all who paid. My most lucrative commission had just come to me, a portrait for a political club of one of its most prominent—and worst—members, and it was giving me a great deal of trouble. To begin with, the man would not sit more than fifteen minutes at a time, and his face was simply horrible.

I painted it first, nearly from memory, in all its brutal reality of low forehead, eyes set far back, and enormous jaw development—a positively bestial thing. And it looked not the slightest like the original.

Then I conceived the idea that a soul was shining through this fleshy mask and put the light of holiness in the eyes, the curve of renunciation at the corner of the lips. When my man called, his own face made its painted counterpart look like the delineation of some kindly saint. That day I devoted myself solely to the hands—veritable Gargantuan paws they were—and after he had left, very discouraged, started to scrape and turn the face. Just as I had eliminated all but chin and forehead the phone rang.

"Hello!" I said crisply into the transmitter with the intonation I have adopted since I consider myself a successful artist.

"Come to dinner, painter-man," drawled Van's voice over the wire. "I have something to show you."

"I'm very busy," I answered loftily; "but I'll try to manage it if you'll tell me beforehand what we are eating."

Van has one idiosyncrasy that is positively ghastly. He is always cooking the most awful, uncivilized dishes concealed in such delectable sauces that you can't help liking them till you find out what they are. At his table I have eaten a lizard creature tasting exactly like delicate chicken, and a savory dish of what appeared to be roasted oysters and was really the larvæ of the black palm weevil.

"What are you busy with?" came over the wire. "If it's a Vulcan, I have a good model for you."

"I'm trying to paint a baboon," I snapped, "and no model will do."

"Surprising," he answered in really animated tones. "I can furnish you with a gorilla, and I have a young cannibal here to go with it."

"Am I to act as a meal for your guests?" I began, but he had hung up.

Van and I dined luxuriously on what I took to be very young lamb and afterward adjourned to the den, on the walls of which are ranged the cases containing his albino collection—the traditional white blackbird, the enormous, glittering, white toucan, the snowy raccoon, the white panther, and that last acquisition in a huge case by itself. There was a roaring wood fire, and before it, partially covered by a snow-leopard's skin, twitched, while he slept, the coffee-colored slim cannibal boy. Once he reached up a long, bare foot and scratched his ear exactly as a dog attends to a flea.

There was a livid, five-inch scar on Van's cheek, and while he talked the blood would pulse to its top, run down underneath the skin, and disappear exactly as an electric advertising sign lights and flashes out.

"Of course you know, painter-man," he began, "that I am in touch with people throughout the world whom I pay to keep their eyes open for the albino phase in animals and birds. The mail daily brings me offers of specimens or word where they may be procured; but, for the most part, they are of species I already have or else out-and-out fakes—I have been offered scores of white elephants. You see, among savages, the abnormal in nature is very often an object of direct worship.

"Contrary to our ideas of religion, the untutored savage has the delicacy not to inflict his beliefs on strangers, and does not, so to speak, wear his god on his sleeve. It is, therefore, hard to get reliable information regarding animals that are white when they normally should be quite a different color.

"It was, as a matter of fact, the very indefinitiveness of the data that sent me on this last expedition. From Libreville, in the French Congo, an Englishman wrote me it was common talk among the Mpangwe, who had recently been driven out of the region at the headwaters of the Gabun River, that their conquerors worshiped and sacrificed to a white woman who walked on her knees and elbows and was covered with long hair. A Dutch trader sent word from Booue that the Fan tribe of cannibals had an old, old man for chief who walked on all fours and was fed entirely on human flesh. A French rubber exploiter in the Sierra de Crystal told one of my agents that there was a large, white monkey in the Ogowé division of the Fan cannibals which was held sacred and accompanied them to war.

"The very meagerness of this information and the improbability of collusion between its widely separated sources gave me something on which to theorize, and I sailed for Libreville. The building of my theory was simplicity itself. The third informant had distinctly stated that the creature was a white monkey. Monkeys are regarded by many tribes in Africa as only slightly modified human beings.

"The final link in my reasoning came from the statement that it walked on its elbows and knees. The gorilla walks, or rather swings itself along, on the back of its hands—the wrist, we would call it—and often turns the toes of its feet under. In short, I hoped for an albino gorilla, and my theory was strengthened by the knowledge that gorillas, when caught young, are docile and easily tamed, in spite of the unquestioned ferocity of the wild, old males. As a matter of fact, we know little more about this largest of all primates than has been vouched us from the fertile imagination of Paul de Chaillu.*

"There are current, in Africa, tales of men snatched from the ground to die a horrible death in the tree-tops; of an African tribe that kept a huge, old male for executioner until it was killed by an Englishman about to be sacrificed, who noticed a swelling over its heart and struck it in this vulnerable spot. At any rate, I had never seen a gorilla in the wild state, and the adventure promised many thrills.

"From Libreville I made a short expedition among the Mpangwe whom the more warlike Fans had driven from the interior. Savages, I have found, Mr. Painter-man, belong to two categories: Those that are honest, trustworthy, and truthful, and those that are the exact opposite.

"The Mpangwe belong to the latter class. They were the worst liars I have ever met, and told me only what they thought I wanted to hear. The hairy woman was endowed with wings and made to lay eggs that hatched into serpents, and when they found it was a monkey I was after, they agreed to a man that she always assumed that form at night.

"There was nothing to be learned from these swindling blacks, and I made up my mind to follow rumor to its source and go up the Gabun River into the gorilla country where dwelt the Ogowé Fans. The local French government, not without a warning against its unsettled state and the absolute lack of positive knowledge of the region into which I proposed to penetrate, finally gave me a permit for a scientific exploring expedition.

"They even went further and provided me with a guard of twenty soldiers—so, you see, I traveled rather *en prince*—and helped to collect the

---

* Anthropologist who, in the 1860's, confirmed the existence of gorillas.

rather large caravan which I required.

"A trip of this nature to one who has been through the same kind of thing before, contrary to the general idea of you city dwellers, is remarkable only for the length of time it takes to reach a given point. There was, of course, the usual revolt of the porters for higher pay, which had to be summarily quelled; the leopard that blundered into my tent-ropes one night, and the killing of a man by a wounded buffalo; also an ill-advised attempt to assassinate me. These are only the incidents one expects in jungle travel, however; and, on the whole, it was rather a dull journey, and a very hot one.

"As we neared our destination the country became rugged with open but shady and damp forests, and there were interminable thickets of scitamines and tree-ferns, on the fruits of which the gorilla feeds. All along the route I made guarded inquiries about my quest, and, from what I could *not* learn, fully made up my mind that a white gorilla, or at least some extraordinary animal, its existence well known to the natives, was in possession of the Fans. I came to this conclusion because every approach to the subject, no matter how indirect, instantly inspired fear, and those interrogated either became dumb or lied wildly.

"One day's journey from our destination I sent ahead runners with gifts to the sorcerer (so is designated the local priest) and to the chief. Of course word of my coming had long ago preceded me, and, partially through curiosity, partially through respect for my guard and my large caravan, they sent back friendly messages.

"The next evening, to the monotonous beat of tom-toms, I pitched camp on the edge of the valley in which dwelt the Ogowé Fans. These savages were quite different from any I had met in Africa. They were not black, but coffee-colored, well made, with thin lips, intelligent faces, and were tall and, according to our standards, excessively slim.

"Best of all, their language was a slight variation of the great Bantu tongue, as spoken by the Zulu Kafirs, and with which I am thoroughly familiar. The women, who were quite handsome, worked in the manioc-fields, while the existence of the men was made up of war and hunting. To a high degree they were both truthful and honorable.

"Savages love ceremony, and our mutual greetings took up all of three days, on the last of which there was a feast with wild dances and much palm-wine. I was not at all sure of the bill of fare, and, in order to be on the safe side, pretexted a vow of fasting, an expiatory rite which they practise, and so understood. My role was that of a sorcerer who had come to study their birds and beasts, but most to consort with my brother priests to our mutual advantage, and I was accepted at my own valuation.

"A liberal gift insured me the privilege of dwelling in their country as long as I pleased, and so well did I get on with my hosts that finally, with the chief, I went through that not unpoetic ceremony of mysterious origin which they call blood-brotherhood. This practical adoption into the tribe so reassured me as to my safety that I sent back my guard of soldiers, much to their horror, and in spite of their protestations, and with them the greater part of my porters, retaining only a few in whom I had implicit confidence.

"I've lived with savages before, Mr. Painter-man, and I must say there is no pleasanter or easier life. To a very great extent every man does exactly as he pleases. Food is the only real necessity, and is largely furnished by the labor of the women.

"Moral and ethical considerations are never personal, but the affair of the high priest (better called sorcerer), and are left entirely in his hands.

"In spite of ideal conditions for happiness, it was distinctly wanting among the Ogowé Fans. There was an undercurrent of dissatisfaction running through the tribe, and an atmosphere of mental discomfort. Quarrels were frequent, and there were several cases of absolute insanity, the victims of which were promptly put to death, tribal law permitting of no mental or physical deficient.

"In my assumed character it was naturally the sorcerer that I saw the most of, and we found much in common. As a matter of fact, the priest among savages represents not only the highest mental, but what we must characterize for want of a better definition, as scientific attainments of the race. My confrere of the Ogowé Fans was a shrewd, middle-aged man, leaning toward asceticism, and a real fanatic in his beliefs.

"He had one daughter, and if you can imagine such a thing as a soft, brown rose glowing in the tropical jungle you will have a fairly accurate picture of her. The Fan faith was a kind of Pan-deism with just a dash of sun worship, interwoven with superstition, its manifestation interpreted by the sorcerer from the actions of various sacred animals. There was also an additional and very unusual way of learning the wishes of their deity.

"The priest was master of a crude but none the less effective form of hypnotism, which he practised on members of the tribe, but principally on his daughter. Through her, while she was 'possessed of the spirit,' otherwise in a cataleptic state, he unconsciously impressed his own will on the tribe.

"I give him absolute credit for attributing divine origin to the words that she uttered, which made him only the more determined in his purposes, in the same way that a man with an honest belief is much more likely to be successful than one who must admit in his own heart that he is a faker.

"The girl was so completely under his mental control that a few moments' gazing into a large crystal, which had been roughly rounded and held a thousand lights, made her mind blank and instantly receptive to any impression from him. This crystal was a very sacred thing, and it was the duty of a different warrior each day to rub at the inequalities with fine sand with the purpose of finally bringing it to a perfect roundness.

"The sorcerer was enough of a man of the world to appreciate the awe he might inspire by means of a few chemicals I gave him and the—to savages—startling tricks I was able to teach him. As a matter of fact, he ruled these frankly cannibal warriors through fear alone; and so great was his mental dominance that, at times, it seemed to me, he held half the tribe in a semi-hypnotic state. There was a bitter feud between him and the temporal chief.

"The latter wished to move on to new conquests; the priest held firm that they remain where they were for a year until expiation had been made by endless religious ceremonies for the 'blinding of the eyes of piety,' a phrase which meant nothing to me then, but which I now understand.

"I was, of course, more or less affiliated with the chief since, with him, I had gone through the blood-brotherhood rite, but my closest friend was his son. He was a youth of some twenty summers, and the most marvelous hunter and tracker I have ever known. Ikstu—that is as near as I can Anglicize his name—accompanied me on all my collecting expeditions, and, what was of the greatest importance, since I was supposed to know them instinctively, told me the birds and animals that were sacred and not to be molested.

"Chief among those taboo were the gorillas, and they throve and were quite unafraid under such treatment, though naturally rather retiring beasts. In the manioc-fields, which the women cultivated, toward evening I have literally seen dozens of them. The males would wander out from the jungle with their two or three mates and family, or sometimes I would come upon a solitary old bachelor, grayish-white, and a very dangerous animal to approach.

"Some would run away, screaming with fright, in a tryingly human manner; but there was one old fellow who never gave a step until I myself retired.

"He was fully six feet tall when standing braced against a tree-trunk, his hands hanging below his knees, the hair on his neck and head erect with rage, and the ruff under his chin quivering. Two great canine teeth protruded from each side of his snarling mouth, and beneath their enormous protuberances his little eyes blazed red in his coal-black face. I learned to hate that animal, and, as he hopped away on all fours, his legs swinging out beyond his arms, I longed to turn and put an explosive bullet in him.

"Policy, that was even a question of personal safety, held me in check, however, and I wisely refrained. Ikstu, who feared nothing else in the world, was deadly afraid of these old males; but, even more than he feared them, he hated the sorcerer.

"As we became better acquainted and I gained his confidence, the reason for this was apparent. I noticed that on several occasions we found two purple orchids, their stems crossed, lying in the narrow trails through the scitamines thickets, and each time this sign appeared I lost my companion for the rest of the day. The connection was obvious.

"The daughter of the sorcerer-priest always wore these orchids in her hair and as a garland—in fact, they formed by far the greater part of her wardrobe.

"Always, however, she was back from these love rambles at her father's hut before sunset; and, after he had made her gaze for a few moments into the sacred crystal, she would hurry off into the jungle with a basket of manioc and fruit of the scitamines on her arm. You may well believe I was curious in regard to these expeditions, but I kept this curiosity to myself. Once I tried to pick up her trail in the morning, and was very nearly impaled in a leopard-trap. That afternoon I received a warning from the sorcerer of the presence of a very sacred and awful spirit in the direction I had gone.

"My excuse for lingering in the neighborhood was wearing thin, and the priest was beginning to look on me with unconcealed suspicion. Meanwhile, there was no hint of what I sought, and the whole tribe was humming with an undercurrent of politics that would have done credit to Tammany Hall during election.

"My time had not been entirely wasted, however, for I had the skin of an albino thrush (it proved new to science), and also a large, white spider of the trap-door variety, the first absolute case of albinoism I had ever found among the *Arachnida*. My camp was ready to be abandoned and my porters to travel, and I made up my mind to start for the coast the moment I had solved the problem of the girl's nightly trip.

"The crisis came sooner than I expected. In spite of the objections of the spiritual power, the chief made a raid toward the sea and returned with heavy spoil and ten captives. There was much rejoicing in the tribe, though the sorcerer was very angry, and the captives were closely guarded and well fed, so that their ultimate, gruesome disposal was only too obvious. The war party gained in strength, and it was decided the matter of moving on to new conquests be finally decided at the Feast of the Gorillas, when the moon was full.

"My position was now not only very uncomfortable, but positively dangerous, and I kept exclusively to my own camp, my only connection with the Fan village being through Ikstu. Time hanging heavy on my hands, I hit on an expedient that I should have thought of long before.

"Through a pair of powerful field-glasses I spied the girl's route each evening until I finally traced her down to her destination, a rocky amphitheater hardly a mile distant from the village.

"That night, darkness came so quickly I could not see what she did, but the next evening the secret of her expeditions and, at the same time, the end of my quest were revealed to me. From the crotch of a great rubber tree I watched her set down her basket and, swaying slightly as people do in the cataleptic state, raise her arms above her orchid-crowned head evidently calling.

"Twice she did this, and then, from a cleft in the rocks, an unbelievable object swung slowly out to meet her.

"Never have I seen so beautiful and so repulsive an animal. It was an enormous female gorilla with fur long and white as that of an Angora goat. Even in a crouched position, practically on all fours, its jet-black face was above the girl on whom it looked down from eyes that seemed, through my field-glasses, milk white.

"One mighty arm rose and rested on the girl, the other groping in the basket at her feet, and thus the two figures stood while the fruits were crammed into an enormous mouth. Then the girl lifted, with both hands, the great paw from her bare shoulder, and before the quick tropical darkness shut them from my sight, I saw her catch the wreath of purple orchids from her own neck and throw it over the brute's head.

"At camp, with his chest bleeding from a knife wound, I found Ikstu waiting for me. Without giving him time to explain his own errand I told quickly what I had seen. He was in no way astonished, and I doubt even if he heard half I said, so full was he of his own troubles.

"The sorcerer had somehow learned of the meetings with his daughter and was keeping her in a continual hypnotic state, so that, quite unconscious of what she was doing or saying, she had actually stabbed him at their last rendezvous and even threatened him with 'the blind eyes of piety.'

"His simple request was that I should take him and the girl away with me after he had killed the sorcerer during the coming feast. I consented without the slightest hesitation, bargaining only that he should tell me, in return, all he knew of the white gorilla.

"Gradually, though it was apparent he feared a celestial thunderbolt, I dragged the story from him. The beast, under the care of the sorcerer, had been the fetish of the tribe ever since he could remember, and figured in every religious ceremony. At the beginning of the Fans' march toward the coast the gorilla had always gone into battle with them and, maddened by a great beaker of the potent palm wine, proved a terror to their enemies. Then, to the lasting grief of the sorcerer, during a night attack, it had lost the sight of both eyes from a firebrand.

"Formerly it had been a docile and friendly animal (when not inflamed by the palm liquor), with the unrestrained freedom of the village; but this accident changed it into a she-devil that dwelt morosely alone and could only be approached by the sorcerer's daughter, and that only when under her father's hypnotic influence.

"It's a wild tale, painter-man, and sitting here before the fire one can hardly believe it actually happened. In the jungle, though, with the blackness of the tropical night wrapped around us like velvet ribbons, the squeak of the vampire bats, the far-away roar of a male gorilla, and the cough of a leopard circling the camp, it seemed perfectly natural and fitting for me to be conniving, with a cannibal, at a cold-blooded murder.

"Besides, I wanted the skin of that albino primate, and I was going to have it at any cost. I believed every word of Ikstu's story, even to divine attributes with which he credited the brute and of which I have not told you—you see, I had seen it, and alive."

Van Dam snapped on the electric lights and turned in his chair to face the glass cabinet which contained his latest acquisition. My eyes followed his and I shuddered to the very depths of my city-swaddled soul. The great monkey had been mounted bending slightly forward, its hands swinging between and far below its knees. In its immense paws it held a pear-shaped crystal larger than an ostrich's egg, which caught and imprisoned the light.

Beautiful, long, silky fur, white as silver, clothed the enormously powerful body, and beneath the low forehead, deep in the black face, were set, in lieu of eyes, two round milky-white agates. The mouth was curled back in a fixed grin revealing the broken, yellow, doglike fangs, repulsive beyond belief by contrast with the beauty and power of the rest of the animal.

"Go on, Van," I said, "you couldn't make me disbelieve anything about that thing. For Heaven's sake, out with the lights, though. I don't want to look at it."

The blood showed at the top of the scar on Van Dam's cheek, slithered down its ragged length, and winked out leaving it livid white. He switched off the electric current and we were left again with only the light of the fire.

"I gave Ikstu no advice as to his killing," Van Dam continued, "because I felt that he was quite competent to carry out his private vendetta in his own way. However, since the next evening was to see the beginning of the Feast of the Gorillas, I moved my camp a mile toward the coast and prepared everything for immediate flight. In the afternoon I made Ikstu guide me by a roundabout route, to the very edge of the rocky amphitheater above the beast's den, and ensconced myself, within easy hearing and seeing distance, in the thick top of a scitamines bush.

"Hardly was I comfortably settled when the sorcerer and his daughter, both heavily laden with baskets, appeared beneath me.

"I don't think I have ever seen anything more beautiful than that girl. Of actual clothes she wore only a white loin-cloth, but her hair was braided full of the purple orchids and garland on garland of the same flower hung from her neck and covered her lithe, brown body.

"The sorcerer was hideously painted in crimson and white and his face was made up to simulate a gorilla, the hair drawn far back and two extra, white eyes daubed on the forehead.

"Immediately the girl, sitting with crossed legs, began to beat a tiny tom-tom, while the sorcerer built a small fire and busied himself with the baskets and three other articles. I recognized them as a leopard skin worn by one of the under chiefs, a mat from a hut, and Ikstu's favorite spear.

"When the fire was going well the girl stood up and called. The third time her voice rose, the white gorilla emerged slowly from its den and hesitatingly hopped and swung down to her. Then, before my eyes, took place the most remarkable performance I have witnessed.

"The man cast some herb into the fire and the girl led the animal into the thick, scented smoke. Time and again it broke from her and rushed to its rocky refuge, time and again it came back to her call. Herb after herb, each with a different odor, went into the flames, and gradually the movements of the great beast became slower, lethargic, till it finally stood swaying, its blind agate eyes turned to the sorcerer.

"Once the girl faltered and seemed to be awakening from a trance, but her father held the crystal to her eyes till they went blank and she again mechanically did his bidding. Now he transferred the sacred stone to the gorilla's paws and began a chant. The words were not of the Bantu tongue but from some language older than the hills. I don't know what they mean, but I remember the sound, mixed with the beat of the tom-tom, as well as though I were now hearing it.

> "Nala *(bong)* Nala *(bong)*
> Nala impi *(bong, bong, bong)*.
> Nala *(bong)* Nala *(bong)*
> Nala impi *(bong, bong, bong)*.
> Nala *(bong)* Nala *(bong)*
> Nala impi *(bong, bong, bong)*.

"Intoned to the sullen beat of the drum till the world seemed to go to sleep and the brain reach forward for the next repetition.

"The great brute began to move slowly in a swaying dance keeping time with the rhythm. One by one the girl held the leopard skin, mat and spear against its flat nostrils while, for each separate article, the sorcerer pressed a hot coal to the slowly shuffling feet. At every burn the beast reared and raising the glittering crystal, to which its paws seemed glued, dashed it down on the object before it.

"Extraordinary as was the idea, I recognized at once that, for the usual passes and crystal gazing used in hypnotism, the sorcerer had first substituted the scent of herbs and then the chant, and actually held the frightful beast in control by that thin thread of sound.

"Still beating her tom-tom with measured strokes the voice of the girl took up the mysterious words, and the sorcerer grew silent crouched over the fire. Night was coming fast. I slipped from my hiding place as the forest shadows blackened the cliff and silently slid down to the very cleft whence had come the gorilla. There I lay in the darkness peering at the three figures before the fire.

"First one tom-tom, another, a third, till their number seemed countless, awoke in the village. There was a high, shrill scream of agony from far away, then the voice of the whole tribe raised in a great chorus, the words growing distinguishable as they grew nearer.

"In English they would go like this:

> "The sun, oh, the sun, from the rising of the sun,
> We go through jungle aisles until the moon is high.
> There's blood within our footsteps, and every warrior one,
> Lifts up a limp, dead body unto the bleeding sky.
>
> "Always before goes the white one.
> (Piety, Piety thou!)
> Leads us in the path of the sun.
> (Piety, Piety thou!)
> Judge at the feast when the red blood runs free,
> Leading the Fans to hot, cruel victory,
> We come for thy judgment, again come to thee.
> (Piety, Piety thou!)

"Meanwhile, under the roar of voices the girl sang her monotonous strain and beat her tiny drum.

"The whole tribe defiled into the amphitheater, chiefs first with the leopard skins, which they alone are privileged to wear—a custom that links them with the Zulus—then the warriors with the prisoners in their midst, now significantly reduced to nine, and last the women and children.

"These bore fagots which they piled in the center and a large fire was soon blazing. The ceremonies began, to the music of the inevitable tom-toms, with a furious dance by the warriors.

"It was a wild scene, the nearly naked savages brandishing their spears and whirling around the fire; the prisoners conscious of the horrible fate awaiting them, cowering in the background; the crouching figures of the great, white gorilla, the hideously painted sorcerer, and the exquisite, brown girl intoning her endless chant.

"As a proper stage setting the heavens began to grumble, lightning flashed across the sky, and a few, big, hot drops of rain fell.

"The dance and the tom-toms ceased with such startling suddenness that the voice of the girl cut sharp as a knife through the murmur of the multitude.

The priest faced the great white brute and spoke:

" 'Piety, against whom the Ogowé Fans have sinned, before we ask thy judgment for the tribe, select from us in expiation. Let the sacred crystal gleam red in thy honor.'

"He raised a close-woven basket full of palm wine to its nostrils, and, while it still held the crystal pendant in its paws, tipped it till it was drained of the last drop. For a moment the white gorilla staggered, then hopping forward, balanced at its full height before the chief. While the girl's song and the beat of the tiny drum alone broke the silence it circled to the right, bent with distended nostrils above the chief whose leopard skin was in the sorcerer's possession, and, quicker than I can tell it, the great paws rose and the crystal came crashing down on the doomed man's skull. Resolved to end the scene then and there, cost what it might, I raised my rifle to my shoulder and then lowered it again at what I saw.

"Sinuous as a snake, stealthy as a leopard, Ikstu, a knife in his hand, was creeping up behind the sorcerer. Warned by some subtle instinct the priest turned barely before the spring. One hand shot out the finger pointing straight at the boy and their eyes locked with nearly an audible snap. It seemed as though invisible bonds held the would-be murderer. He struggled in vain to raise the knife, to go forward.

"The pointed finger described a slow circle, Ikstu's head followed it. Faster it swung and faster. With a great burst of strength the sorcerer snatched the sacred crystal from between the gorilla paws and held it to the boy's face. For a breath Ikstu swayed away from the glittering lights, then his head went forward, and, eyes glued to the shining thing, he sank with it to the ground.

"The sorcerer silently faced the breathless multitude, then deliberately picked up Ikstu's own spear and turned toward him. There was a great crash of thunder and the gorilla, still swaying to the girl's music, groped blindly forward. The priest raised the spear. The girl broke off in the middle of a note and, quicker than light, covered her lover's body with her own.

"Released from the spell of the chant, though suddenly animate, the white gorilla tore the priest into his terrible arms and bore him to the ground. A blinding flash of lightning split the heavens as I fired. Catching the outline of the gorilla I pulled the trigger again, and sprang down into the arena. Every savage had fled save the chief who stood, spear poised, between the lovers and the struggling man and brute. With a back-hand sweep of his long arm, the gorilla ripped open my cheek at the very moment I sent a final bullet through its forehead.

"The sorcerer was quite dead, practically every bone in his body broken by the awful clutch of those hairy arms. The white gorilla still feebly moved though the mushroom bullet had carried away practically the entire back of its head. The girl, the chief, and I alone were alive and sane and until morning, in the hot rain, we labored to strip the skin from that great carcass.

"Then, the girl leading Ikstu by the hand, and the skin swinging between us on a pole, we struck out for my camp. The chief, in silence, watched his son depart, and did not try to hinder us.

"Perhaps he was thinking of the fate of those among the Fans who were found mentally wanting, and, in addition, there was the sacrilege of the attack on the priest."

Van Dam lay back in his chair and carefully lit a cigarette.

"That isn't all?" I asked after a moment's silence.

"That's all," he answered.

"But what's the end of it? What became of the girl and Ikstu?"

"The girl died on the way out. Ikstu lies there before the fire, his mind never came back to him. I have hopes, however, he has taken to worshiping the beast in the case and bowing down to the crystal. Interest in anything is an encouraging sign."

"You have a pleasant way of entertaining your guests," I said, for want of something better. "Cannibalism, murder, madness, everything but starvation."

"We had about come to that, too," Van answered carelessly, "on the way back, when we ran into a great migration of spider monkeys. They make very good eating, we just had one for dinner."

The Albino Otter

MY FRIEND, VAN DAM, HAD SET OUT FOR MIAMI on one of his mysterious quests, so it was there I sent the telegram, announcing that my painting of Hercules, the extraordinary model for which he furnished me, had taken the first gold medal at the National Academy of Artists. I really didn't expect the telegram to reach him; just sent it in the first burst of buoyancy as a written libation to my good fortune. However, an answer came that very same evening:

> You don't say are you going to wear it for a bangle or bang it around your neck at once. Send me here by express ten pounds of round, assorted turquoise, blue and light red beads about the size of a small pea and of solid build, and a pound of the purest arsenic railroads toot man felicitations. VAN DAM.

After I had censored the telegraph company's punctuation with an exclamation point after "say," and an interrogation point after "neck," and translated the apparent enthusiasm of the railroads into "*Vraiment, toutes mes félicitations*," I took up the matter of his commissions.

I never should have been able to get the arsenic had I not happened to mention Van Dam's name in the course of a vehement denial of an intent to poison my neighbors, or at the very least myself. Then, however, the clerk was all interest, and he even directed me to a beadery where I was able to secure the exact articles described. I added of my own volition for good measure some splendidly glittering gold specimens. Despatching the parcel, I returned to the studio and, with the help of three other men, wrote Van Dam the most insulting letter I could compose.

Among other things we asked if the beads were to be his sole costume, and suggested that he swallow the arsenic and feed himself to an innocent alligator for bait. Pretty poor humor, I admit; but I had lost a whole morning of good painting light while making his absurd purchases, and besides, something I had eaten the night before disagreed with me.

At the end of three months I was getting used to the absence of my eccentric friend, when one afternoon the telephone bell rang.

"Hello!" I said in those dulcet tones reserved exclusively for women, millionaire picture buyers, art dealers, and creditors.

"Glad you have regained your temper, artist-man," drawled Van's voice over the wire. "Come and dine with me this evening," and then I distinctly heard an aside that was plainly not meant for my ears: "Lizzie, stop tickling my neck!"

"All right," I agreed, "but you've got to have something to eat that I have at least heard of before."

Van Dam has a way of concocting mysterious dishes that are delightful until you learn of their derivation from some bird, beast, insect, or reptile, quite unknown to the most cosmopolitan menus.

"And shall I dress?" I added as an afterthought.

"Dress! What for?"

"For Lizzie," I answered with sardonic triumph.

Van Dam laughed. "No, don't bother. She won't mind. We'll have a steak, too. Lizzie likes 'em!"

Van Dam's apartments, or diggings, as he prefers to call them, occupy the entire top story of an immense building, and are really a museum of the natural-history collections he has made in every corner of the globe. There his Jap received my hat and stick as imperturbably as though I called every day, and ushered me to the curtains of the dining-room. I pulled them aside cautiously and peeked in at my host. Never have I seen a man so sunburnt! He wasn't red, or brown, or bronze. He was black, and this color was heightened by contrast with the whiteness of a small animal (little larger than a cat) on his knee, which regarded me with inscrutable, malicious eyes.

"If that darned thing is a skunk I won't come in!" I threatened. My knowledge of natural history is slight, and anyway, I distrust all Van's pets.

"Skunk nothing!" he answered indignantly; "that's Lizzie, and she's a white raccoon—the only case of albinoism I ever heard of in her family," he added proudly.

"Cost you a thousand dollars!" I ventured sarcastically. Van Dam is shamefully rich, and doesn't in the least mind paying for his whims.

"I bought her for two dollars on the edge of the Everglades, and she is as gentle as a kitten."

"Like all of her sex," I commented, entering and sitting down. "Where have you been, Van, and how did you get such an awful sunburn? I can't say I've missed you, because it's the truth—and that's bad form. But I am curious to know how you combined those many bead things and the arsenic, and what resulted therefrom."

"I have been acting as Cupid in the Everglades," he answered; "but let's dine first, and then I will tell you of hate, love, mystery, gold, and great wild places that will make your city-bounded horizon seem as limited as the inside of a teacup."

Van Dam's table is remarkably wonderful. He may, and I have no doubt that he does, live on grass and raw animals during his sojourns in the wilds, but at home his cuisine would quickly make a bon vivant out of an ascetic. The steak was a kind of a glorified dish that quite belied its respectable, bourgeois name, and the things that went with it were indescribably good.

During the entire meal the white raccoon climbed impartially over us and

the table, varying its acrobatics by filching choice morsels which it held in
its curious, tiny, human hands and, before daintily eating them, washed in a
glass of water with all the fervor of a religious rite.

"Well," I said, when my pipe was going comfortably and my host had lit
a cigarette, "begin at the beginning. What bleached animal started you this
time, and what happened?"

"It was an otter," he acknowledged shamelessly. "I met a globe-trotting
Englishman at the Old Club who said a Seminole Indian had told him of a
white otter in the Everglades that was supposed to have magic powers and
charm fish with its ruby eyes. I found out the Indian's name, Osceola, after
a former great chief of the Seminoles. With only that to go by, I set out for
Miami, which, as you know, is on the edge of the Everglades.

"Speaking of the Everglades, painter-man, I suppose you visualize them
as an enormous, fertile field, sprouting with corn, watermelons, oranges,
and coconut-trees, and cut by neat Dutch canals. You probably owe this
conception to some one who was trying to sell you stock in the Drainage
Improvement Company Limitless, three hundred per cent profits guaranteed.
Your idea is not exactly correct.

"The Everglades are an enormous inland lake, fifty miles broad and a
hundred and forty long, with a limestone rim ten feet above mean tide level,
and a limestone bottom through which seeps, or sometimes bubbles up,
fresh water. This limestone is covered with more or less mud, nearly entirely
overgrown with saw grass, and here and there are islands. The water is fresh
and pure, seldom over a few feet deep; the mud is from one to ten feet. There
are few mosquitoes since the water moves continually in a northeasterly
direction, and is, therefore, unsuited to the development of mosquito larvæ.
Hence there is no malaria.

"Millions of birds and, I regret to say, an equal number of snakes, some
deer, and a few Seminole Indians—the oddest of all the animal dwellers—
find a home in this strange place. The Indians live on tiny islands in the
midst of the Everglades, or in the impenetrable Great Cypress Swamp to
the north. Since their verbal contract with General Worth a century ago they
have shown no hostility to white men, in spite of all they have suffered. Time
has taught them that in their own protection they must not guide a white
man into their fastnesses, though they are always willing to lead out those
who get lost in this sea of grass, lured on by legends of islands fabulous
in fertility, overgrown with orange and lemon groves, and even harboring
pirate gold.

"You can easily imagine that one Indian name gave me little to go on. It is
true that there are less than six hundred Seminoles left; but they are seldom
seen, and those I did meet could not or would not give me any information
in regard to Osceola, and professed to have never heard of such a thing as

a white otter. I tried in every conceivable way to get a guide, all without avail; the best I could to was to find an Indian who agreed to take me to a rookery two days' sail down the coast. Quite frankly I hoped to overcome his scruples during this trip, and by a large bribe prevail upon him to lead me into the very heart of the Everglades.

"A rookery, painter-man, is where one species or several species of birds nest together in communities. The one I sought was of both long and short whites, referring to the lesser and snowy egret, the plumes of which during breeding-time were once worth far more than their weight in gold. Now, thank Heaven, their sale is prohibited, largely due to the splendid work of Dr. A.D. Hornaday, and rookeries, no longer shot up as they were in the old days, show an actual increase in all species.

"My guide was addicted to liquor, a weakness that might have been the means of furnishing me with some information had he not confined his remarks entirely to the Seminole tongue after the fifth drink. He proved, however, a competent man.

"I chartered a small sloop with a crew of two 'conches'—so the local coasting sailors are called—and dropped down the coast. Inside a long key the guide and I embarked in a small, light boat I had brought along for the purpose, rowed to the mouth of a small creek, and commenced our real journey.

"This was not in the Everglades proper, painter-man, but a coastal swamp. The tiny creek we followed was of brackish water and quite deep, though narrow. Sea fish had penetrated far up in search of food, and the waters fairly teemed with marine life of every description. Silvery mullet actually jumped into our boat on three occasions, and we grounded on a great drumfish whose bulk all but blocked the channel.

"There were moccasins galore, and birds beyond counting. It was evidently some time since a boat had passed that way, and the quick-growing vegetation had nearly closed our passage. Constant labor alone with ax and knife cleared our path, so it was only at evening we reached the rookery, too tired to even look for a dry place to sleep. From the boat, while the light lasted, we watched the birds returning to their nests in the cypress trees and mangrove bushes, egrets, blue and green herons, snaky-necked water turkeys. When it was too dark to see, we withdrew a short distance and ate our evening meal. One thing struck me as rather odd: The birds did not seem as tame as might have been expected after a long period of non-molestation, and were continually hopping nervously to the end of the branches, and even bursting into a snowflake flight that was like the explosion of silver bombs.

"At daybreak we were suddenly startled from sleep. The birds were all gone, and hardly had we realized that it was the report of a gun that had wakened us when our nerves were shattered by two cries of frightful agony.

I yanked away the painter that tied us to a cypress tree, seized one oar, the guide the other, and we pulled toward the sound.

"Beyond the trees of the rookery a small island of scrub palmetto came into view, and lying on the edge of the water was an old Indian, a younger man bending over him and hastily tying a cord around his bared leg. As our boat slid onto the mucky land the trunk of a five-foot, diamond-back rattler, its head shot away, was thrashing among the palmetto leaves.

"The younger Indian never looked up from his task; he was now cutting deeply across two fang-marks in the elder's calf, and I noticed his own shoulder visibly swelling.

"Science, painter-man, has provided an antidote even against the supposedly deadly venom of the rattlesnake, and I labored over both men with the anti-venomous serum we owe to Calmette of the Pasteur Institute, and with hypodermic injections of strychnin, and washed the opened wounds with the wine-colored precipitate of permanganate of potash crystals. It soon became evident that the younger Indian would survive—the poison of crotalis seldom proves fatal if the victim is carried through the first hour—but the older man's recovery for a time seemed very doubtful.

"I fought for his life as I have never fought before, and finally the tide turned in his favor. We were then confronted with the problem of getting the patients back to the sloop. Our own boat was too small for more than three men, but we unearthed a rude dugout for the younger and towed it behind. It was something of a task, and once it turned over and I had to splash around in six feet of water in close proximity to a shark while rescuing the Indian boy. On the sloop we were able to make them both comfortable and hoisted sail for Miami.

"During all this time I hadn't said a word to either of the Seminoles and they had been equally reticent. However, when we were well underway I extracted their story in brief form. Father and son, they had been after sharp-nosed alligators, which is the American crocodile, a sinister, slim, gray-green saurian with black blotches. They had penetrated by an inside channel to the rookery, landed on the scrub-palmetto island, and had slept there that night.

"In the morning the elder man had stepped on the snake, whose rattles had been broken off so it could give no warning, and had been struck. The younger shot off the head, tripped, fell on it, and the fangs entered his shoulder—proving for the hundredth time that a rattlesnake head will bite even when separated from the body.

"By a fortunate coincidence the son was no other than the Osceola I sought. Money, I had found, was of no avail in providing a guide for my quest; gratitude might—and it did. They said no word of thanks until we reached Miami, and then the old man spoke:

" 'My years are many, and it would not have mattered greatly had I died, but my son is young, and life still is sweet to him. You may ask him what you wish; he is your slave till both our debts of life are paid.'

"I know savages, painter-man, and I made no pretense of the ha-ha-it-is-nothing attitude with which so-called civilized people meet even real gratitude, but answered simply: 'I shall ask him much.'

"Osceola seemed to have entirely thrown off the effects of the snake-bite, but his father fared badly. There were signs of gangrene in the wound and his vitality was very low. I thought it best to leave him in a hospital, and he was too weak to make any serious objection. Then I had my interview with Osceola.

" 'I am a friend of your people,' I said, 'but they do not trust me. I wish to go into the Everglades to the place where the white otter is, and look upon it. I ask you to guide me.'

"The aboriginal savage, Mr. Painter-man, may have had a stoical control of his features, but this Seminole Indian certainly did not. Surprise, fear, anger and even horror chased themselves across his face, all to be replaced by a look of bitter resignation.

" 'The white otter, *hokatee osana*, the white otter! I wish *chitkolalagochee* (the rattlesnake) had struck my heart,' he answered, 'rather than I should do this—but, alas, my father has spoken for me.'

"I have never felt anything more intense in my whole life than the hate of that tall, young, good-looking Seminole in the days that followed. It simply radiated from him. He made me feel as though I were about to commit some awful desecration, for there was plainly a mystery, the secret of which he believed I shared.

"Nevertheless he made his preparations, and even went so far as to suggest, since it was evidently a law of the Seminoles that no white man should penetrate into their fastnesses, that I stain my skin.

"One early morning found me, dyed from head to foot, paddling up the Miami River, and outlet of the Everglades. We soon turned from the open water, and when the saw grass finally closed over our heads I doubt very much if many men would have envied me. I was going into a land, or rather into a lake, that had never been really explored, in company with a savage who plainly hated and abhorred me from the bottom of his soul.

"It was hot, hot, hot! The edges of the saw grass cut at the slightest touch—but before me there was always the thought of the white otter!"

Van's eyes glowed fanatically. I could not help thinking that the Indian was not the only savage on that expedition. Surely there is nothing more ruthless than a scientist once he has a definite object to attain!

The white raccoon, to which I was now quite accustomed, curled up between my neck and the back of the chair. Van's low voice took up the tale.

"That day we paddled from early morning until sunset, sometimes along winding channels which were broad and flowing with clear water, but more often through the cruel, cutting saw grass that parted in the mere shadow of a trail. Often we dragged the dugout along limestone or mud bottoms, and there was never, the long hours through, one word from my companion. At last, as the birds were flying to their roosts, and their evening chorus mingled with the insistent croaking of the frogs, we landed on a small island and pulled up our boat. By a lucky shot I neatly decapitated a Florida wild turkey from a live-oak, and elicited the first sound from my mute Seminole, a guttural 'good.'

"I sha'n't easily forget that night. No sooner were the stars out, and my eyes just closing than there sounded from the shores of our islet the bull-like roar of an alligator, to be answered by another saurian in the distance. All night the limpkins yelled—how birds of their size can make such an awful sound is quite beyond me—and the frogs croaked in seventeen different keys, quite unlike any frogs I had ever heard before.

"I slept little, and toward morning, when my eyes had finally closed, in the real rest sleep that every outdoors man knows, I woke suddenly to a frightful, nauseous smell. Turning on my side in the direction of the offensive odor, a luminous mass met my eyes. A huge rattler, its scales shining as though with phosphorus, was piled against the body of the Indian, a raised, triangular head, broad as my two hands, weaving nervously back and forth above its coils. At that very moment the dawn broke, Osceola moved, and the reptile whirred warningly.

" 'Keep still,' I whispered sharply, and rolled sidewise from my rubber blanket. A shotgun was beneath my hands and I snatched it up, tempted the snake to strike with a stick, and blew it in two pieces just below the neck. It was fully eight feet long, and it shone with foxfire. Unlike any other member of its family I had ever seen, the stripes ran longitudinally.

"Osceola lay tense and motionless, eyes wide open, staring up into mine as I bent over him. Even when I dashed water in his face he came slowly from his trance. To my insistent demands as to whether he had been struck, he simply shook his head and went dazedly about the preparations for breakfast and departure. I noticed that his eyes followed me continually, however, as I was skinning the snake, and their look of implacable hate had been replaced by a dumb, dog-like wonder.

"That morning our trail led entirely through the saw grass with no open channel. It was unbearably hot, and we both labored like galley slaves with paddle and pole. Suddenly Osceola broke into feverish talk, and, with his eyes shifting back and forth from mine to the snake skin I had tacked inside the gunwale of the boat to dry, told me the legends of the All-Soul.

"Long, long ago, even before the time of the great chief Osceola, whose name my young Seminole bore, there was but one soul to all the Indians of the Everglades, so no one did wrong, since the punishment must fall on all. *Ollahaw* (the orange), and *shottaw* (the persimmon), were their sole food, and they dwelt in friendship with every bird, beast, and reptile. Came a great wind with darkness, rain, and thunder, and when it had passed, *holwagus* (badness) was among them.

"To one man he said: 'Why do you eat only *ollahaw* and *shottaw* when the flesh of *woodko* (the raccoon) is so much better?'

"So the man slew *woodko* and ate his flesh, and so great was the power of *holwagus* for evil that the flesh tasted good to the man, and his descendants ever after ate of *woodko*. And some *holwagus* tempted to eat the flesh of *chofee* (the rabbit), others *foakee* (the quail), others *hilolo* (the curlew), until all the Seminoles were corrupted save one alone, a maiden.

"And the All-Soul left the Seminoles, taking refuge in her as the only good left among them. The beasts, in horror, hid themselves, save *lakosee* (the bear), *kowatgochee* (the wildcat), and *katsa* (the panther), and they grew claws and teeth for defense, or even attack.

"Then the Seminoles spoke among themselves, saying: 'Let us kill this maiden who will not eat flesh, and the All-Soul will be shared among us again and we shall be happy.' But *holwagus* heard them and gave poison fangs to *chitkolalagochee* (the rattlesnake), making him a guardian of the maiden, because he did not wish her to be killed and take the All-Soul out of the world, but to become bad like the rest of the Seminoles. Man, bird, and beast feared his fangs. All except *holwagus*.

"But the maiden hid in the bodies of animals, going from one to another, until *holwagus* gave up looking for her and went away. He warned, however, that he would come again and steal the All-Soul.

"Osceola watched me very sharply during the last part of this recital, and then, lowering his eyes before mine, complained of his shoulder. I stripped away the shirt to find it badly swollen, and, for a moment, feared that the fangs of the striped rattler might, after all, have touched him. There was no new wound, however, and I put the swelling down to auto-suggestion till my own theory so worked on my imagination that I peeled the snake skin from its place and hid it under my rubber blanket.

"The swelling did not increase, but the fever grew on him until, directing me to steer by a cypress that was the only landmark discernible above the sea of saw grass, he lay down in the bottom of the dugout and promptly lapsed into delirium.

"I pushed steadily on, far from tranquil in mind. The cypress was only visible above the saw grass when I balanced perilously on the edge of the rude craft. Suppose I should lose sight of it and Osceola should die? I should be as hopelessly lost as a compassless mariner in the middle of the Atlantic Ocean.

"However, the cypress began to stand out more clearly, and about two o'clock I was suddenly out of the grass. What a picture was spread before my eyes! First came a hundred yards of open water dotted with the brilliantly colored Everglades ducks and ringed by breaking fish. Then, like a green ribbon heavily embossed in silver and gold, a broad band of water-lilies in full bloom girdled an island—an island that fairly smiled with sunlight, happiness, and peace.

"A grove of lemon and orange trees, pollarded so as to rise little above the level of the saw grass, had shaded out all undergrowth from the clean, gray soil. To the left spread an orderly vegetable garden behind which crouched a low house weather-beaten to silvery gray and surrounded by a multitude of brilliant flowers. Osceola mustered his strength for one look, rose on his elbow, murmured *poyafitsa* (heaven), and fell back unconscious. I paddled to the shore and pulled up the dugout as a very old Indian came from the house to meet me.

" 'He is very sick,' I said, pointing to Osceola; 'we must get him out of the sun immediately.'

"The meaning of the words were plainly unintelligible to the old man, but he understood my gesture. Between us we picked up the fever-stricken boy and carried him to the house, where a couch of fragrant rushes received his burning body.

"For two days, painter-man, I listened to the ravings, half in Seminole, half in English, of that savage, and pity grew and grew in my heart as I fought for his life. The old Indian was a quiet and competent assistant. I was vaguely conscious of another presence in the house, that of a woman, but I was far too busy to even glance at her.

"On the third day the fever broke, thanks to a concoction of herbs the old man brought me which I tried in desperation, and my patient sank into a natural sleep. Wearily making sure that he needed no more attention for the present, I twisted into a blanket, shut my eyes, and immediately fell through unlimited space. While the clock went twice round I slept without waking, save when some one held a cool drink of orange juice to my lips.

"My eyes finally opened to a perfect day. The scent of orange blossoms was in the air and a mocking-bird was trilling from a magnolia outside the window. I looked anxiously over at my patient to find him awake and staring at me.

" 'You all right?' I asked.

" 'All right,' he grunted morosely.

" 'We'll see that white otter soon, then,' I suggested cheerfully.

"For answer he raised his voice and called, 'Ocola! Ocola!' and the old man slipped silently into the room. They spoke rapidly together in the Seminole tongue, and then Ocola disappeared to return in a few moments leading an Indian girl.

" 'There is Hokatee Osana, the white otter,' said Osceola, turning his face to the wall with a groan.

"In my whole life I have never looked on so proud a creature! She stood poised like a butterfly ready for instant flight, her eyes blazing at me, full of hate and fear. She was too small and her features too Seminole to be beautiful, but her hair, showing unmistakable traces of white blood in its brown waviness, was very lovely. Her greatest and most wonderful charm was a birdlike alertness, the lightness of thistle-down, a vitality quick as sunshine.

"I gazed at her, my mouth wide open, I fear, and her eyes finally tore away from mine and sought the figure on the couch. With the change that came over her face as she looked on Osceola the whole situation became suddenly clear to me. I understood the Indian youth's hate, his bitter sacrifice in guiding me to his treasure, grasped the significance of the legend, and the reason it had been told.

" 'Osceola,' I said sternly, 'it is not a woman with a red skin to whom I asked you to guide me; it is to an otter, a real otter, and white. You have deceived me and your father, whose life, as well as your own, belongs to me.'

" 'The animal otter is here,' he answered humbly; 'but it is only a shadow; its soul is in Hokatee Osana, and she is therefore the white otter.'

" 'It is not a soul I seek,' I answered angrily; 'it is a skin, a white skin.'

"The old Indian broke in excitedly with a stream of words.

"Osceola translated.

" 'He says, "Lord, if you take the skin of the real otter, Hokatee Osana dies. Will nothing else please you? He offers what all white men desire—for he knows you are a white man." '

"I wanted time to think. Of course I was going to have my white otter, but I have a fundamental objection to offending the religious beliefs of primitive peoples, and, besides, I know there is something in auto-suggestion—the girl *might* die!

" 'Show me what gifts you can offer equal to these,' I said scornfully, spilling a pound or two of beads (I received your kindly letter concerning them) on the floor. The girl gave a covetous glance at my offering—she was certainly femininely primitive—the old Indian never even glanced in their direction, but beckoned me to follow him.

"Out in the sunshine we went through the orange-grove toward the sound of running waters, and Osceola, stopping near the signal cypress, drew back and pointed.

"What has been bred in us for centuries, painter-man, cannot be eliminated in a moment, and I was conscious of a thrill of covetousness at what was spread before my eyes. The ground was strewn with scores of small chests, some entirely rotted away, some partially whole, and from every one cascaded a stream of gold pieces that blinked dully in the sun. Doubloons, pieces of eight, English guineas, French pistoles, strange octagonal slabs of gold from India and the Orient lay untouched beneath the cypress-tree since the day when their last buccaneer owner had abandoned them.

"I stepped closer and with my foot stirred a mass of metal to that silky rustling that weaves a spell through the rooms of Monte Carlo's gambling palace, and gradually the lust of desire left my blood.

" 'What is this foolishness?' I shouted angrily, unmindful that the old Seminole could not understand; 'I don't want this trash! Show me the real white otter—hokatee osana, hokatee osana!'

"He included all the scattered chests in a sweep of his arm and then swung his hands, palms upward, to me in a gesture of offering.

" 'No, no,' I refused, 'hokatee osana.'

"Again he went through the dumb ceremony of endowing me with all this strangely stored wealth, and again I shook my head and insistently reiterated my request. Suddenly his expression changed from pleading to fury, and snatching a knife from beneath his garments, he flung himself upon me. An old man, it was an easy matter to send the weapon from his hand to the ground, where it fell with the tinkle of metal against metal.

"Unsubdued, he still defied me with his eyes, and our glances locked. 'Hokatee osana,' I demanded fiercely again and again, and at last the spirit broke within him. Slowly he turned and I followed his faltering footsteps across a carpet of gold toward the cypress whence came the sound of running water. A stream gushed from the wide-spread roots of the tree, and, as we looked, a white form slipped from beneath and came toward us. It was an otter, painter-man, an otter, white as snow, with two eyes of red fire—an unearthly, beautiful thing, wonderful— Well, look for yourself!"

Van rose, and, switching on more light, stripped away a sheet from a cabinet in the corner of the room.

In the foreground, posed on a tongue of strange gold coins mixed with sand, stood a creature so wonderfully mounted that it seemed alive.

"Van," I cried reproachfully, "you didn't kill that lovely thing! I can understand the slaughter of gorillas and toucans and—animals; but you *could not* have killed that silver spirit!"

"As a matter of fact, I didn't," he confessed. "Perhaps I shouldn't have killed it, and then again it is quite possible that I should," he added honestly. "You see it is a perfect type of albinoism. The matter was taken out of my hands, however. As it came toward the spot where the old Indian and I stood among the rotted chests, it paused every few steps to gaze at me curiously but entirely without fear from its ruby eyes.

"A spit of heaped gold ran down from us and as its feet touched the first coins something sinuous, deadly, fulvous so as to be nearly indistinguishable from the yellow background, lay in its path. There was a sinister buzz as of some great locust, and I sprang forward shouting. The otter turned quicker than light, but the lash of the rattler's head was a lightning flash—and the beautiful thing was dead when I picked it up."

There was a long silence. Van was gazing musingly into the cabinet.

"Are its eyes genuine rubies?" I asked him.

"Only things I could get to match the real ones," he answered.

"Did the Indian girl die?"

"No."

"What happened to you?"

"I came home."

"See here, Van," I exclaimed angrily, "it's all very well for you to escape alone from places it is impossible to escape from, but you have, in a way, taken me along, and I want to know how you did it? What happened to you next? How did it all end?"

Van's eyes were on the white otter and he murmured absent-mindedly before answering me, "*Lutra canadensis vaga, varietas alba.*

"Where was I?" began Van anew. "Oh, yes!

"Well, I skinned the otter and preserved the pelt with the arsenic you were so glad to send me and began to think of getting home. The situation on the island offered an easy solution for anyone with a grain of imagination. The last rattlesnake incident firmly established my disreputable divine origin, and I simply proclaimed my godhead as a reformed and satisfied *holwagus*, and carried matters off with a high hand. My first decree was that Hokatee Osana—the girl—and Osceola should marry, and I performed the ceremony myself."

"What!" I gasped in astonishment. "How did you do it?"

"Oh, Jabberwocky served my purpose perfectly. The line 'and shun the frumious bandersnatch,' particularly impressed 'em. The rest of my beads I bestowed on the bride and gave the bridegroom my shotgun. Then I asked how I was to get back to Miami.

"It was quite evident that I should have to make the trip by myself, because neither of the men would have dared to trust himself alone with me.

"After a great deal of hesitation Osceola finally confided that by keeping the great cypress in line with a tall, yellow pine barely discernible in the distance, I would strike a deep channel which led, though by twice as long a route as we had come, to the Miami River.

"Next day I found this channel, and only just in time to keep from getting hopelessly lost. They must have begun cutting down the cypress the moment I left, for I saw it fall myself from miles away. No human being save a Seminole can ever again find Poyafitsa Island. The rest of my journey was plain sailing, or rather paddling."

I always make some idiotic remark after hearing Van's latest adventure. It invariably leaves my mind in such a hopeless whirl.

"Didn't you get bitten by rattlesnakes, or frogs, or have to eat curlews or—or raccoons?" I asked.

The animal against my shoulder woke suddenly and bit me severely on the back of the neck.

Lost—One Mylodon

THE FACT OF THE MATTER IS that for a man who makes a profession of exploring expeditions, Pete Wells (which is me) had been in civilization too long. I was ripe to go any place where there were no waiters to be tipped. Certainly Bones' physical charms didn't lure me from my happy table in Old Swartz's Café, Jacksonville, Florida, U.S.A. The top of his head looked like an ostrich's egg, his face was a jungle of straw-colored beard, stiff as the spines of a hedgehog, out of which peeped two innocent blue eyes, and the rest of him was completely globular. In height he was six feet, all but nine inches, and his name was Nicholas Vladmir Versch-and-all-the-rest-of-the-alphabet-well-scrambled.

But, law me, how that miracle of rotundity could talk! The evening from the time I laid down his letter of introduction until next morning came, I simply listened spellbound.

His specialty was bones, the bones of extinct animals, and he wanted me to go with him to a place called Ultima Speranza in southern Patagonia, where there was a famous cave full of bones, and then up along the Chilean Andes prospecting after the remains of beasts that had been dead so long that no one really knew how they looked.

The proposition in itself did not appeal to me—I had tried it once before in a salt marsh on the Brazilian coast and the 'skeeters had nearly eaten me alive—not until after the second drink, anyway, when he really began to talk. Then I started in seeing things. From a bunch of drawings of prehistoric and modern bones he sorted the same kinds together and explained how he correlated them. First he compared the thigh of a common or garden guinea pig to a busted up, second-hand-looking relic of what he called a toxodon, and, before I realized it, so vividly reconstructed a nine-foot rodent, with tremendous, chisel-like teeth, that I reached under my armpit to see if my automatic was loose in its scabbard. Then came pterodactyls, flying reptiles with long, beak-like jaws and an eighteen-foot spread of leathery wings; a cute little atlantosaurus with a thigh bone larger than an elephant's; eighty-foot long diplodocuses.... Honest, I was glad when the morning light filtered in, and only half of my quart of Scotch was gone, too, though the Russian had gotten away with two full bottles of white, blockade liquor—so like his native vodka, he apologized.

Of course I agreed to go with him, just couldn't help myself, and in less than a week we were on board a steamer for Valdiva, Chile.

It was a long trip, and I had plenty of time to size up my companion, and that fat little Russian seemed so simple that I just couldn't believe in him. Apparently his one object in life was the collecting of bones, and his present direct purpose to controvert some German scientist against whom he nursed a royal grouch because of the assertion that mylodons had sat on their haunches while pulling down the tops of trees to feed on instead of standing up like human beings.

I don't mean by all this that Bones was a freak and didn't know anything else. Quite the contrary. I don't think there was anything he didn't know something about, only nothing but prehistoric animals really interested him. He sang in the ship's concerts like a tuneful mocking-bird, if you can imagine a bewhiskered mocking-bird in a dinner coat that would have fitted a hogshead, never laid down two pair to a one-card draw, and took the masculine normal, or perhaps twice the normal, amount of alcohol. He hadn't any use for the señoritas, though. A flock of them fluttered around him, but he let 'em flutter. I suppose they were attracted to him because he was so darned ugly. Women are often taken that way—no better proof than that I have had two romances in my own life, both ending happily.

Valdiva is some little city. We put up at a hotel that even a commercial traveler couldn't have criticized. Bones slid out to look for the consul and a lot of people to whom he had letters, while I spread myself all over the waterfront trying to pick up a craft for the rest of our journey down the coast.

Gosh, but that was a punk lot of shipping! There was enough paint spread over rotten wood and rust-honeycombed iron to decorate several battleships, but not one thing I'd care to trust myself in off a lee shore. Had to give it up finally, it was getting so dark. Besides a kind of a crowd had collected after I handed one to a skipper who demanded a hundred pesos from me for jabbing a knife into his schooner below the waterline—claimed I'd ruined it, which was probably true.

Back at the hotel I found Bones down in the lobby, surrounded by a group of what it took no finesse to identify as reporters. They were asking him the usual fool questions: how he liked the country, how it compared with Russia, and so on, and they were calling him Count. He introduced me to the bunch, but, being only a plain American, I didn't make any big hit with them, so I bought a drink just to show how much I cared and went up in the elevator.

"Can't stay in this town long, Pete," the Russian announced as he came into our apartment, "or we'll be done to death socially. I was simply forced to accept a dinner invitation for us."

"All right, Count," I agreed amiably; "I'll go down stairs and rob a waiter of his glad rags. Never be it said I deserted the aristocracy in their need."

It went at that. Somehow he never was much stuck on my horsing; didn't seem to get it.

Annexing clothes proved no trouble, and when I came back the little man had hung medals all over himself.

"Gosh!" I cried in admiration, "you certainly look the part! Sure you are only a count, not one of those grand dukes?"

He answered rather shortly that his family had always been respectable, which kind of had me guessing exactly how he meant it, and then we were whisked away in a large touring car to a club.

It was a men's dinner. If I had known that in advance I should have worn my own clothes—and felt like a fool in them, too, since every one else wore evening dress, mostly with some decoration. The food was fine, the drink better, and Bones was sure the whole cheese. An old chap, with more medals than a baking-powder advertisement, made a long speech about how honored they were at having the great scientist, Count Vladmir, in their midst, and the Count got up and said in a few well-chosen words he was darned glad to be there. Then we ate some more and drank a lot more, while the orchestra played "There'll Be a Hot Time in the Old Town To-night," which seemed to have just struck that burg and struck it hard.

To be perfectly truthful, I didn't have a roaring good time. The man on my left did nothing but eat. The man on my right would only converse in English, and all he knew was "You tak' lil' drink wis me?" which I did, until he couldn't talk at all. The feast finally ended, however, and we motored back to the hotel, only hitting one lamp-post on the way.

The next morning I was off to the wharves again, and with no better result. Finally, though I hadn't the slightest hope of securing it, just on a chance, I had myself rowed out to a dandy little steam yacht in the offing. Who should come to the rail but my right-hand neighbor of the night before with his "You tak lil' drink?" I did, and then, since he consented to talk Spanish, I explained my predicament to him.

Easiest thing in the world! His yacht was quite at our service. It really would be a favor to him to use it, since he was forced to visit his *hacienda* in the interior for several months. He was tickled to death to be able to serve Count Vladmir. The crew was on board, the yacht provisioned.

He really meant it, too, and, congratulating myself on a piece of pure luck, we had another "lil' drink," and I beat it back to the hotel.

It was a long steam down the roughest coast I have ever seen until we swung in back of Desolation Island, and we simply never should have arrived at Ultima Speranza fiord had it not been for the luck of finding that perfectly appointed yacht with its pilot who knew the channels. As it was, within those land-locked waters we had to nose cautiously further and further inland, to the anxiety of a nervous captain and with a crew harassed by endless soundings and perpetual lookouts until, somewhat below 50°, Bones was contented to go ashore. The yacht was dismissed with orders to return in two months, and, hiring two sturdy white men from the little settlement to pack our supplies, we began our hunt for the cave.

It was an extraordinary country and, from my point of view, not a pleasant one. For a long way back from the sea the land was arctic, bare and very rough; then came forests of enormous trees, above which rose the mountains, with silvery glaciers twisting from their sides like ribbons of burnished steel. We froze at night and boiled during the day, while the humidity was so great that mists were always rising from hidden valleys or streams, like the smoke of volcanoes.

Somehow it all depressed me—gave me a feeling as though time had stopped, as though there was no going forward, no looking back—as though there was an inertia in all things.

I lost that feeling after we found the cave, though. It isn't quite correct to say we found the cave. What we really did was to stumble on a little farm where dwelt an old, old white man, who directed us where to look. He claimed that within his time an immense piece of skin covered with greenish hair unlike that of any known animal, had been brought from there and, together with several barrels of bones, sold to men who came in ships. Then there had been some trouble with a wandering tribe of the big Patagonian Indians, and the cave had been gradually forgotten.

It was a terrifically hot and muggy day when we reached the place. From the outside it did not look like much, merely a symmetrical black half moon set in the green of the hillside. Inside, however, it opened up into a hundred-foot chamber, with walls fully thirty feet high, and the dry, sandy floor showed signs of having been disturbed in the center. It appealed to me principally as a place to get out of the sun, but the Count went straight up in the air as soon as he was within.

Exactly as it had been described by Dr. Nordenskjöld! Humid atmosphere, but not too humid to reduce everything to peat. Cave dry—might find anything there!

He grabbed one of the two pointed shovels which, with a couple of mattocks, were our only collecting impedimenta, and dashed it into the undisturbed sand close to the wall. And promptly he did find something, the skeleton of a man about seven feet tall.

I didn't like it. It's all very well to dig up prehistoric animals, but I don't approve of meddling with grave-yards, and a grave-yard it proved to be. All along the edge of the cave, hardly two feet beneath the sand, were the skeletons of men and women, not one measuring less than six feet.

"Look here, Bones," I said. "Cover up those giants and let's get out of here. I absolutely refuse to dig up dead men, even in the interest of science."

"I don't understand," he answered, more to himself than to me. "Skeletons of comparatively modern savages, Patagonians according to the cranium. They have no business here. We'll try the middle of the cave, Pete."

I shoveled back the sand along the edges while he dug in the center, cussing quite fluently the while. It became evident that all the middle of the cave had been worked over, and his labors were rewarded only by the rib of a guanaco and a pointed sliver he claimed had been fashioned into an eating utensil from a dog's leg bone. Disgusted, we sat down, and realized for the first time that both our white bearers had disappeared, leaving their packs behind them.

After hallooing outside for a time, we saw night was falling and went back into the cave to escape the heavy dew. There was no wood for a fire, and as we sat in the darkness munching hard tack I for one heartily wished myself back at Old Swartz's.

"It's been cleaned out," finally sighed my companion. "Our only hope is that farther in it may be untouched. Are you afraid to explore the entire cave to-night, Pete?"

Darned if I wouldn't have refused if he had put it any other way. The skeletons were on my nerves, but I didn't propose to be bluffed by any foreigner, not if he had so many medals he had to wear them on the tails of his coat.

"After you, my dear Count," I answered, fishing our electric torches out of the packs, together with a half-dozen balls of twine.

Beyond the faint moonlight from the mouth of the cave it was black dark—not the darkness of out of doors when there are neither moon nor stars, but the enclosed blackness of the inside of a camera before the cap is taken off. I tied one end of a ball of twine tightly to a shovel driven in the sand, and followed the rotund form of my companion.

Around the walls we went, and then, bending our heads, dived under a shallow arch, walking on living rock. One ball, two balls, three balls of twine unwound as we explored a narrow passage which opened up finally into a small chamber with sandy floor.

"Here's something!" exclaimed the Russian, dragging a bone from the soil. "Another guanaco," he finished disgustedly, and we went on. To the left the darkness became opaque, and there was the sound of slowly dripping water. A broad passage opened before us, and suddenly above our heads, through an aperture high, high in the rock, appeared a luminous body, the moon. We swept the place with our torches, and nearly at our feet a tiny spring seeped up through the sand, flowing down an incline of white, luminous slime into the darkness. Bones took one step forward, lost his footing, fell, and, dropping his torch at my feet, rolled swiftly out of sight down the sloping way, his round body picking up the clay like a snowball adds to its bulk as it hurtles down a hillside.

To save my soul I couldn't help it—I roared. There was a crash in the distance like the breaking of dry branches before a fleeing deer, and then the Count's voice:

"Laugh, you damned hyena," came cheerily up to me; "I've fallen into a boneyard. Wrap my torch in your shirt and throw it down to me."

"Hadn't I better come down?"

"Don't! don't!" he yelled; "it's slippery as ice! You'll have to get a rope to haul me out!"

I raised my own light high above my head and, putting his torch into a bundle with my shirt, threw to where I could dimly discern his figure, a glittering white globe below me. The bundle fell short. In vain he tried to climb up the slippery incline to it, while I howled with laughter; then, abandoning his attempts, he began to dig steps in the slime with a large, pointed bone. In half an hour he had progressed to where my shirt lay, and then, as the easiest mode of locomotion, rolled back to the bottom again.

The snapping on of his light showed the walls clearly. It was nothing more than a shoot down which he had fallen, a shoot paved with luminous, white, phosphorescent clay all the way to the bottom, where it ended in a chamber twenty feet in circumference and literally filled with bones. They were banked up the sides, protruding from the ground. The little fat man was standing on them.

As he pulled the gruesome relics about the Russian growled out short sentences: "Damned guanacos again! Rabbit! A jaguar femur—what should that be doing here? Pete! Pete! I've found it, and part of the skin on it! A *mylodon!* A *mylodon* without question!"

"Hurrah for the *mylodon!*" I shouted enthusiastically. "I'll go back now and get a rope, and meanwhile you work as far up the slide as you can. Tomorrow we'll arrange some kind of a light in here and dig the whole thing up."

"All right!" he yelled. "Hurry back, though! It isn't pleasant being left alone in the bowels of the earth!"

I tied the cord to a projecting piece of rock and turned back, letting the twine run through my fingers as I walked. Not twenty feet around the next corner my torch suddenly went out, the battery exhausted. Great God, but it was dark! The sweat poured from my bare shoulders in spite of the fact that it was far from warm. For a moment I thought of turning back, and then realized that it would only mean leaving Bones alone in the darkness if I took his torch, and there were other batteries to recharge the lights in our packs. Slowly, both hands cramped to the cord, I went forward. It seemed as though I had been groping on for centuries. Once the string snapped out of my hands, and I threw myself on the ground panting with fear until I found it again. At last, after I felt I had been long enough in the cave to be classed as a prehistoric animal myself, the cord slackened, light showed ahead, the flickering illumination of a fire, and I instantly decided our white bearers had returned. With a shout I dropped the limp cord and ducked into the main cave. I had only time to see seven tall figures facing me around a fire, when strong hands grasped me on either side. Furiously I struck out, then tried to drag my automatic from under my left arm. Down I went with two big men on top of me, and in less time than it takes to tell I was trussed up like a fowl and dragged to the fire.

There were nine great Patagonians, seven men and two women, grouped about me, dressed in mantles fashioned from guanaco skins and armed with knives, old muskets and bolas.

Beside the fire, nearly at my feet, lay a tenth savage, an immense man, but thin to the point of extreme emaciation—dead.

The younger woman (she was a right good-looking savage for all of her six feet of height) whispered excitedly to the elder. The men regarded me silently.

"What the devil does this mean?" I sputtered in Spanish. "Turn me loose at once!"

"You'll have to get your devil to turn you loose," a man sneered at me in the same tongue. "We shall not. You have come into the cave of the Sacred Moon and disturbed those who were sleeping. To-morrow you die in honor of the one who lies before you."

Nice, wasn't it? End of Pete Wells, Esq., sacrificed to the glory of a Patagonian stiff with no clothes on, and buried in a cave haunted by the ghosts of prehistoric animals! I lost my temper.

"You don't say?" I remarked sarcastically. "Well, my devil *will* be here, and he'll make you turn somersaults under the 'Sacred Moon.' "

"Aren't you afraid?" curiously asked the man nearest me.

"Not of you," I answered furiously, and, twisting one leg free, applied my foot forcibly to the pit of his stomach.

It was a fool thing to do, and he was on me in a second with raised knife. I thought my last moment had come, but the others pulled him away.

"No blood must be shed in the cave of the Sacred Moon," said the elder woman sternly. "To-morrow we will see to him. Now let us bury our dead."

Muttering evilly, my assailant stepped aside. Raising the dead man, the others carried him to a shallow depression near the wall and unceremoniously scratched sand over him. Then, the men standing in a circle and swaying before the dying fire, the girl began to sing in the corrupted Spanish that seems to have taken the place of the Patagonian tongue, if there ever was one:

> *"Night has come that ends not,*
> *Night has come to thee,*
> *With the Great One quickly*
> *Thy spirit wanders free.*

Body lies in sacred ground,
Spirit will fly soon
Where the light is softest,
Up to the bright, round moon.

"Where the light is softest,
Up to the bright, round moon."

The other savages crooned in unison, swaying back and forth and then settling to the ground.

There was a long silence, and the girl's voice again rose:

"Night has come that ends not,
Thou wilt go on high
Where the light gleams always
In the darkest sky.
Earth will hold thy body,
Ever and for ay;
Spirit goes a floating
Where the moonbeams play.

"Spirit goes a floating
Where the moonbeams play."

intoned the others, rocking back and forth on the ground.

I shifted my position painfully and felt something hard beneath my elbow. It was the shovel to which I had tied the guiding cord for our expedition into the cave, and, rolling further over, I sawed the rope that bound my arms against its point. The edge of the moon came down over the top of the entrance to the cave, and again the girl began to sing:

"Night has come that ends not,
But she comes, her light,
Silver sparkling pathway,
Guides thy steps aright.
Sacred, O most sacred!
Shines on sea and dune,
Sacred, O most sacred,
Bright and shining moon.

"Sacred, O most sacred!
Bright and shining moon,"

from the other voices.

The silvery disk outside lowered, filling the foreground of the cave with light. The ceremony evidently over, the Patagonians rose to their feet, and two of them stepped across the dead fire towards me. The rope about my right arm was sawed through. With numbed fingers I tried to draw my automatic from under my left armpit. The shovel slid from beneath me, began to progress into the darkness at the end of its cord. With a flash of inspiration I pointed my free arm towards it.

"Look!" I howled. "Look! I send the senseless wood and iron for my devil! Tremble, fools, he is coming, the devil, the devil . . . from the moon?" I added as a happy afterthought.

Came a roar of fury from the blackness behind us.

"What in hell do you mean by leaving me this way, Pete? What is all this row?"

There was the glare of an electric torch, and from its light emerged Bones. Great Cæsar's ghost, but he nearly scared me! His whiskers were plastered with mud and blood running from his freely bleeding nose; his great round body was one luminous mass of shiny white clay, and he lurched forward like a Bacchanalian moon, spitting curses at every step.

With a simultaneous yell of terror the savages dived for the entrance of the cave. I jerked out my automatic and fired at the rock above them, bringing down a piece in their midst. The mouth of the cave cleared like magic, and Bones stood over me, throwing his light on the motionless figure of the girl who lay stunned by the fragment of rock that my bullet had brought down.

We revived our captive with a dash of water in her face, none the worse save for a lump on the side of her head, and decided to hold her as hostage for the present in case any of her friends returned. As a matter of fact, she showed no inclination to escape—just sat still watching Bones with awe-filled eyes. Even when he had exchanged his glittering, clay-coated garments for prosaic khaki it was evident she still looked on him as some kind of a god—or devil.

We slept across the entrance of the cave, guns beneath our hands, and save that the Russian conversed steadily about mylodons in his sleep, it was a quiet night.

Morning found us penetrating into the cave, the Patagonian maid walking ahead with both packs our bearers had abandoned. She picked them up unbidden, and didn't seem to consider their weight at all. Also the darkness evidently caused her no fear, since she kept on the very edge of the illumination thrown by our torches.

The top of the slippery clay chute where I had left Bones the night before presented an entirely different appearance in the daytime. The sunlight streamed down through the aperture in the rock above, and even lit the cell-like chamber at the bottom of the incline. The rude steps by which Bones had escaped were now overrun by the slimy clay, but we found it a simple matter with our shovels to dig a somewhat slippery but practical stairway to the bottom.

Then we really began to work. Not a bone was missing from the skeleton of the mylodon, and, furthermore, there were six square feet of skin, vivid green, and studded on the inside with small bosses of bone, showing, the Count said, that the animal had a rudimentary protecting shell beneath its fur, something after the fashion of an armadillo.

It was a happy fat man that collected this fifteen-foot skeleton, the bones in perfect preservation, even with pieces of sinew attached.

By relays, the girl silently doing more than her part, we transported the pieces into the main cave, and then it was noon. Lunch quickly gobbled, we went back to our excavating, and not another thing rewarded us. The rest of the bones, down to solid rock, proved to be of guanacos, jaguars, dogs and rabbits, not one single remnant dating back even a few thousand years.

"Don't understand it at all, Pete," complained the Count. "Why should a mylodon's bones be mixed with those of modern animals? I can understand their being well preserved, because of the extraordinary conditions in the cave, but why mixed with modern animals, when all authorities claim mylodons have been extinct for a thousand years?"

"Simple enough," I answered. "Why couldn't one of your little pets have survived until recently, and then have been driven to suicide through loneliness and jumped down that hole?"

"Why isn't the moon made of green cheese, as you English say?" disgustedly asked Bones.

"In the first place, I am an American, *not* an Englishman," I flared up, on my ear at once, "and, in the second place, how are you going to prove the moon isn't made of green cheese or bacon rinds, as far as that goes?"

"It simply isn't," he snarled.

"How are you going to prove it? How are you going to prove that there isn't a mylodon sitting outside the cave this minute? You've got to *show* me."

The Lord knows it was silly, but we were both red hot by that time and shouting at the top of our voices. Glaring at one another, we both opened our mouths again at exactly the same time, thought better of it and snapped them shut. Then we went back into the main cave, where the Count began to wrap his treasures in yards of thin, oiled silk, and staked the piece of skin out flat on the ground to dry. I built a fire from wood the girl collected and started to cook our evening meal.

All day long that Patagonian woman had toiled with us, carrying enormous burdens, collecting fuel, and had never once opened her lips to speak. So noiseless and unobtrusive had she been, in spite of her great height and splendid proportions, that we really hardly noticed her. Subconsciously

I had been aware that she seldom took her eyes from the little fat man, and when we had hauled out that piece of green fur I felt, rather than saw, her start. Now that the skin was pegged out flat and Bones had come to the fire, I could dimly discern her in the darkness kneeling by it, her arms stretched up to the roof of the cave.

We finished our meal and lit our pipes, when there came from behind us a soft crooning:

> *"Ou-ou, ou-ou, ou-u-u,*
> *Ou-ou, ou-ou, ou-u-u."*

Then, very softly at first, growing in volume with every note, the savage girl began to sing:

> *"Moon, moon; moon, moon,*
> *Bright with fire and white with snow.*
> *Moon, moon; moon, moon,*
> *Look down here below.*
> *By thy sacred sheep I kneel,*
> *Lest some wicked one should steal*
> *What is thine— Heed my appeal!*
> *Moon, moon; moon, moon."*

Bones started to rise, but I pulled him back. A beam of moonlight showed the kneeling figure, face bowed to the green skin. Once more she raised her hands above her head, and again her lips opened:

> *"Messenger to earth thou sends,*
> *Moon, moon, O sacred moon,*
> *Lowly to him my heart bends,*
> *Moon, moon, O sacred moon.*
> *I, thy daughter, soon will go*
> *Through the cold, and ice, and snow,*
> *Where the molten streamlets glow,*
> *Where thy sheep are grazing slow,*
> *Sacred flocks to tend."*

Her voice sank at the end. Came the softly crooned "Ou-ou, ou-ou, ou-u-u," then silence.

"Let me talk to her. I have an idea," I whispered to Bones, a wild suspicion growing in my mind, and I called out in Spanish.

She came at once and stood before us. Straight as a mountain pine, six feet tall, head high, and great eyes fixed on my face, the woman was without fear, without servility, and yet was dominated, in the grip of a power she could not understand. Her apparent mental attitude might perhaps be paralleled with that of a child who obeys willingly, though it knows not why. She was really beautiful, too, that dark, splendidly strong girl, beautiful like a heroic statue.

"Do you want to go back to your people?" I asked.

"My lord's servant knows I cannot since I have looked on him," she answered, turning her great eyes towards Bones.

"What will you do when we leave here?"

"Tend the sheep of the Sacred Moon with those so old they are no longer of the tribe."

"Where are these sheep?"

"Beyond the snow, and ice, and fire."

"We will go with you in the morning. Sleep now."

"As my lord wills," and she drew back into the darkness of the cave.

"What do you make of that?" I demanded excitedly of the Russian.

"Well, I don't know. The tribe has sheep some place that the very old people tend. I suppose the girl is kind of taboo through associating with us. Don't see why we should waste time running after the sheep, though."

"What kind of sheep do you suppose the sheep of the Sacred Moon are?"

"I don't know. You can't mean . . . oh, you're crazy, Pete!"

"Crazy or not, I'm going to find out," I answered. "What was she singing about, if not that Irish-colored fur? I'm going to see those sheep. Can't prove the moon isn't made of green cheese, but I can and will run this down."

The silk-wrapped bones and piece of skin were left at the little farm with the old, old man, who when he heard we were going down the coast with the girl announced that they would come in handy for fertilizer—said we wouldn't return to claim them. Even the Patagonians who went that way were never seen again. With this cheerful prophecy as a send-off, packs stripped down to the bare necessities, but still with our shovels and mattocks, we set out.

I have been on many a hike in my life, but never one to touch that. Our guide first led us several miles back from the sea and then turned due north. All day we followed a trail along the barren rocks of the coast zone—rather a line than a trail, since it was but three inches wide. The Patagonian easily covered the ground, walking, as do most savages, with a swing to her hips that enabled her to put one foot almost directly in front of the other. To us, following that narrow path was like walking a tightrope. How the fat man did it I really don't know; it must have been an agony of effort for him. Nevertheless from sun up till dark his great round body progressed steadily on before me.

That night we slept in a cave where bubbled up a spring of sulphur-laden, boiling water, and we slept hard.

At dawn our trail wound up through the forest from which we emerged; at noon the mountains towered high above us. Crossing a swampy tundra, we descended a gentle dip, and stood on the edge of an immense glacier, smooth, straight, reaching down in steep incline to where sparkled, miles and miles away, the waters of the Pacific.

Here the girl paused and, pointing out a peak across the ice, indicated that a path must be cut towards it. Our mattocks and shovels came into play, and while the woman and I hewed a way in the ice the Russian shoveled out the fragments behind us, tossing them on the smooth surface, along which they slid towards the sea, their tinkle growing fainter and fainter until swallowed up in the distance. Darkness caught us still laboring, and we were forced to spend the night on the edge of the glacier, doubly cold through comparison with the glowing reflection of a volcano on the sky.

As soon as it was light enough to see we were at it again. A great wall of vapor or steam rose on the opposite side of the glacier, ending abruptly at the point where our path was aimed. By two o'clock we were safely across, and paused in awe at the panorama spread before us.

The glacier was held by a thin ridge of rock, on the other side of which ran a broad stream of boiling water gushing out from a cavern beneath our feet. Above hung a cloud of vaporous steam, spreading out over a valley and completely hiding it, while on every side towered snow-capped mountains. The whole place looked like a great pit filled to the top with snow.

"How long do you suppose the rock will hold the ice back from the valley?" I asked Bones in a whisper. Somehow it didn't seem right to speak aloud in the immensity of all things.

"Don't know," he answered. "The ice has been grinding at one side, the stream wearing at the other, probably for thousands of years. I'm half inclined to believe in your crazy dream, Pete. This place seems like the beginning of the world."

We crossed above where the boiling spring gushed out from the cavern, and found grass growing luxuriantly not ten yards from the glacier. Along the bank of the stream the girl led, with us following, the land sloping gently downward, the precipice rising higher and higher on the opposite bank. Once the Count touched my shoulder and pointed to a great fissure in the rocky wall fully a yard wide, seemingly created that very moment, ice squeezing through it at the top and melting, drop by drop, to fall hissing on the seething water below. The grass rose to our thighs, to our shoulders; trees appeared, then dense thickets, tangled, lush, green. Our leader turned at right angles and plunged into the vegetation. The cloud of vapor seemed to be resting on the tree tops. It shut off the sky, and, condensing, fell steadily in an infinitesimally fine rain. We walked in a humid, breathlessly hot mist. The trail opened into a broad, hard-beaten road, flat as though crushed down with a roller. On either side rose enormous trees hung with lianas and orchids, beneath them a nearly impenetrable tangle of underbrush thirty feet high, sappy, living green, save for splashes of the white, crimson or gold orchids.

"Here pasture the sheep of the Sacred Moon, here shall I dwell forever," spoke the girl.

"Where are the sheep?" I demanded.

As if in answer came a crash close to the road, and the underbrush swayed. Breathless, I glanced at Bones, but his staring eyes were riveted on something above my head.

"Wheet-wheet, wheet-wheet," came a tiny voice from the tree tops, and I looked up straight into a face peering down at me. And what a face! The round, yellow, foolish eyes were set well up in the narrow, greenish forehead, two flat, sniffing nostrils expanded and closed above a thick-lipped, vacuous mouth, from which protruded a long, slender, blue tongue, like a piece of satin ribbon. Never have I seen anything that portrayed such complete imbecility as that face!

"The utter damned fool!" I heard myself say aloud.

"Wheet-wheet," came the ridiculously tiny voice, the underbrush parted, and an immense bulk moved out into the open.

If you could have forgotten the idiot face (which you couldn't), I suppose the mere size of the animal would have made it impressive. It was as big as an elephant, as an elephant sitting on its haunches. The hind legs were enormous, doubled under it, and ending in great, flat paws; the back was curved, nearly humped; the forelegs were short, powerful, and armed with stupendous claws; the neck was long, a cord dangling from it, and topped by that fool head, maddeningly out of proportion to the bulk of the rest of the animal; while the entire body was covered with short, very green fur.

"Heavenly saints!" breathed the Russian, "it's a mylodon come back from the birth of time—utterly different from what we have conceived, but a mylodon; yes, a *mylodon*; a *mylodon*; yes, a *mylodon* . . ."

He kept repeating "A *mylodon*; yes, a *mylodon*," till my nerves snapped like cotton thread.

"Nobody said it was a teakettle!" I roared. "Supposing it is a mylodon, what in hell are you going to do with it?"

"We'll go on further," the little man answered, as though talking in his sleep, and paying not the slightest attention to my words; "perhaps we'll find something else."

"Heaven forbid!" I piously ejaculated. "This is enough for me!"

The creature let itself down on all fours, and with a final silly "Wheet-wheet," half hopped, half walked into the jungle, while we continued down the road in the dripping mist.

The ground rose and the trees became more scattered. A great cave opened in the mountainside and, pausing before it, the girl called out.

From within came eight Patagonians, seven men and one woman, or rather eight relics of the past. They were the oldest human beings I have ever looked upon—bent, gnarled, wrinkled, not one could have been less than a hundred years old. Peering out from age-bleared eyes, they blinked at us like an assembly of galvanized mummies.

"I come to watch the sheep," the girl said tonelessly, "and he"—pointing at Bones—"is a messenger from the Sacred Moon who would see how we tend our charges."

"You are over-young to leave the tribe never to return," the withered hag mumbled.

"My lord brought me here," the girl answered simply.

Within the cavern it was dark as pitch and dripping wet. Another pleasant discovery we made was that nothing would burn. Tree and shrub were too full of sap; there was no dead dry wood, just wet decay. The Patagonians evidently lived entirely on fruits, and it was on fruits that we dined.

Dusk was approaching, indicated by an evener opaqueness in the mist and less condensation into rain. The nine Patagonians, our guide included, moved off down the road. The Count busied himself putting his camera to rights, grumbling aloud meanwhile about the difficulty of taking pictures in that perpetually cloudy atmosphere and cursing the fates that he had but one flash-light powder. I pressed the moisture out of my clothes between two flat stones.

Suddenly a perfect chorus of "Wheet-wheets" broke on our ears, and the most extraordinary procession man has ever looked upon defiled up the road.

Each of the old, old Patagonians was leading—yes, *leading*—a mylodon by a rope around its slim neck, the girl bringing up the rear with a cunning little one, evidently very young and merely some six or seven feet tall. The other eight colossal, green beasts ran in size from fifteen to twenty feet, the largest, the only male in the bunch, having a kind of a crest of upright bristles along its back. Past us they wheeled into the cavern—round, yellow eyes gazing aimlessly in every direction, blue, ribbony tongues hanging from vacuous mouths.

"Hea-venly days!" I ejaculated, and sat down in a puddle. The Count's eyes were popping from his head, and he began to repeat something in Russian that may have been a prayer, but sounded like the sputtering of a dynamite fuse. I recovered my senses first.

"Come on!" I commanded. "Let's see the little dears tucked into their beddies—and then drink the bottle of brandy we brought along for medicine.

I know I'm sick—symptoms, a strange belief in things I *do* see but that *can't* be true."

We followed the procession into the blackness, electric torches in hand, and came to a further cave that was nearly dry. Here the Indians were slipping the ropes loosely about stakes driven in the ground. The great beasts loomed up under our lights like green mountains, and the glare of the electricity brought forth a disturbed chorus of the ridiculous, tiny cries. Their guardians angrily motioned us back, and we retreated outside.

"This, Pete, is the greatest thing that has happened in science for five hundred years!" exclaimed Bones. "Let's bend every thought and energy to getting the most out of it. We'll find out all we can from the girl, and then when the savages are asleep steal in and take a flash-light of that sleeping flock of prehistoric survivors."

As we talked a change came over the sky. The cloud of vapor caught the rays of the setting sun and reflected them through in countless rainbows of every color in the spectrum. Out into the beautiful illumination came the Patagonians and, grouping in a circle, with the old hag in the middle, sang a kind of an evening hymn:

> *"O sacred moon now rising,*
> > *(Alas, we cannot see!)*
> *All day we faithful tended*
> > *Thy holy flocks for thee.*
> *Now night comes in its glory,*
> > *Forget us not below,*
> *Remember thy great promise*
> > *That death we shall not know."*

After this lyric rendering we called the girl to us and put her through a long interrogatory. It was rather difficult to get things straightened out, because she assumed we knew so many things of which we were ignorant. Finally, however, a more or less linked chain of information was evolved.

When first she knew of the vapor-hidden valley there were only two mylodons. The other seven sprang from the original pair. The legend was that as long as there were mylodons so long would those who tended them live, and the Patagonian race as a whole survive. Their ever-present anxiety was that something would happen to the old male, the only representative of his sex, all his progeny having been females. Of course, Patagonians died outside the valley and were buried in the cave of the Sacred Moon, the girl conceded, and sometimes those within the valley, through their infirmities, became tired of living and slipped quietly into the boiling stream, but no one there was obliged to die. Within the records of the tribe the old woman had been there a hundred and then forty snows. Once a year all the Patagonians came to the valley to count the moon sheep. They were due very soon now, she concluded, and would worship the messenger of the Sacred Moon with song and dance.

After the girl had retired we sat outside the cave steaming in the hot, wet darkness, and talked things over. Without an argument we agreed that it was too great a risk to trust to Bones' clay-created godhead for our safety and await the arrival of the able-bodied Patagonians. What we had to do must be done quickly. That very night we would take the flash-light photograph within the cave, and the next day use the balance of our films in the forest.

For two hours, in order that the savages might all be asleep, we waited, and then, slipping off our shoes, stole within the cave. The way was easy to find even without a light, our feet feeling the solid path beaten by the weight of the monsters, and we knew at once, when we were inside the second cavern by a roaring like the sea, the snoring of the great beasts. Then I snapped on my torch so Bones could set up his camera. With the flood of light first one then another of the mylodons awoke and rose to its feet, looming up monstrous shadows whence came weird twitterings. I stepped back of Bones and spread the flash-light dust inside my tobacco pouch, the only dry thing I had. Match after match refused to light, then one flickered and blazed up, and I dropped it into the powder. There was a puffing blind of light showing the terror-stricken eyes of the immense animals turned toward us, the click of the camera shutter, then darkness shaken by a mighty tread. I pressed the button of my torch and jerked Bones, the camera in his arms, against the wall of the cave. The mylodons were thundering down on us like an avalanche, and the air was full of their shrill calls, while from the distance came the frightened cries of the Patagonians.

Hours we leaned motionless against the rock, scarce daring to breathe, then stole silently to the entrance of the cave and, rolling in our wet blankets, waited for dawn.

No matter how great the excitement sleep will not be denied to tired, healthy men, and we both dropped off just as the vapor outside began to whiten. The next I knew I woke to a wailing as though of lost souls, sat up to find it broad daylight, and Bones bending over me.

"Something terrible has happened from the sound those savages are making," he whispered. "Keep your gun ready and let's go see."

I followed him out into the fine drizzle and we turned down the broad road. The old, old Patagonians were rolling on the ground and raising their hands to heaven in frantic sorrow. Before them lay the male mylodon dead, its neck broken where it had collided with a giant forest tree in the darkness.

The mourners paid no attention to us; just kept up their horrible wailing interjected with broken plaints:

"The father of the sheep of the Sacred Moon is gone, is gone, and soon we, too, shall be no more. . . . We must die, must die. Perhaps ages hence, but still we must die. . . . We shall watch the last one die, and then we, too, shall die. . . . We, who hoped to live forever, must die. . . ."

Leaving the frantic savages we went back and got the camera, passed down the road unmolested, and plunged into the jungle. It was easy to locate where the monsters were feeding from the crash of breaking trees and the swaying of the underbrush, but quite another matter to photograph them. In the first place their color blended so perfectly with the lush green of the forest that, in spite of their bulk, it was very hard to see them; then again, we could never get all of a mylodon at once because of the thickness of the vegetation. Finally, when we reached the spot where the first monster had been seen on our entrance into the valley, we decided that the only practical plan was to lead one out into the road and snap it there. Plunging into the underbrush we fought our way through to where the tree tops were waving, and I took hold of the rope that hung from a mylodon's neck, not without inward quakings. It followed me like a lamb. Nearly out of the underbrush Bones raised his hand.

"Wait," he whispered; "I hear something."

So did I. From the direction of the glacier came the sound of many voices singing. Nearer it came, till we could distinguish the words:

> "Children of moon are we,
>   Fear not the darkest shade,
> Trusting, O moon, to thee,
>   Of darkness unafraid.
>
> "Come to thy cloudland
>   Where thy flocks be,
> There, hand in hand,
>   To worship thee."

Peeking out through the tree trunks we saw an entire tribe of splendid Patagonians file by—warriors, women and children, and not an adult under six feet.

We lay still in the woods until the mylodon began to graze and nearly pulled a tree down on top of us.

"Oh, hell," I broke the silence; "we're in for it now, Count. There isn't a chance of getting away if that bunch gets after us. All we can do is to shoot as many of 'em as we are able before going under. Let's lead Irene here to the road. You snap her till you're tired, and then we'll beat it."

Out in the open I tied the cord to a tree, and standing behind Bones, whistled so the beast would turn its idiotic face toward us. The Count took picture after picture from every angle, and while he was doing it a mad plan flashed through my mind.

"Look here, Bones," I stuttered; "let's take this prehistoric silly with us. She'll serve as a breastwork to get behind if we have to fight. I know it's like stealing a whole church, but I'll try anything once."

The Russian gave a whoop of joy.

"Pete, I never thought of it! If we get your Irene to the coast we'll be the most famous men on two continents. If we don't . . . well, we'll have tried something, anyway."

Down that road we went, Bones leading, through the brush and out by the flow of boiling water, the mylodon following docilely at the end of the rope. Across the hot stream the crack in the side of the precipice was now twenty feet wide, and great masses of ice were pushing through. I saw Bones glance at it apprehensively and shake his head. Over the rock, whence gushed the water, we climbed, and out on to the path we had cut in the glacial ice. And here we had to go more slowly. The beast's great pads kept slipping on the smooth surface, and her foolish face was contracted with fear at the cold beneath her feet.

"Stop a minute," I suggested, "and let Irene rest."

"All right. I'll take a snap of you leading her, with the glacier for background."

I felt the ice tremble under my feet as the camera clicked.

"Get up, old girl," I clucked, jerking at the cord.

The mylodon did not move. She lifted from the ice first one enormous cold foot, then another, swinging her foolish head from side to side, and uttering her inadequate, plaintive cry. Then she started to lie down.

"For God's sake, don't do that," I yelled, jerking at the rope; "you'll slide clear to the coast."

Paying no attention to my frantic yanks, down she went on her side, lifted her feet in the air and turned on to her great, round back, then rolled ponderously over and tried to scramble to her feet. She slipped, the rope pulling through my hands; recovered herself, slid, whirled about and went swiftly down the steep incline, gathering impetus with every second.

There was a mad chorus of yells behind us. The Patagonians were climbing on to the ice. I felt the glacier heave. With a terrific crash the barrier of rock on the shore gave way. Half the glacier, splitting from the main body, went over into the boiling stream, carrying our pursuers with it.

The mylodon was a speck in the distance, growing rapidly smaller against the sparkle of the Pacific.

How the Count and I reached solid ground I do not clearly remember. I have some vague recollection of hitting him on the point of the jaw to keep him from following the mylodon, and then running across the ice, his hand in mine. Anyway, when we were up on the bank, the glacier splitting into fragments below us, he was crying like a child. And cry he did for two whole days, never speaking a word, just crying and wringing his hands, his mind seemingly quite gone.

I lost the trail we had followed coming in, and had to strike for the coast by compass. The rest was one long agony of going forward, always forward, through the forest, across another glacier, over a bleak, boulder-strewn land, and then coming to a little white settlement on the seashore. There a British tramp steamer picked us up and landed us at Valparaiso, where for two months I nursed Bones through a raging brain fever that all but finished him.

An end comes to everything if you wait long enough. Time found us on a passenger steamer for San Francisco, but we were not the same men. At least the Russian wasn't the same. Every recollection of what had happened to us had been wiped from his mind. He knew who he was, who I was, and was rational in every other respect, but he didn't know where he had been or why, and he wouldn't let me tell him about it.

When I called him rational in every respect I told a lie. He had gone plumb dippy over women. Before we landed I found out that he was engaged to all three of the unmarried girls on the boat.

At San Francisco I took the train across the continent to Jacksonville. Bones hated to have me go; begged me to come to Russia with him at any salary I cared to name; said he was going to get married and settle down. I told him that, with his fund of feminine appreciation, Russia would never do for him; he'd end up in Turkey, and I'd never be able to live happily in a land where the women wore trousers.

At parting he presented me with a magnificent watch (I have eleven others that people have given me), and I never saw him again.

Jacksonville certainly looked good to me. The second evening I sat in Swartz's Café, with the old Dutchman himself across from me, and started to tell him of my adventures. As a preliminary I passed over the flash-light of the mylodons Bones had taken in the cave. Swartz looked at it a moment, and then asked:

"A new kind of a mice, *nicht vahr*?"

I picked up the photograph and examined it. There stood the mylodons just as I had seen them when the powder flashed, but, unless you had known it, there was no means of gauging their size, nothing in the picture with which to compare them. I opened my mouth to explain, and then shut it again.

"Yes, a new kind of mouses," I agreed. The story of my wanderings I improvised.

Up in my room that night I gazed for a long time at the snapshot of me leading Irene, the lady mylodon, across the glacier. Then, with a sigh, I hid it in the very bottom of my trunk.

What was the use?

(((✦)))

This tale might easily be true. About 1906 Dr. Nordenskjöld found on the shore of Ultima Speranza, in Southern Patagonia, an immense cavern from which the white settlers had removed an enormous piece of skin, covered with greenish brown hair, and studded on its inner side with little knobs of bone. It was unquestionably the skin of a mylodon that had survived until modern times. The remains of more than twenty mylodons were removed from this cave by Dr. Moreno, of the Museum of La Plata, and by other persons.

I state this on the authority of Sir E. Ray Lankester, M.A., LL.D., K.C.B., F.R.S., late director of the Natural History Department of the British Museum. He says further: "Possibly, though by no means probably, the mylodon is still alive in similar caves in this region as yet unvisited by man." (See *Extinct Animals*, page 124.) There exists also a great deal of evidence that tends to show that these mighty beasts were held in entire or semi domestication by prehistoric man.

The brain cavity of a mylodon is surprisingly small, indicating a very weak intellect. Many (or most) large ruminants, the giraffe, for instance, have blue tongues.

Southern Patagonia to this day is *terra-incognito*.

All these things being so, how could I help writing "Lost—One Mylodon"?—ELMER BROWN MASON.

Black Butterflies

The name of Elmer Brown Mason is a talisman that never fails to open the door to weird adventures in weird places with weird animals and men. In this fascinating tale of the jungles and mountains of Borneo, Mr. Mason has excelled himself. The pupæ of the ordinary honey-sucking butterfly look like angels, or souls in transition, says the author; but those of the Black Butterfly looked exactly like the devil!

I

THE MOUNTAIN SPIRIT

IT WAS THE OBSTINACY OF TREVOR DILLINGAME, the stark, sheer obstinacy and conceit of the man in his power to handle any situation, solve any jungle secret, that brought us under the shadow.

'Tis a fault of the English. Where a Scotchman is firm, an Englishman is obstinate. Where a Scotchman simply realizes his powers, an Englishman puts no limit to what *he* may accomplish.

Not that I didn't like the man. Losh, who could help it from the mere good looks of him? though I do not put undue faith in male beauties. But he was such a whale of a laddie, six feet tall, four across the shoulders, cold blue eyes, tread as light as *plandok*, the tiny mouse-deer; and big hands, that could crack a cocoa-nut or hold a butterfly without bruising its wings.

Butterflies were his line, and he knew as much as anyone in the world about them. I'm a cautious man and I'll go no further; he knew as much as anyone in the whole world about butterflies.

'Twas in the low swamp belt of the coast of British Borneo that it all began. We were collecting pretty nearly everything for a lot of stay-at-home scientists who could afford to have the jungle wonders sent to them to be tagged with Latin names at their leisure. It did pay, but it was hard work, dangerous work. The jungle leeches sucked blood from every uncovered inch of our bodies and our flesh was raw from mosquito bites. There were poisonous insects, snakes, and more snakes, and then the heat—moist, deadening; sapping your vitality like the final rounds of a long, long fight.

Shifting uneasily from foot to foot, and tearing away the jungle leeches that would pop onto their bare skins, three little Dyaks stood in the checkered shadows. Trevor Dillingame was bending over a great flower-stalk, around the top of which were symmetrically clustered the red and black caterpillars, with their one creamy segment, of *Cethosia hypsea*, creating a living, wriggling bloom.

A red thing sailed through the air—a bird, I thought—and settled in a low nipa palm. I saw it was a tree frog at the very moment that a green-and-gold, whip-like strand swung down from the tree-tops and caught it in its narrow jaws.

"*Chalaka, ular Tuan!*" (Very wicked snake, sir), shrieked one of the little Dyaks.

From the olive green of a rattan thicket stepped out a woman, naked to the waist save for wreaths of jasmine, the two wings of a coal-black butterfly pasted on her forehead. Her hands flew to the slender neck of the snake, twisted quickly, and the head with its red prey was left between her fingers.

Dillingame stood stock still, staring at her. Laughing up into his face she flung away the serpent's head, stripped off a jasmine garland, cast it about his neck—and was gone.

Both Trevor and I knew enough of the mythology of Borneo to realize at once that we had looked upon a *hantus*, one of the spirits that lived on the top of Mount Kina Balu and reappeared as the female priests of the country.

That was all very well; but such things can't be—they *aren't*, whether we had seen one or not; and the woman had been very beautiful.

"Yon's a bonnie lassie who favored you with the flowers," I remarked as Dillingame began to strip off the garland.

"That I leave to your Scotch susceptibility, Andy Freeman," he answered. "But did you get a good look at those butterfly wings she wore on her forehead? an eight-inch spread to each of them, and black as jet! A new species, a new genus—perhaps even a new family of Lepidoptera. What do you suppose a specimen of that butterfly would bring in Paris or London? A fortune!"

As we talked we picked our way carefully along the back trail toward where a boat waited us on the water of a sluggish stream that ran to the coast. We did not expect to see the Dyaks again; they had fled in wild panic, but we did hope my Chinaman would still be there and would have enough knowledge of the channel to pilot us to the sea without becoming lost in some backwater. Besides it was getting dark, and a night in a Borneo swamp jungle is enough to make the most seasoned explorer shudder.

The boat and Chinaman were waiting, as we had hoped; but as for getting out in the darkness Lee San positively refused to attempt to guide us. Outside of the great probability of being lost he claimed that our craft would arouse countless devils of the night by disturbing the waters.

Strange cuss, that Chinaman! He had been with me for over two years in Sumatra, Sarawak and Dutch Borneo, and never before had pretexted superstition for disobeying an order. He was unusually intelligent, too, and I had given him a large share of my confidence, and gained much interesting inside native information in return. The Chinese are the traders of all that part of the world and know more about the Dyaks, Muruts and other tribes of Borneo than any white man.

We poled the boat out into midstream and dropped anchor, preparing to make the best of a bad situation. Fortunately there was enough dry wood on board to build a good fire on the dirt hearth so we could boil some water and attend to our countless leech wounds with ammonia. Of course the light lured hordes of bloodthirsty mosquitoes, but we stoked up on quinine (Lee preferred an opium pill), and smoked hard beneath our 'skeeter nets.

Sleep was quite impossible. Even if the heat had not put it out of the question the jungle noises would have kept a dead man awake. From a hundred yards away, as regular as the striking of a clock, a bull alligator roared out his love call; *samburs*, the big blue deer of Borneo, belled in the distance; great fruit-bats cut the air with a mighty swish of their leathery wings; and underneath all came the chorus of tragedy from the forest floor, the agonized squeak of a small rodent as it was borne off in triumphant jaws, the snarl of some cat animal that had missed its spring, the ceaseless snuffle of the rooting wild hogs.

"Whisky," I said to Trevor—it's bad stuff in the tropics, but the night was unendurable—and he passed the bottle.

"Quinine," he demanded, and we both took ten more grains.

In the bow of the boat Lee San's teeth began to chatter.

"What matter, boy?" I sang out.

"No got mo' opium," he answered.

"Come here and drink some whisky," I ordered.

"No can," he objected—the Chinee doesn't often touch it, doesn't seem to like it—but he came down to the stern, just the same, and swallowed the big slug I had ready for him.

Silence for a long time, silence that every one of us wanted to break, but each was waiting for the other. Finally Dillingame's thoughts broke out in a torrent of words.

"Andy, how could that woman be real?—and yet you *know* she was! How did she dare grab that deadly tree-snake, that can turn and bite in its own skin, and twist off its head? And why did she do it? Where did those butterfly wings come from? You know no such insect exists in lower Borneo; you know we, or others, would have found it were it here. And if it came from the mountain country, what were its wings doing in a lowland nipa swamp on a girl's forehead? I'd give all we have collected on this trip for one specimen of that black butterfly!"

"So would I," I replied, ignoring his questions, since they were unanswerable. "But I think you are on the right track. It must be a mountain species or we would have found it. Pass the whisky."

We all had another drink. Lee did not demur this time.

"I move, unless we are down with fever in the morning, that we go back, look for the woman, and, if we find her, try to buy those wings—or at least try to discover where they came from. A black butterfly, Andy—"

"Lee savvy black butte'fly," chanted the Chinaman. "You want know, you no tell!"

"Sure not," I agreed, and the Englishman grunted an affirmation.

I sha'n't try to repeat Lee's exact words, for the story filled the entire night; but this is the meat of what he told us: Long before the English took over North Borneo, before Sir James Brooke came to Sarawak, even before the Dutch had seized their portion of the island, the Chinese looked upon all Borneo as their own private treasure-house. From it they exported rattan, teak, precious and semiprecious stones, and gold—quantities of gold—the source of which no Aryan nation has ever been able to discover in after years. And the power, head, moving spirit of the Chinese in those days (as now) was centered in a tong—a tong so mighty that it had no name.

The emblem of this tong was a portion of a butterfly's wing, never a whole wing, but just a fragment; and this fragment was always round and always black. Even now the gold that came out of British Borneo passed only through the hands of the Chinese—the Chinese that belonged to the old, old tong that had the round piece of black butterfly's wing for emblem.

The whisky passed back and forth many times during this recital, a strange one, indeed, to come from an Oriental (they never speak of their secret societies), and Dillingame, leaning toward me, whispered:

"He's lying!"

" 'Tis the whisky," I whispered back.

"No lie, no whisky!" vehemently protested Lee San—his ears must have been devilish sharp. "China boy *pantong* (taboo)—mus' die in twenty day for makee tong mad. No sendum body back to ancestors, jus' scatterum ashes. So no care what come. Tellum tluth!"

"Where do the butterfly emblems come from?" asked Trevor.

"My no savvy. Way off, mebbeso. Seeum only in Blunei town."

A terrible rumpus broke out on the bank of the stream. Gruntings, howls, roars, screams. The light was just breaking, and we could dimly discern vague shapes dancing frantically about. Suddenly the sun shot over the horizon, and we saw a great python lurch into the water, leaving a crowd of big, frantically chattering, long-tailed red monkeys on the bank.

It rained dismally as we retraced our trail of the day before. The *mise en scène* was unchanged. The head of the tree-snake, already half decomposed, lay on the ground, but the red tree-frog was gone from between its jaws. The prickly thicket of rattan whence the *hantus* had come, and into which she had disappeared, was as impenetrable as a solid wall of barbed wire.

I lifted up my voice and called. A deer snorted near by, a flight of hornbills sawed the air with their heavy wings. No other sound broke the silence save the drip, drip, drip of the wet jungle.

Morose, and hardly believing what we had seen the day before, heavy from the night's vigil, we retraced our steps to the boat and dropped down stream.

II

GOMEZ, THE PORTUGUESE

Brunei is built on piles and roofed with thatch, and has all of twenty thousand inhabitants. A globe-trotter once called it "the Venice of the East." There is an English quarter, of course, with a resident who lives in card indexes and considers it low to have anything to do with the natives.

We were not of his favorites. He told us on one occasion that our lack of dignity in mingling with the aborigines lowered the caste of every white man in the East. Dillingame promptly chucked him into the water, and he retaliated by revoking all our collecting permits. It was a nuisance to have to forge others; and then, too, we spelled his name wrong on them. The first real government white man we met in the interior laughed at us, corrected the spelling and passed us on.

It was humiliating, though.

In the Chinese quarter, where all the business was done, they knew us well and, as near as you can gage the feelings of Orientals, liked us. We shipped all our stuff through them, and they cashed our drafts and even lent us money.

Among the Kadyans and Dyaks, in the native quarter, we were rather lords. Dillingame crumpled up all their wrestlers and astounded them with feats of strength. I told them stories in the different vernaculars.

There is absolutely no use in a white man trying to match wits with a yellow one if he wants to find out anything. I went straight to the biggest Chinaman of the lot, told him where and how we had seen the black butterfly wings, and asked him point-blank whence they came. He answered me with apparent frankness that he did not believe such an insect existed to-day, though it may have in the past. Goods (he did not specify what kind) that came from the mountainous country around Kina Balu often were accompanied by a fetish in the form of a black butterfly's wing, but that wing was made of paper—and to prove it he gave me one.

This, to my mind, closed the incident.

Dillingame, who had been getting together supplies and packing our stuff for shipment, greeted me cheerfully.

"Hello, dead man," he called, "I have just been informed that any one who sees a *hantus* is due to cash in the same quarter of the moon. One of our Dyaks ran amuck when the three got back, and was hacked to pieces by his friends; the other two have been gloriously full of arrack ever since. What did you find out about the butterfly?"

I repeated what the Chinaman had told me, taking out the paper wing and laying it before him.

I think I said before that Englishmen are obstinate. Trevor Dillingame absolutely refused to believe a word of it. He pointed out that the paper wing showed an arrangement of veins and a frenulum quite different from that of any known species of butterfly, and stoutly maintained that such a species did exist and the paper counterpart was just a typical oriental plot to throw us off. I tried to show him that there could be no reason why the Chinese would object to us sashaying all over the island after butterflies, since we always attended strictly to our own business; but he wasn't to be budged from his plot theory.

"I'm going to have that butterfly if I rake over all the mountains in Borneo," he announced, "and I'll bet you I will have it within a year—or rather that we will; because you are naturally coming along."

"You mean you *may* get it, not *will* get it," I corrected.

"I mean I *shall* get it," he insisted. And yet people say the Scotch don't understand the difference between shall and will!

Brunei is civilized in that it has one white hell where foregather the captains and mates of the trading ships, globe-trotters and men who have made their pile in the black country; in short, every white who has the price. You pay your money and you get what you order. To a certain point you do as you please. Beyond that point a Malay kriss ends the evening's entertainment and the tide takes you out to sea without further trouble to your friends.

A Chinaman ran the place, of course. He called it the House of Unending Happiness and Delight. White men called it the Devil's Club.

Neither Dillingame nor I is a saint. We like our bit of fun as well as any one. 'Twas to the Devil's Club we planned to go that evening; first to talk to one of Rothschild's orchid-collecting agents, then to enjoy whatever happened along. We didn't anticipate much from the agent. He was an evil little rat of a Portuguese who bought low and, in all probability, turned in his purchases at four times what they cost him. Also he was a careful lad with the money, never known to buy a drink could he help it.

Lee San had laid out clean white clothes for us in our nipa-thatched hut, and seemed to be lingering about with something on his mind that he lacked the courage to unload. I gave him a lead, and, explaining that only nineteen days more of existence remained to him according to the sentence of the tong, he asked for his pay covering that full period.

It's fatal to pay a Chinaman in advance, so I naturally refused and suggested, as a substitute, that he come with us into the interior, thus running away from his fate.

The idea of escape had evidently never occurred to him—tongs even do their thinking for most Chinamen—and I left him to turn it over in his mind.

The entertainment furnished at the Devil's Club is rather unique. Everything starts with a good dinner, of course, and plenty of drinks. Then comes gambling on a rickety roulette wheel, fan tan, or just drinking. If none of these amusements appeal to you, you watch the show.

Dyak girls, teeth blackened and ornamented with tiny gold stars let into the enamel, ears bored around the edges with holes from which dangle rings and pendants, wave their long hands, the nails dyed to a crimson, and dance to the slow beat of the native instruments. Chinese girls, always smiling out of their slanting eyes, play toy-like banjos and never cease to wonder at European kisses. Perhaps there are wrestlers, or two sailors from rival ships put on the gloves and fight to a knockout while men from every corner of the earth stand around the ring.

These various kinds of evenings, with their next mornings' headaches, were old stories to us; but this evening furnished something surprisingly new. Gomez, the Portuguese, not only invited us to dinner, but actually paid for it. Then instead of going into the back room to smoke opium, he sat out with us watching the dancing and talking about everything under the sun. 'Twas plain that the lad wanted something from us, but to save me I couldn't figure out what it was.

Finally, as the crowd thinned out, dropping into or being carried to their boats, he suggested that he accompany us to our own hut, as he had something of importance to take up with us.

Lee San set out the whisky, and as soon as he withdrew, the Portuguese hauled a little package out of his inside pocket.

"Can't handle this alone," he remarked as he began to remove the paper wrapping, "but there should be enough in it for all three of us," and he laid a porcupine quill and a small round object, about the size of a half crown, on the table.

I picked up the transparent quill. The weight together with the color of the contents told me at once that it was filled with gold. Dillingame gave a low whistle over the round article and handed it to me. It was a kind of a locket, holding beneath its thin film of glass a round section cut from the wing of a black butterfly.

"Where did you get these, Gomez?" I demanded.

"What does it matter as long as I know where the gold came from, and we can get more?"

"It matters so much that if you want us in with you you'll have to tell us."

"I found them on the body of a Murut who had been bitten by a snake," he answered sulkily. "He told me, before he died, that he brought gold down from the mountains each year, that there was plenty of it there."

We hadn't the slightest desire to take Gomez with us, but other considerations besides our personal feelings had to enter into the calculations. It costs like blazes to get to the back country; mainly because one has to carry all the rice for the porters, as well as everything else, and the Portuguese seemed to have lots of cash. Of course we realized the source of at least part of this wealth. Not for a moment did we believe that a single quill of gold was all that had been taken from the dead Murut, any more than we swallowed the story about the poor devil having been bitten by a snake. Gomez had no reputation save that of an excellent shot and being death quick with a knife. We insisted on one reservation, namely, that all entomological specimens should be our exclusive property—oddly enough it was the black butterfly that appealed to Dillingame's and my imagination even more than the prospect of gold; and then went into the project, each taking a third.

III

THE RED FROGS

It's devilish hard getting into the interior, but it can be done by determined men who know the jungle. A couple of weeks later found us under the shadow of Kina Balu, its fourteen thousand foot summit towering high above us. The natives had not bothered us at all; indeed, we hadn't seen much of them, and our supplies were holding out splendidly.

All that day we toiled up the old course of the Tarnpassuk, collecting as we went, and we certainly did well. Everywhere were beautiful green papilos—the Saranak Beauty—and frail, black-spotted *Hestidae*, while lovely, velvety black-and-green male *brookcani* went swiftly dancing by. Also the orchids were something unbelievable; *grammatophyllums*, golden-brown spotted flowers on stout two-yard-long spikes; a greenish-yellow flowered *dendrobium*; clusters of tubular *aesclynanthus* like scarlet jewels beneath the great, leathery, aroid leaves; and the enormous moth orchids with their hundred snowy flowers.

Already we could easily see a profit on the trip from what we gathered if we continued to do even half as well, and were all as happy as crickets.

That evening we camped on the bank of a half-dry stream, and while

Dillingame and I figured out how much further we could cut down the loads for the mountain climb, Gomez washed the sands for gold—his favorite amusement, no matter where we stopped. Lee San (he had accepted my suggestion to accompany us in defiance of his tong) was cooking our supper, and the jungle was as quiet as a high-limit poker game.

Night came quickly, as it does in the East; a black curtain rolled suddenly across the sky through which the stars would later punch their twinkling holes, and we gathered around the fire. From far off in the jungle came the bellowing of wild cattle; a flying lemur cut a straight line against the horizon across the curves of the circling bats.

Then, in the Ida'an tongue, and with the sudden crash of an orchestra, came a roaring chorus:

> *"Little red flames that flit so fast*
> *Through wet, green leaves till day is past—*
> *Little red flames in the tree-tops shine*
> *Where the hungry, green-gold serpents twine—*

> *"One and all, great and small,*
> *We carry you up the mountain tall,*
> *Down where the jungle's hot and dim,*
> *Under the world's far, farthest rim,*
> > *To HER, to HER,*
> > *Where red waters stir,*
> > *And the lilies float*
> > *O'er the gods demure."*

Weapons ready, we stepped out of the circle of the fire and stood in the shadowy edge of the jungle. The moon swept up over the tree-tops and down its silvery path filed a long procession. They were Ida'ans from the mountains, the taint of them on the breeze, and each of the fifty men was loaded down with a wicker basket whence came a volume of sound like the splashing of countless, tiny waterfalls.

Again crashed out the song:

> *"Little red flames that feel as cool*
> *To burning hands as the shaded pool—*
> *Little red flames through the jungle fling*
> *The breath of freshness while you sing—*

> *"One and all, great and small,*
> *Never cease your piping call,*
> *Down where the jungle's hot and dim,*
> *Under the world's far, farthest rim,*

While you go to HER,
Where red waters stir,
And the lilies float
O'er the gods demure."

"They are going to, not coming from, the mountains," whispered Gomez, "so they haven't any gold. Let's stay hidden."

"Want to know what is in those baskets. They'd see our fires anyway," spoke up Dillingame, and stepped out of the shadow toward the last of the passing men.

It was an idiotic thing to do—I don't believe in hunting trouble—but I followed him, of course. The entire column halted. It was probably the first white man they had ever seen; certainly the first wearing khaki, puttees and an immaculate helmet, and I called for the *orang-kaya* (head man).

A little wizened Chinaman was pushed forward, whom I proceeded to interrogate sternly on the purpose of the expedition just as though I were a government officer.

I got away with it, of course. They were returning from a religious pilgrimage into the lowlands after having washed away their sins in some sacred stream. I said I got away with it, but not with bells on. Indeed, the Chinaman seemed somewhat inclined to interrogate me as to our destination and purpose in that part of the country, a tendency that I promptly suppressed. I also gave him orders to camp well away from our party and not to permit his men to stray in our direction.

During this conversation the fresh sound as though of running water continued to come from the baskets the natives were carrying. Trevor stepped to the nearest one and threw up the lid. It was loosely packed full of green leaves, among which sang hundreds of little red tree-frogs.

Back in camp I cussed the Englishman proper for advertising our presence to the natives, and we speculated in regard to the red tree-frogs. I knew the Ida'ans considered rats a table delicacy, and the frogs might be in the same category. The strange part was that an expedition should penetrate into the lowlands to collect them—they aren't found far from the coast—and that the expedition should be the in charge of a Chinaman.

After all it did not concern us directly, and gradually, one by one, we dropped off beneath our mosquito nets. The jungle noises blurred from separate sounds into a droning whole, I was drowsily conscious of a pair of large, bright, yellow eyes—a slow loris, my brain lethargically telegraphed— and I slept.

I woke, with the first morning light, to the song of birds. The sun popped up over the horizon, and the chorus from the tree-tops increased to an ecstasy of harmony. In prompt contrast to all this joyousness came a wail of fright from behind our tents, followed by shouts of surprise and fear from the porters.

Jumping into my boots, clad only in pajamas, and an automatic in my hand, I rushed toward the sound of the disturbance. Lee San, surrounded by the Muruts, was raising his voice to high heaven and holding his upper garment away from his body—and from that upper garment fluttered a long piece of paper covered with Chinese characters and signed with a crudely inked butterfly's wing.

"Stop that fool howling," I yelled angrily, tearing away the fluttering strip that was evidently the cause of his anguish, "and tell me what this all means!"

"Lee San on'y t'lee day to live! That tong sign. No can get 'way!" and he roared anew.

Grabbing him by the throat I choked the noise back into his gullet.

"Where did that laundry ticket come from?" I demanded.

"Pin to clo' when Lee sleep," he moaned.

I was sorry for the little Chinaman, of course; but couldn't let him go on bawling forever. It might stampede my dozen porters any minute. Naturally I surmised that one of them was in tong employ, and had pinned Lee's sentence to him while he slept. I should have liked mightily to ferret out the guilty one, but didn't dare take the risk of the bunch quitting on me.

Pretending a wrath I was far from feeling and threatening Lee San with immediate death, I sent the men to cooking their breakfasts and returned to my tent.

We made good progress the next two days, passing several Ida'an villages, the inhabitants of which viewed us with an uninterested stolidity that made me rather nervous, and on the second night camped just below the timber line on Kina Balu.

Gomez claimed that the gold came from the western slope, but it was easier to go over the mountain than to try to thread the impenetrable jungle around its base.

We took many rare butterflies, those days, including the *Euthalia magnolia*, known only from Kina Balu; another beautiful local species with a six-inch spread of velvety blackness and a broad band of pea-green across the wings; and then, just before pitching camp, I netted an entirely new species, soft gray with little squares, as though of isinglass, set in its wings, and both veination and frenulum identical with the round fragment of black wing that Gomez had shown us in the little locket.

We had out this talisman and compared the two—after which I slipped the little round thing into my pocket—and it was easy to see that we had a species for an entirely new genus; two species, if we secured the black butterfly. In spite of the rain that began to fall that night Dillingame and

I were jubilant, though we could not get Gomez to enthuse—he was after more valuable game.

The altitude and cold rid us of mosquitoes and we turned in early in anticipation of a full night's sleep. Scarcely had I closed my eyes, however, when I was wide awake again and sitting up. Clear as a bell, through the darkness, came the whistle of a kite—and kites don't fly at night—to be answered from the other side of the camp by the drawling snarl of a tiger cat, followed by the unmistakable sound of a girl's laugh.

On my feet in a flash, I stole out beyond the light of the fire and lay down in the shadow, straining my eyes through the blackness. It had stopped raining and not even an insect disturbed the perfect stillness. Suddenly, to my right, a single voice broke into song—a voice so filled with contemptuous raillery that it made me grit my teeth in anger.

> "Orang puteh, * *what dost seek*
> *Toward Kina Balu's lofty peak*
> *Where the dead troop free*
> *'Neath Lugundi's tree*
> *In the sacred lake*
> *Whence the spirits flee? . . ."*

I raised up on my left elbow and fired twice in the direction of the sound. A mocking laugh came back to me, then silence, save for the waking of the camp. Quieting the men, I told Dillingame and Gomez not to bother me with questions that night, and, turning in, slept till daylight.

IV

KRATAS THE PRIESTESS

It was deadly cold in the morning, and Lee's teeth chattered as he built our fire. I sent him over to wake the porters, only to have him back in a second, hands trembling and face ashy white.

"Come," was all he could say. "Come!"

My twelve porters lay their feet to the dead embers and on each man's left cheek was stamped in black a butterfly's wing.

There was no holding them, of course, when they awoke and saw the mysterious emblem that had been placed on their very flesh while they slept. Furthermore the marks would not wash off—left an indelible stain that seemed to penetrate the pores of the skin. I threatened, bribed, cajoled, all in vain; and, accepting half what I had promised them for wages, my Muruts

---

* White man.

fled down the mountain.

Nice fix we were in! All our goods and chattels dumped high on the side of Kina Balu, and no one to carry them! There was only one thing to do; go back to the nearest Ida'an village and hire local carriers—and a villainous lot they proved to be when I finally managed to get ten of them at an exorbitant wage in cloth. Then it was noon before we got started again, and our nerves were on razor edge.

Lee San helped the situation by bewailing the fact that it was the last day on earth allotted to him by the tong, and stuck so close to me that I finally lost my temper and made him lead the column.

Over the shoulder of Kina Balu the character of the country changed. Jungle grew high up a mountain slope so precipitous that we never should have been able to descend had it not been for a narrow, winding trail. There were no butterflies, the giant trees meeting overhead and shutting out the light, but never have I seen such a riot of orchids, or so many gorgeously colored birds.

My porters balked twice, demanding their wages as having gone far enough; and the second time I was forced to make good my threatenings by knocking one flat. It was beastly hot and sticky, the ground fairly crawled with leeches, and the trail was cut every hundred yards by wild pig runs, along which we three times went astray.

I joined Lee San and we kept well ahead of the column, progressing downward as best we could and clearing the way. The Chinaman had recovered his spirits with the realization that sundown would see the end of his fears—tong law considers a man dead, no matter whether he is or not, after the date for his execution has passed, and no longer molests him.

The trail became narrower and narrower. I stepped over a liana that stretched across about a foot from the ground, and turned as Lee brought down his jungle knife to sever it. There was a swish overhead and a weighted spear plunged down, entering the man's neck, piercing the length of his body through the thigh, its point going into the ground and holding him upright.

Lee San opened his mouth in an attempt to speak, his head flopped forward, and death claimed him before the words could come.

Dazed for the moment, I stood motionless, my eyes on the spear shaft along which slowly dribbled round drops of blood. A ray of sunlight filtered down from above and played over the dead man. Sable black, two feet from wing tip to wing tip, an enormous butterfly darted straight for the crimsoning spear, poising against it with swiftly fanning wings.

I grabbed with my bare hand, but it dodged, circling about my wrist, to relight on the dead man's bleeding shoulder. Again I lunged for it.

There was a rustle behind me and an arm went round my neck, flinging me flat on the trail. Beautiful as an orchid in her wreaths of fragrant jasmine, a woman caught the sable butterfly between her fingers, jumped lightly over my body, and disappeared into the jungle, while through the great tree trunks came a low, mocking laugh.

Half stunned, I stumbled to my feet, tearing away a great leech that had fastened to my lip, and the first of the porters came down the trail.

It was a trap for wild hogs that Lee San had blundered into, and I sprang two more of them, with a long pole cut for the purpose, within the next mile.

We buried the Chinaman beside the trail—tropical jungles do not admit of delay in such matters—and I certainly did feel cast down over the loss of such a good cook. Also he had been with me over two years and I was very well used to him.

I did not mention the sable butterfly or the woman before Gomez, saving up the incident for Dillingame alone. Perhaps this was because of the rather humiliating role I had played. Anyway I did not say anything about it at the time to either of them.

Two miles farther down the trail the jungle opened up into a park of enormous teak trees with no underbrush on the forest floor; just a meadow of short grass with a stream running through the middle, on the bank of which we camped. Being completely devoid of confidence in the porters, I had all the waterproof-canvas-wrapped loads piled in a great heap, pitched the two tents, one on each side, and then the three of us matched to see who should cook. Gomez got stuck, much to his disgust; so he had to forego his customary evening's amusement of washing for gold.

Hardly had we finished our supper, and a rotten bad meal it was, when the Ida'ans appeared and asked pay for the full week I had hired them with an additional bonus to the one I had manhandled. As is always the case with natives, and inspired by arrack, they started at the top of the pitch beginning with demands and working down until they reached the pleading stage.

Their argument was based on the fact that we had not climbed Kina Balu as they expected, and as had other white men, but had led them down into the Land of Blood where the spirits stole men's souls. Their spokesman assured me that no one who went into this jungle ever came back, that it was the abode of spirits and devils who, like gigantic leeches, fed on the blood of the living.

In the end I drove them to their fire, and we turned in, agreeing to keep watch, turn by turn, during the night. Dillingame took the first period and I went promptly to sleep.

Then I began to dream: the *hantus* woman stepped out of a rattan thicket and laughed up into Trevor's face. He gathered her into his arms and bent his lips to hers, when a flock of great, black butterflies swept down, forming a cloud about them. I beat at them with my hands to reach the voice calling, "Andy! Andy!"

Some one was shaking me by the shoulder. "Wake up, for God's sake, Andy, wake up!" whispered Dillingame. "This place is enchanted!"

Outside the tent it was light as day. A luminous mass came hurtling through the air and fell at my feet. I kicked it and a great fungus broke into a thousand pieces, each glowing with fox fire. More fungi were hurled into the open space about the camp. I rolled down several of the canvas-covered loads and we crouched behind them. The Ida'ans, near the dead fire, were standing huddled in a close group whence came no sound.

The shower of luminous fungi ceased. There was a pop like a champagne cork leaving the bottle and one of the porters staggered and fell on his face, a tiny arrow quivering in his forehead.

"Lie down, you fools!" I yelled, and pumped a bullet into the edge of the jungle. A shower of tiny arrows rattled among the packs. I picked up one and showed its point, smeared with some pitchy poison, to Trevor.

"No use staying here to be shot down like trapped hogs," he snapped. "Let's make a break for cover. Where is Gomez?"

"Here," came the little man's voice from my elbow. "We're in a tight fix, is it not?"

"We're in all of that," I answered. "Draw their fire, and after the shower of arrows, grab a pack and get into the jungle near them. I'll toss one of those flares we brought for trading where they seem thickest and we'll try to get enough to give them a permanent scare."

One of the Ida'ans rose cautiously to his knees. Came the pop of a blow-gun and he went down screaming, his hands to his face. Trevor fired in the general direction whence the arrow came. A storm of the little darts rattled about us, and then we were all running, packs held before us, toward the edge of the jungle.

Safe in its shadow, I touched a match to the flare and flung it whence had come the last volley. There was a yell of fear, and we turned loose on a bunch of black outlined figures, long bamboo blow-guns in their hands. Some went down, but about twenty started across the open.

"After them and get as many as you can," I shouted. "We've got to make this a lesson!"

Under the cover of the trees we ran, shooting as we went, until they crossed the stream and were lost in the blackness beyond.

Something stirred behind us, and Trevor jumped into the underbrush. There was a brief struggle and then he swore.

"Gimme a light," he demanded. "I've got something queer."

I struck a taper match and held it above my head. Dillingame had two slender wrists grasped in one of his big hands, and as the flame flared higher, my eyes followed his other hand to where it was twisted in a woman's hair— the woman of the nipa swamp, snake and red tree-frog, the woman who had snatched the sable butterfly from Lee San's bleeding shoulder!

Gomez switched on an electric torch and we all stood staring at her. Man, but she was beautiful! Short grass skirt, leather sandals bound half way up her legs, the upper part of her body bare save for wreaths of jasmine. Her skin was as white as the flowers of the great moth-orchid, her lips crimson as red blood, her eyes blazing violet, swimming with flecks of gold, and her hair beneath Trevor's hand was black and soft as silken thread.

Losh, but she was beautiful as she stared back at us, her little hands twisting helplessly in the Englishman's big one, her body tensed.

Then, before we could find words, her form relaxed, her eyes flew to Trevor's face and she laughed up at him. Not a wild, hysterical laugh, just a soft, amused little one with an undercurrent of contempt in it—the sound a woman makes over a child who has done some silly thing.

Out of the corner of my eye I saw Gomez cross himself and shift forward his automatic.

"Laugh, you vixen," said Dillingame, but his eyes were not unkind. "She jabbed a knife into me and fought like a wild cat," he flung us in an aside, then turning back to her, "Do you know I ought to kill you, shoot you down in your tracks?"

Of course the woman did not understand, and again she laughed up at him, her lips curving back over her white teeth, her violet golden eyes half shut.

"Santa Maria!" gasped Gomez. "Let me shoot her and then we'll burn her body in the fire. Don't you see she is a *hantus*, a witch? She will enchant us all and the leeches will suck our bodies dry. I am afraid—me!"

"Don't be a fool," I advised gruffly, stepping in front of him, for he was fingering his pistol nervously. "Bring your captive lassie to the tents, Trevor. I'm thinking we won't be troubled with those poisoned darts while she is with us. Gomez, go over and tell the porters to keep down on the ground. If there is one of those blow-gun men simply wounded, haul him in and we'll see what we can get out of him."

It had begun to drizzle. I threw wood on the fire and piled the packs in a barricade, the two tents for ends. Meanwhile Trevor tied the woman's wrists together, holding the end of the rope in his own hands; nor did she resist. Gomez came back driving a small figure before him and, as it came into the firelight, I nearly yelled.

It wasn't a man, it was a beast, a human ape! There was a *sarong* around its middle, but the rest of the body was naked and evenly covered with a generous growth of reddish hair, arms ending in tiny hands hung below its knees, and its head jerked from side to side with the lightning quickness of an animal while it whimpered over a wounded thigh where a bullet had barely creased the black skin.

The only human thing about it was its hair, which was elaborately dressed high on the head and through which were stuck several of the tiny poisoned arrows.

Suddenly it caught sight of the woman, and going down in a cringing heap, lay motionless, its face against the ground.

"Five dead," reported Gomez laconically, and took his seat as far as possible from the Englishman and his captive.

I addressed the girl in the Ida'an tongue.

"Why did you lead your slaves to kill us? Have we done you harm?"

"You come for gold as do all white men—our gold is pledged. About that I should not care, but you take the souls of the dead, the butterflies. Not even do you respect the souls of the sacred priests that sail on sable wings!"

"Who are you that talk of souls!"

"Kratas, priestess of the Land of Blood, who knows not death, who lives forever."

"Yon lassie is wrong in her head," I said to Dillingame in English. "Let's try and find out something from the beast-man," and I heaved him to his feet.

What came next happened quicker than words can tell it. Raising her hands to her lips the woman severed the cords that bound her wrists with one snap of her white teeth. Trevor caught her around the shoulders and, whirling, she bit deep into his hand.

"You'll pay for that, my girl," he snarled, gathered her into his arms, bent, and kissed her lips. One second she relaxed, clung to him, then twisted free, caught a tiny poisoned arrow from the crouching savage's hair, drew the point in a long scratch across his back, and leaped over the packs. Trevor sprang after her just in time to slap Gomez's automatic from his hand as he fired.

A taunting laugh floated back out of the darkness.

The beast-man died from the poisoned scratch, toward morning, with many twistings and writhings. With the first light our Ida'ans disappeared up the trail and we could not catch them. They left three dead behind, victims of the poisoned arrows, and we found six beast-men in the jungle and five in the open that had stopped our bullets.

It took some time to dig a pit large enough for all those bodies, and, after we had stamped down the dirt, we sat on the packs and looked at one another.

Gomez broke the silence. "Money I like it much, but if I am dead or crazy it does me no good. Let us go back as quickly as we can with what provisions our shoulders will carry."

"That's all very well for you," spoke up Dillingame; "you have a stake tucked away. Freeman and I have our all in this venture. I move we linger on and try to pick up something else. What do you say, Andy?"

"There is food for a long time," I answered judicially, "and we are more liable to be attacked on the back trail running away than if we stay boldly here. I'll not say it were best to go on, nor will I say it were best to stay, but—"

I broke off, and dived for my net. A gray butterfly of the new genus was floating just outside the barrier of packs. I caught it in midair. Then I chased another, and another till, with eleven perfect and four damaged specimens, I finally returned to the tents. Dillingame had the real luck, though. He brought in forty of them, all taken over a crimson orchid, and netted an immense Hestia besides.

As we removed our catch from the cyanide bottles and folded them, wings back to back, into envelopes before packing them away in our waterproof collecting boxes, we easily calculated with what we already had we'd break better than square on the expedition.

Gomez was not there when we returned, but he drifted in with his gold washing pan shortly afterward, and an I-have-eaten-the-canary expression on his face.

"You found it!" I guessed at once, and could see his under lip stiffen for a lie.

"I have found traces," he answered; "it may be here, though probably in very small quantities. Anyway, I'm brave enough to stay on a little while even if you gentlemen are not."

Dillingame's face went purple, but I spoke before he could explode.

"Sure, we'll stay on. After Trevor and I have done a little more collecting we'll all turn in and pan the stream, and if there is gold we'll find it. Meanwhile let's match to see who cooks to-day!" And there the matter rested.

V

THE TALISMAN

I'm a cautious man—being Scotch—and haven't been every place in the world, so I'll no say there are not collecting grounds equal to where we were, but under oath I'll swear these were the best I had ever seen.

We found no further new species of the larger butterflies, but the microlepidoptera would have kept a systematist busy classifying them for an entire year. The unnamed orchids were legion, and we took skins of two new pheasants, not to mention the Argus, Bullwer and Fireback ones; a rare yellow shrike, gorgeous red and yellow sunbirds, and a cream-white lemur. All day we were off in the jungle so interested in our own work that we paid little attention to Gomez.

Gradually it dawned on us that the Portuguese had developed a virulent grouch, wasn't even civil. One morning when it was raining torrents, so it was impossible to leave the tents, matters came to a head. It all began by Dillingame detailing our harvest of butterflies, orchids and birds for his benefit, a cataloguing which he terminated by the statement that the next day we would join in the gold search.

Gomez promptly answered with a snarl that he'd attend to his business and it would be healthier for us to keep to ours, that we needn't be afraid he wouldn't make a fair division even though we had lured him on the trip under false pretenses and made him do all the work. And then, without the slightest warning, he jerked out his gun and barely missed the Englishman. Furious, Dillingame made a jump for him. The Portuguese fired again just as I hauled the tent pole down so the two of them were wrapped in its folds. From the outside I gathered the little man into a neat bundle of canvas, Trevor crawled from beneath, and we undid Gomez with a gun pressed to his stomach, and then tied him hand and foot.

There was no doubt he had intended to kill both of us, and he expected no gentler fate at our hands, especially after we had searched him and found fully a pound of dust in a belt strapped around his waist. There was nothing of the hero about him, and he began to whine for his life, offering the bribe of showing us the exact place he had found the gold.

I'll not deny that the Anglo-Saxon is the greatest of all races, but being one has its disadvantages at times—we talk when we should act. To save a cartridge Gomez should have had a knife stuck into him, and a savage would have applied that practical solution to his problem. White men are civilized beyond logic, however.

I sat down by the trussed up, treacherous little rat and explained to him carefully that if he appeared at Brunei without us there would be no possibility of any explanation he might offer getting over, that he would have a mighty short time to enjoy his gold before some of our friends got him. Then we turned him loose.

Trevor kicked him once, and, according to the custom of fool Anglo-Saxons, after that we acted as though nothing had happened.

Our combined search for gold was without result. Gomez had taken his from a single pot-hole in the bottom of the creek—he showed us where. There were traces everywhere, but no place worth a second panning. The formation was unusual, the water flowing over a thin bed of sand beneath which was solid rock. The creek itself sprang from a swamp, half a mile up the mountainside, and for the two miles we followed it down, ran between high banks on which grew short grass and mighty teak or cocoanut trees exactly like the place where we were camped.

Since the immediate neighborhood had been thoroughly raked over both for specimens and gold, it seemed best to move on, and the banks of the stream offered open going without the trail danger of being ambushed or speared in a pig trap. We cached nearly everything, including the orchids and bird and animal skins, swinging them high in air by ropes over the limbs of the immense trees, and with our butterflies (which took up little bulk), ammunition, some food, and a small pack of trading stuff, the three of us started down stream.

For three miles the character of the country did not change, and then there was an abrupt dip. The stream broke into rapids and went brawling downwards, both grass and trees disappeared from the banks, their places being taken by immense boulders, stretches of bare rock and sandy beach. Half a mile from the stream, on either side, rose the barrier of the jungle, and it was dry, broiling hot.

We progressed along the sandy beach until well into the afternoon, stopping every now and then to pan the edges of the stream, but getting no color. Before us rose a cloud of vapor that I took at first for smoke and then decided must be mist above some great waterfall.

We camped early. Wood had to be brought from the jungle half a mile away, but the ground was smooth, so we dragged an entire dead tree to the beach without much difficulty. A cool—too cool—wind sprang up at dusk, driving away the mosquitoes, and by the time it was dark we were grateful indeed for the fire.

I suppose it may seem queer to any one who has not felt the spell of the unexplored wilderness that we should go on and on facing known as well as unknown dangers. Really it was the perfectly logical and natural thing, considering the men we were. Gomez was spurred on by his insatiable lust for gold. Dillingame and I told one another that we must have that sable butterfly; but the real reason lay in that lure, irresistible to men of our race, that Kipling so well expresses:

> Something yet beyond the ranges,
> Diddle, diddle, diddle come,
> Something calling, something calling,
> Diddle, diddle, diddle dum.

I don't remember the exact words.

After supper we sat around sleepily watching the bats swoop through the flames and listening to the roar of life from the jungle. A great beetle blundered into the fire and toppled over on the ground at our feet. Dillingame and I bent over it. There was a gasp from Gomez that made us look up.

Sitting on a boulder within the circle of the firelight was Kratas, the priestess; two sable butterfly wings on her forehead, neck and bosom wreathed with jasmine, and an oblong, palm-leaf-wrapped bundle between her small hands.

"Welcome, priestess of the *orang utan* (wild men)," I said, shifting my automatic well forward under my fingers. "Many times welcome, wearer of the sable wings."

She did not answer me, just sat motionless, her fearless eyes, filled with curiosity, resting on each of us in turn. Gomez shifted uneasily in his seat, Trevor picked up the floundering beetle and held it between his long, nervous fingers. I slipped the strap from the trading pack.

"Do you, then, love to play 'neath the shadow of death that ye linger here, or have ye eaten of the blue root of madness?" she asked.

"Death dare not approach us," I boasted.

She seemed to accept my words as a mere statement of fact.

"And yet there was blood beneath my teeth when they sank into his white flesh," she mused, looking at Dillingame. "My lips were salt with it till his lips ravaged the taste from mine." Then, abruptly changing her tone: "I bring ye the gift that all white men crave," and she tossed the compact palm-leaf bundle at my feet. "Let it be *salaamat jelan* (good-by). I bid ye go whence ye came before three suns."

"Tell her we haven't the slightest intention of leaving until we take some of those black butterflies," broke in Trevor obstinately.

"I'll tell her no such thing," was my answer, but the woman had gathered some of the meaning from the tone of his voice.

"Let him remain if he desires it more than life," she said softly, and, gliding to the Englishman, held her lips up to his.

"We, too, offer gifts," I hastened, to attract her attention, tumbling an alarm clock, gross of earrings and bolt of pink calico out of the pack, but she did not even glance at them. Drawing her lips back from his, she laughed up into Trevor's face, and was gone into the night.

"Andy, I don't believe any man but me has ever kissed that woman," he sighed.

"Holy smoke! And who cares if a hundred had?" I demanded.

Gomez tore open the palm leaf bundle and its contents slipped to the ground—twenty hollow porcupine quills filled with gold.

"Fools we were not to keep her once we had her," he cried, gathering up the hollow tubes, avariciously. "There are probably quantities where this came from. A cord around her temples or a little fire. . . . What's that for?" he howled, as Dillingame's boot caught him in the side.

In the morning we started down stream toward the vapor that hung in the sky. I listened for the crash of falling water as we approached, but there was no greater sound than the murmur of the stream. After a mile the stream itself switched abruptly to the left while the vapor cloud rose dead ahead and close to the edge of the jungle. We were walking on solid rock that dipped in a series of remarkably symmetrical spaced steps, so it was like going down a very shallow pyramid.

Nearer, the vapor took definite form, one thick jet going straight up into the air, and touching each side of this central column were two misty, broad, rounded clouds.

"Santa Maria!" gasped Gomez. "It looks like one of your cursed butterflies!"

And so it did, the body clearly defined and the wings spread out and moving in the slight breeze.

A hundred yards farther on we halted in amazement. At our feet a narrow flight of stone stairs ran down into a valley, or rather an enormous amphitheatre, since it was plainly the work of man. Half a mile broad and three-quarters of a mile long, it was sunk fifty feet deep in the solid rock. Immediately below us three springs boiled up about a central tank, springs of hot water, judging from the steam that rose and traced the butterfly in the sky. The floor was bare rock, save on the opposite side where a belt of jungle had gained a foot-hold and flourished luxuriantly.

At the end of the amphitheatre, to the left, a hundred-yard-broad flight of easy steps led us to the plain—and, gazing in that direction, I yanked both my companions flat on the ground.

Coming down the steps was a strange procession. In the lead four bearers carried a closed litter, or palanquin, on each side of which marched attendants with long palm fronds in their hands, by means of which they created an artificial breeze for its occupant. Six men brought up the rear, muskets over their shoulders. As they reached the springs immediately beneath us we saw that all were Chinamen.

The palanquin was placed on the ground, the curtain drawn, and out stepped a mandarin, the largest Chinaman I have ever looked upon. He must have been all of seven feet tall, very broad, and in addition, enormously fat. The attendants pitched a small tent in the steam of the springs and, after the tent flap had been respectfully held back for the big man to enter, the last of them joined his fellows in the shade thrown by the litter.

Plainly the mandarin was quite some dog and his preparation for a hot bath a real ceremony.

Before us, the giant amphitheatre for a stage, action developed like the plot on a moving picture screen. From the edge of the jungle directly across trotted out a large bull rhinoceros, its guardian angel, the Buphagus bird, flying ahead. The coolies were squatted behind the palanquin, their master still in his tent, and the great beast approached entirely unobserved.

Twenty yards from the springs the rhinoceros bird flew back to its charge with a harsh cry of warning. The animal stood stock still for a moment, sampling the breeze; then with a squeal of rage it charged ponderously down on the empty palanquin, behind which the attendant Chinamen were sheltered from the sun.

Howling with fear, the servants fled toward the broad stairway. The horn of the furious pachiderm became entangled in the curtains of the palanquin, and it paused long enough to smash the frame to bits. The tent flap swayed back, revealing a half-naked mandarin who, taking in the situation at a glance, plunged into the tank between the hot springs. Whirling on the tent the rhinoceros trampled it flat, then stretched its ugly head into the steam through which the figure of the immense Chinaman loomed dimly.

I rose to my feet, our heaviest rifle at my shoulder, drew a bead on the spine at the base of the short neck, and pulled trigger.

A rhinoceros hide may stop an ordinary bullet, but it's no proof against a steel-capped projectile, cut to mushroom, and fired from above. The great bulk heaved one step forward and then flattened out, stone dead, while the guardian bird circled around, still uttering its warning cry.

"Come on," I commanded, rising to my feet, "let's go down and get thanked. The Lord knows what we are in for next, the only way to find out is to keep going ahead."

We left our packs where they had dropped and climbed down the narrow stairway. The Chinaman had emerged from his forced plunge, his skin so pink as to indicate the water was slightly too hot for comfort, and, gathering up some garments from the wreck of the tent, stood ready to receive us, the dead rhinoceros at his feet.

As I approached, the size of the yellow man became more apparent. He must have weighed all of four hundred pounds, and there was something queer about his face, something horrible! To begin with a black butterfly was tattooed on his forehead, his eyebrows had been shaved, and each eye was circled by a broad ring of crimson. But it was his mouth that made the shivers run up and down my spine, for the lips had been cut away square in front, showing all his yellow, flat teeth, with two fangs, like those of a dog, at the ends. And he had no ears.

I spoke the Ida'an words of conventional greeting, and the monster mumbled their answer. Gomez and Dillingame came up behind us, and I heard the latter exclaim, "My word!" Then there was a silence painfully drawn out.

Finally the Chinaman spoke, the words hissing through his teeth.

"Whence came ye?"

I waved my hand in the general direction of the west. To tell the truth, his apparently complete absence of gratitude for preventing a rhinoceros from sharing his bath began to irritate me.

"Why come ye here?" he demanded arrogantly.

Thoroughly angry now, I jammed my hands in my pockets, determined not to answer, even by gestures. My left hand touched something round, and, feeling to see what it was, thin glass shaped beneath my fingers. A sudden inspiration came to me. I drew out the little locket I had taken from Gomez, which held the round section of black butterfly wing, and, shaking off the broken glass, stepped to the dead rhinoceros and held the talisman up to the haughty mandarin standing on the other side.

Have you, perhaps, seen one of those balloons the bairns buy at fairs slowly collapse, the skin loosening, wrinkling, finally sinking into crinkled folds? That is what happened to the man before me. His eyes started from his head, his head sank between his shoulders, and his whole, enormous body seemed to shrink, sinking in on itself. With a groan he spread his hands before his face, salaamed thrice, forehead to the ground, and his voice was a toneless whisper when he said:

"Make known thy bidding! I see the sign and am thy slave."

VI

IN THE TEMPLE

Even in after days I never fully understood why Lo Chan (thus did the mandarin name himself) caved in so utterly at the sight of the talisman. I found out before I had been long in the Land of Blood that this same small, round locket accompanied the Murut (never a Chinaman, always a Murut) who brought the tribute of gold dust to the tong head on the coast.

Why, in my hands it should have such potency, remains an unsolved problem. I evolved the theory, for want of a better, that the breaking of the glass above the section of black butterfly wing had some special meaning in the complicated and mysterious ritual of the tong.

Such speculations have small significance, however. What really mattered was the fact that the mandarin recognized in the talisman a power that he feared and dared not disobey, and was, in his own words, immediately my slave.

Lo Chan stepped over the dead rhinoceros and blew a blast on a silver whistle, carved in the semblance of a dragon. The coolies reappeared at the top of the broad stairway and came timidly down to the springs. Evidently assuming that we wished to be taken to his headquarters, the Chinaman ordered his servants to pick up our packs, and himself led the way out of the amphitheatre.

It was apparent that walking was not the mandarin's favorite form of exercise, and I was rather sorry for that enormous bulk of a man toiling ahead in the burning sun, sorry as it was possible to be for any one so utterly repulsive physically.

From the sunken amphitheatre we continued in the direction of the stream, which we struck after two miles of heavy going through sand, and then followed over a road, always sloping downward, paved with large blocks of stone, their surfaces worn as though by innumerable feet. Vegetation reappeared, gradually thickening into jungle, and in the distance rose what I took for a hill of bare rock.

The stream lost itself in wet, swampy ground on either side of the stone causeway; tree-tops met overhead, shutting out the light, and we came at last to a long house of bamboo, set upon piles. Ladders admitted us beneath the thatched roof, and we were in Lo Chan's home.

Certainly that fat mandarin did not believe in discomfort. The house was no different in construction from the usual Ida'an dwelling, a single sixty-foot room with no partitions or front; but its contents were of a richness none of us had ever dreamed of. Silk rugs of brilliant colors strewed the floors; on the walls were hung embroideries heavy with gold; there were inlaid taborets, vases as high as a man's head, and low couches heaped with pillows.

A corner, hidden behind silver-embossed screens, held the complete paraphernalia of the opium smoker, and a great gold-and-red curtain, whence came feminine rustlings and whisperings, barred off one end of the long room.

Behind this curtain Lo Chan retired with a last profound salaam, and we were left alone.

Dillingame began to laugh. They are feckless people, the English; I could see no joke.

"For a cautious Scotchman as you claim to be," he announced, it seems to me you are taking big chances. That piece of butterfly's wing is a frail excuse for bossing a mandarin."

"You're a fool," stuttered Gomez, "a reckless fool to run us into this. Do you suppose for one minute that you can trust that mandarin? Do you know what the mutilation of his face means? He has been guilty of the vilest crime a Chinaman can commit; he's a parricide! Had he been a coolie he would have been burned to death. His rank saved him, but not from mutilation that all his race might know and scorn him, and he has plainly been banished to this corner of the world. Give me back that piece of butterfly wing before you get us into more trouble. It's mine, anyway!"

I think I have already said that I am a Scotchman, and therefore firm—not obstinate, firm; and once I have set myself to follow a certain course I am not to be turned aside. Besides, the Portuguese showed an awful cheek in trying to run matters, considering his general reputation and what we especially knew of him. I promptly told him to mind his own business, that I had brought him to the very source of the gold, and that I'd keep the talisman.

Dillingame backed me up, of course, and together we quickly silenced the vicious little runt.

With sundown came a meal the like of which we had not tasted for many a month. Lo Chan did not reappear, and we slept that night through in absolute comfort.

In the morning there was a council. Gomez urged a direct demand for gold and a quick departure. Trevor had no suggestion to make except that we do something at once. I proposed to let matters develop along their own lines, trying to pump our host without arousing his suspicions that we really hadn't the slightest idea what we were doing.

We called the mandarin in and I asked him for a report on his stewardship. Of course I had no idea what I meant, but it seemed a safe question. He answered that the coolies had been unable to wash out the usual quantity of gold, the workings were not half as rich as formerly, but that the temple tribute came in regularly every full of the moon.

Not much information in all this. The only thing I could think of was to take a look at the temple, and I ordered him to lead the way.

The wet jungle was cut by numerous stone causeways, between which, I soon decided, had once been rice fields, now grown up save for occasional patches of paddy, to great trees. Everywhere were indications of a once flourishing city, stone roads, ruined houses also often of stone, and the worn surface of the rock on which we walked.

Finally the jungle opened, revealing what I had taken for an elevation of naked rock, and we halted in amazement. Built of blocks of stone, the size of which made it seem impossible they could have been moved by human hands, rose an immense, pagoda-like structure of three great stories, the topmost crowned with a single enormous block of glittering stone.

Strange beasts were carved on the overhanging balconies, and plaques of metal hung down in clusters, tinkling musically in the slight breeze. A small pond, surrounded by a rampart of stone, its edges overgrown with white lilies, spread out in front of the temple, and the water in its centre, bubbling up ceaselessly, was red as blood.

In every cranny where the tropic vegetation could find a foothold it flourished, but not even the great rending power of its growth had been able to move the enormous blocks, and bring to the ground that astonishing edifice. And there was a queer air of emptiness about it, as though it had just been deserted by a multitude that might swarm back at any moment.

Into dim coolness we entered through a lofty square portico. There was absolute silence save for two sounds: the hushed clink of the swaying metallic plaques and a muffled murmur as though of running water. The ground floor was a great, bare room of solid rock, with an aperture in the ceiling opening up all the way to the sky through the successive floors, and down which came a thin shaft of light. A strong ladder led up to this aperture, and towards it I pushed the mandarin. But he drew back with an exclamation of horror.

"It is not permitted!"

"Mount," I ordered, and he preceded me, obedient, though trembling.

The next story was full of vague rustlings from a floor knee deep in green foliage. Something moved at my feet, and I bent down. Seven inches long and black as jet, a thick caterpillar was eating ravenously into a camphor tree leaf.

Dillingame picked it up between his long fingers and together we examined it. Never have I looked on anything more repulsive than that twisting, worm-like creature. Unlike any caterpillar I had ever seen, it was furnished with heavy, piercing jaws—it was a flesh-eating, predacious thing that could have bitten through a finger.

"Pretty, isn't it?" commented Trevor, snapping it back disgustedly among the leaves.

At the end of the room were piled great wicker baskets whence came the sound as though of running water. We knew what those baskets held, of course; the red tree-frogs from the coast. To make sure I threw back a lid. A crimson cloud floated about me as the little piping things sailed out, to fall among the leaves on the floor.

Then happened something horrible. Like lightning, black caterpillars fastened their ugly jaws to the tree frogs, paralyzing them so that in a moment all were silent and still. It was plain that these joyous, crimson travelers were tit-bits indeed to the black larvæ—undoubtedly brought from the coast for this purpose.

Rather shaken, I shepherded Lo Chan before us down the ladder and we hurried out into the warm sunshine. The blood-red pond with its border of snow-white water lilies heaved and bubbled as some great body swam across it barely under the water so as to leave a swirling wake. Half running, half hopping along the causeways, bent figures sped before us. One of them swarmed up the trunk of a tree with all the agility of a monkey. Nearer, we saw that they were those same beast-men whom Kratas, the priestess, had brought down on us in the jungle.

"Let's go back to the house," urged Dillingame, "and kind of orient ourselves before we see any more horrors."

I motioned to Lo Chan to lead the way, and we retraced our steps. The Chinaman kept glancing back at me, and I knew instinctively that something was wrong—I had blundered in some detail, and he suspected I was not really what he had first taken me for.

Gomez broke out again as soon as we were alone.

"What's the use of all this waiting?" he demanded. "Why not ask the mandarin for all the gold he has and get out of here? I'm afraid—me! There is magic all around us, black magic. . . . Those frightful worms!"

"Shut up and let me think," I answered crossly. "We have got to make up our minds to some definite plan of action—though I'm hanged if I know what!"

"The first thing to do is to go back and get some of those caterpillars," broke in Trevor. "I'll wager they are the larvæ from which the black butterflies develop, even if predacious butterfly larvæ had never been heard of before. Also I'll wager we run into Kratas before long."

The Portuguese shivered.

"I'm not going back to that place of evil," he announced decidedly, "especially if there is any chance of meeting the witch."

"Besides, we must look into that red pond and find out what that big thing swimming under water was," continued Dillingame, paying no attention to the interruption.

"Let's have a pow-wow with the Chinee first of all," I suggested, and clapped my hands to summon him.

Lo Chan emerged from behind the red-and-gold curtain, and salaamed. It may have been imagination, but I seemed to detect that there was not quite the same degree of reverence he had shown in the past.

"I desire to look into the matter of the gold," I announced, making my statement as indefinite as possible.

"This afternoon we will go to the diggings," and he salaamed anew.

"What's he saying?" demanded Dillingame, and I translated.

"We're going back to the temple this afternoon," the Englishman insisted obstinately. "Put off the other trip till tomorrow."

"Why not let me go with him," eagerly suggested Gomez, "while you two attend to other matters?"

For a moment I hesitated. The Portuguese was not to be trusted, and I did not know what he might hatch out against us. On the other hand, since he could speak no Ida'an or Chinese, how could he plot with the mandarin? Ashamed of my fears, I gave my consent and advised Lo Chan that only Gomez would accompany him. Again he bowed and withdrew.

Then, since the sun was at its height and it was insufferably hot, we stretched ourselves on the cool *kajang* matting for a noontime siesta.

VII

KRATAS ASSERTS HERSELF

We were not destined to visit the temple that afternoon, the next day, or the day after; nor did Gomez get to the gold diggings. After an hour's uneasy doze we woke fairly gasping for breath. The heat lay over the world like a heavy blanket, there was not a breath of air, and it was rapidly growing darker. Came a moaning in the tree-tops, gradually rising to a roar.

Coolies clamped heavy shutters over the open front of the house and then scurried for shelter.

The roar increased to thunder, a breath of cool wind slipped in through the loosely woven walls, and then came the rain, a solid sheet of water crashing onto the ground as though hurled from above.

The coolies brought lights and, unable to make ourselves heard in the awful tumult, we settled down to wait for the end of the storm. Gomez began cooking opium pills and was soon lost in oblivion. Trevor found some rice-paper and I tried to teach him more of the Ida'an dialect (he had picked up quite a bit by himself), spelling out the words phonetically.

It rained without ceasing the next day and the next; then at sundown the storm came to an end as quickly as it had begun. The shutters were removed from the front of the house, Gomez emerged from his opium trance, and Trevor and I could hear each other speak. All ground between the stone causeways was under water and every curved leaf was a miniature fountain of silvery spray.

For half an hour we stretched our legs outside and then returned for the rest that had been impossible during the roar of the rain. The sun sank, the birds became silent, and my companions' deep breathing soon told me that they had found sleep.

From the jungle, clear and pure as a silver thread, floated a voice:

> *"Gone is the wind, the rain is past,*
> *The moonlit night is here at last.*
> *I wait, all longing, wait for thee,*
> *Come fast, my love, come fast to me.*
>
> *My skin is pale as the jasmine flower,*
> *(Oh, haste you love, 'tis the sacred hour!)*
> *My breath is sweet as the areca bloom,*
> *Where its purple cups in the darkness loom!"*

Trevor snorted in his sleep and I stirred him with my elbow. "Wake up," I whispered. "You are being serenaded. You or that other handsome laddie, the mandarin."

> *"As the* epidendrum *holds the* anguska *tree,*
> *Musk-scented, my arms shall twine 'round thee;*
> *As the teak is held by the clinging vine,*
> *Thus shall thy lips be held to mine!"*

"It's Kratas," exclaimed Dillingame, sitting up, "and she isn't serenading that fat Chinaman, either! What did that last verse mean?"

> *"Leave this place as quick as you can,*
> *I much prefer the fat Chinaman,*
> *Or I'll have to jab a poison dart*
> *Straight through the middle of your heart."*

I translated obligingly—this love affair seemed to me to be verging on the serious.

"You're a liar," he answered promptly, and stepped out into the darkness.

"Come back, you fool," I called after him. "You'll get a knife stuck into you!" But he had disappeared.

Groaning at the stark idiocy of it—Trevor had never shown himself a ladies' man before—I followed down the ladder. Somewhere in the blackness the girl laughed. My foot went off the causeway and I plumped down into the water.

Crawling out again, and cussing beneath by breath, I listened. There was no sound. Disgusted, I climbed back, shed my wet clothes and rolled up in a blanket. Again came the girl's laugh from out of the night. The ladder creaked beneath Trevor's weight and he scratched a match. Around his neck was a jasmine wreath and he held a small palm-leaf package in his hand.

"Did she kiss you?" I asked disagreeably.

"None of your business, but I couldn't get close enough to her," he growled. "She just chucked the flowers around my neck, gave me this bundle and vanished. I couldn't think of the Ida'an for 'come back,' either."

In the tropics the morning after a storm is always beautiful. The coolness still lingers, and everything is fresh green and has generally grown about a yard. We woke full of energy; even Gomez seemed to feel no ill effects from his opium debauch, and decided to carry out our original programme of visiting the temple while the Portuguese accompanied the Chinaman to the gold diggings.

I was just about to clap my hands to summon Lo Chan when he lurched from behind the red-and-gold curtain. Evidently opium had also been his solace for the last two days, and the effects had not worn off. At any rate, he omitted the customary salaam and began a rather heated harangue.

According to the laws of the tong (so he said) certain privileges were due him, and I had given no intimation that I intended to grant them. For example, even if I had been sent to take his place, I should have told him at once of the manner and time of his death—it was his right. Also where was the acknowledgment of the last tribute of gold sent to the coast, and his written sentence from the tong?

More and more inflamed by his own words and still swayed by the poppy drug, he began to wave his arms and a fleck of foam came to his lips.

How did he know we hadn't stolen the black butterfly talisman? That we weren't impostors? What kept him from calling in his coolies and having us strung up by the thumbs?

This sort of talk couldn't go on, of course. The drugged man was lashing himself into a fury. I gave Dillingame a signal (he always did the fighting for both of us), and the Chinaman went down to an uppercut nicely combined with a trip.

"Dog of a parricide," I thundered, "you shall die a death unnamed, nor shall I tell you when! Who are you, scum of the earth, to question the black butterfly's wing?" and I hauled it out of my pocket.

Lo Chan got slowly to his feet and salaamed, all the fight knocked out of him.

" 'Twas a madness," he mumbled. "I do my lord's bidding."

Gomez was scared to death of the big Chinaman after this outburst, but his desire to see the place whence the gold came prevailed over his fears, and away the two then went, surrounded by a guard of coolies.

The very first thing Trevor and I did when we were alone was to open the little package Kratas had given to the Englishman the night before. Inside the palm leaf wrapping was a soft piece of native cloth, which we unrolled, bringing to light two eight-inch-long cocoons, jet black, their fine silk-like threads woven as closely as a piece of linen. Dillingame split one open with the sharp blade of his knife and the pupa tumbled out on the floor.

Most pupæ of butterflies make you think of angels or souls in transition. This one looked exactly like the devil disguised in the form of a dragon.

"Let's see that butterfly talisman," he demanded, and I laid it before him while he was trying to dissect out the embryonic wing. The pupa was not sufficiently developed to show wing veination, though, so he carefully replaced it in its silk cocoon and did it up with the other.

"Keep the talisman," I suggested, "and try to ask Kratas about it in the intervals of your unholy love-making."

I overhauled our weapons carefully, as became a cautious man, before starting for the temple, and we set out heavily armed. There was water on either side of the causeways and the stones beneath our feet were steaming wet. A little wind fanned the tree-tops and the whole world seemed a waving silver-and-green symphony.

It was not a deserted world, however, as it had been on our previous expedition. The little beast-men were trotting along the stone roads, pressing timorously to the edges while we passed, and all converging in the same direction toward the temple. They lined the rampart around the pond, no longer blood red, in which we had seen the mysterious ripple, and the square in front of the portico was one solid mass of them. There must have been two thousand of the ape-like beings, and from this great multitude came not a sound.

"Go on or hang back?" I interrogated Trevor.

"On, since we started," he answered. "Besides, they haven't even their blow-guns."

The crowd opened silently before us as we strode toward the entrance of the temple. Inside it was as empty and dim as when we had first visited it, save that a single, thin shaft of sunlight came down through the aperture above.

"Come on," called Dillingame, and I followed him upward. The sides being shuttered in, it was quite dark at first as we stood on the top rounds of the ladder and tried to pierce the gloom. The bar of light broadened and I saw the edge of the sun overhead. Dimly we made out that the foliage had been removed from the floor; then, as the light increased, we saw the walls hung everywhere with the long, black cocoons, the resting stage into which the black caterpillars had entered.

The sun came square over the hole at the top of the temple, shining down so brightly into our eyes that we were blinded; and at the same moment came a murmur from outside as though each member of the crowd had drawn a single, simultaneous deep breath.

"Next act. Let's see it," I suggested, and we backed down the ladder, shielding our eyes from the glare.

Along a causeway to the left, where were turned all the beast-men's faces, slowly advanced a group of strangely clad figures. Closer, we made out that they were old, old women, wrinkled, bent, tottering, clothed in strips of many-colored cloths that fluttered from their scrawny shoulders. Immediately before the temple they halted and opened out. In their midst appeared one of the beast-men, and bound to his back was the wizened Chinaman we had met leading the Ida'ans whose baskets contained the little red tree-frogs.

Suddenly the old women broke into a cackling chorus:

> "Pale is the pool with the silver rim,
> Pale should be red,
> So we send you to him.
> When the sun has painted the world to gold
> Pale shall be red as it was of old.

"Pale is the pool with the silver rim,
Hungry is he,
So we send you to him.
When the sun has painted the world to gold
Pale shall be red as it was of old."

Straight through the crowd came Kratas till she stood among the shrinking old hags. Catching the beast-man, who bore the Chinaman bound to his back, by the hair, she led him to the edge of the lily-bordered pool.

"Pale is the pool with the silver rim,
Waiting is he,
So go to him.
When the sun has painted the world to gold
Pale shall be red as it was of old,"

chanted the cracked voices.

The captive shrieked and struggled on the beast-man's back. With a mighty heave Kratas sent them over the ramp into the water, their impetus carrying them beyond the border of white lilies.

The centre of the pool bubbled as they sank. Up they came, something tipped with pink, something on a thick black stem pushing them half out of the water and fastening to their bodies. For a moment the miserable bound creatures were above the surface; then were drawn slowly under, the water reddening about them.

It all happened so quickly, was done so mechanically, that it was doubly horrible.

"Pretty sweetheart you have," I managed to gasp, "feeding live men to some water monster!"

Dillingame's eyes were popping from his head, but at my words his jaw set.

"Criminals, probably," he stuttered. "She was only seeing justice done— and the pool had to be red."

"Look here," I cried out in horror, "are you defending that—that witch? Have you gone crazy?"

He did not answer; his eyes were on the girl, who was coming through the scattering crowd. I plucked at his sleeve.

"Let's go from here," I begged.

I so hated, and still do hate that woman—indeed I think she has made me hate all women—that my conscience forces me to do her justice in spite of the wrong she did me. As she stood before us smiling at Dillingame she was beautiful as a dream of Paradise, a goddess of the golden age, Eve, the first woman whence all after drew their charm. I forgot that she was a savage, forgot her beast-men had shot the harmless Ida'an porters, how she had wantonly slain one of them with the poisoned arrow; even forgot the tragedy of the two bound wretches cast to a horrible death in the water-lily-bordered pool. All I could see was that she was beautiful, desirable beyond the whole world.

Paying no attention to me, she halted not a hand's breadth from Trevor, and spoke:

"I am Kratas, priestess of the Land of Blood, who knows not death, who lives forever. The lives of all men—your life—are between my hands.

"I am Kratas, the priestess, guardian of the souls of the dead. Even the sable butterflies are beneath my law.

"I am Kratas, who guards the yellow dust all *orang putehs* desire.

"I am Kratas, all-powerful, and I come at set of sun to take you to my house as my slave and mate."

"I don't get that last part," complained Dillingame, turning to me.

"Merely a proposal that will not take 'no' for an answer," I explained. "Shall I tell the lassie you'll think it over?"

"She's very beautiful," he sighed, letting his eyes stray back to her.

"The Great Lord from Afar has already a wife whom he loves," I explained hastily in Ida'an, "and *orang putehs* have but one mate."

Her arms were around his shoulders now, and she gave me one venomous backward glance.

"Her blood shall fatten hungry leeches," she hissed, "and he will forget . . . forget. . . ." Her lips found his.

VIII

THE LITTLE SCHEME OF GOMEZ

Dillingame and I quarreled bitterly when we got back to Lo Chan's house. The man was mad, bewitched, and in his stark obstinacy defended himself. Hadn't he a perfect right to kiss a pretty girl if he wanted to? Hadn't she spared us when she might have wiped us out any minute? Wasn't it through her that we hoped to get the black butterfly—and gold?

There was no arguing with such a maniac, and I told him so.

Gomez came back alone, around four o'clock, and in a most disconsolate state of mind. It seems that the gold diggings were in the bottom of a dry creek and the rain had brought down an entire bluff on top of them. The little man was in despair, whined and bemoaned his fate that he had ever come with us, and declared himself ruined.

To tell the truth, we paid little attention to him. Dillingame was stretched out on one of the *kajang* mats looking exasperatingly comfortable and complacent. I was sulkily packing up our belongings at the other end of the house—and it was to me that Gomez gravitated.

The trouble with villains is that they are apt to consider the rest of the world as bad as they are, especially when it is a question of gold. Gomez proceeded to tell me that as soon as he had found out Lo Chan understood Portuguese he had pretended to conspire with him just to discover what he could. He suggested to the Chinaman that Dillingame and I be murdered, and, the piece of black butterfly wing in their possession, they grab all the gold in sight and flee to Dutch Borneo.

Lo Chan had been delighted with the murdering idea when he learned that the talisman was Gomez's property—"had to tell him that, you know"—explained the little man ingenuously—and confided to him that, without it, he would be unable to collect the tribute from the temple.

As to fleeing to Dutch Borneo, however, he did not want to because of the difficulty of transporting his three wives.

"My plan now is," the little villain continued, "to pretend to be hand-in-glove with Lo Chan, and through the black butterfly locket—which seems to be the key to the situation—hold him in check. I will let him have the talisman to collect the tribute, then we'll kill him and return to Brunei."

Fine arrangement, wasn't it? All Gomez wanted was to get the little round locket in his hands and then it would be good-by to us. I lost no time in passing all this up to Dillingame, and he lost no time in kicking the Portuguese down the ladder. It was not a diplomatic thing to do, but I couldn't altogether blame him.

We paid for it later, as you will see.

Gomez did not return, and Trevor and I picked up our quarrel where we had left off. I argued for an immediate return to Brunei; what we had already collected would show a good profit on the expedition. Further intercourse with the Portuguese was all but impossible. Dillingame obstinately stood out for waiting till we had secured a specimen of the black butterfly—in other words, until the pupæ had developed in the cocoons and emerged; and added that he might trade for some more gold from Kratas—that she seemed to like him.

Seemed to like him! I should say she did! That was my main anxiety, combined with the fact that *he* "seemed to like" *her*.

We argued, if facts being presented by me and denied by him can be called arguing, till nearly dark, and then we ceased speaking to each other.

Behind the gold-and-red curtain at the end of the house a woman screamed, and the sound was cut off short as though some one had grabbed her by the windpipe. Instinctively we jumped for our weapons. Without the slightest warning the curtain went down, unmasking a huddled crowd of coolies armed with muskets. I yanked Dillingame to the floor just as the house was filled with the roar and smoke of a volley.

"Got me through the shoulder," he gasped, and rolling over, turned loose with his automatic. I pumped my rifle into the thick of the smoke, and then they were upon us.

The first Chinese face that loomed up before me changed to a blur of blood beneath the butt of my gun. With my foot I slid a couch in front of us and then hauled the Englishman to his feet.

In a yellow avalanche the coolies piled over our frail barricade. Dillingame, swinging a heavy tabouret, cleared the floor in front of him. I literally blew men from the mouth of my pistol. The smoke rose. I tried to slip in new shells, but there was no time. Over the motionless or squirming bodies of their companions they were on us again. The Englishman went down, dragging a half a dozen of his assailants with him. Forced against the wall, my arms were twisted upward, a cord slipped around my wrists, binding me helpless, and my knees were pinioned.

The fight had been voiceless, just a silent striving punctuated by the firearms, till this moment, when there was a scream of deadly fear from a coolie. In the open front of the house stood Kratas, her face a mask of rage. From beneath the jasmine wreaths that clothed the upper part of her body she snatched a long knife, and, light as a butterfly, sprang over the couch to where Dillingame lay.

Three times the knife fell, dripping red after each stroke, and she rolled three dead Chinamen from the body of the unconscious Englishman. Then, with one sweep of her round arms she swung him to her shoulder, spat out some words I did not understand to the cowering coolies, and heedless of my frantic yell for help, went swiftly down the ladder with her limp burden.

The house was a shambles. There were no less than a dozen dead and wounded men lying about, not counting the three Kratas had knifed. Floor, walls, couches and overturned screens were splotched with blood, and the air was heavy with gunpowder and the smell of death.

Gently enough, though I cursed them, I was bound to a bamboo couch, a cushion even being slipped under my head to ease it. The gold-and-red curtain at the end of the room was replaced, dead and wounded were carried away, and I was left in the darkening twilight.

Not for long, however. I heard Gomez speaking in Portuguese at the bottom of the ladder.

"I hope they are both dead, damn 'em. You may take the talisman from Freeman and keep it, for all I care. Just give me a load of gold and I'll find my way down into Dutch Borneo somehow."

"True friend," purred Lo Chan, "it shall be as you desire," and they both came up the ladder.

"You turn me loose, Gomez," I roared, "or I'll beat you to death later."

"I'm going to kill you slowly as soon as I have taken away that talisman," he snarled, "you all-virtuous, heavy-handed fool!" and he began to investigate my pockets.

I shut my jaws tight and let them search me. Finally they stripped off most of my clothes and literally tore them to pieces.

"Where's that butterfly thing?" demanded the Portuguese furiously.

"I gave it to Dillingame," I answered in Portuguese so both would understand.

"Dillingame is dead, thanks to me," said Gomez, also in Portuguese. "We'll just take a look at his body, Lo Chan."

"He's not dead, as you will soon find out," I interrupted. "Kratas carried him off and the talisman is with him."

"Santa Maria! That witch again!" and the little man crossed himself.

His perturbation was nothing to the terror that convulsed the mandarin's frightfully mutilated face, making it doubly hideous.

"If Kratas gets that talisman, I shall die the unknown death," he wailed to me. "Go, go at once to Dillingame Tuan and beg it of him for me! I will send you from here unharmed, I swear it by the sacred black butterfly, and with all the gold three strong men can carry!"

"What of this swine?" I asked, jerking my head toward Gomez. "Speak Ida'an so he may not understand."

"He shall be burnt over slow fire for your imperial pleasure, or thrown into the silver-rimmed pond. You may see him torn with hot pincers or fed living to the fire ants of the jungle. . . ."

"Enough," I commanded, and translated carefully into English for the Portuguese's benefit.

"Get the sable butterfly's wing and we will kill the Chinaman," he whined back at me. "You wouldn't have a fellow Christian done to death by a yellow heathen, a companion murdered in cold blood!"

"Nothing I'd enjoy more," I answered heartily. "Now, turn me loose."

On my feet, freed of bonds, I restrained myself, though with difficulty, from kicking the little man—it had brought us bad luck before. Food appeared, and with it two iron-bound chests that were humbly laid at my feet. Raising the covers I saw they were filled to the brim with raw gold-dust.

Again, his eyes on the yellow metal, Gomez began his plea that I join him in murdering the mandarin and make away with this fortune. I had just finished translating this for Lo Chan's benefit, just so everything would be nice and friendly, when Kratas stepped in from the darkness.

Without as much as a glance at the other two men she beckoned to me, and I followed her down the ladder. Catching my hand she guided me through the shadows along the causeway. Before the red pond she stopped for a breath, and pointed.

"If he dies—*you go there*," she hissed.

Past the temple we went and into the black jungle. Ahead of us a voice began to sing, and the words were in English.

> *"They stuck him full of pins to remind him of his sins,*
> *And still he swilled down beer and rum together.*
> *So they cut off his fool head and filled him full of lead—*
> *And a boy's best friend is his mother."*

"He prays to his gods," sighed Kratas, dragging me on faster.

I sprang up the ladder into a torch-lit house and hurried to Trevor's side. He was tossing on a broad bamboo couch, a bandage of crushed leaves against his wounded shoulder, and his eyes hot and wild with fever. For a moment he recognized me.

"Hello, Andy, old top! Come to preserve the proprieties, hey? You're a hell of a chaperon. . . .

> *"Oh, Andy married Margaret,*
> *Oh, Andy married Jane;*
> *He gave his name to Mary,*
> *Eloped then with Elaine . . ."*

and he was in the clutch of the fever-devils again.

Thirty long anxious days Kratas and I nursed the Englishman, nursed him with the care and tenderness that a man receives only from his best friend and the woman who loves him.

Each morning Gomez appeared before the house and begged for the butterfly talisman, and each morning I cursed him and bade him be gone.

Kratas, beautiful as a dream of bliss and tender as a mother, never left the sick man's side save twice, and both times I heard the cackling chorus from the direction of the lily-bordered crimson pond.

> *"Pale is the pool with the silver rim,*
> *Waiting is he,*
> *So go to him.*
> *When the sun has painted the world to gold*
> *Pale shall be red as it was of old."*

The thirty-first day Dillingame's lever broke, and he knew me, reaching out his hand with a little unsteady smile. Kratas knelt beside him and her lips brushed his as lightly as a passing butterfly, Then he slept.

IX
THE PRICE OF MY FREEDOM

Once Trevor was on the road to recovery his progress was rapid. In a week he was up and could walk about, though still woefully thin and white. Kratas was unceasing in her devotion and had a retinue of old women—the priestesses clad in the strange garments of strips of colored cloths—waiting on and cooking for him.

Our traps had been brought from Lo Chan's house, and I found time to do quite a bit of collecting, always in the opposite direction from the temple. I couldn't even think of that place without a shudder.

Conditions would have been ideal for a man who loved the jungle and found happiness in solving its secrets had it not been for one thing: Kratas was jealous of every word I spoke to the Englishman. He had made marvelous progress in the Ida'an tongue, and they held long conversations together, part of which Dillingame retailed to me, throwing some light on our situation.

Kratas' story of her own life was extremely simple. She calmly asserted that she was the first woman that had been put on earth, and that she would live forever.

Years ago there were many brothers of Lo Chan in the wilderness, who had built the temple and washed out great stores of gold, which were buried beneath it. Then they had all died, and for a long time there were no Chinamen. Finally Lo Chan and his coolies appeared with the black butterfly talisman to vouch for them, and had started to wash for gold.

Each full of the moon, according to the age-long custom, he was given as many quills of the precious metal as he could hold in both hands; but while in past years the dust had been collected by the beast-men, it was now drawn from the horde beneath the temple. This tribute was then sent to the coast by a Murut, who carried the round piece of butterfly's wing as a passport.

The messenger had not returned from his last trip (Gomez could have told why), but he was expected any moment, since the time of tribute was but two days off.

In regard to the lily-bordered pool, the information was extremely sketchy. It was there dwelt the God of Blood, father of the black butterflies; but what exactly that god was Kratas did not make clear.

"You see, Andy," Trevor explained to me a dozen times, "what we consider cruel bloodthirstiness in the girl is nothing but custom—a heritage from her ancestors. Since she has always been supreme, the life of a miserable beast-man means nothing to her. Consider for a moment how frightful it must seem to her that we catch and kill butterflies—the souls of the dead!"

He was teaching her to speak English, too; though I hardly saw the necessity of beginning with "darling" for the first noun, and "love" for the verb.

Gomez had not appeared for several days, but that morning he came to the foot of our ladder with an entirely new plan. Lo Chan had promised to send out the gold by him if the Murut did not return—"as I know well he will not," he interjected—if he could secure the black butterfly talisman, which, once recovered, Lo Chan had sworn should never again leave his hands. Instead of going to Brunei we could simply steer for Dutch Borneo, the Portuguese explained, and make away with the gold. He begged and pleaded for the talisman, but I only cursed him while Trevor laughed and tantalized him by holding it up so he might see it.

A pretty pair they made, Gomez and Lo Chan, cold-blooded murderers, both of them, and each continually plotting to destroy the other. Lo Chan's plot, in this instance, was perfectly plain to us. Gomez and his gold would never leave the Land of Blood without the black butterfly wing talisman.

That evening the three of us were sitting in the dusk, and Trevor and I were engaged in a long argument regarding the possible food plants of some new species of butterflies. Twice Kratas had spoken to the Englishman and, absorbed in what we were discussing, he had not answered her.

Without the slightest warning she was on her feet with a snarl of rage.

"Offspring of the wild hog, killer of the souls of the dead," she shrieked at me, "you have dared too much! You would steal my Lord Tre-vor from me. Now you shall die. I have spoken who cannot unsay my words!"

Quick as a snake she sprang at me, and I caught the bare blade of her knife in my left hand so it cut deep into the fingers. Dillingame threw himself upon her and I wisely retreated down the ladder. For a long time he tried to soothe her, but quite in vain. She was absolutely determined on my death—she had spoken who could not unsay her words.

Finally he got her calmed and willing to let me live for the present—and he won this concession with kisses.

My hand bled freely, the blood even soaking through a bandage, and I lay down on my bamboo couch near Dillingame with the pleasant feeling that I should probably be murdered in my sleep beneath my mosquito net.

I woke at dawn to a pang of agony from my wounded hand. There was a great hole in the mosquito net and a soft black thing brushed my face.

Wide awake, as the pain increased, I looked down on a sable butterfly, a foot from wing tip to wing tip, poised above my head, its powerful jaws tearing and biting through the bloody bandage until they reached the live flesh beneath. Light as air it evaded me; then I smothered it beneath folds of the netting, giving it that pinch that every butterfly collector knows, and it went limp. Marveling at the wonder of those sloe-black wings and fierce jaws, the like of which had never before been known among butterflies, I pinned it, finally, in the cyanide poison box. And it was borne in on me that this winged creature was a cannibal thing that came to human blood.

At intervals all through the next day Gomez came to our house and, standing at the foot of the ladder, pleaded desperately for the talisman. The next day had been set for the payment of the tribute at the temple, and he was wild to bring the tong emblem to Lo Chan and receive the gold. There was no insult we spared him, we so hated the noxious, fawning, venomous little fiend; and again Dillingame taunted him with the sight of what he sought, then returned the talisman carefully to the little chamois bag he wore around his neck.

Kratas would not speak to me that day, only glared; and Trevor was plainly disturbed. At last she set out toward the temple and twice we heard the chorus that indicated another wretch had gone to the horrible unknown death in the blood-red pool. It was an anxious twelve hours, and in the evening Kratas simply sent me out of the house while she talked with Trevor.

It rained that night as it rains in the tropics, the drops coming down so that the world held no other sound but their crashing fall. I could not sleep, more than alarmed since I had not been able to get one single word alone with Trevor. Even now Kratas, awake and motionless, crouched in the dark between our bamboo beds.

Hours slipped by and suddenly I was conscious of a spot of shadow against the darkness moving silently nearer and nearer to where Dillingame slept. On my feet I touched the girl's bare shoulder and she sprang forward as though shot from a bow.

The rain drowned all sound of the struggle and I struck a light. Gomez, his hands twisted behind his back, lay on his face, a broad-bladed knife by his side. Dillingame moaned in his sleep and the girl hastily dragged her captive within the house.

"Lo Chan sent him to murder Trevor," I shouted to her above the noise of the tumult.

She nodded, her face black with fury, and quicker than a wildcat twisted the Portuguese onto his back, burying her knife in his throat. An imperative hand bade me be gone, and as the match flickered out I saw her slip an earthen vase beneath the couch to catch the blood dripping from the dead man's severed jugular. When morning came she was still crouched, wide-eyed and grim, by Dillingame's couch, and all our weapons had disappeared.

Not a word would Kratas let us exchange, her knife at my throat whenever I turned to the Englishman, and the sun was just rising when she led me down the ladder.

"This looks like the end of Andy Freeman," I shouted back to him.

"Kratas, if harm befalls my friend I, too, die," called Dillingame. "Here, take this, Andy," and he flung at my feet the chamois skin bag that held the black butterfly talisman.

The same painfully silent crowd of beast-men was before the temple. Inside the ladder to the second story had been removed and a thin shaft of sunlight came down through the hole in the ceiling, gilding a pile of porcupine quills, through whose transparent sides winked the glint of gold. The old hags with their garments of multi-colored strips of cloth filed in, the leader carrying a covered earthenware vase, which she laid at Kratas' feet. The ray of sunlight from above broadened and the priestesses began to sing:

> *"Fill up thy hands with the golden thing.*
> *Both hands cram-full of the dust we bring*
> *From the secret horde alone we know,*
> *Stored up by thy brothers long ago."*

Lo Chan, his horrible features dead white, entered the temple alone and stood before the pile of porcupine quills.

> *"The moon is full, thy people pay,*
> *Lord of the Pool, on this thy day,*
> *Tribute to those who long did raise*
> *This temple to thy glorious praise."*

Through the aperture above came a solid shaft of sunlight, filling it to the edges. A sable butterfly sped down this golden stream of light; another, and then another, until the air was black with their wings. Lo Chan bent down, burying his hands among the heavy quills; and at that very moment Kratas poured the contents of the earthenware vase over his back and shoulders, soaking him from head to foot with red blood. The Chinaman straightened up with a startled cry.

First one and then a swarm of black butterflies darted upon him till his body was all but concealed beneath their quivering wings. He staggered toward the door, beating with shrieks of anguish at the monstrous flying things that fastened to his wrists, his lips, his face. The hole above vomited out a solid column of the horrible insects, and Lo Chan was smothered beneath them.

The mass of quivering wings rose from the ground, hurtled out into the sunlight. Once the man broke free and rushed toward the lily-bordered pool. Then they were on him again, whirled him in their midst above the water.

The surface broke and a pink thing protruded out into the light, a gaping pink mouth a foot broad attached to seven feet of flat, inky body that now lay on the surface—a loathsome, gigantic leech.

The butterflies raised their victim ten feet in air, then slowly sank down with him toward the water. The pink head of the leech went blindly groping among the sable wings; then man and butterflies together disappeared beneath the bubbling water that soon had changed to a livid pink.

For a moment they reappeared, then sank once more, and only the ripples rocking the big white lilies disturbed the calm of the blood-red pool.

"Let us go back," I begged Kratas, a great nausea coming over me.

"*You* go back to the land whence you came," she answered, "living only through my infinite mercy."

Before the bamboo house were waiting five of the beast-men loaded with my baggage. I attempted to mount the ladder, but Kratas jerked me back, and herself ascended.

"It's no use, Andy," said Trevor from above. "You have to go or die. I can not move the girl, and our weapons are gone."

"But aren't you coming?" I whispered, a great horror over me.

"No," he said. "No. It is only by staying that I bought your life. The talisman will protect you on your way out."

Behind him Kratas leaned against his shoulder and snuggled her cheek to his.

"Come back—some time," he said, looking down at me. "I sha'n't be unhappy here, but—come back—some time."

The jasmine-clad girl slipped one beautiful, warm arm around his neck and raised her face to his. Their lips met. . . .

Red Tree-Frogs

*Fourteen years have elapsed since Andy Freeman,
Scotchman, naturalist and explorer, bade a reluctant farewell
to his old friend and comrade, Trevor Dillingame, and at
the command of the amazingly beautiful and savagely cruel
priestess, Kratas (backed by her army of beast-men), turned
his back upon the mysterious lost Chinese temple hidden
deep in the impenetrable and deadly jungles of Borneo, and
took up his sad and lonely trek back to civilization—the
civilization that Dillingame had bartered forever for the
love of his savage goddess. In this new story you will follow
the hardy Scotchman once more into the fetid jungle, where,
lured on by the call of the strange red tree-frog, he plunges
again into a maelstrom of amazing adventure.*

I

BACK TO BORNEO

ONCE THE JUNGLE HAS CAST ITS SPELL OVER YOU, once you have sweated to
torture in the wet, enervating gloom of its tropic growth, you are lost forever
to the world of cities with their dull skies and flat pavements over which
stream unceasingly the endless, white-faced throngs. Those who have the
jungle in their blood must go back to the jungle, or they will die.

I, Andrew Freeman, a Scotchman and therefore cautious with words, say it.

All may seem to be going well, and then, some night, you wake to the
patter of rain outside and it comes back to you: the sappy smell of growing
green things, the drip, drip, drip from every overburdened leaf, the great sigh
of wind through the trees as though the whole, hot, restless world moved in
its sleep. There is no resisting, no escaping. 'Tis the jungle calling back her
own, and 'tis best to go then, at once; for sooner or later you *must* heed that
call.

There was more than this to lure me from my comfortable berth in the
British Museum where, all day, I mounted butterflies and moths that other
men had gone to the ends of the earth to secure, and checks came each month
so that, frugal Scotchman that I am, my bank account soared to figures I
had never dreamed. In the unexplored wilds of Borneo had not Trevor
Dillingame's last words to me been: "Come back—some time. I sha'n't be
unhappy here but—come back—some time," when he had bought my life
by staying behind to mate with Kratas, priestess of the Land of Blood, and

beautiful beyond dreams?

The sable butterfly-wing talisman, emblem of an all-powerful Chinese tong, had brought me, with my five beast-men porters, safe through many perils to the coast. The beast-men had faded back into the jungle to return to that strange land where great stores of gold were hidden beneath a temple raised by age-long dead Chinamen, and victims were sacrificed by Kratas (who claimed she would live forever) to "the father of the sable butterflies," a gigantic leech that dwelt in a white-lily-bordered pool like to a fair mirror mounted in silver.

Then for ten years I wandered through the East: Sumatra, Sarawak, Java, New Guinea, collecting birds, beasts and insects. Always I meant to return to Mount Kina Balu and the Land of Blood; always something took me into some other remote corner of the earth, till at last, after a fearful bout with jungle fever, I found myself in London.

There it seemed natural to slip into my place in the British Museum, and for three years I was content.

The change came in the night. When I woke the wet, gray, London mist was streaming in and a voice from my dreams still echoed through my brain.

"Wake up, for God's sake, Andy, wake up!" it called. *"This place is enchanted!"*

With a rush it came back. Dillingame shaking my shoulder to rouse me against the attack of the beast-men; the velvet darkness lit, here and there, by luminous fungi; the rush for shelter into the jungle. My soul sickened, London roared at me through the open window as though with Homeric laughter. The four walls of my room changed to four walls of a tomb from which I must escape at any cost, escape and flee to where there was space, where there was silence, where the choked jungle hid many things that I must find!

Till morning I roamed the streets, my scant belongings packed for storage, my traveling kit ready; and then walked into my laboratory in the Museum. The grizzled old entomologist for whom I mounted specimens did not raise his head when I entered.

"Good morning, Mr. Freeman," he said. "There are some *hestiae* from Borneo." Then something made him look up. He gazed at me a moment before he spoke.

"Humph! I see. The best *préparateur* we ever had, too. When do you go, and where?"

"Now. British Borneo, Mount Kina Balu and thereabouts."

"Will you wait for a list of the Lepidoptera we should like to have from there?"

"No. Send it to me at Brunei, care of the Resident," I answered, and turned to go.

"Here's some mail for you."

I took the small, square package he handed me. It had been posted at Brunei, British Borneo, to an address in Sarawak; then followed me all over the world, five, six, seven months on the way. I tore it open hurriedly.

Inside was a scrap of paper and a shriveled, crimson thing, a red tree-frog, the kind that Kratas, the priestess, had brought in from the swampy coast-jungle as food for the predacious larvæ of the sable butterflies.

I turned over the slip of paper. There were only a few lines on it.

> The red tree-frogs seem to have been wiped out by some epidemic. The black butterfly caterpillars have nearly all died through want of this food. It looks as though this species of papilio might be extinct in another year.
>
> DILLINGAME.

'Twas the sheer, stark obstinacy of the Englishman! He could not write me if he wanted me, needed me, but had to send just such a message so I might read into it what I pleased.

Brunei, principal town of British Borneo, with its twenty thousand inhabitants, looked exactly as it had fourteen years before. I cruised between its nipa-thatched huts built on piles to that rendezvous of adventurers, sea captains, and derelicts, called by its Chinese proprietor the House of Unending Happiness and Delight, and by white men the Devil's Club. I wanted to pick up the gossip of the land, find out where to buy provisions, and especially to learn if anything had been heard from the back country concerning Trevor Dillingame.

At my first innocent question anent supplies I sensed something wrong. In one breath I was informed that porters were not to be had for love or money, that the back country was full of orchid and other collectors, that the natives were very unfriendly!

Of course this was all poppycock. Porters are always to be had, there aren't a dozen collectors in the world who would care to go into the interior of British Borneo, the natives are always as unfriendly as you will let them be, no more so. It was plain I wasn't wanted in the back country, that was the answer, and I could not definitely make up my mind why.

There was nothing to be gained by making known my intentions at this stage of the game, however, and I got into a boat and went to call on the British Resident.

I found him as I had left him, immersed in card indexes—he was fey on indexing everything—and he wasn't pleased to see me. Trevor Dillingame had chucked him into the water once when he commented on our friendliness with the natives as lowering the white caste throughout the East.

"Where is your friend, Mr. Dillingame?" he asked, after he had indexed my commission from the British Museum and regretfully written me out (and indexed) a collecting permit.

"Somewhere around Mount Kina Balu."

"So I have heard, so I have heard," and he continued pompously. "Several complaints have come to me, Mr. Freeman, in regard to him. Several complaints! It seems he has acquired a pernicious power over the natives in—er—the part of the country where he is. There are some Chinese interests—mining, I believe—in that—er—region, and through his influence the legitimate owners were not allowed to work them. They have complained to me. This will not do at all, Mr. Freeman, not at all! The Chinese are wealthy and influential members of this community. I have listed here several hundred who"—he turned to his beloved card indexes.

I fled.

There is an old, old Chinaman in Brunei, very rich, who used to cash our drafts and even lent us money on occasion. I went to him for information when we set out with the Portuguese, Gomez, after the sable butterflies, and he had tried to lead me away from my purpose by a typical Oriental trick. Nevertheless I knew he would not actively lie to me, though he would have no scruples, if it suited his interests, about deceiving me. Also I was sure that he was the real head of the tong, which bound together all his compatriots in the East.

He came last on my calling list.

When I left Brunei he had been an old, old man, but now he looked like Methuselah. His face was so wrinkled and lined it resembled the closely drawn contour map of very broken country, and his eyes were so sunken that they gleamed out with the glitter of water in the darkness of a deep well. Opium had taken its toll in the shaking of his hands, the nails of which were fully five inches long, a sign of very high caste indeed.

He was just the wee bit doddery, though, and I could plainly see that his sons did not like my request to talk with him alone. Without preamble I went straight to what I wanted to know—it's useless to try to match wits with an Oriental.

"Why am I not wanted in the back country; what is happening there?"

"Where is Dillingame, Fleeman?" he parried.

"He's the other side of Kina Balu, as you know."

"You no go to him," the old fellow warned. "He catchum tlubble. Gold come evely full moon, then gold no come."

"That's all right," I interrupted, "but it was Gomez murdered the Murut who used to bring out the gold, and also took the black butterfly talisman from him. I have it now," and I showed it. "You can't take gold out of that country without this talisman. Kratas, the priestess, won't let you."

"My savvy, my savvy," the wrinkled Chinaman answered, and then became silent, musing after the fashion of very old men. I did not speak. Finally he raised his head.

"You want catchum gold?"

"No."

He nodded as though in confirmation of his thoughts.

"Dillingame, he your flien'?"

"Yes."

He nodded again and then began to speak slowly, more to himself than to me.

"Gold! All wantee gold! Never catchum 'nough. My no care, but young man, who rule after my go back Chinaway to ancestors, he wantee catchum plenty gold. He send. Dillingame no let. Now many go catchum Dillingame, get allee gold."

"Then he's in danger?"

"Yes."

"Look here," I said, "I suppose you have passed one of those tong sentences on him. I know you are all-powerful in the tong, and I'll give you the choice of two things: either I'll go out with all the men I can muster and fight this expedition that has been sent in to kill Trevor Dillingame, or I'll give you plenty gold, all I've got, a thousand pounds, if you'll guarantee his safety."

The old man sighed.

"My no wantee. You love you' flien'?"

"I'll not say no," I answered with Scotch caution.

"My makee save him life, no can do mo'. Only big China climinal, worse kind climinal, killum fathah"—he shuddered—"sent in there because temple makee curse heap long time."

He rose and moved to the inevitable sandalwood chest that is found in the sanctuary of every rich Chinaman, and, returning with something between his fingers, laid it on my palm. It was a tiny red tree-frog, about the size of a sixpence, and fashioned from some very light metal. While I was examining it he drew brush and ink-pot to him and painted some characters on a fragment of rice paper, signing with the semblance of a butterfly.

"You take. That give Dillingame back life. Now you go, my wantee smoke."

You can't ever thank an Oriental. He doesn't understand it and detests it. I went.

By myself, I wrapped the red tree-frog and precious scrap of paper in oiled silk, cut a hole well up the heel of my boot, and plugged the little package inside.

There wasn't the slightest difficulty in securing porters, that lying proprietor of the Devil's Club notwithstanding, and I got hold of six good men, all of whom had been with me in the jungle before. It was mighty few for the distance I was going, but I armed them well, we could travel very fast, and I knew I should find food when I reached Dillingame at the ruined city of the temple in the Land of Blood.

How quickly the jungle takes one back, and, how you hate it and love it at the same time! It was a dry year; that is, it only rained once a day, and the jungle leeches were as bloodthirsty as tigers. There were (as Dillingame had written) desperately few of the little red tree-frogs whose piping sounds like the fresh dash of falling water. I saw only three, all of which I captured as food for the caterpillars of the sable butterflies, should those extraordinary insects yet survive in the Land of Blood.

There were plain traces of a very large expedition having preceded us, and we followed the trail they had broken. Toward nightfall I always went ahead of my men after we camped, as a precaution.

Day after day the spoor became fresher, and when we were beneath the shadow of Kina Balu, I knew that we were not two hours behind whoever had gone before. The men pitched camp near a trickle of water, and I walked on for my evening's reconnaissance.

It was unusually hot even for that region. The sun hung like a red copper penny just above the horizon, and it seemed as though it would never sink and let the cool breeze down from the mountain. The air was alive with the flutter of butterflies, and I pushed into the underbrush after a gorgeous yellow and green swallowtail. Reaching high I netted it in air. A dry twig snapped behind me. I swung half round, and a gun-butt crashed down on my head—then oblivion.

I came to slowly, lying on the ground. My ankles were tied together and my hands bound behind my back. I could feel a leech fasten to my middle finger-tip, another was hanging from my cheek. It was a big camp, fifty, seventy-five, possibly a hundred men. Five Chinamen were huddled over a fire, their backs to me.

For a long time I could not realize what had happened, and then I remembered—and boiled. The attack was gratuitous, unprecedented. Strangers in the jungle, especially if they are white, do not fall on a man and bind him hand and foot for no reason at all. It isn't done, it is not according to etiquette!

A Chinaman turned his face from the fire toward me, and the indignant words died on my lips. The face was mutilated horribly, the lips cut away square from the teeth, the ears gone, a black butterfly was tattooed on the forehead, crimson circles around the eyes. Thus do the Chinese mark those of too high rank to be put to death for the most horrible of Oriental crimes, patricide.

The marked man was speaking—and I understand Chinese.

"It must be the other one, and yet I hesitate to kill him. We might force him to guide us to the gold, use him as a decoy for the Englishman, Dillingame."

"Perhaps he can explain that night song," said another, and shivered.

"Let's get him out of the way," suggested a third voice. "They say he is without fear, and he might lead us into an ambush even at the cost of his own life."

"As you will," answered the patricide indifferently, and rising, a knife in his hand, stepped from the fire. I tried to pray, but all I could think of was the doxology. He failed to see me in the darkness, and called impatiently for a light.

Then he froze in his tracks.

From the jungle came a high, mocking laugh, twice repeated, and then words in the Ida'an tongue, not exactly sung, but chanted, and with studied insolence as though the singer had spat in one's face:

> "Tired his feet on the jungle trail,
>> When shall ye find a place to rest?
> Leeches' food when the night is pale,
>> Would ye sleep on the jungle's breast?
> Lianas twining in and out
> Weave naked bones around, about
> Of those who deemed the jungle free,
> Free to their steps, men such as ye!"

I glanced at the men near the fire, stricken motionless by fear, and a great thankfulness welled up in my heart. At least Dillingame was warned even if I had to die.

The voice from the darkness was that of his mate, Kratas, priestess of the Land of Blood, the most beautiful thing the jungle held.

II

DILLINGAME

The project for my immediate murder did not materialize. The patricide stepped quickly back to the fire, and the five Chinamen were soon deep in a discussion of the weird chant that had come from the jungle. I gathered that this was the fifth consecutive night they had been serenaded.

They were a hard-bitten lot who, according to their own standards, should have been immune from superstition. No one is, however; even I dislike meeting a black cat, especially when it is raining, and you can't force a Welshman to kiss a red-headed girl on a Friday.

They did not in words put down the chant to supernatural origin, and yet, in their inmost souls, they were not sure. Kratas' little sandaled feet left no track in the jungle, and things that leave no trail—

It was growing late. There were leeches at each of my finger-tips, so numb now that I could scarce feel them, and one had crept inside a legging, fastening to my calf.

"What shall we do with that out there?" asked a voice, the man nodding into the darkness in my direction.

"Leave him till morning. His fighting blood should be thinned by then, and we might get something out of him before he dies," answered the patricide.

Some one else laughed, and they all went to their tents.

A black and white lemur, its round, night-seeing eyes bright as lighthouses, sniffed me from head to foot, and, when I hissed at it, scuttled off into the darkness with piggish grunts of surprise. An ant crawled half into one nostril, and I suffered agonies before it decided to withdraw, walking across my chin down inside my shirt. More leeches came to me.

I debated in my mind whether it would not be easier to end things then and there by yelling until some one came out and killed me. Then I shut my lips firmly; they might only gag me, and no yellow man should ever have the satisfaction of knowing that I was afraid.

I counted fourteen thousand nine hundred sheep jumping over a high stile. A beetle worked into my ear, and the pain was so intense that I could feel myself weeping silently like a little, frightened lassie.

"Freeman, *tuan*," came a guarded whisper, and I whispered back, "Here!"

One of my Muruts crawled cautiously to me and cut my bonds. For a quarter of an hour I had to lie where I was, slowly working back the circulation into my numbed limbs. Then, my hand on his shoulder, we slipped into the jungle.

I found my other five men waiting, ready for the trail, and gloriously excited. These Murut laddies love a fight, and have been great head-hunters in the past. They were anxious to swoop down on the sleeping camp at once and account for as many enemies as possible before disappearing back into the jungle. Also they possessed such unqualified faith in my prowess that they hadn't the slightest fear as to the outcome of any such attack.

I was strongly tempted to make a raid on the tents of the five Chinamen who had so coolly discussed putting me out of the way, but discretion prevailed, though I *would* have liked to tie them up properly for a little while, and sprinkle a few leeches over them.

Noiselessly we circled the camp and hit the trail up Mount Kina Balu, traveling fast till noon. Then, just beyond a big Ida'an village, the inhabitants of which looked at us askance but offered no hindrance, we lay down among some rocks to the sleep of thoroughly exhausted men.

Night was coming on again when, warned by some sixth sense, I suddenly found myself wide awake. Peering over the rim of rock in the dusk I made but vague figures creeping in from all sides.

Silently I roused my men and put weapons in their hands. Then we waited. There was a long whistle and the Ida'ans came forward in a howling mob. I swung a pump-gun, loaded with small bird-shot, in a half circle, and my men turned loose, mostly at the stars. The crowd broke with howls of pain and surprise, scuttling for cover, and we were left alone save for a few figures writhing outside in the semi-darkness.

I wasn't especially alarmed. There was little likelihood of the attack being resumed, and I sincerely hoped none of our antagonists were actually dead. Aside from the fact I dislike killing savages, it would be unpleasant to be stalked by the deceased's relatives on our way back.

Still the situation was not without its elements of danger. I did not know the trail up the mountain well enough in the dark to risk an ambush, and, by morning, if they made a forced march, the Chinese might be upon us.

I couldn't quite account for the Ida'an attack either. We had done them no harm. It must have been the temptation for easy plunder offered by the small size of our party.

In spite of the improbability of a second attack I kept watch all night. Nothing happened, and as the sky was beginning to pale, I caught up a blanket, intending to snatch a few minutes' sleep. Some one stumbled in the darkness; there was the clink of metal falling upon rock, followed by the flash and staccato report of a rifle.

This time our first volley did not check them. The mechanism of my pump-gun suddenly jammed; the Muruts fired at the sky with much noise but little execution, and several Chinese coolies along with the Ida'ans were on top of us, the fight quickly resolving itself into a series of individual struggles in which we were outnumbered ten to one.

I caught a Chinaman, whom I had just shot through the head, to my breast, and, using him for a shield, emptied my automatic. A hatchet kept my opponents at bay for a moment, and then the sun popped over the horizon full in my eyes, blinding me. The hatchet was wrenched away and I was dragged down.

There was a whistling singing in the air—the flight of poisoned blow-gun darts—cries of terror, the grip on my throat relaxed. Triumphant as a soaring lark rose a voice:

"Quick is the death born upon wings,
Sings through the air, the upas juice stings.
Souls down to Hades. . . . Fly, all ye; fly!
Comes She, the priestess, who never may die.
Comes She, the priestess, blood turns to flame
With the hot poison sent in her name.
Scatter and flee, in deep jungle hide,
Food for the leeches, lest worse you betide!"

"Andy, Andy, are you all right?" roared Dillingame's voice.

"I'll tell you in a moment," I called back, heaving the dead coolie off my chest and feeling myself cautiously from head to foot. There seemed to be nothing worse than bruises, and I stood up. Trevor Dillingame was making his way towards me among the dead bodies, but if I hadn't heard his voice I never should have known him.

Most Anglo-Saxons the jungle curses, weakening them with fever, flaying them with malaria till they are the color of gold leaf; but once in a century this same jungle takes a white man to her breast, feeding him the vitality of the teeming earth, cooling his blood with wild fruits, giving him the strength of the great lianas that choke forest trees in their folds.

Trevor Dillingame was this man. His yellow hair, bleached nearly flax-white with the rain and sun, was down about his shoulders that seemed even broader and mightier in their brown nudity than I had remembered them; his arms, tapering to slim wrists, and long, sinewy hands, were like twisted cables; the muscles in his thighs bulged, and played back and forth beneath his skin like a sail bellying to the wind; his whole body was pink brown, and he was nude as Mercury save for a native *sarong* around his waist and buckskins bound half way up his calves.

But it was his face that caught and held you; the obstinate, full red mouth, the eyes blue as steel, the sweep of silky, flaxen beard that, somehow, did not seem to hide the skin beneath, and over all a look, a stamp, a something that breathed the full-throated, deep-bosomed life of the jungle, the free, wild sweep of wind through the tree-tops, the limitless vitality of every growing thing.

Perhaps the old, pagan wood gods looked that way, but I doubt me were they so bonny.

"You're a mad-looking thing," I managed to gasp. "Where is Kratas?"

"My *wife* is herding the beast-men back into the jungle," he answered, emphasizing the second word. "She does not like you; thinks you have come to take me away. How far behind are those damned Chinks?"

His wife, mind you! A wild woman of the wilderness whom we had watched offer sacrifices of the half-human beast-men to a heathen god in the form of a gigantic leech, beautiful as a dream of paradise, but none the less a savage of the jungle! It was just like Trevor Dillingame; he never did anything by halves. Mated with her that I might go alive from the Land of Blood, and now he took pains to impress upon me that she was to be respected, was to be thought of only as his wife! Losh, but it's a queer world!

And yet I was proud of the man for the very way he looked at it!

"The Chinks, possibly a hundred of them, are near if not here already," I said. "Mrs. Dillingame's mind may be at rest: the jungle has agreed with you too well for me to dream of luring you from it."

Every last one of my Muruts was dead. I gathered together all the fire-arms and ammunition, abandoning nearly everything else. Once over the shoulder of Kina Balu we plunged downward, soon meeting the jungle, and stopped, at last, in a grove of enormous teak trees through which ran a stream, the very place we had been attacked fourteen years before by the beast-men under the leadership of Kratas.

III

THE SON OF KRATAS

Of course I did not get the entire history of the fourteen years I had been separated from the Englishman all at once. At his best he was not a very communicative laddie; 'twas a part of his obstinacy. Gradually, however, I pieced the story together, and here it is:

After I had been banished from the Land of Blood, the fever again took hold of Dillingame. Kratas and her retinue of old, old women nursed him carefully and, in the intervals, fed all the miserable Chinese coolies, who had survived the fight with us, to the gigantic, sacred leech dwelling in the lily-bordered pond before the temple.

Then, of a sudden, the fever left him; he began to mend, and being a live man, reached out for something to occupy his mind.

The thorough exploration of the temple kept him busy for a time, and deep under its foundations he found the great store of gold washed out, by long-dead Chinamen, from the bed of a creek now buried beneath an avalanche.

It did not impress him especially, so he told me, this treasure hoarded up through the ages, grain by grain, only to lie hidden in the heart of the jungle. What really did interest him was the strange architecture of the part of the temple beneath the earth including an ingenious mechanism that I was to learn more about later.

Next he turned his attention to the repair of the stone causeways that threaded the water-soaked jungle, using for this purpose seven Muruts who were allowed to dwell in the Land of Blood. The beast-men were incapable of such labor; indeed they were of the very lowest intelligence, timid, fearful, moving about only during the night, and obeying Kratas alone, whom they feared and reverenced in equal parts.

Many months went by and finally Dillingame's soul sickened of the jungle. He made up his mind to escape from the Land of Blood, and took the Muruts into his confidence. Selecting a morning when Kratas was busy with one of the endless temple ceremonials, he slipped away with the Muruts, traveling till late, and then, when nearly to Kina Balu, lay down to rest.

"Hardly had I shut my eyes," so he told the tale, "when I heard her voice singing. It wasn't exactly singing, either, it was the plaint, infinitely tragic, of a lost soul. The words I can never forget.

> " 'Fold up your petals, every flower
>   And hide your sweetness, joy is dead.
> Sink to the earth, O birds; this hour
>   Marks the all end, and hang your head
> Red, gold-eyed frog, that piped to me
>   From out of the tree-top blithesome. '

"I thrust fuel on the fire so it blazed up, and called. Kratas stepped slowly from the darkness within the circle of light. She was nude to the waist, did not even wear the wreaths of jasmine that you will remember always served her as upper garment, and her beautiful, golden body was smeared with ashes.

" 'Have you come to hail me back to the Land of Blood?' I demanded.

" 'No,' she answered softly.

" 'Then why did you come?'

" 'To bid you farewell and wish you happiness.'

" 'Farewell, then,' I said, 'and happiness to you, O Priestess,' and I turned away.

"She continued to stand there, voiceless, proud, and at the same time pitiful.

" 'Is there anything further?' I snapped. Something inside me had begun to ache.

" 'Will my lord look upon me,' she whispered, 'look upon me who am Priestess of the Land of Blood and shall never die, and yet—and yet am a woman?'

"Hand in hand we went through the jungle, and never, since that time, have I been tempted to leave this land.

"I might state, in passing, that though Kratas was gentleness itself to me, every last one of the seven Muruts disappeared and I was wise enough to ask no questions. I noticed, however, that the gigantic leech floated on the surface of the lily-bordered pool for several days, always a sign that it had been well fed. There have been no further human sacrifices since that time, however; not even of beast-men, and the sacred leech has had to content itself with an occasional *sambur*.

"My son was born the month following, and Kratas believes she has transmitted to him her immortality. He has been old enough to hunt with me for several years. Beyond the Land of Blood there are no other tribes, only the half-human beast-men; but there is game a-plenty: rhinoceros, *sambur*, bear, elephants. Some day I shall capture and tame those elephants so as to use them for rebuilding my causeways."

In regard to the Chinese he told me that a year back, several of them had come into the land under the leadership of a mutilated patricide. They had demanded a tribute of quills of gold which Kratas refused to grant because they did not have the little black butterfly talisman (it being in my possession), and tried to run things generally with a high hand.

Finally Dillingame had a fight with two of them and killed both. The rest were driven out of the Land of Blood up Mount Kina Balu to the Ida'ans, whom they seemed to have corrupted into friendliness.

The present Chinese expedition was no secret. Kratas had been spying on it for days, and it did not especially bother him. He hadn't the slightest doubt that, if it could not be scared away and came to a question of fighting, the beast-men could completely destroy it with their poisoned blow-gun darts.

He was much more concerned over the possible extinction of the black butterflies, since he could not procure the necessary food for their caterpillars, the little, red tree-frogs from the coast, even at an offer of a quill of gold a piece; and he accepted gratefully the three specimens I had taken.

Next morning we followed the stream from the teak grove till we struck a stone causeway of very ancient origin, and, at night fall, reached the low, wet jungle of the Land of Blood. As we passed the temple with the lily-bordered pool in front of it, some one came through the dusk to greet us.

"My son," said Dillingame, and stood back, smiling at my amazement.

I could easily figure the boy was thirteen, or thereabouts, but he looked eighteen if thews and sinews are to be taken into account. Furthermore, he had the best from both his father and mother; the delicacy of her beauty, the strength of his manhood. Losh, but he was wonderful to look upon, a fawn of the Golden Age, so lithe, so lightly poised upon his well shaped feet that he seemed capable of floating up to the tree-tops on the slightest breeze.

"Have you taught him English?" I threw in an aside to Dillingame, while the boy's eyes, level with my own, smiled upon me.

"Why should I?" he answered. "He knows a few words, but that is all."

Come to think of it, why should he? What was the use of burdening this thing of the jungle, as much a part of the jungle as the birds that flitted through the trees, with a useless tongue?

I remembered Kratas as very beautiful, but the years had somewhat dimmed in my mind her absolute gloriousness, so that its actuality was really a shock. They were a group, that woman, man, and boy, to make a painter gasp and then throw down his brushes in despair at the sheer impossibility of reproducing it on canvas. I should have liked a photograph of them: framed in a wreath of immortels it would have been a handsome thing indeed.

It took some time to persuade the priestess that I had not come to take her Lord Tre-vor from her, but only to warn of the Chinese expedition and see my friend. Even then she looked on me with suspicion and dislike, and I privately made up my mind to cut my visit as short as possible.

You see I easily realized that my place in Trevor Dillingame's affections had been usurped; twice usurped, making me a bad third to his mate and their son. And it is not a pleasant thing for a man, especially a bachelor getting along in years, to find that a woman has more than taken his place in the heart of a friend.

That night we all slept in Kratas' dwelling, built upon piles above the wet ground; the very place where Gomez had tried to assassinate Trevor Dillingame, and where he met his well deserved end at the hands of the priestess.

Toward morning we were awakened by the chatter of beast-men, and stepping to the open front of the house, looked down upon a crowd of them carrying torches, a very calm Chinaman walking in their midst. Before us they halted and the Oriental spoke up to Kratas, his harangue, or rather demands, simple and to the point, namely that all the gold from beneath the temple, together with Dillingame's head, be brought to the teak grove between the next two suns.

The sheer audacity of his request rather took our breath away. Then Kratas, her knife bared, jumped lightly to the ground before we could hinder her. The Chinaman did not move a muscle save to draw one hand from his sleeve holding out to her the black butterfly talisman of which I had been robbed.

For a breath she hesitated, just long enough for Trevor to reach her side, and there they confronted him, beautiful woman, and her no less beautiful mate. Dillingame, silencing her with a gesture, spoke:

"Gold you shall not have. As for my head it is yours when you come and get it. Send no more messengers into the Land of Blood, others might not return. Now, get you back to your people, thanking your sainted ancestors that you are yet alive!"

Stepping forward he snatched the black butterfly talisman and flung it out into the darkness.

"We give you between two suns," the Chinaman said imperturbably to Kratas, ignoring the Englishman entirely, and strode away into the night.

"It seems to me that you are not taking this matter seriously enough," I told Dillingame. "They wouldn't go to the expense of sending in an expedition of a hundred men unless they meant business. Besides it certainly had a bad effect on the beast-men. I could see it, this bearding of you in your—er— this insulting of you before them. It would have been better to tie up that nervy individual for a time and give him a scare." (I remembered how the Chinamen had treated me.)

"Nonsense," answered Trevor obstinately, "we'll shivaree them all over the country to-morrow night. The beast-men don't like me, but they obey Kratas implicitly."

"Have it your own way," I grumbled, "but I misdoubt me no good will come of it."

Kratas and her son were up and away with the dawn. Almost at once the little, misshapen beast-men with their odd, hopping gait, began to arrive before the temple, and, chattering to one another, milled about nervously beneath Dillingame's and my scrutiny.

"Queer swine," he commented. "There must be a couple of thousand of them hidden back in the jungle. They hunt, eat, sleep, and attend the temple ceremonials, and that is their life."

All morning we watched them assembling, and toward noon Kratas walked into their midst with her retinue of old, old women, and leading a *sambur* buck.

"Listen, now, and you will hear something worth while," whispered Dillingame. "It's the rallying song."

There was a hushed silence and the voice of the priestess rose, silvery, clear:

> *"A jungle breeze sighed to the angusta tree,*
> *'Where are the orang-utans, where can they be?'*
> *The angusta tree bowed to the jungle breeze*
> *While answered in chorus all the trees:*
> > *'Under the palm leaves,*
> > > *Down by the pool,*
> > *Deep in the jungle,*
> > > *Where the winds blow cool,*
> > *Here, there, and everywhere,*
> > > *That's where they be!'*
> *Are the orang-utans ready?"* (crescendo)
> *"Ready are we!"*

chanted all the beast-men in a crashing chorus.

> " 'Their priestess is calling,' the jungle breeze spoke,
> 'Calling to save them from a tyrant's yoke.
> Will they obey her, still remain free?'
> Answered in chorus each nodding tree:
>   'Naught do they fear
>   The wide wilds hold,
> When she is near
>   Beat their hearts bold.
> Always unconquered
>   They will live free.'
> She will they follow?" (crescendo)
>   "Follow will we!"

came from every beast-man's throat.

The *sambur* was driven into the lily-bordered pool, the gigantic leech came to the surface, fastened to its prey, and sank beneath the waters that grew slowly red.

"We bring fear, O orang-utans, to those who dare the jungle," cried out Kratas. "Follow your priestess who lives forever, who cannot die," and the whole assemblage melted up the causeway out of sight.

"They plan to reach the teak-grove only at midnight since they have first to collect a lot of luminous fungi," Dillingame informed me. "Suppose we go on ahead and spy out the Chinese camp before it gets dark. I know a short-cut."

I won't soon forget that short-cut. It may have seemed a legitimate road of travel to him dressed, or, rather, undressed as he was; but it wasn't an easy matter, or cool, for me to go through the very heart of the jungle.

At any rate it brought us to the banks of the stream running through the teak-grove, and there we mounted, by pegs driven into the bark, to the top of a gigantic tree, whence we could look down upon the camp.

All was activity there. The packs had been arranged in a great circle to serve as a partial defense, and a barrier of saplings, with their leaves still on, was being rapidly raised as a screen for what was happening behind. Two poles, driven in the ground about thirty feet apart, were connected with a wire from which hung, in loose, crinkly folds, some kind of a paper contraption of brilliant colors.

We speculated at length, but in vain, as to what it could be before it was hidden behind a screen of leaves. Dillingame had at once recognized the patricide as the same Chinaman he had driven from the Land of Blood a year before, and this discovery evidently made him rather nervous.

"That Johnnie knows all about the country," he complained, "and got quite chummy with some of the beast-men, rather made a study of them."

Night came and the camp beneath us apparently went peacefully to sleep.

Here and there winked a tiny brazier, the kind Chinamen always carry along no matter where they go, but no camp fires were lit.

I ensconced myself comfortably in a crotch to wait. Trevor climbed down the tree to prospect around, as he called it. A little, spotted owl fluttered to a limb above me and glared down vindictively.

Then I went to sleep.

Dillingame woke me. The full moon flooded the camp with that deceptive radiance which looks like light, but really is very far from it.

"The beast-men are all posted and Kratas and my son are here," he whispered. "Better come to the ground and see the fun."

Not a leaf stirred when I reached the forest floor, the jungle might have been entirely empty of men for all I could see of them, and yet I knew that more than a thousand were concealed all about me. Finally I made out Kratas, the boy by her side. And just as I located them she began to sing:

> *"Tired feet on the jungle trail,*
> *When shall ye find a place to rest?*
> *Leeches' food when the night is pale,*
> *Would ye sleep on the jungle's breast?*
> *Watch the witch-fire softly glow,*
> *Heed my warning, quickly go*
> *Whence ye came; unless ye do,*
> *The jungle grass shall grow o'er you!"*

> *". . . unless ye do,*
> *The jungle grass shall grow o'er you!"*

thundered out the beast-men, and were as suddenly silent.

Not a sound came from the camp, and there was no perceptible movement behind the screen of leafy saplings.

"They don't seem to scare," I whispered to Dillingame.

"Huh!" was his only answer.

Kratas raised her hands, trumpetwise, to her lips, and gave the shrill whistle of a soaring kite. Instantly the air was full of the luminous fungi hurled toward the camp. And there was a prompt answer, the crashing volley of a hundred rifles.

Twigs rained down on us from overhead as the bullets whined through the trees, but one, at least, found its billet. I saw Dillingame's son stagger and clutch at his throat.

Kratas threw her arm around him with a cry of mingled fury and anguish, and I was by her side. A shot had drilled clean through the boy's neck and he was bleeding profusely.

From the camp came a shower of rockets, followed by the most deafening din I have ever listened to, drums, rattles, the blaring bray of enormous Chinese horns, and it all ceased as quickly as it had begun. A paper snake unwound its green length in the sky, lit from within, and then vanished in a puff of fire; hideously painted birds and beasts rocked in the air; and then, rising slowly, fully thirty feet long, a gold-and-red dragon with flaming, crimson jaws and silver crest, floated up toward the tree-tops, while the jungle all about us became alive with rustlings.

"Shoot, shoot, O orang-utans!" shrieked Kratas. "Kill! Kill! Let not one yellow dog escape!"

But there was no answering flight of poisoned darts in obedience to her command. The beast-men had fled.

Another volley cut the underbrush about us. I plugged the boy's wounds with some soft grass and, half walking, half carried between the priestess and Dillingame, we haled him through the jungle toward the Land of Blood.

IV

THE ATTACK

Not a beast-man did we encounter during the long night journey. Instead of going to Kratas' hut, Dillingame led us straight to the temple. You see, the palm-thatched house would not have offered the slightest protection against bullets, but the temple was a different matter.

An immense, pagoda-like structure, it was built of solid blocks of stone so large that it did not seem possible they could have been raised by human hands without the aid of machinery. There were three great stories, each about forty feet high, the topmost crowned with a single enormous block of glittering stone.

Strange beasts were carved on the overhanging balconies, and plaques of metal hung down in clusters, tinkling musically to the breeze. In every cranny where it could gain a foothold grew tropical vegetation, but even its tremendous rending power had failed to move a single block of this astounding edifice.

A square portico gave entrance to the ground floor, which was nothing more than a bare room of solid blocks of stone with a small aperture in the middle of the ceiling admitting to the story above. A bamboo ladder led up to this orifice and could, of course, be easily removed. The weaknesses of the second story for defense were its sides, open save for split-bamboo curtains, and the height of only forty feet from the ground making it an easy matter, against but four defenders, for a large force to carry it through the medium of ladders.

The third story was also reached by a hole in the middle of the ceiling, and its eighty feet of height precluded a ladder attack. It was there, early in the morning, we established ourselves, and spent half the day hauling up ammunition, food, and water.

Kratas had no eyes or ears for anything but her son. The boy was getting along nicely, sleeping soundly from exhaustion, and without a particle of fever. Still it was obvious that, with two holes in his neck, he certainly would bear watching. His mother crouched by his side, motionless, silent, statue of immobility save for the fire that blazed in her eyes.

We took the simple precautions necessary for defense, and then I turned to Dillingame.

"Seems to me we are in a pretty bad fix," I suggested. "We will be starved out of here, or driven out by thirst, in a few days, if nothing worse happens to us. Wouldn't it be more sensible to give up the gold—which neither of us wants—and take to the jungle?"

"And throw in my head for good measure," he added crossly.

"I've attended to your head," I answered, nettled, "though I doubt me you would be just as well off without it," and I pried the little, oiled silk package containing the small, red, metal tree-frog and scrap of Chinese-inscribed rice-paper from the heel of my boot. To my explanation of its significance the Englishman only vouchsafed a grunt, stuck it in a fold of his *sarong*, and bade me follow him.

Once the walls of the third story had been painted with brilliantly colored reproductions of Chinese ceremonials in which a figure of Buddha was carried through endless jungle adventures. The paint had mostly flaked away, but one spot, depicting several Orientals kneeling before a gigantic red tree-frog with golden eyes protruding from its head, was still comparatively fresh.

Against one of these protruding eyes Dillingame pressed firmly and a four-foot-thick slab of rock as high as my head swung noiselessly inward, revealing a flight of descending stone steps. A blast of air, fetid and damp, blew from this aperture, but *blew*, nevertheless, showing it was safe to enter; one could breathe.

"How did you discover this?" I demanded.

"I'll tell you about it when we have seen it all," he answered.

We went down a very dark, spiral stairway to emerge in what, by the light of my electric torch, proved to be a large chamber.

"We are now under the temple foundations," Dillingame volunteered, and led to the right. A passage opened into a corridor, some eight feet square, the walls of which grew wetter and the air more oppressive as we advanced. It ended at a blank wall formed of two blocks of stone between which water slowly oozed.

"This is beneath the very center of the leech pond in front of the temple," my companion announced. "I bring you here so you may more easily understand the rest," and he turned to retrace his steps.

We went past the entrance to the chamber by which we had come in, straight down this strange corridor, the air growing better with every step, and the floor now quite dry. A gleam of light, like a very small, dim star, appeared in the distance, and the tunnel suddenly contracted. And this contraction was caused by hundreds of two-foot-long cocoanut-husk bags, each one sealed with red wax in the shape of a tree-frog, and each one filled with gold—there was more of the precious metal in that one place than in many a government mint.

"Losh!" I exclaimed. "Losh, but you're a rich man, Dillingame!"

He laughed and led on without as much as a glance at the treasure, turning to the left just where the piles of sacks came to an end. There was a four-foot square side-room, and my flash-light, playing into it, revealed two enormous bronze levers.

"This," said Dillingame, laying his hand on it, "opens the very bottom of the lily-bottomed pool in front of the temple, so that the entire volume of water rushes down the passage-way we have just traveled. The other lever opens up the floor beneath the gold and precipitates it into the lower drain—for the whole thing is nothing more than a drainage system for the rice fields that were formerly cultivated between the stone causeways—and the water sweeps into the second drain, which empties into a swift-flowing river some two miles away.

"You see, it is possible, at one and the same time, to scatter the gold over half of Borneo and block the upper end of the underground passages with a solid wall of water.

"There is another entrance under Kratas' hut, and an exit a mile away in the jungle, where the tunnel ends at a small stone house, the hiding-place of the gold before Kratas moved it here. This stone house the Chinamen probably know of, so I have, by removing a block of stone, made another way out, leading into the jungle within sight of the temple."

"Are you sure the levers will work?" I asked.

"Tried them less than a year ago. Carried the gold back in the passage, opened up the place on which it is now piled, and emptied half the pond."

"Is there any secret in regard to how you found out about this, to say the least, unusual mechanism?"

"None at all," he answered promptly. "Kratas showed it to me. Let's go back and see how the boy is. Besides the Chinks should be turning up very soon."

We walked past the treasure, turned into the large chamber, and climbed the spiral stairway. The block of stone swung noiselessly open to pressure on the golden eye of a tree-frog painted on the inside wall (identical with the one painted on the outside), and we stepped into the third story.

A very pretty picture greeted us. The boy's eyes were open, his splendid young body relaxed, and he was smiling up at his beautiful savage mother who was crooning over him:

> *"Awake, little godling, to sunshine awake!*
> *The parrots are talking, and out on the lake*
> *The wild ducks are feeding, while through the soft air*
> *The swallows go swooping—sunshine everywhere!*
> *Awake, little godling,*
> *Sweet godling of mine,*
> *To the treasures of daytime.*
> *To joy and sunshine."*

Late afternoon came before there was any sign of the Chinese expedition. Then there was the sound of a trumpet, followed by the crash of what the Orientals are pleased to call musical instruments. Far up a causeway we could see them advancing, a great, green paper dragon born at the head of the column. They halted in the distance, and a single man, a white flag in his hand, advanced toward the temple.

"Go down and meet him, Andy," Dillingame directed, "and play for time. As soon as the boy is fit for the jungle, we'll go where the beast-men are and rally them. But play for time now."

It was the same imperturbable Chinaman who had delivered the first message, and he greeted me in perfect English.

"Mr. Freeman, I believe? You must excuse me for saying that you are in bad company. I have come to deliver an ultimatum that it will be well for you to heed. We will give you twenty-four hours to surrender the gold, not a second more; and Mr. Dillingame must be in our hands within that time, dead or alive."

"Suppose we resist?" I suggested, trying to simulate uncertainty.

"It would be madness. What could two men, a woman, and a boy do against a hundred? For you must realize that the beast-men have been too badly scared to attack us again. I might also call to your attention the fact that the gold rightly belongs to us.

"Also, it will be much to your personal advantage to see that we get it—and Dillingame. If there is no resistance I shall make a point of seeing that you receive your share of the treasure. You may have Kratas, too, if you want her, though I rather had my eye upon her myself." He licked his lips. "If there is resistance, you will die with the others."

I'm afraid I'm no diplomat. I had fully intended to temporize, to try and gain time; but the double insult in the bribe was more than I could endure.

"You yellow cur," I hissed. "I'll see you in the hottest depths of hell before you have as much as a sight of the gold! As for Dillingame, come and get him!" And, trembling with rage, I turned my back, striding toward the temple. The third step I stumbled and nearly fell, and it was well I did. A bullet whistled through my hair, the Chinaman crying out triumphantly, "One less enemy for the tong!"

A rifle popped from the third story of the temple, and I turned to see my assailant running swiftly up the causeway, his left wrist, from which blood was dripping, held in his right hand.

Safe in the temple (I pulled up the ladders as I mounted each successive story), rather shamefacedly I told what had happened. Dillingame only laughed.

"It's just as well to know they are going to attack," he said, "because I haven't the slightest doubt they would have done so anyway, in spite of the alleged twenty-four hours' truce. We'll hide Kratas and son under the temple, and see what they have up their sleeves. If worse comes to the worst we can always escape into the jungle."

The priestess and boy were banished through the secret passage, the woman carrying her boy without the slightest difficulty; and, lying flat on the ornate balconies, we kept a sharp lookout.

It was dusk before anything happened. Then a coolie tried to steal across the open space into the temple. He died half way.

For a time all was quiet, and then a volley came from the edge of the jungle, the bullets whistling above our heads and flattening on the ceiling. Evidently the Chinese were figuring on a lucky shot ricocheting down on us.

Night came, and again a coolie tried to reach the entrance, carrying a load of wood on his head for protection. It cost three shells to stop him, the darkness making uncertain shooting. There was an uproar at the other side of the temple, and we rushed across to the opposite balcony, but could see nothing.

"A ruse," called out Trevor with an oath, and we hurried back to our former positions. A ruse it proved to be. The open space below us was full of Chinamen hurrying into the temple with great bundles of wood on their heads. We shot hard and fast, but few fell. In a moment the place was bare, and another volley came whistling over our heads. Dillingame gave a cry of pain, half anger.

"Did they get you?" I called anxiously.

"Only a scratch," he growled, and stood up, revealing a bleeding cheek, across which a bullet had torn a ragged furrow.

There was a smell of burning in the air, and smoke began to eddy through the hole in the center of the room. I rushed to it, and a bullet whizzed up past my head.

"We're fools," bitterly exclaimed Trevor. "We've let them reach the second story. They can haul up fuel without danger from us, and smoke us out like rats in a hole."

The smoke grew denser, and the stone floor beneath our feet got uncomfortably warm. I tossed a handful of cartridges down into the fire, and they exploded in a chorus of yells of pain. A tongue of flame licked up into sight. The heat became unbearable.

"Best get out while we can," Dillingame suggested, and crossing over to the painted, red tree-frog, pressed the golden eye. I scattered some shells on the floor, to explode when it became hotter, so the Chinamen would think us still there, and followed down the secret stairway.

Gasping for breath between the heated walls we reached the square chamber, scurried into the corridor past the sacks of gold, and stopped before the little recess that held the bronze levers. Kratas was crouching there in the dark crooning over her boy. As my flash-light picked her out of the blackness, she held out her arms in an adorable gesture.

"All goes well with him, our son, my Lord Tre-vor," she said.

Dillingame stepped quickly to her into the circle of light, and her eyes fell upon his bleeding cheek.

Never have I seen a face change from all softness to such absolute fury!

"They dared, they *dared*, spawns of unclean fathers, lusters after yellow dust!" she shrieked; "they dared to harm my Lord Tre-vor as well as our son!"

Again she shrieked, and foam came to her lips.

"I go to rally the orang-utans. The kites shall feed full and the lizards play between bare ribs picked clean!"

Dillingame raised his hand to stay her, but I spoke quickly:

"Let her go. We are in pretty desperate case. The sooner the beast-men appear the better."

Kratas slipped out into the darkness of the jungle through the exit the Englishman had made; then the three of us—Trevor, his son, and I—went further along the rock tunnel, coming out finally in the little stone house where the gold had formerly been stored. The boy, thanks to his wonderful vitality, was perfectly able to walk, and, indeed, his wounds had already closed, so we felt no compunction in leaving him there to recuperate more quickly than in the fetid air underground.

Hardly had the revolving stone that readmitted us to the tunnel closed behind us when there was a roar of voices from outside dominated by a sharp command in Chinese:

"Don't kill him! We'll hold him for ransom against the gold."

As quickly as two big men can move we were back again in the stone house, only to find it empty. Through the door we saw some thirty Chinamen, the boy in their midst, defiling into the jungle; and I caught Dillingame around the waist just in time to keep him from plunging after them.

"Think, think, you fool!" I managed to gasp, as he struggled with me. "There is no chance of rescuing him; you'll only get yourself killed, and we can buy him back."

For a wonder common sense prevailed over his usual obstinacy, and he heeded me. Back in the tunnel, we planned, and planned in vain, what was best to do. Then, in a flash, the whole thing came to me; a desperate expedient it is true, but a possible one should all go well.

"Look here," I demanded, "when will Kratas be back with, or without, the beast-men?"

"Not later than to-morrow, dusk."

"Have you lost that little red-metal tree-frog and the scrap of paper I gave you?"

He fumbled in the folds of his *sarong* and produced them.

"Very well. Now listen carefully," and I proceeded to outline my plan. The next afternoon, as soon as we spied the five head Chinamen together, Dillingame was to walk boldly into camp and give himself up, trusting his life to the tree-frog and the scrap of paper. In return for the release of the boy he was to offer to lead them to the treasure. Were the boy freed, he was actually to fulfill this promise, and, furthermore, let them carry off the gold.

He opened his lips to protest at this point, but I swept on.

Should they play false and still hold his son, he was to lead them to the treasure anyway, through the entrance beneath Kratas' house, as many of them as he could get to follow him. When they came to the gold he was to dash ahead past it, and then I would first pull the lever that opened up a gulf beneath the sacks into the drain below; next the one that would precipitate the water of the pond into the corridor, sweeping all before it through the lower drain to the swift river, two miles away.

Then we should have to trust to luck, and Kratas' success in collecting the beast-men, for freeing the boy. But at the worst, some of our enemies would be out of the way.

Desperate and as improbable of accomplishment as this plan seemed, we could think of no better, and on it, perforce, we finally agreed.

There was a long wait before us, and to fill in the time, under the guidance of the Englishman, we stole through the jungle within sight of the temple.

What time had failed to accomplish in many years, fire had brought about in a few hours. The upper story had fallen in, and even from afar we could see that many of the immense blocks had split apart from the heat. The Chinese camp was pitched around the smoking ruins.

V

THE PATRICIDE

Came at last the evening of the next day, and there was no sign of Kratas. Together we made our way toward the temple, and waited within the edge of the jungle until the five head Chinamen were together. Then Dillingame walked calmly across the open.

I saw him show the red tree-frog and scrap of paper, saw them bend over it, then made my way back into the tunnel.

Time seemed to stretch out into countless ages as I sat in the darkness, my hands on the bronze levers. Surely a day must have passed! Something must have gone wrong! I became parched with thirst. Then it must be another day, I told myself, and speculated on how much longer I could live without water. Men had gone for a week, I remembered reading somewhere. There was a faint sound from the corridor. It grew nearer, increased in volume, resolved itself into many footsteps.

"We'll be there in a moment," spoke Dillingame's voice.

"I told you to keep silent," came an answer, followed by the sharp snap of a fist striking on bare flesh.

"Pull the levers, Andy, pull, pull!" shouted Trevor, and there was the sound of bodies dragging past me in the darkness.

I threw my weight against the levers, snapped on my electric torch, and, gun in hand, bounded into the corridor. There was a crash as the heavy bags of gold went down into the lower drain, cries, shrieks, the roar of the coming water driving the air before it. Dillingame was struggling on the ground, each wrist bound to that of a Chinaman. I fired into the face of the patricide and ground the head of the other, the cool messenger, beneath my heel.

"Don't kill him," gasped the Englishman. "My son is bound in his tent, and I want to repay the blow he struck me when I was helpless."

I slashed away the cords from his wrists, and tying the surviving Chinaman's hands behind his back, we drove him before us. Kratas' voice greeted us at the exit.

"Is all well with my Lord Tre-vor?" she queried anxiously.

"Yes, yes," he responded impatiently. "Are any of the beast-men with you?"

"All of them," she answered simply.

"Quick, to the temple then!" he commanded. "The leaders are dead, save this bound one, and we have only to deal with coolies, but who hold our son captive."

Not a sound betrayed our presence, as the beast-men were stationed around the camp. At a signal the luminous fungi were hurled, and the place became light as day. The terrified coolies sprang from their sleep, only to fall before the deadly blow-gun darts.

"Why butcher all of them?" I called to the Englishman. And he answered: "I'll find Kratas and put an end to it. The beast-men will not obey me."

But Kratas was not to be found and, furthermore, neither was our prisoner. He had escaped, bound as he was, in the confusion. Once I thought I saw him trying to rally the coolies, and then he was lost again.

I'll draw a veil over the rest of that night; the writhing figures on the ground, the shrieks of some poor wretch who had reached the protection of the jungle, only to fall into the hands of the beast-men.

Till morning the butchery—it could not be called a fight—went on, and through the hours I searched in vain for Kratas. Dawn broke over the silent camp, and then, nearly at my side, wailed out her voice:

> *"Where are they who greeted the sun,*
> *So many, so proudly, last day begun?*
> *   Where are they, where are they?*
>
> *"Where are they who dared the jungle shade,*
> *Came to the Land of Blood, bold, unafraid?*
> *   Where are they, where are they?*
>
> *"The kite whistles high in the morning sky,*
> *'Come to the feast, brothers,' his cry.*
> *   Where are they, where are they?*
>
> *"The worm thrusts his head from the jungle mold.*
> *What does he mouth, so stark and cold?*
> *   Where are they, where are they?*
>
> *"Gone where the evil spirits play,*
> *Gone where their food is molten clay,*
> *And there is no drink—gone, gone are they!*
> *Gone to the last one, with break of day,*
> *Gone, all gone, are they, are they."*

It was a dreary scene the sun rose upon, and in harmony the storm-clouds banked high in the west. The ruins of the temple still smoked, the pond before it was empty of water, and in its slime writhed the gigantic leech, an obscene, horrible thing to bare to the light of day. Dead men were everywhere.

Kratas stood with her hand on her son's shoulder, and Dillingame and I rocked on our feet with weariness.

"Let us go hence," said the priestess. "I am sick of the smell of death."

"Yes. Let us go back to the house—if it has not been burned down," said Dillingame, and we turned. I yanked out my automatic, but not in time. The escaped Chinaman lowered his smoking pistol as Kratas fell into my arms.

"Give me your gun," gasped Dillingame, snatching it from me, and ran forward in zigzags, the muzzle of the Chinaman's weapon steadily following him.

Once the Oriental fired and, staggering, Trevor sprang aside; a second time he pulled trigger, missed. Then with an inarticulate roar of rage the Englishman had him between his hands.

Catching his throat and middle he whirled him high in the air, brought him down across his knee, and I could hear the bones snap. Again above his head he hurled from him the broken-backed thing into the slime of the empty pool where groveled the loathsome leech.

"Come to me, my Lord Tre-vor," cried Kratas, her voice growing weaker at every word. In his arms she gave a little sigh of content and turned her face against his shoulder.

"My lord knows that I—that I—priestess of the Land of Blood—can—cannot—die. But I—am—very—weary—and—would—rest—against—his—heart."

There was a blinding flash of lightning, the crash of thunder, and the rain came. I followed Dillingame, his dead mate in his arms, to the house in which they had so long dwelt. There he laid her on a bamboo couch and knelt by her side. For hours he neither moved nor took his eyes from her face. Once I touched him on the shoulder and said: "You had better lie down and rest, old man." But he shook off my hand. Once the boy screamed out aloud, and I hushed him gently.

Dillingame neither heard nor saw. Outside the lightning flashed and the thunder shook the heavens, while water fell in such torrents as I have never dreamed.

The rain ceased, the clouds fled, the whole world gleamed fresh, clean, full of sunshine, beautiful as it only is after a tropic storm.

Dillingame gathered his mate into his arms and smiled at me.

"She is very cold," he said. "We must take her out into the warm sunshine."

I followed him to the temple, knowing neither what to do or say.

The water was level with the causeways, and running furiously into the pond, now brimming full, its center a whirlpool where it sank into the tunnel.

Dillingame paused on its brim and turned to the boy.

"Child of the jungle, go back to the jungle," he said gently, and reaching out, touched his son's arm with that awkward caress man offers to man.

"Andy, you are a good friend," he flung over his shoulder, and stepped into the flood.

"What are you doing, Trevor?" I shouted. "Come back here!" But the water had caught him, whirled him about.

I saw his arms tighten around his beautiful, dead jungle mate, and the whirlpool sucked them down, to be borne in the clean, brown water to the river that flowed swiftly no man knows where.

The boy and I lived together in Kratas' house for a week. Then he was gone into the jungle all one day. He came back in the evening and handed me the black butterfly talisman that Dillingame had snatched from the Chinese messenger and flung away. A beast-man had found it and given it to him.

The next day and the next he was off in the wilderness, and when he returned he did not weep over the empty house as he had other nights, but told me a strange tale of an elephant with a broad gold band beneath its belly.

Dillingame's son was beginning to forget. At first it hurt me horribly, and then I suddenly realized that he wasn't a man, in spite of his splendid body; wasn't even a boy, just a twelve or thirteen-year-old child.

The next time he was gone a full week, and came back with more jungle tales, also wreathed in jasmine garlands, such as Kratas had worn. I said good-by to him then. He was divided in mind between sorrow at losing me and anxiety to be on the trail of a white *sambur* which the beast-men had told him about.

On the ship that bore me back to England, to my place in the British Museum where I should for the rest of my days contentedly mount butterflies that other men had gone to the ends of the earth to take, I thought a great deal. Then one night I took the black butterfly talisman and dropped it over the side into the sea. Without it there would be little chance for any man to reach the Land of Blood; certainly should one by some miracle attain it, there would be none at all of ever leaving it alive.

OFF-TRAIL PUBLICATIONS
Specializing in the era of American pulp fiction

THE WEIRD DETECTIVE ADVENTURES OF WADE HAMMOND
By Paul Chadwick
Volume 1: 10 stories, 180 pages, $18
Volume 2: 10 stories, 172 pages, $18
Volume 3: 10 stories, 202 pages, $18
Volume 4: 9 stories, 232 pages, $18

> *The Wade Hammond stories complete in four volumes. In these chilling adventures, all from the classic 1930's pulps,* Detective-Dragnet *and* Ten Detective Aces, *freelance investigator Wade Hammond battles a series of weird enemies. Some of the best of 1930's pulp fiction.*

DOCTOR COFFIN: THE LIVING DEAD MAN
By Perley Poore Sheehan • Introduction by John Wooley
8 novelettes, 178 pages, $16

> *Weird stories from* Thrilling Detective, *1932-33. A former character actor who faked his own death, Doctor Coffin runs a string of mortuaries by night and fights crime at night. One of the strangest detective series.*

SUPER-DETECTIVE FLIP BOOK: TWO COMPLETE NOVELS
From the pulp *Super-Detective*:
"Legion of Robots" (November 1940) by Victor Rousseau • Introduction by John McMahan •• "Murder's Migrants" (March 1943) by Robert Leslie Bellem and W.T. Ballard • Introduction by John Wooley
2 short novels, 174 pages, $18

> Super-Detective *started as a Doc Savage-like adventure pulp, then changed format to hardboiled detective. The* Flip Book *features a novel from each of the two phases with intros exploring the historical background. Exciting!*

PULPWOOD DAYS: VOL 1: EDITORS YOU WANT TO KNOW
Edited by John Locke • 180 pages, $16

*Numerous articles from the writers' magazines by and about pulp editors, with ample biographical profiles. Editors include: Frank E. Blackwell (*Detective Story, Western Story*), Ray Palmer (*Amazing Stories, Fantastic Adventures*), Edwin Baird (*Weird Tales, Detective Tales*), and many more.*

GANG PULP
Edited by John Locke • 19 stories, 294 pages, $24

Hardboiled stories of the criminal underworld from the first year (1929-30) of the gang pulps: Gangster Stories, Racketeer Stories, *etc. These violent tales came under immediate censorship pressure; the history is explored in an in-depth essay. "A remarkable work of popular-culture scholarship"*—MYSTERY SCENE, *Fall 2008.*

THE GANGLAND SAGAS OF BIG NOSE SERRANO
Volume 1: DAMES, DICE AND THE DEVIL
Volume 2: HORSES, HOBOES AND HEROES
Volume 3: HELL'S GANGSTER
By Anatole Feldman • Introductions by Will Murray
Each: 4 novels • **Volumes 1-2**: 266 pages, $20 • **Volume 3**: 224 pages, $18

The complete Big Nose Serrano novels from Gangster Stories, Greater Gangster Stories, *and* The Gang Magazine, *1930-35. Feldman was the best of the gang pulp authors, and Big Nose was his most inspired creation, the berserking king of Chicago gangsters.*

THE CITY OF BAAL
By Charles Beadle • Introduction by John Locke
7 stories, 240 pages, $20

Authentic stories of African adventure from an author who had traveled the lands he wrote about. Lost cities, strange tribes, jungle magic. Six stories from Adventure *(1918-22) and one from* The Frontier *(1925).*

CULT OF THE CORPSES
By Maxwell Hawkins • Introduction by John Locke
2 novelettes, 150 pages, $13.95

Two weird detective stories from Detective-Dragnet *(1931) by a forgotten master. Introduction discusses the weird-detective trend of the early '30s, and the career of Maxwell Hawkins.*

THE OCEAN: 100TH ANNIVERSARY COLLECTION
Edited by John Locke
20 stories, 234 pages, $18

Munsey's The Ocean *(1907-08) was one of the first specialized pulps, a sea-story magazine. The best adventure stories are included here, along with 30+ pages of nonfiction material: a history of the pulp, and extensive author profiles.*

FROM GHOULS TO GANGSTERS
THE CAREER OF ARTHUR B. REEVE
Edited by John Locke
Vol 1 (fiction): 21 stories, 264 pages, $20 • **Vol 2 (nonfic)**: 260 pages, $20

Reeve was the leading American detective-story writer of the early 20th Century, with his scientific detective, Craig Kennedy. The astonishing breadth of his career is explored for the first time here. Vol 1 includes a cross-sction of fiction from all phases of career, including many never-before-reprinted pulp stories. Vol 2 provides a 40-page biography; an extensive Art Gallery of cover repros, interior illos, ads, etc; a 75-page guide to Reeve's work in all media; and more. An "excellent piece of scholarship"—MYSTERY SCENE, *Spring 2008.*

AMAZON STORIES
Volume 1: PEDRO & LOURENÇO
Volume 2: PEDRO & LOURENÇO
By Arthur O. Friel • Introductions by John Locke

Vol 1: 10 stories, 222 pages, $18 • **Vol 2**: 10 stories, 286 pages, $20

> *Collects Friel's first twenty stories from* Adventure *(1919-21), following the strange experiences of two Amazon Basin rubber workers as they explore the jungle. The best of pulp adventure fiction.*

GROTTOS OF CHINATOWN: The Dorus Noel Stories
By Arthur J. Burks • Introduction by John Locke

11 stories, 194 pages, $16

> *The complete adventures of Dorus Noel from* All Detective Magazine *(1933-34). Burks' Manhattan Chinatown is a place of dark mystery, riddled with secret passageways, menaced by hatchetmen. Introduction discusses the history of* All Detective *and the career of the Speed-King of the Pulps, Arthur J. Burks.*

Shipping: $3.00 media mail; $6.00 priority
Check or MO to:
Off-Trail Publications
2036 Elkhorn Road, Castroville, CA 95012
Paypal: offtrail@redshift.com